A TOUCH OF THE FAMILIAR

A NOCTURNAL TRINITY SERIES BOOK (BOOK THREE)

LEONARD D. HILLEY II

For my wife, our two children, and our two grandchildren. My love for you always.

CHAPTER 1

Kailey awakened, tied to a chair and blindfolded. Her parched tongue and throat indicated a cloth had been stuffed inside her mouth to prevent her from calling for help. She was gagged and help-less. As much as she loved Brady, she knew this *wasn't* one of his playful kinky games. This wasn't even in his nature. He objected to handcuffing her, even when she *begged* him to do so on occasion.

Despite her droggy state, she was alert enough to know she was in danger. This much she understood. A normal reaction would have been to fight and struggle against the restraints, but such an attempt would also be futile since she was only human. Her mind raced, but she remained still, hoping that through her thoughts she might determine who had taken her and ... *why.*

After she had anonymously posted several preternatural blogs about the vampires' irrational need to rule over humans, werewolves, and demons, her blog on her website was bombarded with threatening comments. And some of those threats had been on her life. Worse, a few of the messages detailed how she'd be bitten, fed upon, and after a long agonizing period, she'd be turned into what she feared the most: a vampire. Then, she be tied and left outdoors until the sun rose.

Since her website blog was encrypted and ran through various IPs around the world, she didn't consider the threats as serious. She was quite

"

confident no one could trace the exact location of her IP. But Brady's police officer mentality took the threats more seriously. He warned and insisted that she shut her site down permanently. The risks were too great.

Brady had enemies, and since she was the person he loved the most, those enemies would be more apt to take her in order to torture him. And after the remaining four vampire siblings that had founded Nocturnal Trinity forbade the union of werewolves into the council, Micah fled. No one had seen the Alpha since. Not even at his luxurious estate. Half of the pack members chose to follow Brady because Micah could not be trusted.

Brady wasn't certain of the exact number of pack members that remained loyal and followed Micah except for Ashley. A good number of the elder werewolves never met with Brady after Micah vanished. Jacob remained loyal to Brady and continually tried to contact all the former pack members without much success. At best, a dozen of the young strong werewolves placed their loyalty in Brady. The rest of the pack must have scattered.

Micah was no longer a friend Kailey could confide in or trust. He was unpredictable, full of rage; and for a lack of a better word: deranged.

"Shut down the website," Brady had said. "Should Micah happen to read your blog, he'll recognize that this is you. Irina and her siblings would, too, although it's doubtful they'd ever discover it on their own. But, even if no one else figured it out, Micah would know."

Despite Brady's warning, Kailey continued posting. She possessed a driven need to warn others about the dangers and the existence of the preternatural creatures preying on society.

On occasion, she wrote pieces about the troubles within Nocturnal Trinity's infrastructure, which was no longer a *trinity* since Alec—the eldest vampire in the Council—had dissolved the unity. After Forrest staked Flora—at the insistence of her siblings—the witches were forced to leave the Circle of Unity within Nocturnal Trinity. The four remaining behemoths were to have been slain like Diaboch with the Wrathbone. No one knew if the vampires had followed through with the proposed promise or not.

Brady was relieved in the nullification of the forced agreement Micah had established within the hierarchy of Nocturnal Trinity. Werewolves should never be in a covenant with vampires. The cracks in the Council's foundation had been exposed. Had the vampires not initiated the disbanding of the inner factions, Brady would've found a way to dissolve their forced agreement anyway.

Brady viewed the solitary nature of the werewolves as part of their sacred way of life. The last thing werewolves needed was to be confined as a part of a union with vampires and demons. Playing nice with direct enemies was a charade to create a false reputation in the nightclub. He wasn't that good at acting, and his facial expressions often revealed his emotions. He didn't like the idea of constantly looking over his shoulder whenever he entered Nocturnal Trinity, which was how the situation could've been if the werewolves remained in the union.

Alec let Brady know that he wasn't welcome in the nightclub except whenever a police officer was called to break up a scuffle or to arrest troublemakers, which suited Alec fine.

Still dazed, halfway between sleep and consciousness, Kailey's head throbbed. Papers shuffled. Footsteps scratched the rough floor. She fought any sort of struggle against the restraints because she was no longer alone. She sensed at least two men in the room with her. One stood close by, looming over her. The heat of his face radiated against hers. He was too close.

Heavy breathing rasped near her left ear and the tip of a man's wet tongue slid down her cheek toward her mouth. She lolled her head slightly to turn away, as if she were still asleep, but his stern hand gripped her chin, preventing her from doing so.

The heat of his lips lingered near hers. His breath reeked of gin and menthol cigarettes. Both cheap brands. She fought the nausea threading at the back of her throat and was relieved when he finally backed away without pressing his lips to hers. She doubted she'd prevent vomiting on the man.

His large calloused hands tightly gripped her bare knees, forcing her legs apart. The tip of his nose trailed up her inner thigh as he sniffed. Under the present circumstances, she didn't know if she still wore undergarments or if she'd been stripped of her clothes.

"The stench of the werewolf lingers on her," the man's voice hissed angrily. His accent was old, ancient, and similar to Flora's. He pressed his hands against her knees, hesitated, and pushed himself to his feet. His shoes scuffed the floor as he stepped away from her. "She's been with him recently. For that alone, we should kill her."

"No. Our orders are to keep her alive."

"But she's allowed herself to be defiled by one of … *them*."

"How many humans have allowed themselves to be defiled by us, Costel? The world over, human minds are weak, and easily preyed upon. Americans prove to be no different. Thousands voluntarily plead to be turned into the undead or some sort of shifter. They're not pleased being humans, thinking that what the supernatural possesses is far greater. They're hasty in their decisions, which later most regret."

"But what we are is greater, Serge," Costel said.

"Of course it is."

Kailey wanted to interrupt them and demand answers, but she understood she'd get more information by pretending to be unconscious. She wondered if they were vampires from their conversation, and if so, were they aware she was already awake?

Vampires could detect the change in a heart's rhythm, and since she was awake, they should have noticed the sudden change in hers. But if they weren't vampires, *what* were they? *Why* had they taken her? They were under strict orders to keep her alive, which meant someone had given the command to take her.

"Come on," Costel said. "She's still out. Probably will be for several more hours. Let's do an outer perimeter walk."

"You think others might find where she's been taken?" Serge's raspy voice lingered near her ear.

"Doubtful," Costel replied. "But let's not take chances. If all is clear, we go find local food truck and get lunch before he arrives."

Serge placed his hand to her cheek. She fought not to stiffen or flinch at his touch, to remain limp, and hope they continued to think she was unconscious.

"I'd have loved to have eaten her," Serge said in a harsh whisper. The drool in his voice was evident and she was not mistaken at what he implied. "Had the precious fruit not been tainted and spoiled."

"Come on, Serge," Costel said angrily. "Keep it in your pants."

"No worries there," Serge replied. He spat on the floor. "I'll never follow where a wolf has been."

The door closed, their hard-soled shoes grew fainter, and when she was certain they had left, she sobbed and tightly pressed her knees together. Her feet were cold, but for whatever reason, her legs were not bound to the legs of the chair. She rubbed her right foot against her left calf and was relieved that she was still wearing socks.

Kailey tugged at the restraints. By touch alone, she determined that her wrists were tied together with an abrasive rope and not handcuffs, which was good. The rope wasn't overly tight, but at least with enough effort, she might work the rope loose, provided she had enough time.

CHAPTER 2

"*K*ailey, don't try to speak aloud. *Think* your responses to me."

Stunned, Kailey held her breath.

"Raven?" Kailey thought, straightening in her chair. The tight blindfold prevented her frown and in spite of the blindfold, she involuntarily turned her head as if she might see her.

"Yes, it's me. Don't speak aloud."

"Hard to do with a gag in my mouth," Kailey replied.

"Uh, right."

"*How* are you speaking to me? You're dead."

"A solution that pleases you, no doubt."

Regret swam through Kailey. Her chest tightened and fresh tears burned her eyes. It was difficult not to speak aloud and to project her thoughts. "No. I never wanted your death. I never wanted you turned into a vampire, either. But your hatred toward me and Brady … and the fact that you tried to *kill* me and Luna. Out of jealousy. And while I can understand your reasons for being jealous, the fact you tried to kill me—"

"I'm sorry, Kailey. Truly, I am. You have to understand that the motives weren't solely mine. Yes, I was resentful and jealous, but I was a new vampire, too, and well, every emotion, every one of my senses, were heightened beyond my reason and understanding. I had no control. I succumbed to my full rage. I was out of my mind. It took my … death, for me to under-

6

stand how horrible I had become. I regret all those actions. I do. I'm so sorry."

"How are you speaking to me? Or is this simply a delusion from my guilt or hallucinations from a drug?"

"No. Although I was a vampire, I was first a powerful witch, and I wanted to die. The urges to kill and commit violence bombarded me. I wanted to be staked so I could be free, so I cast a spell that could bind my consciousness to the earth for several weeks until I found my soul. That's how I'm able to speak to your mind. Trust me, you're not crazy."

"Some days it's hard to tell," Kailey thought.

"Not to make light of your situation, but you have no idea how much seeing you tied and gagged turns me on."

"Raven!"

"Sorry, couldn't resist."

Even though the joke was distasteful, it was definitely a remark Raven would make.

"It's *really* you. Why would you want to roam the earth after you'd been staked?" Kailey asked.

"I sought to find my soul. When I was turned into a vampire, my soul was ripped away."

"And you found it?"

"Yes."

"How?"

"Another story for another day, provided we're given that much time. But my heart hoped to find and speak to you so I could apologize. I didn't want your last memories of me … to be the way I was at the end," Raven said. "Regardless of all the bad blood between us, I still loved you. I still do, even in death. I've missed … *you* … and what we had."

An acrid taste came to the back of Kailey's mouth. Raven sounded the way she had when they first met at college. But Kailey was having a difficult time shaking the coldhearted nature of Raven's last actions before Cassie decapitated Raven with the Wrathbone. Perhaps her guilt was the true reason for this unexpected conversation? After all, the only reason Raven had come to Seattle was to help Kailey. Instead, Raven reaped the worst of every possible curse a human endured from the vampires.

Yet, Kailey kept projecting her thoughts to temporarily ignore the situation she was in, if nothing else. "It's good to hear your voice, but I may be joining you in death soon. I'm afraid they're going to kill me."

"Killing you defeats their purpose," Raven said.

"How do you know that?"

"Because these people work for Micah."

Kailey swallowed hard. "Micah? No, that's not possible."

"Yes, they do. He was in the outer room earlier."

"You're certain it was him and that they work for him?"

"Yes. You don't think so?"

"Aren't they vampires?"

Silence followed the question. Cold silence that added to Kailey's isolation. Fear crept into Kailey's mind.

"Raven?" Kailey said, suddenly finding herself desperate to hear Raven's voice again, even if only in her mind. Was this all a bad dream? Was her mind playing tricks on her? Was this the result of the drug they had used to keep her sedated ?

"I'm here," Raven's voice whispered soothingly. "What makes you think they're vampires?"

"They mentioned that I had been defiled by one of *them*," Kailey thought. "The emphasis and distaste in their voices indicates that they aren't werewolves."

"They can't be vampires," Raven replied.

"Why not?"

"One of them went outside to smoke and it's near midday."

"Maybe they're a vampire's servants? Raven, they're not from the U.S. Their thick accents are Romania, like Flora's."

"It's possible, which makes matters worse for you."

"How?"

"Micah has allied himself with vampires," Raven replied.

Kailey shook her head. "I find that difficult to believe."

"I saw him."

"Did you see him talking to these two men?"

"No."

"Perhaps you're mistaken then. Micah's hatred for vampires is too much for him to cast aside."

"Maybe so. But these two men aren't vampires. I know of none that can walk into sunlight. Of course, I wasn't a vampire long enough to have met a great number of them."

"Where am I?"

"I am not certain. The building and alleyway didn't look familiar to me," Raven said.

"Please find Forrest or Brady and tell them I'm alive," Kailey pleaded. A knot tightened in her throat and the blindfold was wet from tears. Snot dripped from her nose, coating the gag protruding from her mouth.

Kailey sensed the anger in Raven's sudden silence. She shook her head slowly. She shouldn't have mentioned Brady's name. She worried that Raven might have left for good.

"I'm sorry, Kailey, but that's not something I can do."

"Why not? Sorry. I shouldn't have asked. The pain is still too raw."

"No, it's not that. I'm free now. The anger and bitterness have washed away."

For some reason, Kailey didn't believe that was true. When it came to Brady and Kailey's relationship, those wounds were still tender for Raven. She sensed the pain in Raven's tone and her death had not changed that completely.

Raven said, "My incantation only allows *you* to hear me. He couldn't hear me, and I'm unable to physically move objects or I'd untie you from the chair."

"Am I still dressed?" Kailey asked. A lump rose in her throat.

"You're wearing the gym shorts and sports bra that you always train in."

Kailey sighed.

"I watched and worried as he sought your scent."

"Not half as much as I did. I had just awakened. Could these men be *were* from a different pack?"

"Anything's possible, as you already know. We saw a lot of odd things in Salem, but Salem's tame compared to Seattle, or have you forgotten?"

"I remember," Kailey said, playing along. "We shared some good times together."

"We did," Raven replied.

"You should go."

"I'll not abandon you."

"But there's nothing you can do to aid me. Why watch me suffer?" Kailey thought about her question and winced. She suddenly wondered if that was the true reason for *why* Raven was watching—to watch Kailey's suffer.

"I'm thinking, Kailey," Raven replied. "My magic worked well enough that we can communicate by telepathy or whatever this is. I still have a few days to figure this out."

"*You* might have that long. I don't think I do."

"You heard what they discussed, didn't you? They're under orders *not* to bring any harm to you."

"Since when do criminals obey rules or laws, Raven?"

Raven laughed softly.

"Really? You think that's funny?"

"No, sorry. But you're right. They don't, *normally*."

"What makes you think this is different?"

"The expression on Serge's face indicates severe penalties will befall him by whomever rules over them should any harm come to you."

"It's good that you're on a first name basis with them," Kailey said.

"Snarky and bitchy," Raven whispered inside Kailey's mind. "That's why I love you so."

Kailey frowned, but she doubted Raven noticed. "What do they look like?"

"Does it matter?"

Kailey shrugged her shoulders slightly. "Maybe? What are they wearing? Any tattoos? Jewelry?"

"They both look to be in their mid-forties, maybe early fifties. Serge has several deep scars on his face. He's been in a lot of fights apparently. He has a neck tattoo of the Roman numeral thirteen."

"Any other tattoos?"

"I don't know. He's wearing a leather jacket so I cannot see his arms. He's also wearing worn jeans and black hiking boots. They look new."

"Are they wearing any silver?"

"No," Raven replied.

"So they could be *were*?"

"Possibly."

"But not wolf were," Kailey said.

"What makes you say that?"

"The way Serge said that he'd never follow a wolf."

"Ah, yes."

"But that's another reason they couldn't have sided with Micah—"

"I saw him, Kailey. I remember what he looks like."

"I know. Just projecting my thoughts." Kailey gave a muffled sigh. Nearly gagging, she leaned forward and forced air up her windpipe, causing the cloth to move forward in her mouth. With her tongue, she pushed the cloth partway out of her mouth.

"I wish I could help," Raven said.

Another push with her tongue, and she spit out the gag. "If they're with Micah, which I highly doubt, they're not anyone I've ever met. I'd recognize those names or accents had I encountered them. Brady's never mentioned them, either."

"Ah, dear Brady—"

"Don't start, Raven."

"He and Micah had a falling out?"

"Yes. The pack divided but not in equal numbers. Eighty percent or more chose to stay with Brady. Others chose neither side, and Micah fled. Brady should've killed Micah," Kailey said.

"I thought you were against murder."

"Murder in the conventional sense, yes. But I've come to accept the fact that survival comes at a heavy price sometimes, and when you're dealing with the undead or *weres*, some are too unpredictable to let live."

"Like me?"

"Not like you."

"I vaguely remember the hatred and disgust in your eyes when you almost pressed the stake into my heart. But you held back. You couldn't do it."

Kailey remembered the cold evil that blackened Raven's eyes, but she chose not to bring that up. She didn't have the heart to tell Raven that had Cassie not decapitated Raven, Kailey wouldn't have hesitated to plunge the stake into Raven's heart. "Well, I never hated you before Nicodemus turned you. I honestly would have given my place for yours."

"Let's not get hasty."

"But it's true."

"Drifting around in one's consciousness isn't what you'd imagine."

"I suppose not."

"I mean, I can see and hear you, but I've lost the ability to touch, and I'd love to feel you, to wrap my arms around you again. To smell and taste you—"

"Raven—"

"I didn't mean it like that. Your kisses, back when we were *briefly* intimate."

"Not to make you hate me more," Kailey said.

"I could never hate you."

"I let things escalate too quickly between us," Kailey said. "I feared doing so would ruin our friendship and it did."

"No, it didn't. I'm here, aren't I?"

"I want to believe so," Kailey said.

"You don't think this is real?"

"I don't know. I want it to be, but there's still the chance that I was drugged with LSD or knocked unconscious and have a concussion."

"I assure you that I'm here," Raven said.

"Said the delusional mind."

"Me?"

"No, me."

Raven said, "I'll be back in a few minutes."

"Where are you going?"

"I'm going to try to find someone to help you."

Nervousness tightened Kailey's chest. "Please hurry."

"Hold tight … sorry. Be back soon."

CHAPTER 3

Cassie's eyes flicked wide open; her crimson irises blazed like fiery, bubbling blood. She seldom slept long but lately, what little sleep she got was less and less due to Micah's meddling with the Nocturnal Trinity Council. His unreasonable demand to have the werewolves unified with the Order had caused tensions to rise even more, but Alec had been quick to dissolve such a union. In fact, he disbanded the trinity altogether, causing the distrust between the factions to critically magnify, brewing toward an inevitable clashing battle.

Some witches and demons sought to regain what they had lost in Nocturnal Trinity. Not that they had much to gain except prominent notoriety in Seattle's underground.

"Kailey?" Cassie whispered.

The succubus wasn't certain why Kailey's welfare was Cassie's first waking thought, but a supernatural tug informed her of Kailey's imminent danger. For some strange reason, thoughts of Raven popped into Cassie's mind, too, even though Raven had rightfully met her demise. Cassie's stomach twisted with uneasiness. By impulse, she reached for her cellphone and called Kailey.

The phone rang until Kailey's voicemail requested that Cassie leave a message. The dread inside her intensified, so she dialed another number.

When the party answered after several rings, Cassie said, "Brady?"

"Yeah. Kinda in the middle of—"

Cassie said, "When's the last time you've spoken to Kailey?"

"A few hours ago. Right before I left for work. Why?"

"So she was at home when you left?"

"Yes, why?"

"Something's amiss," Cassie said.

Brady was silent for several moments. "What do you mean? Has your demon intuition gone haywire again?"

Cassie pursed her lips and glared into the phone, wishing she was video chatting so he could see her scowl. "Haywire? Have I ever been wrong before?"

"Why do you think there's a problem?"

"She's not answering her phone."

"She's probably showering."

"How close are you to your apartment?" Cassie asked.

"A half hour? Give or take five minutes."

"With your lights and siren, you can make it in ten."

Brady lowered his voice. "I'm in the middle of a murder investigation. I can't leave the scene based on one of your hunches."

"Hunches?" Cassie hissed. Her demon anger rose inside. She was close to spewing her wrath through the phone. "I've never been wrong when my impulses inform me someone's in danger, especially when it comes to Kailey. Where's Forrest?"

"Um, he's here, too."

"Forrest's at the murder scene? Why?"

"Because it's … bizarre."

"In what way?"

"Medieval torture device on the mutilated body," Brady whispered. "The body was completely drained of its blood."

"Vampire?"

"That's what Forrest seems to think, at least by the way the body was drained. Except, there are no puncture marks. No traces of blood left behind. Not a drop. According to Forrest, only an ancient vampire would have the access to such a device in order to perform such a ritual."

Cassie frowned and clucked her tongue. Her mind raced. "Not one of our locals then, huh?"

"No. Probably far worse than any vampire in Seattle. Older than Flora's family. Forrest has implied that the vampire might be one of Dracula's children or grandchildren."

Cassie's heart raced. She placed a hand over her chest. "Seriously?"

"I wouldn't joke about this."

"You never joke about anything."

"Then you understand why I can't leave yet. Can't you do that demon teleport-thing and check on her?" Brady asked.

Cassie sighed. "Yes. But doing so drains my energy, which is why I only do so on rare occasions."

"See? You've been wasting valuable time. You could've already gone there and spoken to her."

Cassie's fangs showed as she snarled. "I only called to find out when you had last spoken to her and what you might know. I'll pop over to your apartment and check on her and get back to you."

"Thanks. Look, I'm certain you're overreacting. Maybe you had a bad dream—"

"I don't have nightmares," Cassie replied. "I *become* other people's nightmares when they tick me off."

"Like me right now?"

"How'd you deduct that, Sherlock?"

Cassie disconnected the call. "Bastard."

CHAPTER 4

Cassie stared into her bedroom's full-length mirror and transformed into her favorite human form. She visualized tight leather pants that hugged her shapely hips and legs, a crimson terry cloth halter top that matched her irises, and a black leather jacket. A few seconds later, she tied back her curly red hair into a ponytail.

Deep down she knew Brady wasn't a *total* jerk, despite his cold reaction to her near frantic call. His recent attitude toward Cassie was somewhat justified, but his reasonings were not entirely her fault. However, he'd never acted the same toward Cassie since she'd used her succubus wiles to plant a lustful fantasy into his mind about the three of them together.

The only reason she had done so was because Brady had insisted his will was too strong to be tempted by her seductive powers. His belittling of her capacity to sway men and women into lasciviousness by her intuitional charms had been a direct challenge. She believed he had only openly taunted Cassie in front of Kailey to prove his loyalty to Kailey, which he *didn't* need to do. But the challenge had been made.

Cassie never retreated from any challenge to prove her mental abilities or her powerful enhancing pheromones far worse than a cupid's lust-inducing arrow, but in retrospect, she now understood that she should've thought her actions through more than she had.

The rigorous illusion Cassie projected into Brady's thoughts was overwhelming, far greater than she'd meant, and Brady was left shaking and profusely sweating. He'd reached a mental and physical height of ecstasy without any physical contact, which wasn't what Cassie had intended to happen.

Most men might have walked away shaking from their need to find immediate relief for their arousal, but for Brady, it triggered an appetite he didn't even know lived deep inside. Of course, those urges were due to his werewolf nature, and she had not taken that fact into account when she projected the fantasy.

Brady's struggle to shunt away those yearnings awakened his inner beast. Cassie was forced to take Kailey to stay with her for several days at Brady's insistence until he regained control of his raging lust. The situation between Brady and Cassie afterwards had never fully recovered. Although she apologized multiple times, and he silently shrugged it off, he continued to keep Cassie at a distance.

The lesson learned was that even a werewolf was incapable of setting up a mental barrier to thwart a succubus' ability to enter his mind. The embarrassment he suffered weighed heavily on his ego. The aftermath was his lingering anger; more toward himself than Cassie. Cassie wondered how long it would take for Brady to get past the episode, if he ever did at all.

Cassie sighed and closed her eyes, focused on Brady and Kailey's townhouse apartment, and teleported right inside the front door; what was *left* of the door, that is.

Her heart froze and she stood like a stiffened corpse. Listening, she hoped to detect some movement in the apartment, because if the intruders were still there, she'd give them a physical example of what it meant for them *to have Hell to pay.*

No sounds interrupted the silent atmosphere inside the apartment.

No heartbeats.

No breathing.

Whoever had broken through the door was already gone, but knowing Kailey, she had not given in easily. She wouldn't have surrendered to intruders. She'd have fought back. Perhaps they were unable to take her. She was much stronger than her short stature hinted.

Cassie eased along the foyer wall, glanced up the polished wooden stairs, and in a flash, she stood at the top.

"No more of that," Cassie said, leaning against the wall to balance herself. With her vertigo skewed, her surroundings spun. Teleporting twice so quickly was more taxing than she could afford, especially if she happened to confront someone inside the apartment and needed to fight.

Her senses indicated that she was alone. Kailey was gone. Where? Who had taken her? Or had she escaped?

The strewn bedroom indicated that Kailey *had* fought back, but whether she had been successful in getting away unhurt was something that even she couldn't detect. Yet, she had fought.

"That's my girl," Cassie said softly.

Upon closer inspection, she found no blood. The sheets and blankets were clumped at the end of the bed, and both nightstand lamps lay broken on the floor.

She sniffed the air. Whoever had been in the room had not been demons, and since it had occurred after Brady had left for work, she safely ruled out vampires. But their scent was odd. Different. Nothing like she had encountered before.

Nowhere could she find fresh traces of Kailey's barefoot prints. The intruders' heavier imprints pressed over hers into the plush carpet were made by two different sized work boots.

The harshest scent she detected in the room was the stench of man sweat. Well, a partly human odor. The permeating odor lingered and an entire bottle of Febreze couldn't have erased it. Such pungent sweat usually meant that the individual smoked and drank heavily. The men, or whatever they were, had either been nervous in their duties to abduct Kailey or their endorphin levels had heightened from their struggle to restrain her.

With the apartment door being battered down, they had not taken Kailey totally by surprise. But their actions must have been quick, as she didn't have time to call Brady or Cassie. A busted cellphone lay on the carpet near the wall. One of her attackers must've thrown it hard against the wall.

Cassie picked up the shattered phone. "Useless. Damn."

She tossed it on the bed and took out hers. She snapped several pics and then sent them to Brady before calling him again.

"Yeah?" he said.

"Sent you pics," Cassie said. "*Never* underestimate my intuition again. Kailey's gone. Someone took her."

She disconnected the phone before Brady could reply, but she sensed his immediate pain in his last breath before she had done so.

Her festering anger was too extreme to remain on the phone, and she didn't want to lash her words at him like a scorpion flung its poisonous barb when cornered. Her anger was more at the two men who had fled with Kailey than Brady, and the last thing Cassie needed was to endure more contention with him. Their bridge of friendship needed mended, not further deconstruction.

Brady immediately called back, but Cassie ignored his call. She needed a few more minutes in the apartment to use her demon powers and *hope* she found more clues before the city officers arrived at the scene. But she had little to go on, other than these men were not quite human.

In a city filled with vamps, witches, and demons, the men could be working for any one of the factions. And since Forrest Wollinsky had settled in Seattle, the best bet was vampires had hired someone to take Kailey in retaliation for Forrest staking two of the six vampire elders that were the founders of the Nocturnal Trinity nightclub. Even though they had willingly surrendered Flora to him to be staked, enough time had passed that they might have considered their sacrifice hasty and wished Flora was still with them.

Which meant, the best place she could solicit information was at the nightclub before night settled and too many outsiders made nuisances of themselves. Because she had befriended Kailey, few workers at Nocturnal Trinity wanted to be seen talking to Cassie, but Cassie possessed ways of making them reconsider.

CHAPTER 5

"*D*ammit!" Brady said. He slid his cellphone into his back pocket after trying to reconnect with Cassie several times. The pit of his stomach twisted, ached. An acrid taste came to the back of his mouth, and he fought the urge to vomit.

Fear wasn't something Brady ever let get the best of him, even after he and Micah became the most unfortunate enemies. But when it came to the thought of losing the one person he loved more than life—Kailey—fear struck harder and more unexpectedly than he'd ever imagined possible.

Forrest—a bear of a man at three hundred pounds of lean muscle and a towering, six-foot four inches tall— stood dressed in a long leather trench coat in the cold cellar room. He looked away from the blood-drained corpse and faced Brady solemnly. Beneath the brim of his hat, Forrest's eyes narrowed as he studied Brady in intense silence and partial scrutiny. He ran a hand through his short graying beard. He didn't need to ask, but he did, Brady assumed, to break the still atmosphere shrouding them inside the eerie cellar.

"Cassie again?" Forrest asked.

Brady nodded. His face paled and his eyes became haunted and darkened. He took a deep breath and scratched the back of his head. A sheen of sweat covered his face, in spite of the cold cellar room they stood inside. Brady fought to maintain his composure, but his fear was giving way to his festering anger to find who had taken Kailey and enact the rightful justice his badge didn't allow. He closed his eyes and took a deep breath. The last thing he or Forrest needed was for Brady to become a ravenous beast.

Forrest frowned with concern. His deep voice thundered and echoed, even at a low whisper. "What's wrong? Kailey's okay, isn't she?"

"Someone's taken her."

Forrest's face tightened. "Let's leave this body for now. With the chill of this room, he won't decompose at a rapid rate. I'm certain he won't become a vampire as he has no bite marks and the people who did this knew exactly how to use the torture device and what they were doing. They wanted him to suffer, but they wanted his blood more. Their intentions weren't to turn him. It takes a skilled individual to perform this effortlessly and without mistakes. I'm done here. I'll go with you to find Kailey."

Brady shook his head. "No. You stay and see if you can find more clues or evidence. We need to know all we can before I have another team of officers and forensics come to the scene."

Forrest glanced at the drained corpse and shook his head. "There's nothing else to look for. We know the how and why. We just need to find out *who*. Such a torture device ... I've not seen this in over a hundred years, and that was in the old country. Even then, no one had used such a device in over two hundred years to my knowledge."

Brady stared at the lifeless eyes of the dead man stretched out on the grimy stone floor. Not a drop of blood remained. "All right, Forrest. We leave him for now. Come on. I'll send forensics—"

Forrest shook his head. "No. You don't want anyone else to examine this body. You certainly don't want the press to get wind of how this poor individual was killed and the type of weapon used."

Brady nodded in silence, his eyes vacant and deep in thought, and then he turned and walked up a short spiral set of stairs that led to the basement of an abandoned warehouse near the bay. Forrest followed.

"Then how do I let the mayor know that one of the city council members is dead?" Brady asked.

Forrest paused on the stairs and looked back at the corpse. "He's on the city council?"

"*Was*," Brady said.

"Hmm. Can you be so certain the mayor didn't offer this man as a sacrifice to spare his own life?"

"What leads you to believe the mayor's involved?" Brady asked, glancing back in surprise.

Forrest shrugged and returned to climbing the stairs. "It's been a rumor for quite some time. I'm certain you're aware."

Brady opened the old metal door. The rusted hinges squealed. "I've caught wind of that, too."

"And?"

"I don't like the possibility of such a rumor being true."

"How did you know to look here?" Forrest asked, pulling the heavy door closed behind himself.

"An anonymous tip was left on my desk," Brady said, taking his keys from his pocket.

"Does that happen often?"

"No."

"Any reason why they'd leave a note?"

Brady hurried to the old entrance door with the shattered window that stood open for any number of homeless vagrants to come and go as they pleased. Old, bent and rusted, metal barrels that once were used for night fires were cold and collecting dust. No fires had been made inside this warehouse for months.

The homeless seldom entered the old building anymore, and it wasn't due to the posted city ordinance signs forbidding them, either. Since the growing activity of vampires had gone rampant on the less fortunate of Seattle's society, and two dozen victims had been found inside the warehouse one morning, those without safe homes chose to reside under the piers near the choppy Elliott Bay, despite the cold.

Brady sighed, waiting for Forrest to squeeze through the doorway. "I imagine to prevent anyone from recognizing his or her voice. And to prevent their number from being traced. Either way, it leaves me without any clues."

"You have the weapon," Forrest said.

Brady got in his squad car and unlocked the passenger side door. Forrest leaned slowly inside and sat down. His weight caused the passenger side to lower slightly.

"The weapon ... ah, shit! I forgot to—"

Forrest smiled and held up the barbed collar. "I didn't forget it. You don't want anyone other than us to know about it."

Brady nodded and revved the engine, gunning across the narrow street near the pier. He shook his head. "So there's significance for not taking the weapon? Why would someone decided to do this … now?"

"Yes. Leaving the device behind is a clear signal that someone high in power wants us to know he or she has come to Seattle. It also means this individual knows I'm here, as I'd recognize the weapon immediately. But, be warned. Should the mayor be involved and you report the bizarre murder to him, you might be the next on his list. You might be anyway."

That made sense, Brady thought. Then, "Why would they want me to know?"

"Fear. Intimidation," Forrest said. "That's how ancient vampires behave. Notoriety is something they thrive on."

"Are you implying the mayor is—"

"No."

"Then why would you mention ancient vampires?"

"This weapon is rare, and only an ancient vampire could have access to one?"

"You're sure?"

"Positive."

"Can someone not steal one from a museum?"

"Not in Seattle. Hell, probably not in any museum in the U.S."

Brady sighed. "I still don't see a connection for why someone would want to silence me by using this weapon to kill one of Seattle's council members. If an ancient vampire has arrived in Seattle, shouldn't we see if one of Flora's sisters or brothers knows about it?"

"You could ask, but it's doubtful they'd tell you."

"Why not? They should extend some help since I disbanded the were-wolves from Nocturnal Trinity."

"Look, an ancient vampire will have Flora's remaining siblings groveling and begging to do his bidding. Her brothers and sisters could combine their strengths and still not defend themselves against an ancient."

Brady frowned. "I thought Flora's brothers and sisters were ancients."

"They're old, but they're not *that* old. If this ancient is a direct descendant of Dracula's bloodline, he's royalty to them. Her family was royals at one time, too, but they view the lineage of Dracula as sacred, as he's their father's father. Without hesitation or question, they'll do whatever's commanded of them. The sooner they satiate the ancient one's needs and desires, the sooner the ancient one returns to his old country," Forrest said.

"Why wouldn't they simply reside in Seattle since they have greater power?"

Forrest half-grinned. "Nothing's greater than one's own home country, especially for the eldest vampires. I suspect this calling card was left by one of Dracula's immediate family members. A direct descendant is far more powerful than any of the vampires or undead in America. Even I'd hesitate in approaching such an elder vampire."

Brady took a sharp breath. "They're that bad?"

"I've dealt with a few vampires that had been turned by Dracula's children and his grandchildren. Even as new vampires, Dracula's neophytes were much stronger, quicker, and deadlier than vampires that had been around for a hundred years. Somehow, those chosen by Dracula's descendants advance more quickly than the outliers, which is why Dracula's family rarely turns others. To remain higher in the hierarchy, they limit their *gift*, so to speak. Dracula's children have no desire to share their thrones of power with anyone and even Flora and Nicodemus are viewed as mongrels or lessers since they are not direct descendants."

Brady said, "Is Dracula really dead?"

"In history's version of his life, yes. In reality? No," Forrest said, looking out the side window.

Brady took a sharp breath. "How do you know he's still alive? Nothing's ever been reported to the contrary."

Forrest chuckled. "And nothing ever will be. You cannot live for hundreds of years unless you're excellent at keeping secrets. Pretending to be dead is the best misdirection one can have."

"So he's still alive?" Brady's hands tightened on the steering wheel.

"And protected at all costs by his family," Forrest replied.

"With your skills as a vampire hunter, could you kill him?"

Forrest moved uneasily in his seat and didn't respond for several minutes. Finally, he said, "Even if I were able to locate *where* he resides and killed all his guards, servants, and the family members protecting him, I'd never get close to him."

Brady frowned. "Why not?"

"The power he possesses is far more than you could imagine. It's highly unlikely I'd get past two guards before he killed or captured me since he can magnify the strength and cunning of those nearest him."

"If he's still alive," Brady said, "why did he allow the world to think he'd been killed?"

"Because armies would've continued coming to dethrone him," Forrest said. "None could have succeeded. Such a bloodbath would be of no benefit to him and his vampiric family. They not only need humans as a food source, they need them for servants as well. You can rest assured that any dictator over the years that has recklessly killed hundreds of his citizens has been under the influence of one of Vlad's children. Terrorizing people unfortunately brings about loyalty."

Brady flipped his patrol car lights on, but not the siren. "I see. So tell me, since I was the one who received the anonymous tip to find the councilman's body, you think I'm possibly a target?"

"Could be. I'd view it as highly suspicious. It's how you react to the councilman's body as to what they might do next or if they attack you."

"Like taking Kailey?" Brady's jaw tightened. His anger and apprehension increased.

"While that might be something they'd do, at this moment, I'd consider it a coincidence and nothing more. At least until you get more information."

Brady blared his horn at an intersection, cut through the light, and turned left. He was only a block from his apartment, but he already knew his arrival didn't change anything. Kailey was gone and he might never see her again.

CHAPTER 6

Raven drifted through the front door of the building where Kailey was being kept. Although she loved the benefits of being a spirit capable of going through walls and doors, she hated that she was unable to physically touch or move any objects at all.

Mentally, she was happier than she'd been in months. Happier because she had finally been able to talk to Kailey and apologize, which she'd been unable to do as a vampire. When she was a vampire, all her senses—*except taste*—and her emotions were magnified, including her bitterness and resentment. These two emotions, for reasons she didn't exactly know, masked all the others. She sought to kill Brady and even worse, she wanted to painstakingly torture and kill Kailey, watching her writhe and beg for mercy.

Raven's only explanation for her bloodlust was not only from vampiric needs and desires, but she believed she was under Flora's compulsion. She wasn't capable of resisting Flora's commands and followed them with the utmost obedience.

Flora despised Kailey far greater than Raven did. Nothing would have pleased Flora more than seeing Kailey ripped and torn apart by Raven. When Raven fought Kailey in the MMA ring, Raven nearly beat Kailey to death. She tried *not* to hit Kailey, she attempted to pull punches, but she had no control over her fists and feet. Raven wasn't even seasoned as a fighter and never would have considered fighting anyone, at any time or anywhere. Raven cried whenever she'd chipped a nail or accidentally burned herself with a curling iron. It wasn't in Raven's nature to abuse others physically, which was why she constantly berated Kailey's interest and training in the sport. She was seasoned with her poison tongue to hurl insults and degrade people she disliked or viewed as *fake*, like Luna and Brady, but now she realized the error of her ways.

Sadly, Raven's death was what caused her to realize the degree of Flora's mind control grasp. Raven wondered why she never saw the depths of Flora's hold. Now that Raven was no longer undead and her soul was restored—rejoined to the essence of her spirit—she hoped Kailey believed her sincerity, because Raven meant every word she'd said. And if Raven could find a way to apologize to Luna and Blaze, she wanted to make amends with them, too.

She'd been too jealous while in her physical body and incapable of giving Kailey the freedom her best friend desired. Such jealousy was unbecoming between friends and violated her oath of being a witch. Raven should have been sending forth blessings instead of venomous curses.

Raven simply couldn't accept Kailey's breakup and rejection. And seeing Kailey's desire to be with Brady shortly after their breakup had crushed Raven's ego. The whole situation still stung, her ego remained bruised, but not nearly as badly as before. As a spirit, she didn't have any other choice but to move on.

Raven's former attitude of *if I can't have you, no one can,* was now: *I'm happy to see you happy and I regret all the bad blood between us.* Admitting this was still a difficult pill to swallow, but after becoming undead and getting staked, nothing was worse than wandering the ethereal plane alone. The isolation forced her to dwell on all the mistakes she'd made, and if she didn't own up to them, she'd have an eternity of regret, constantly reliving the events over and over in her mind.

In hindsight, Raven didn't know if she'd have done things differently or not. She hoped that she would have. Her blindness toward Kailey's needs was simply part of her personality during that time. Anything less than the ordeals Raven suffered would never have given her the insight she possessed now.

Outside the building, Raven tried to figure out what part of Seattle she was in. Another bad thing about being in spirit form was her inability to carry a foldout map. Her short time living in Seattle hardly made her a resident. She was still a tourist in her ability to identify major landmarks, so even if she were able to find the name of the building or a street, such information still proved unhelpful.

The best she could determine was that she was near the bay. In the distance, a foghorn bellowed its low tone, far louder than she'd heard when she stood outside Nocturnal Trinity. The bay was close-by.

Fog settled along the street. Raven drifted in the fog, and even if she weren't invisible, she'd have blended into the mist with the same effect.

After several minutes, she found herself in a dim alleyway. She wasn't certain of the actual time of day. With the taller buildings and the rolling fog, seeing the sun was nearly impossible. She needed to find a way to help Kailey escape before night fell since vampires didn't roam the streets during the day. She knew from her own experience that being aroused during the sunlight was practically impossible. Sleeping during the day was equal to being fully comatose. Little could be done to awaken a vampire in this state, which was why vampires kept devoted human servants to keep guard of the caskets. Vampires, regardless of age, were most vulnerable during the day.

While vampires weren't an actual threat to Kailey at the moment, she still wasn't safe from the other monsters like werewolves and demons.

Raven had recognized Micah, and she held no doubts to it having been him, despite Kailey's insistence that it wasn't. Raven wondered if he might have made some pact with vampires *outside* of Nocturnal Trinity since he'd been ostracized by his pack and Nocturnal Trinity's Council. The strangest part of seeing him walk past the spot where she hovered was his sudden pause and turning his head in her direction. His eyes narrowed and his nostrils flared. He sensed her presence and although he posed no real threat to her since she was a ghost, a bit of fear lingered in Raven's mind.

Her impression of Micah when she first met him at his magic supply shop had been positive. She held no fear of him. In fact, she admired him for his walk in the path of enlightenment. He was attuned to the light, as she once was before she'd been turned. But he was a werewolf alpha with many secrets. The worst of which, at least she had thought so at the time, was the spell he placed over his pack to prevent the members from turning during the full moon. The pack members suffered horrific agony during each full moon without any mercy being given by him. He held control over them, which slowly festered resentment from several pack members, including

Brady. A challenge to Micah's authority was not unexpected. It was inevitable.

When Micah finally relented in releasing them and himself from his spell, something inside his mind shattered. The release of his *were* beast revealed the nastier side of Micah. Or perhaps, the image Micah portrayed to others had also been veiled by his spell and his true demeanor emerged once that spell dissolved.

A clatter and the rattling of metal ricocheted in the darker recesses of the alley. Raven went to investigate. On the ground lay an empty metal food service tray tarnished by misty rains and the accumulation of crud and grime.

A pair of green nervous eyes peered from beneath the battered, rusted dumpster. A frightened mew and then a sudden hiss spat from the stray black cat's mouth. To Raven's amazement, it could see her.

Raven laughed. Of course, it *saw* her. A witch's best friend was her familiar. Before the frightened cat sprinted into the foggy alleyway, Raven thrust herself faster than a dart and entered the cat.

Opportunity came in unusual fashions sometimes. This proved no different.

CHAPTER 7

*C*assie strolled into Nocturnal Trinity, despite the slight attempt by the musclebound bouncer who tried unsuccessfully to convince her that she needed to come back after the club opened. When she informed him of who she was, he then insisted she leave, as she was on the 'not welcome' list. After crossing his thick arms, he spread his legs, filling the door with his body.

Needless to say, in less than several seconds, the bouncer sat on the floor beside the door cradling his right wrist and forearm. She was almost certain she hadn't broken any bones, but for the moment, she didn't care. His ego had probably suffered more than what physical damage she'd inflicted.

Kailey's welfare was Cassie's top priority and unnecessary delays only ticked her off more. Since he was one of the new bouncers hired after Nocturnal Trinity's renovation, she hoped the incident taught him to display better manners in the future. She should have, at the very least, won the wary respect she deserved. Pretty women could be provoked. Of course, few men could have detected she was actually a demon in disguise.

She smiled. *Live and learn.*

Cassie headed toward the Demon quarters of the club where Jinn stood behind the counter taking inventory. Though she slinked quieter than a cat's paws sinking into thick plush carpet as it walked, Jinn detected her approach without glancing in her direction. He set down his clipboard, releasing a slight growl.

Rolling his eyes, Jinn threw his hands upward, and turned toward her. "I suppose the bouncer didn't give you the message?"

Cassie cast a sly grin. "Oh, he tried. That's a decision he'll reconsider ever relaying to me for a long time."

"Dammit, girl," Jinn said, shaking his head. His long braids slung back and forth. He glanced at the door. "You didn't kill him, did you?"

"I've never killed any of the bouncers at Nocturnal Trinity." She playfully frowned and scoffed. "You know that."

"Might as well have," Jinn replied. "All of the recent ones who've met you … they quit the next day. Do you have to rough them up?"

"No, but then where's the fun for me? All these goons they hire to deter unwanted guests … You ever seen those signs at the gym or in a dojo? You know the ones: Leave your ego at the door?"

Jinn crossed his muscled arms. His knife-carved tattoos illuminated slightly from his agitation. "I have no need to workout in a gym. Nor do you. Us being demons and such. But yeah, I've seen those signs."

Cassie grinned. "You need to post a sign like that over the door."

"No, we need *you* to stop injuring our bouncers."

She slid atop the barstool and leaned onto the bar. With a wink and scrunching her perfect cute nose, she said, "Take my name off the unwelcome list and all your problems concerning me are solved."

"Don't try to entice me with your succubus wiles, girl. You know that doesn't work on an incubus. And you know *I* can't get your name off that list," Jinn said. "Even if I wanted to, I can't. Lately though, I have to say that I *don't* want your name removed. You've been nothing but trouble, more than any normal demon."

"Still sore over the death of the Diaboch?" She formed a bridge with her hands and rested her chin atop them.

"Hell, yeah, you *know* I'm still pissed about that," Jinn said. His orange-yellow pupils flickered like windblown hot coals, revealing his burning anger. "You betrayed your own kind, and to make matters worse, I'm lucky the other behemoths only peeled my skin from my body and rolled me in salt for Diaboch's death."

Cassie winced, thinking of the immense agony he must have suffered. "I'm so sorry, Jinn."

Jinn shrugged. "I healed, albeit slowly."

Cassie frowned. "Wait. I thought the vampires killed the behemoths."

Jinn shook his head slightly. He swallowed hard and lowered his voice. "No, they're still here. And to top that off, you helped kill Flora. Your friendship with that vampire hunter and his girlfriend demon-killer—"

"Penelope *isn't* my friend."

"No? You know her first name. Hell, that's *more* than I knew. Regardless, you've lost your chances for ever tending bar here again."

"I've set my goals for higher aspirations, my dear," she replied.

Jinn cocked a brow. Frustrated, he sighed and grabbed a towel to wipe the bar. "You've a bizarre choice in friending others."

"Forrest? You talk to him all the time. He's never been turned away at the door."

"Yeah, well, you know the size of that man, and that he can turn into a were-bear whenever he gets pissed … Few folks, myself included, could ever turn him away. Not with words, at least, and probably not with ten bouncers better than Cliff, whom you just met. Besides, Forrest's walking on razor-thin ice. It's a matter of time before it cracks and he meets his doom. And with you cozying up to them after sending Diaboch deep into the abyss, you've created more enemies than you can imagine."

"Didn't Forrest and Alec reach some type of mutual coexistence agreement?"

Jinn flicked his gaze to meet hers and nodded. "By word of mouth, yes, but Forrest tends to overstay his welcome. Kinda like you."

Cassie shrugged and pouted her lips. "What happened, Jinn? We used to be good friends. We had one another's backs, even when Diaboch had to be taken down, you were there for us, for me."

Jinn's gaze softened. He stopped wiping the bar and glanced both directions, checking to see if anyone had entered the room. "My feelings toward you have never changed. You know that, but if I want to live on Earth's surface and not be returned to the abyss like Diaboch, I've an image to uphold, ya know? Which doesn't include playing niceties with you."

Cassie read the conflict in his eyes. "Sorry. I understand."

Somewhat relieved, he slid a topped shot glass of Devil's Rum to her. Before she reached for it, he pointed a stern finger and said, "Drink it and leave. Tell Forrest it's best he doesn't show his face in this nightclub again. Vamps are looking to kill his ass. They want revenge."

Cassie downed the shot and then patted her chest as the liquid burned its way down her throat. She blinked hard, squeezing out tears, and chuckled. "He's almost a hundred and forty years old and has slain vampires since he was a child."

"Yep, his time's long overdue."

"The odds are he'll outlive you and I," Cassie said with a smirk.

Jinn leaned across the bar and whispered, "I'd have taken that bet a week ago, but not now. Not today. I'm not safe, and honey, you certainly are not safe, either. Understand that you and I aren't the ones they're gunning for. However, the more you're in his company, the more likely you'll become a casualty."

Cassie shifted on the barstool in response to the sudden uneasiness in his voice. "Forrest's a seasoned vampire hunter."

Jinn said, "Against normal vamps, yeah, or the neophytes, Forrest can easily kill them. But … um, and don't speak this aloud, but some bad blood, if you'll pardon the pun, has reared its ugly head in Seattle. Won't do any of us any good to stand beside Forrest, unless we *want* to die."

Cassie frowned. "Other vampires? Relatives of Flora?"

Jinn shook his head. His strange eyes harrowed with nervousness. "No. These vamps … they're far worse than Nocturnal Trinity's founders. Baby, these are so nasty that the remaining four founder vamps cater to their every want and desire. I'm guessing these visitors are royalty or something we've never seen the likes of before. But … you didn't hear this from me. Got that?"

Cassie nodded.

Jinn leaned back and huffed, feigning his spite toward her once again. "Now what do you want so I can watch your fine ass saunter toward the door before the higher-ups notice you talking to me? I'm not going through the torture with the vamps and the behemoths again over *you*."

Cassie pursed her lips, leaned back on the stool, and crossed her arms. "Kailey's missing."

"And how's that *my* problem?" His words were harsh, but his worried eyes revealed his sorrow. Cassie knew Jinn held a soft spot for Kailey. "She's the whole reason this nightclub has been turned upside down. It'd be best for all of us if she vanished for good."

Cassie's jaw tightened. "Jinn—"

"Easy now," Jinn said, lowering his voice and leaning atop the bar to move closer to her. "Just tugging your chain. I know she's important to you. What I can't figure out is *why*. You two got something going on that I've not sensed yet?"

"No," Cassie said. "And even if I did, you'd never hear about it from me."

"I see how you look at her."

"It's no different than how you look at her," Cassie said.

"Maybe so, but somehow she favors you enough to reverse her want to kill you and now becomes you bff?"

"Look, she's missing," Cassie said, resting her fists atop the bar. "Have you heard anything about—"

"'Bout someone taking her? Nah, I haven't," Jinn said. "It could be any of our factions, although that's highly unlikely right now. With the fallout that she initiated, the list of those who'd love to hurt her in various ways would be a long one. Might take days or a few weeks to check off each one."

Cassie sighed. "So nothing other than your rumored thoughts?"

"My hopes and dreams," Jinn said. "I wanted her the moment I saw her, but hell, now that she's with Brady, I've no interest in crossing that line. Hell no. Not only is his bark and bite nasty as a werewolf, but he has the law on his side. I never push boundaries like that. Never."

"Brady's not a dirty cop," Cassie said.

"You been in his bedroom yet?"

Fury darkened Cassie's eyes. Her crimson irises flamed. She found no humor in his comment. "No."

"No? Then you don't know *how* dirty he can get."

"You've been there?"

Jinn's lips pursed a moment before he broke into fierce laughter. "Girl, I told you I won't dare cross that boundary. But, you've thought about it though. Right? The three of you ... but hey, since you've not been there, you don't know how dirty a cop he can become, handcuffs and all."

"You know that's *not* what I meant."

"I know. Don't get all bent out of shape. Teasing you into fits of rage is I the least I can do for the punishment I endured by the vamps and demon council members."

"I'm sorry you had to go through that. I ... I didn't know."

Jinn shrugged. "Wasn't a thing you could do about it anyways. Look at me. See? I recovered. Well, physically. Mentally ... that's another story. Let's just say I'm wary of a lot of things. Being around you is number one, as long as Forrest is part of your posse."

"If the resentment toward me and Kailey is that severe, Forrest is the best backup we have."

Jinn nodded. "That might be. Just know it limits … *us*. You and I. It tilts the friendship scale too far in the wrong direction. Can you get that?"

Sadness came to Cassie's eyes. "I understand. I'll leave as soon as you tell me if you've not heard anything about Kailey."

"Girl, I already told you that."

"Tell me again, and I'll leave. I need to know."

"Deal. Nothing's been said about Kailey at all," Jinn said. He thought for a moment and frowned. "When did she go missing?"

"This morning."

"And Brady knows?"

She nodded. "He does now. I called him before coming here."

"Hell, ol' cop boy knows no one's considered missing until *after* twenty-four hours has passed."

"In most cases, that's true, but not when you have vampires and demons for enemies."

"Valid point." Uneasiness overshadowed him again. "But if someone just took her, there's not been any talk since we're *hours* away from opening. I'll keep my ears perked once the bustling begins. Now, is there anything *else* I can help you with?"

"If you hear anything?"

Jinn looked solemnly into her eyes and nodded. "Even though in my heart and mind I know I shouldn't, if I find out anything, I'll let you know. Probably nothing will be spoken. Given that humans aren't too smart, loose lips run rampant after happy hour though. Booze does that. People boast, even when they shouldn't. Now, since you're dressed to seduce and kill, turn that fine ass around and let me watch ya walk to the door. Make me wish I was a drooling human."

Cassie's brow tightened. Her eyes narrowed until Jinn's wide grin let her know he was only saying it in case they were being watched, which was highly probable. Needless to say, if she were in his position, fearful of the founders watching her every move, she'd have no choice but to pretend to be hostile to someone she favored when she had been ordered not to speak to that person, vampire, or demon.

She held his gaze for several long moments. Regret shrouded their eyes and slowly, she turned away.

"Mmphh!" Jinn said.

Cassie blushed and laughed inside, but she refused to glance over her shoulder. She wasn't certain if *that* remark was his playacting or not.

Although she didn't have information about Kailey, she did learn something. Forrest's guess of ancient vampires coming to Seattle wasn't farfetched. Even Jinn knew. They had come to Seattle for a reason. To settle an old score? Maybe. Or had the vampire founders of Nocturnal Trinity requested their aid in ridding the threat of Forrest?

Jinn had given her information he shouldn't have, or … Had he given her information he was ordered to give by the founders? As much as she wanted to trust him since he had always been a close friend, she wondered if she could anymore? How much pain had they inflicted on him for his role in helping send Diaboch into the abyss? Did they break him? Was he under vampire compulsion?

For a demon to be compelled, his psyche had to have been shattered, and he partway revealed that to be the case. And since Alec and his remaining siblings had lied about killing the other behemoths, the behemoths were capable of breaking Jinn thoroughly.

She shuddered as she thought about the behemoths and that they were still alive. A cold stabbing pain shot through her. The Wrathbone—the one weapon that could pierce the flesh of a behemoth—had been given to Alec because he had promised to send them back to the abyss.

Since the behemoths still resided inside Nocturnal Trinity and Alec had the weapon, Forrest, Penelope, and all the others who stood behind Brady were defenseless in any confrontation where the behemoths challenged them.

Without realizing it, Cassie picked up her pace, heading toward the door where the bouncer scooted away in fear at her approach. He held no desire to confront her again. Normally, his fearful and terrorized expressions would've given her great pleasure, but she barely noticed and certainly didn't have the time to enjoy the satisfaction. She'd been in Nocturnal Trinity too long and the walls seemed to be closing in.

Kailey was in true danger, and Cassie's demon intuition screamed that she was, too.

She glanced back at Jinn. He smiled broadly with what should've been interpreted as a friendly smile. However, she couldn't take anything at face value now, especially a demon's smile, no matter how close of friends they had once been. Humans would've taken his smile as warm and endearing, which was most likely a deceptive guise. Cassie had played the role of a human for too long, to the point that she was susceptible to think like them and vulnerable to respond with the same type of emotions. Her demon side knew better and an epiphany shone like a beacon in her mind as she studied Jinn's lingering grin. Her demon instinct kicked in hard, and she needed to get out of Nocturnal Trinity immediately.

There was no honor between demons.

CHAPTER 8

*A*fter Raven entered the black cat, her vision spun and blurred, and she—for some unexplained reason—found herself near unconsciousness, which did not seem possible for her spirit form. However, since she had possessed the little black cat, she was no longer in spirit form.

The spooked cat's first initial reaction was to flee. The cat's spirit fought against hers. She was an intruder and it wanted her … OUT! Bolting into a full sprint, it met a brick wall head on. The smack was enough to sprawl the cat on the pavement near the dumpster.

Groaning with pain and panting while writhing on its side, the cat struggled to regain its senses. Raven felt the cat's pain as though it were her own, and since she occupied the cat, it was hers, too. Until the cat opened its eyes, Raven was swallowed in darkness.

Trapped inside the feline, Raven felt claustrophobic. She had no way to coax the cat or attempt to tame its wild nature. They scuffled against one another. Had the cat been capable, it would've pushed her out. She feared they'd never share the body peacefully, and she didn't know how she could exit. The cat was too hostile, but she understood why.

If the cat could understand that it benefited from having Raven as a mutual occupant, matters between them could lessen quickly.

Feral cats, like Raven's new lodging quarters, weren't easily enticed by kind words. And without knowing it, Raven could never meld their dual personalities and spirits into one. She was human. The cat was a beast. They could never be fully compatible, but they could live complementary with one another. The fact the cat was female didn't change matters, either. Raven hoped to refine their differences, at least enough to where they held a common purpose.

The cat rolled over and lay scrunched on the dirty alley. It breathed through its open mouth and panted with its tongue hanging partway out.

While it tried to gain its bearings, she slowly adjusted as well. With no possible way to explain how this phenomenon was taking place, she experienced whatever the cat felt. She might never fully gain control of its every movement, but she discovered she could manipulate it to move and act through her mental impulses.

Raven focused on its right forepaw and stretched its leg forward. With a bit more effort, she got the cat to expose its claws and scratch at the pavement. The cat resisted, but Raven's will was stronger.

"Easy," Raven whispered, wishing she possessed a physical way to comfort the cat with gentle pats or rubbing behind its ears. "I'm not going to hurt you."

Viewing the outside world through the cat's eyes was odd. Most everything was a grayish hue that lacked the brightness of vivid colors. For a cat, that didn't matter. For Raven, a world without color seemed a curse for any human to endure.

Raven caused the cat to turn its head to the right and then to the left. The cat somehow began to trust her, perhaps realizing it was stuck with her until Raven decided to vacate, so it allowed her partial control.

She wasn't certain how much time elapsed before they understood one another. The cat relaxed and as it did so, Raven became even more conscious of its pains and needs.

Its stomach tightened and rumbled, aching with hunger, and that was the reason why it was pilfering through the dumpsters. It needed food, and she guessed it hadn't eaten in more than a day. She didn't want to imagine what garbage it might have consumed in its desperation. She pitied it. And because it was hungry, she craved food, too.

"You poor baby," Raven said, projecting her thoughts to the cat.

The cat mewed slightly. She wondered if whatever thoughts she issued, the cat would try to voice them. Or had it simply been the cat replying in its own way? She hoped it was the latter, as her thoughts tended to ramble incessantly, especially since she was trying to make sense of her spirit walk. So if the cat attempted to speak her thoughts continually, any person would think the cat was diseased or had rabies. It was already shunned by society, and no doubt, a frantic cat mewing with every breath would probably freak people out even more.

"Let's find you some food," she said.

This time the cat offered no mews or cries, which relieved her. It offered a brief, slight purr instead. It saddened her to think that her voice might have been the gentlest tone anyone had used toward the stray in a long time.

For several minutes, the cat staggered worse than a drunk having no control over his legs. At first, Raven feared the strange vertigo occurred due to striking its head against the brick wall. It became evident the cat was only showing its true lazy nature by not offering any help in walking or keeping its balance at all. Raven became frustrated because she was having a difficult time maneuvering its four legs, which was far more complicated than she'd ever considered.

Once Raven figured out how to walk smoother and almost normal, they were halfway down the dim alley. Other sensations heightened in addition to its hunger. Her back and belly prickled with irritating, tickling tingles. She shivered at the maddening waves of movement that suddenly made her itch all over.

She sat down and scratched vigorously but it didn't lessen. The jagged, sharp claws ripped open old scabs and the sudden pain made her stop scratching. She dropped to the ground, rolled back and forth on a pile of dirt and debris, trying to scratch her back with the scrap paper and bits of glass, but still the crazy creeping tingles persisted. Rising to all fours and shaking slightly, dust and small bits of paper fell from her fur.

The itching sensation turned to violent, needle-pricking stabs.

Fleas!

Now she felt even more sorry for the cat, and herself. No wonder the poor cat edged more toward the wild side than ever holding trust toward a human. The biting, crawling fleas were already driving her insane and she was unable to ignore them.

A passerby probably never considered the complete agony a homeless cat endured.

"Help me," Raven whispered to the cat. "And I promise to make your life somehow better."

CHAPTER 9

Kailey remained tied to the chair. She stopped tugging the ropes because she could find no weaknesses in the chair's metal frame or the thick rope. It was only a matter of time before she'd be taken elsewhere to face her fate, which most likely ended in death.

The air held a lingering scent of cigarette smoke from the two men who had left her alone. Blending with the harsh tobacco aroma was an earthy, musty scent. Mold too, maybe, as the air seemed moist and cool.

She sat in silence. Perhaps silence wasn't the proper word. Absolute silence would've relieved her, but she wasn't enclosed inside a vacuum. The blindfold kept her in darkness, and amplified her hearing.

Every minor sound became magnified and irritating. The scratchiness of the tied rope against the chair each time she moved, her every breath, each dry swallow, her heartbeat, and the settling of the rafters overhead bellowed an overbearing orchestrated tone that relentlessly serenaded her ever closer to delirium. She strained to hear outside noises, hoping to find a clue as to where she was being kept prisoner. But the walls seemed too thick or she'd been taken to an isolated area where no one could hear her scream.

That was a frightening thought. To scream but no one could hear, no one could intercept, and no one could try to rescue her. She tried to push the notion away.

She thought it odd that hearing louder sounds would've somehow been more comforting. At least then she knew someone might have found her whereabouts and come to rescue her. Although her captors had abandoned her for the moment, she didn't think they'd gone far. Her time and luck slowly dwindled with each passing minute.

Fighting further tears, Kailey wondered if she had truly heard Raven's voice inside her head earlier, or had she stepped to the brink of despair, wishing for any bit of optimism to overshadow her dilemma, even with illogical, delusional thoughts? Of course, the whole conversation might have been due to the side effect of whatever drug they'd used to keep her incapacitated. A number of combined factors might have contributed to her *hearing* Raven. She wished she had the faith to believe Raven had actually spoken to her, but her skepticism overshadowed and crushed her optimism. Yet, she took one thing to heart: the *enlightenment* of a premonition.

Pondering her interactions with Raven—provided their conversation wasn't merely a figment of jumble thoughts crashing inside her mind—Kailey accepted that the person most likely to have taken her hostage was Micah. His hatred toward Brady was extreme enough to use her as a pawn in their power struggle. But during the struggle between the two Alphas, Raven had been under Flora's control. Could Raven have known of their power struggle? Or had Raven learned about it *after* she'd been staked?

During their undergraduate years as roommates, Kailey had not fully accepted Raven's spiritual path as a witch. She wanted to, because she considered Raven to be her best friend. However, a part of her doubted it was real until Raven pointed out that Kailey's brother had fallen prey to a succubus. Even then, Kailey didn't believe in the paranormal or supernatural. Not until *after* her brother's murder and Kailey flew to Seattle to expose the truth. Kailey's investigation flung open a plethora of supernatural beings she had denied existed.

The reality of the truth nearly killed her. Kailey suddenly had enemies that were witches, vampires, and a succubus. Had Raven not flown to Seattle and intervened, sacrificing everything including her own life, Kailey would've died. Raven loved her that much. So, even though she was having a hard time believing that Raven somehow lingered in her spirit form, she knew Raven would do just that. She'd wander as a ghost if she discovered a way to do so, in order to keep Kailey safe.

Kailey couldn't ignore that level of dedication. Most people would sacrifice everything to protect the person they loved the most, which was why she believed Micah was the one behind her abduction. It remained the most logical possibility since Forrest had turned Flora to dust. No other acquaintance of Kailey had any reason to take her.

Micah knew Brady quite well and the best ways to manipulate him. By taking Kailey, Micah intended to lure Brady into a full-fledged fight for dominance over a divided pack. She supposed Micah was hoping Brady would become an emotional wreck in trying to find Kailey, which could tilt the advantage of the fight toward Micah. There was also the chance Micah didn't want to fight against her and Brady since she trained to fight in MMA bouts. Of course, Micah's actions might work against himself should Brady be enraged by his threats.

Brady generally kept a level head during intense moments, but over the past month or so, their relationship had deepened. No longer were their intense heated nights of intimacy guided by pheromones and lust in fulfilling their bodies' primal urges. They had also bonded inside a comfort zone where each could confide in the other without worry or judgment. Their protective barriers they'd housed themselves within for years slowly melted away, allowing each to have a depth of trust neither had known before. They were complementary and unified one to the other. Neither wanted to picture life without the other, and they entertained the idea of marriage and their potential future together. As for children, she didn't know, and Brady worried what their children might be since he was a werewolf.

An odd sound broke through the monotonous melody she was slowly beginning to ignore. The creaking sound came from the rafters above, but since she didn't have a clue what type of building she was in, the ceiling might be as low as ten feet or as high as fifty feet above her head. She didn't know. Of course, the sound could be nothing more than pigeons moving and getting ready to fly out to search for food. She was almost certain the sound wasn't from a pigeon, as no cooing sounds were a part of the noises.

The air shifted above. Something pattered against metal with a slight ticking sound.

Kailey almost spoke Raven's name aloud, but then bit her tongue, in case the sound was the result from one of the men returning. She didn't want them to know she was awake, but by now they'd most likely expect the drug to have worn off. Even if she pretended to be asleep, they'd most likely try to arouse her. She couldn't pretend any longer, and that worried her. Being restrained, she was helpless.

Cooler air funneled downward, sweeping across her hot face, offering a few moments of relief.

Kailey …

"Raven?" Kailey said.

Shh. Yes, project your thoughts.

"What did you discover? Where are we?"

I don't know.

Something warm rubbed against her hand. Instinctively, Kailey tugged her tied hands from its touch.

Easy, it's only me.

"How are you—"

A cat felt sorry for me and was kind enough to take me in, out of the cold.

"What?"

Okay, so I invaded it.

"You possessed a cat?"

Raven laughed. *I suppose you could put it that way.*

Kailey shook her head. "Let me get this straight. You're *inside* a cat?"

Yes.

"What color of cat?"

Black.

"Of course, *black*. I should've known. You being a witch and all."

You just did that eye-roll under the blindfold, didn't you?

Kailey smiled. In spite of the situation, she found a tinge of laughter. Raven always hated when Kailey rolled her eyes and mocked her for doing so. "Guilty."

No need to own up to it. I already knew.

"So why have you housed up inside a cat? What did it ever do to you?"

I needed a way to touch objects. The cat I found in the alleyway and took the opportunity. I hope I can help you get free. Hold still.

"What are you doing?"

If you'll hold still, I'll try to use its jagged claws to weaken the rope. No way I can untie you and I'm pretty certain I can't cut through the rope completely. But I might be able to fray the rope at its tightest junctions.

Kailey almost burst into laughter but was afraid by doing so it simply enforced how close to a mental breakdown she was. Or was she still asleep under the hallucinations of a drug? If Flora had not been staked and turned to dust, this whole ordeal could have been one of her sick, twisted practical jokes. With everything Kailey had witnessed since moving to Seattle, why couldn't she just accept that Raven had returned as a ghost, reclaimed her soul, and was possessing a black cat?

Stringing along the thoughts into one question caused her to giggle. Her body shook as she tried to kept from laughing aloud.

What's so funny? Raven asked.

"Everything," Kailey replied. Her tight smile gave way and she burst into a fit of laughter.

Shh! Stop it! It's hard enough to fray the rope without your tied hands jerking and tightening the rope further.

Kailey tried to suppress her laughs but her body kept spasming. "A part of me still believes you're a delusion."

Is this a delusion?

"Ouch! Dammit, what the hell, Raven? You *scratched* me?"

Be quiet! Think your thoughts to me. Otherwise, those two pricks are going to hear you and come in here and it won't end nicely for you.

"Sheesh, Raven," Kailey projected. The scratch burned like liquid fire. "You've probably given me some weird cat disease or distemper."

This cat has problems but distemper isn't one of them. So hold still. You got to promise me one thing after you get loose.

"Okay, what?"

Food. This poor kitty hasn't eaten well in a long while.

"Deal. Done."

And perhaps one more thing?

"Like what?"

A flea bath.

"Seriously?"

Yes. Either that, or find a way to release me. I'm itching to get out of this fur coat.

"Okay, I'll get you to a vet, flea bath, food, shots, the whole works."

About the shots ...

"Oh, after the scratch, you're *definitely* getting the shots."

Still vengeful?

"Hardly," Kailey thought. "I just don't know how I'll explain you to Brady."

Tell him I'm your familiar.

CHAPTER 10

Curled into the corner of her red-silk cushioned ottoman, Irina sat with her feet tucked beneath her butt. In her right hand, she balanced the stem of a large goblet of blood between her fingers and cupped the bowl into her palm while she propped her elbow on the polished ottoman arm.

Still hours before the sun set, she sat in the windowless room where no sunlight had ever penetrated. Everything was shaded a drab color; even Irina's outlook on the future of her eternal living death was no brighter.

After witnessing Flora's demise, Irina had become more sullen than normal at the death of her sister. The cold Seattle rains painted the perfect background, for which at night she could easily blend into perfectly unseen, if she chose. The somber mood weakened her desire to return to Nocturnal Trinity, even though her two remaining brothers and one sister had called upon her to make an appearance.

Irina ran her left hand across the smooth silk cloth of the ottoman bench, and for brief moments, her mind traveled back to Hirshmacht when she and her siblings had fled their father's castle in fear and haste for their lives during the dead of a cold December night. Had it not been for the intense blizzard, they might have all fallen victim to being staked by a group of vampire hunters that raided Hirshmacht Castle.

A decade after their abrupt departure from the Black Forest, Irina sent a few of her human servants to gather her belongings, including the ottoman, and ship the items to Seattle. Of course, the servants also fulfilled other duties by slaughtering the Baron who had stolen their father's rightful estate. Lorcan, their father, had never been seen or heard from again.

She pondered his fate from time to time, often wondering if he'd manifest his presence elsewhere and exact his revenge. Since he hadn't, she assumed he'd died. And the true blame, though her brothers and other sister seldom brought it up, fell on Flora's shoulders.

The memories of home in their old country and those of her father seldom comforted her. She possessed no desire to ever return. She held no fondness for the past and remained ever spiteful toward the future. The Black Forest's cold bitter winters bit to the bone. The purity of the white snowy blankets shrouding the forests, caking the bark of trees and their castle seemed a hostile betrayal to the hollow darkness that consumed her internally. Worse than the frigid blight, she still despised the decades of isolation she endured inside the castle.

Because of her father's harrowing rule, she'd never held the luxury of venturing outside the castle into the taverns and shops where she could see how the lower class lived. Her curiosity ate at her, but she was never able to satiate the craving. She envied the peasants, their simple lifestyles, their abilities to live life in all its modest splendor, and secretly she wished she'd been born like them, instead of being an aristocrat.

She'd have traded all her silken gowns, jewelry, and her title in the flicker of a blinked eye, if only she could have lived a modest life like them. A normal short life with a normal death was far more suitable. The world changed continually, but never for the better. All the riches in the world meant nothing when she was not permitted to leave the estate.

Her father ensured her isolation and her two sisters' for nearly forty years, making them live like prisoners instead of treating them favorably as heiresses. Their brothers, however, were granted protection to travel to various cities in Europe, to see the trading ports, the cathedrals, and other wonders in the world. They ventured to places her heart was denied. Her anger and resentment festered, but never toward her brothers or sisters. She despised Lorcan, her *father*, more than she craved her freedom, and she had plotted his death on numerous occasions. She wondered if he had ever detected her murderous plots she vested at him, and perhaps he had, because he managed to stay his death by finally granting her the courtesy to leave.

If he hoped for forgiveness, her bitterness forbade she grant him any sympathy or absolution for his treatment of her. She smiled a dutiful smile while loathing him with every stolen breath of undeath she inhaled.

Lorcan granted her a small territory to allow her the sense of reigning, but the guise fell through and she discovered the small, former viscount's castle was nothing more than a cold, near-empty mansion with a few servants. The reality was that she ruled over no one except in name.

But not so in Seattle where she and her siblings owned—and in a sense —*ruled* in prominence at Nocturnal Trinity. Thousands of visitors came, often pleading and begging, to spend the evening as one of the fortunate, *chosen* guests. Those chosen were more than grateful to do whatever the founding vampires demanded. They were willing to sacrifice their lives to satisfy the vampires' needs. Even the peasants of olde weren't so foolish and understood quite well the curse of the undead. Nothing about being a vampire was considered a blessing. Peasants rightfully viewed vampires as the true monsters they were. Despite their blind flaws of accepting the Church's canons, which could be equated to succumbing to a different set of monsters wearing crimson robes, claiming to be of purity, the peasants feared vampires. They held enough sense not to cater to the tainted undead.

Irina had never known happiness before Nocturnal Trinity, and now, that happiness was souring, rotting with the stench worse than a festering decaying corpse. She no longer took joy in watching the groveling wannabes wallow in despair. Their pleading bored her, as did almost every-thing else. The absentminded humans didn't recognize how grateful they should be for not being chosen by her or her siblings. The supposed honor was never a charade. The reputation of Nocturnal Trinity was not concealed and fully understood. Those chosen might never return to the sunlight without receiving the *gift* of a vampire's undead kiss. The majority were completely drained and served as blood feasts for visiting vampires from neighboring states that her brothers invited. And yet, the fools continued to flock in long lines every night. They deserved whatever fate they received, which was not what most hoped for. Few were *ever* turned, as her brothers were most selective.

Irina released her hairpin, allowing her long red hair to spill down her shoulders like threads of gorgeous shining silk. Her hair covered the alabaster skin of her almost bare breasts and her back. She turned slightly to lessen the tightened pressure of her underbust corset's squeezing hold on her ribcage.

She couldn't believe after nearly two centuries she still wore corsets to enhance her modest breasts into more than what she'd been gifted. At least the modern corsets like those young women wore to the nightclub were far more comfortable than those she recalled from her youth. Not as binding, but yet, they were still an unpleasant ordeal. Wearing it wasn't necessarily obligatory to boost her self-esteem, even though her attire was eye-catching to both male and female guests entering Nocturnal Trinity. Her clothing was more for the traditional sense and decor. The true mood of the time she had known ceased to exist, so she wondered why she bothered placating the façade further.

Styles faded, only to return as fads several decades later, but even the revamped style never matched the former. Weakened memories cheapened the quality and new generations thought they knew more than the previous ones, especially in what was regarded as trendy. Irina's closets were lined with dresses and gowns that would someday again become the *in* fashion to flaunt. Why *ever* throw them out?

Nightly, Nocturnal Trinity attracted the strangest crowds, but mostly what those people considered aesthetic only appeased themselves or repelled what was considered the norm of society. This was what they thought the gothic times had been, and they never could have been more wrong.

The piercings, tattoos, and odd clothing were nowhere similar to what she recalled, what she lived. These trinkets would have been viewed as strange even then. And the plastic surgery, breast enhancements particularly, was something Irina never understood. All of these things seemed shallow to her, dismissive, and proved more of the insecurities of those who sought them than how others perceived them.

A slight draft breezed through the cased opening that led into her sitting room. A guest? At this hour? Well before sunset? Since her servants had been sent away for the day, she surmised one of her siblings had arrived via the underground tunnel.

Irina sighed and waited. Couldn't she even enjoy her boredom alone?

CHAPTER 11

Irina took a sip of blood. The silence inside her home echoed loudly, even with the presence of her unanticipated guest. The faint scent of jasmine caught her attention, which indicated her sister, Nikolina, had come to visit.

"Sister!" Nikolina said, standing in the cased opening before her. Her long blonde hair flowed in feathering locks. Her ice-blue eyes shimmered as she studied Irina. "You're not fast asleep?"

Although startled, Irina remained calm and collective without the slightest flinch for the intrusion. "Nor are you, it seems. You traveled through the underground tunnels so early?"

"Yes."

"I must suppose you've urgent news to arrive unannounced. Surely you did not intentionally come to find me slumbering away in my coffin?"

Nikolina pursed her lips. "Well, it's been days since we've heard or seen you. You've not answered our calls. I—I was beginning to worry."

"As you can see, I'm quite well for a breathing corpse." Irina forced a tired smile. A slight hint of her fangs protruded with the widening of her mouth. "I've been busy."

"Busy?" In a flash, Nikolina crossed the room and plopped softly on the ottoman beside Irina.

Irina swirled the thick blood in the goblet. "Thinking."

"Ah, I see." Nikolina feigned a smile. "I didn't expect to find you home. I thought you might be with Alec since he's also been unavailable for the past few days."

"Alec's the last person I want to be around," Irina said, bitterly. She sipped blood from the goblet, leaned forward, and placed it on the glass table.

"Why's that?"

"Need you ask?" Irina's narrowed eyes matched the coldness icing her tone.

Nikolina sighed. "Ah, I suppose not. But no sense sitting at home alone. Why not return to our VIP at Nocturnal Trinity? Some of our guests have been asking about you. At least the wannabes would fawn all over you. You might enjoy having some fun at their expense."

"They sicken me. They offer nothing new. It's a repeat of the same crowd night after night. Is this what concludes our long lives, sister?"

Nikolina looked surprised by the question. "Whatever do you mean?"

"We haven't sought adventure in ages. Nocturnal Trinity's *not* what we initiated it to be," Irina replied. "The excitement faded long ago. At least, for me. Our nightclub no longer feels cozy. It bores me."

"Are you in one of your ... moods?"

"My moods?"

"Sister, you've often displayed your despair and your distaste for our prolonged lives. Is that what you're experiencing now?"

"No. This *isn't* a mood. Nocturnal Trinity has lost its focus. I feel like a stranger there. I miss how it was before—"

"Before Flora's death?"

"Yes." Irina didn't need to fight tears. She couldn't even remember the last time she'd cried. Her cold heart reflected in her tone of voice and her outlook on their existence. No tears flowed past her frozen callous dam. Although she loved Flora because they were sisters, she held no sorrow. She did, however, suffer the loss in ways she'd not expected.

"Of the lot of us, I'd have thought you thrilled to see her gone," Nikolina said.

"Gone? Yes. To Europe or Asia or to another far off region of the world. Not turned to ash where I'll never see nor hear her again. Regardless of what I thought of her, she was still our sister, a part of our strength."

A sly hint of a smile clung to Nikolina's lips. "That's an odd reflection, even for you. After all, you despised Flora more than the rest of us."

Irina shrugged. "*Despised* is a bit harsh of an evaluation, don't you think?

"Then what would you call it?"

Irina bit her lower lip while she mulled her defense. "I never truly despised her. I wasn't fond of her. I held a … strong distaste toward her, but I never hid that in her presence."

"Nor ours. Why was that, Irina? Because she deemed herself as father's favorite? Is that why you despised her?"

"She didn't need to boast about her closeness to father. He made it abundantly obvious without us venturing a guess. His little faithful pet. It always bothered me that he chose to flaunt her before the courts."

"But not you?" Nikolina asked.

"Flora, the *flower* of our father's heart. The one who never did anything wrong in his sight. Flawless in her outward beauty, she acted haughty because she knew how exquisite her features were."

"You and I are equal in beauty, and in some ways, our features overshadowed hers."

Irina wasn't moved by the compliment, nor did she believe it. "You possess such traits, sister. Not me. I'm surprised father allowed her to etch into his massive ego. He was never favorable of competition."

"Their personalities were near replicas of one another, I agree, but that's not why he favored her."

"Then why?" Irina straightened in her seat. Her curiosity gleamed in her eyes.

"She was cunning and more ruthless than the rest of us. Well, not nearly as bad as Nicodemus. But Father used that to his advantage whenever Counts and Countesses visited the castle."

"I remember," Irina said. Bitterness tightened her throat. But Nikolina was right. Flora was only more cunning and ruthless because she didn't hesitate in performing dark twisted acts and murders. Irina entertained a lot of ruthless murderous ways in her mind toward their father, painful ways to make him suffer, but she didn't have the fortitude Flora possessed. Irina never followed through. She held back her actions and cursed herself for her weakness.

After long moments of silence and reflection, Irina finally said, "I lost count of how many princes she was betrothed to without ever marrying."

Nikolina laughed and playfully placed her hand on Irina's knee. "That was an impossible scorecard to keep, wasn't it?"

"Yet, she never married."

"None of us did, dear. Why should we when we have such a gift? I can't imagine living centuries with the same spouse. Or outliving numerous *non-vampire* spouses. The gods forbid. That would weigh heavily on one's soul." Nikolina shook her head and laughed with a lofty giggle. "On one's *mind*. Soul? It's a sure sign I've been around these sorrowful humans much too long by incorporating *that* into my speech. I must say that a few humans over the decades have nearly captured my heart, making me entertain the idea of marriage."

"I almost married," Irina said softly, looking away. "Long ago."

"Really?" Nikolina eased back into the cushioned ottoman and folded her hands atop her knees. "Do tell! You've never mentioned this. To whom?"

"A young man named Franz," she replied.

"The peasant boy?"

"He wasn't a *boy*."

Nikolina waved her hand and nodded. "You know what I mean. But he was a peasant. I faintly remember him. Whatever happened between the two of you?"

"Father found out."

"He disapproved?"

Irina sighed. "He disapproved of most anything I longed for. Do you not recall?"

"Did you tell him your wishes … about marriage?"

Irina nodded. "Of course, I told father, but not that it mattered. I had not been a vampiress but a couple years when Franz and I met. How I wish it had been *before*."

"Ah, I see." She scooted to the edge of the ottoman and reached for Irina's blood goblet. "So father thought it best to end the relationship before you drained him during a bloodlust?"

"No. It had nothing to do with that. I never fed from Franz. I never revealed to him what I am."

"Because he was a peasant and you an aristocrat?"

Irina shrugged. "I doubt that's even part of the reason. All I know is that I ended up locked in my tower room like a fairytale princess for decades."

"Really?"

"Don't pretend you didn't know." Irina flicked an angry glare at Nikolina.

"Honestly, sister, I didn't until now."

Irina frowned. "How could you *not* know?"

"My dear, we all lived in the castle but its vastness made it difficult to know who was where and doing what at any given time. Sometimes weeks passed before I saw Flora or any of our brothers. I asked father about you numerous times, as I wished to travel with you into the city."

Irina's gaze softened slightly, but she wondered if her sister was telling the truth. "And what did he say?"

"Something about you being in the Orient."

Her brow rose. "And you believed that?"

Nikolina shrugged. "Seemed like something you'd have enjoyed."

"Enjoyed, yes!" Irina bolted to her feet and flung her hands above her head. Her voice lowered to a growl and she turned, almost theatrically pointing a finger at her sister. "But no! He never allowed me to leave the castle."

"I'm sorry, sister. I honestly didn't know."

Irina's hands tightened into fists. Her eyes showed her fury. She huffed and turned her back to Nikolina.

"Irina, I didn't realize the heavy burden you've been carrying all these years. But it was so long ago." Nikolina rose from the ottoman and eased to her sister's side, slowly turning and pulling Irina into a soft embrace. Irina clung to Nikolina and shook. But still no tears surfaced. Nikolina shushed into Irina's ear, trying to calm her like she might a small hurt child, had she the humanity to do so.

After several minutes, Irina loosened from their embrace and lowered her arms, stepping back. After pulling back the long strands of her red hair, she allowed it to fall down her back. She took a deep breath and slowly released it. "Apologies, sister, for my behavior."

"No apologies necessary." She beamed a smile, placing her hands on Irina's shoulders.

"With Flora's death, I've allowed my mind to revisit the dark places I've dammed up to forget."

Nikolina smiled and nodded. "A dam only holds back so much before it eventually cracks and bursts open. All the ugliness flows out and drowns the lovelier things. Don't be a victim to your past, dear sister."

Irina nodded.

Nikolina stepped past Irina, returned to the ottoman, and sat down. She motioned for Irina to do the same.

"I suppose so. You don't find Flora's absence disturbing?" Irina asked.

Nikolina studied Irina with a shrewd hesitant stare, which meant she was attempting to pry into Irina's mind to read her thoughts. Irina hated when she did that. But Nikolina's intense glare also indicated she seemed to have taken Irina's question as accusatory.

"Do you regret our decision in having Forrest stake Flora?" Nikolina finally asked.

"Don't you?" Irina asked.

Nikolina looped and curled a strand of her long blonde hair on her index finger while lightly pressing the tips of her fangs on her lower lip. Her sparkling blue eyes shimmered. With no emotion in her tone, she replied, "No."

"No?"

Nikolina smoothed her silken gown. A few seconds later, she took Irina's goblet of blood from the table and sipped.

Irina sighed. "Nicodemus and Flora are gone forever. Nothing we do brings them back. Ever. The power we held has lessened due to their absences. We can't return to the power we had."

"They were both fools," Nikolina spat. "Spoiled like the humans we allow to patronage our nightclub. Nicodemus and Flora failed to understand that repercussions occur, *even* to us. They flaunted their strengths far more than they ever should have, setting targets on themselves. After Nicodemus' death, you'd have thought Flora would've stopped her bullying pursuit of Kailey, at least for a short period. We didn't have any other choice but to stop her once and for all. She was drawing too much unwanted attention to Nocturnal Trinity and setting a reputation we didn't need. We're lucky we were not part of the casualties."

$\mathcal{I}$rina sat silent for a few moments, wishing Forrest had staked her instead. She almost laughed at the absurdity of it all. Could she possibly be the only suicidal vampire in all of history? She wondered if Flora had found peace. Irina doubted she ever would, as long as she was tortured with this living death.

"Can't you see that Flora brought all of this upon herself?" Nikolina asked.

"I know," Irina said. "But when we offered the opportunity for Forrest to stake Flora, I never thought he'd actually stake her."

"Nor did I," Nikolina said.

"That was the only reason I had agreed," she said in a regretful tone. "I truly thought Forrest wouldn't see the task through. They loved each other at one time. You know that, don't you?"

Nikolina laughed, releasing the curled strand of hair. "You say that as if it was some huge secret."

Irina smiled. "Whatever love they shared was lost decades ago."

"Because of father."

Irina's brow furrowed. "Really? Father seemed to meddle in ruining any romantic relationship within our family. What part did he play in theirs?"

"I don't believe father knew about them. His hand in their friendship was purely coincidental. Father hired Forrest to kill another vampire, clearly because he feared Forrest had come to the Black Forest to kill all of us. So father clearly set Forrest up. To father's surprise, Forrest survived the encounter, but Forrest's father died. There's no quieting such rage after that," Nikolina said. "His rage toward father spilled over into hatred for the rest of us."

Irina pondered.

"You don't remember?"

"This may have occurred during the time I was locked away in my room. If not, a lot of my youth I have blocked from memory. Of course, it *could* be my old age," Irina said with a sly grin.

"Oh, now, you don't look a day over thirty," Nikolina said, playfully waving her hand, dismissing the statement.

Irina's eyes grew fierce. "*Twenty-five.* That was my age when father turned me, dear sister. Even though you were born several years after me, I'll always remain younger since he waited until you were in your thirties to offer the gift to you."

"Touché." She placed a hand over her heart.

"Do you think Forrest will keep his end of the truce?"

Nikolina shrugged slightly. "One can never predict what a vampire hunter or a vampire will do from one day to the next. But, in fairness to Forrest, either he's mellowed over the years or he'll abide by the agreement."

"You think he's mellowed?"

"We're all still alive. The Forrest I remember would never have walked away from a group of vampires unless they were piles of dust."

"He's over a century old, but like us, his age doesn't show in his features."

"He's a true Vampire Hunter."

"I don't think he's mellowed," Irina said, her eyes growing distant. "I think it's something deeper."

"Like what?"

"He's more calculated, wiser. As old as we are, he's not foolish enough to have taken us all on at the same time. Young hunters are full of themselves and fail to fully evaluate the odds."

Nikolina frowned, deep in thought. "You think Forrest's awaiting a better time to slay us? Perhaps one at a time?"

"That would be the smartest thing to do, wouldn't it?"

Nikolina looked even more troubled for several moments. "Perhaps, but Forrest's a man from a different generation. His word means something. It's his honor. A badge unlikely tarnished by deceit. Unlike people today, where words are meaningless and freely given without weight or merit, Forrest won't break an oath."

"And you know this how?"

"When he and his father arrived at our castle, Forrest was on a mission then. He was delivering the half-blood vampire, Varack, to the Archdiocese in Freiburg."

"Because he had vowed to do so?"

"Yes. Even though the oath contradicted everything a Vampire Hunter stood for. Other hunters turned and pursued Forrest, attempting to kill the child and Forrest for protecting the child. None of the hunters succeeded. If he had been willing to go against his own to fulfill a promise, it's highly unlikely he'll break his oath to us."

"I hope you're right."

"As do I. But, just in case, we should probably not isolate ourselves like you have these past few days. I'd hate to lose you."

Irina studied the seriousness in her sister's eyes. "May I ask a question?"

"Most certainly."

Irina craned her neck while listening and watching the door. When she was confident no one stood outside eavesdropping, she said, "Do you trust Alec?"

Nikolina sat in silence for several long moments. Her eyes gazed at the floor while her mind seemed to struggle in how she should reply. "Irina, your solitude these past few days has plagued your mind with all sorts of doubts about everything. Why would you ask such a question?"

"Tell me. Do you trust our brother?"

Nikolina licked her lips slowly. "By the question, I've the assumption you *don't* trust him?"

"Just answer the question," Irina said, her eyes darkening.

"I trust him more than I did Nicodemus or Flora," she replied. "And that says a lot."

"But not with your eternal life as a vampire?"

Nikolina shifted slightly on the ottoman. Her hand nervously went to the emerald pendant on her necklace. She rubbed the stone between her thumb and index finger.

"You've lost your faith in him, too, haven't you?" Irina asked.

"Why are you asking this?" Her eyes looked to the door and then around the room with keen suspicion. "Is he hiding here, listening?"

"No," Irina said, shaking her head. "No, I'm alone. I even sent my servants away for the rest of the day."

"You sent them away?"

Irina nodded.

"Why?"

"I needed the silence. No heartbeats. No breathing, other than my own. I've been sorting through the vaults inside my mind."

"So why are you pressing me for an answer?"

"Because I want to know. I *need* to know. Your nervousness reveals that you doubt your faith in him."

"He's assumed Nicodemus' place, so I've no choice but to place my trust in him. Are you implying I … we … shouldn't?"

Irina said, "He was the one who insisted we hand Flora over to Forrest."

"He brought up the idea, but we all agreed. You never offered a word of protest. None of us did. Now, you're whining about your regrets."

"I explained my reasons for siding with the rest of you concerning her fate. Understand one thing. I'm not whining, but the more I've thought about the situation, the more uncomfortable I have become."

"Why?"

"Alec presented her to gain back a peaceful hold over Nocturnal Trinity."

"Yeah, so? That's a good thing. He got back the nightclub for us, the true founders."

"Don't be so certain," Irina said. Her jaw tightened.

"What do you mean?"

"Alec also promised Forrest and Brady that he'd kill the behemoths, remember? But they're still alive. He's setting us up to be killed, too."

"Don't be preposterous," Nikolina said. "The last thing we need is for each of us to turn on the other. Such accusations are dangerous, Irina. You know that. Further division in our family will become our doom. You're sowing seeds of doubt, so bite your tongue!"

"I'll not bite my tongue! But what do you expect? We offered up Flora. Her absence has weakened our power, like it or not. How does that lessen the chance that Alec might offer you or I or Orvoso to prevent his own slaying? Think about it, sister. Nicodemus was already dust."

"Nicodemus caused his own death. Alec had nothing to do with it."

"No, I agree with you about that, but Flora was offered as a sacrifice. Our sister."

Nikolina nodded. "Yes."

"He readily gave her up and convinced us to do the same. Yet, he has allowed the behemoths to live. He holds the only weapon known to kill their physical earthly bodies and send them back to the Abyss. And I'd wager the behemoths still reside under Nocturnal Trinity. Since Alec possesses the weapon, those demons hold allegiance to him."

"I can't believe you've allowed your paranoia to fester beyond control. You need to go to the nightclub and mingle. Distract your mind from this nonsense. You've remained cooped up far too long." Nikolina stood. "I'll hear no more of this cunning—"

Irina shook her head. "You don't believe me? Ask Alec where those demons are. Ask him for yourself."

Nikolina stiffened. She sat in silence.

"See?" Irina said. "If what I'm saying is true, the most dangerous thing you could do is confront him about those demons' fate. Doing so would make you the next in line to be staked."

"Alec wouldn't do that."

"Which part? Hiding the behemoths or staking us? He's already proven that we're sacrificial with how he handled Flora's fate."

Nikolina frowned. "Her death was a group decision."

"Keep telling yourself that lie. It doesn't change the truth. It only reinforces your belief. My part was in reluctance because I didn't think Forrest would stake her."

"Then you should've stated such during our discussion."

"Alec wants us to believe the decision was all of ours, that we share the same guilt. I think he'd still have done it without our approval."

"This is absurd," Nikolina said, heading toward the door.

"Is it? If you won't ask him, then how about we do what you suggested."

"What's that?"

"You want me to go to Nocturnal Trinity tonight? I'll go, but only if you accompany me. We'll explore the lower levels under the nightclub and see where those demons are. If you're right, we've nothing to lose, now do we?"

Nikolina's eyes widened. After giving the proposal more thought, they narrowed and she nodded. "Very well. After nightfall, you and I shall investigate."

CHAPTER 13

Forrest followed Brady into the apartment. He paused only to study the remnants of the splintered door. By his estimate, the damage occurred less than two hours earlier. The lingering musk and nervous sweat permeated the entranceway. An odder scent coated the busted door.

"They wrecked the place," Brady said, hurrying up the stairs.

Forrest nodded but kept his silence. His heavy footsteps thudded as he walked up the stairs. The steps groaned beneath his weight. When he peered through the open bedroom door, he watched Brady nearly crumble when he picked up a small framed picture of he and Kailey seated at a restaurant, eating.

Brady carefully took the busted cellphone off the bed by the edges to avoid smudging fingerprints. The bedroom window was open. A cold gentle breeze rattled the Venetian blinds.

"Why's the window open?" Forrest asked.

Brady shrugged, still looking at the cellphone. "I don't know. We never open it during the winter."

"They destroyed her phone?" Forrest said.

Brady shook his head. "It's not Kailey's phone."

"Then it's evidence. Might be useful."

Brady took a plastic Ziplock bag from his rear pocket and slid the phone inside. "Maybe, if I can find a trustworthy tech to search its data."

Brady's eyes roamed the room and his jaw tightened. His eyes shimmered and his fingernails turned black and pointy. Dark coarse hair rose on his hands and his face. His back muscles tightened, popped.

"Hold back the rage, Brady," Forrest said in a deep, even tone.

"I'm trying," Brady said, his voice more beast than human.

"You must."

"This is far greater than the times prior when I had to restrain my beast due to Micah's spell."

"If you lose your composure, and should your neighbors see or hear your transformation, you've a lot of explaining to do. I doubt explanations will be enough."

"You're right." Brady closed his eyes and took a deep breath. He seemed to whisper words to himself. After a few moments, he calmed. His eyes returned to normal. "Who'd do this?"

Forrest sniffed the lingering pungent aroma drifting in the room. "We've already discussed the possibilities, but those who came into your apartment aren't *weres*."

"Were they human?"

"No, not human. I'd almost say they're human except … there's something odd about their scent. Different. Their human form masks what they really are. You don't pick up their scent?"

"Not as well as you."

"What do you detect?"

"Horrible body odor, but it's worse than a gym locker that hasn't been cleaned for months," Brady said.

Forrest nodded. "Yep. But there's something more."

"What?"

The creases on Forrest's brow deepened. "I almost want to say it's magic, but I know that's not the energy that lingers inside the room."

Brady appeared concerned. "What do you mean?"

"I've befriended many witches over the years. I recognize the energy they draw for magic. This is far different. Stronger, but it's not magic. Yet, it's familiar to me."

Forrest detected two males had been in Brady's bedroom, but these individuals had not broken down the door. Until he figured out why he remembered the unusual scent, he planned to keep the information to himself.

"You encountered this recently?" Brady asked.

"No, long ago, when I was much younger in the old country, which is why I'm unable to discern what was here."

"But you don't remember?"

"It may take some mind-searching to recall, but once I remember, you'll be the first I tell."

Brady scratched the back of his head and growled.

Forrest said, "At least we can take a few clues from the scene."

"I don't see much."

"Being daylight, we can cross out vampires."

"True," Brady said.

"But not vampire servants."

"Are you always so pessimistic?"

Forrest shrugged. "You have to look at all possibilities."

"I know, but right now I don't see much hope of finding her. My rage is battling my despair."

Forrest placed his giant hand on Brady's shoulder and squeezed. "I've been where you are, but for me, it was a burden I carried more than a hundred years over Penelope."

"That's not something I can do, Forrest. Not only because I don't have your lifespan, but my rage will consume me."

"That's understandable," Forrest said, softly.

"How did you survive that long?"

"I focused on the task at hand. With each vampire I hunted, I used the pursuit to distract me from the pain of my loss. Each time I drove a stake through the heart of a vampire, I pretended it was the one responsible for Penelope's disappearance."

"After so much time, didn't you ... give up on her still being alive?"

"At times, yes. But your situation is far different than mine."

"Different how?"

"I've the suspicion that whoever took Kailey wants her kept alive, at least until he or she is able to confront you."

"Micah?" Brady's jaw tightened.

"That's possible, but I don't detect his scent here. Not even on the ones who burst through the doors to get to her."

Anger flared Brady's nostrils. His eyes darkened. His shoulder muscles swelled as did his arms and back.

"Brady," Forrest said in a deep soothing tone. "Calm yourself. You must."

A soft rap came against the open door. "Brady?"

Brady quickly turned his back to the person to prevent her from seeing his partial transformation.

Forrest stepped between Brady and the nervous young lady at the doorway. His large body blocked her view of Brady. "What do you need?"

His deep voice and his towering, intimidating frame caused her to take a step back.

"I didn't mean to intrude," she said. She brushed her purple bangs from her pale face.

"Demi, could you come back another time?" Brady asked. "This is police business."

"I—I understand, but that's what I wanted to talk to you about."

Forrest said, "Did you see who did this?"

Demi nodded. "The sound of the crashing door downstairs awoke me. I partway opened my door to look out. I didn't see them come in, but on the way out, one of them was carrying Kailey's limp body over his shoulder. I called the police immediately, so they must've told you, which is why you came so quickly. When I saw you pull up, I thought I should tell you what I had seen."

Brady turned toward Forrest with a questionable stare. Then he looked at Demi. "What did you see? How many?"

"Two men dressed in leather jackets and jeans took her. Another one waited in the car. He was the driver. Once the men flung open the back door and they crawled in with her, he drove off."

"Did you recognize any of these men?"

She looked nervous and nodded. "That's what I wanted to tell you. The driver is a friend of yours. I've seen him visit you several times, although that was a long time ago before Kailey moved in with you."

Brady frowned. His eyes narrowed. "Who?"

"I don't know his name. But he always wore that strange robe-like jacket. I think he owned a magic shop?"

Forrest exchanged glances with Brady. Together, they said, "Micah?"

CHAPTER 14

Cassie exited through Nocturnal Trinity's main door and hurriedly pulled the door shut since the bouncer probably had no intention of going to the door until he was certain she was long gone.

Her head ached and her legs felt rubbery. She wished that she hadn't teleported twice earlier. Her strength still had not recovered, and she held the nagging gut feeling that she needed to teleport immediately. She needed to get far away from Nocturnal Trinity as quickly as possible.

Cassie usually held remarkable balance on her stiletto heels, but she kept rolling her ankles. No matter how hard she tried to focus on walking, the heels were an obstructive enemy. She unstrapped them and slipped them off her feet, hoping that she could move quicker. Her steps continued to falter. She placed her hand against the storefront walls to steady herself, still pushing rapid steps to get away from the nightclub.

Her vision dimmed. The world spun. She looked over her shoulder to see two men step outside the nightclub. She recognized them. They were busboys in the demon section of the club and whenever situations got out of hand at the bar, which happened more than not, they were the ones who broke up the fights and escorted the unruly guests to the door. Due to their large size, she always suspected they weren't hired as busboys. They only assumed the role until they were needed.

The anger on their faces meant that someone inside the club wanted her brought back. She tried to increase her pace but her growing dizziness overtook her.

Cassie shook her head. Her vision spun. Was this the result of teleporting twice in the matter of minutes? Or was she too nervous at the information Jinn had given her? The draining of her energy and a sudden adrenaline rush might have set her off-kilter, but she suspected something else. Forcing a few more steps, it suddenly dawned upon her.

The free drink Jinn had given her! Devil's Rum.

"Damn you, Jinn," she whispered through gritted teeth.

While the advice wasn't something she shouldn't ever need to remind herself, she had allowed herself to ignore the obvious. Demons seldom were trustworthy and were only allies when it best suited them. Apparently, the behemoths had tortured Jinn to a level where he feared opposing them and as such, he drugged her and sent these two goons to nab her. She was fortunate the drug hadn't incapacitated her inside Nocturnal Trinity.

Gasping for breath, she leaned against the wall. The stilettos slipped from her fingers and dropped to the concrete sidewalk. The two men's hard-sole shoes scraped as they ran. She wanted to run, but it was better that she didn't. By running, she'd simply cause the drug to work faster and she'd lose consciousness. She needed to remain awake at least until she knew who inside the club wanted her.

"You're coming with us," the one man said, grabbing her elbow and jerking her toward him.

"Is that any way to treat a lady?" Cassie asked with a flirtatious smile. She didn't struggle or attempt to pull free of his hold. Instead, she licked her lips and the gleam in her eye caused him to weaken his hold. "How'd you know I like being manhandled? Please, don't disappoint me. Be rough. I can take it."

The man's chest swelled. His face flushed red, and for a moment he almost released her arm. He was stunned by her words and attitude.

"She's bewitching you, Jim," the other man said. "Look away."

"Jim? Jimmy. You've worked in the club long enough to know I'm *not* a witch," Cassie said.

"Yeah, we know what you are," Jim said, trying to regain his hold on her.

"Do you?" she asked. She staggered to him and grabbed his shirt tightly to prevent herself from falling face-first on the sidewalk. She wished her clumsy action had been fake, but her equilibrium had deserted her, which lessened her confidence in escaping without resorting to her charms.

"Yes," he said, grabbing her other arm and pulling her away from the wall and closer to him, even though she made no attempt to escape his tight grip. She pressed her body against his and looked up at him.

"Don't you want to search me for weapons?" she asked, fighting her dizziness. "Frisk me? Nice and slow. I know you want to touch me. You might enjoy it. I know I would."

The hardened intent in Jim's eyes vanished. His heartbeat hammered with such force she felt his pulse through his skin. Leaning back from him, she smiled, rolling a playful purr off her forked tongue. His lustful eyes left her gaze and lowered to study the slight swell of her breasts barely hidden in her low cut top. She pulled away so he could see her better. His hungry gaze moved past her tight abs and eagerly set upon the curves of her hips. He grinned and drooled like a mesmerized fool.

"Jim!" His friend tugged Jim's arm. "Don't."

Jim pushed Terry away with a violent shove, sending Terry into an awkward stumble. He prevented his fall against the brick wall. "Terry, look at her. She's gorgeous. And her making an offer like that, you know I can't refuse. Besides, we'd be fools if we took her back inside and she had a weapon."

Cassie's gaze turned toward Terry. Her pheromones permeated the air. With a sweet seductive voice she said, "I don't think he can handle the search all by himself. He needs your help."

The agitated expression on Terry's face turned to sudden nervousness, but after inhaling her scent, he swallowed hard. He released a gasp of excitement. An eager smile curled his lips and his pants bulged.

For several long moments, the two men stood contemplating what to do. She knew their thoughts were no longer focused on how they'd take her into custody, but on what each of them fantasized about doing to her.

Cassie smiled. "How long have you two worked together?"

"Five years," Jim said.

"That's a long time," she said.

Enthralled, they both nodded unaware of her slow transformation into her succubus form. The tip of her long tail eased around to Terry's head and gently turned him to face Jim.

"And all during that time, the two of you never revealed the lust you have for one another?" she asked. While the statement was untrue, her wiles and pheromones ignited the fictitious desires to explode into a fantasy that seemed to stir in past memories between them.

Jim's eyes indicated he was lost by her charms. He hung on every word that flowed through her perfect lips. He shook his head, but instead of trying to unchain her planted thoughts, he lowered his restraint until his need gleamed in his eyes.

Her tail slinked past Terry and turned Jim's head to face him. "Perhaps the two of you should start first. Get things heated up between you, so you have me all worked up and fully turned on. Then, I'll join you. After all, if you can't get swept away in your passion for one another, why should I allow the two of you to enjoy me?"

Spellbound by her words, Terry's lips parted. He stared at Jim with agonizing lust. Jim rushed to Terry and the two kissed hard. They embraced in passion, pulling one another closer, fiercer, and Cassie slipped back several steps, using the last of her energy to teleport.

She didn't know where she'd end up, but she believed anywhere was safer than where these two lovebirds had intended to deliver her. In a blink of the eyes, she left them, but didn't have enough energy to laugh about the situation. Wherever she ended up, the fear crept over her that she might not awaken for hours and she'd be at the mercy of those surrounding her.

CHAPTER 15

*A*fter questioning Demi for fifteen more minutes, Forrest followed Brady back to the patrol car. The ominous sky spread further gloom to the aging day, as though the gray clouds somehow reached around the sun and forever choked out its light and energy. Seattle days were like that, leaving folks to wonder if the sun would ever make its appearance again.

Forrest sat in silence while Brady fumed. Brady released a line of fierce obscenities, occasionally hitting the steering wheel before driving away.

"Micah?" Brady growled. "I suspected he might have a hand in this."

"I'm not so certain he does," Forrest said.

"Why not? Because he's related to you?"

"He's my kin, yep, but I'm riding with you, aren't I? I chose which side I am on. That's with you, Kailey, and Cassie. Blood-ties have nothing to do with my current analysis. Throughout my life I've been betrayed by many, and some of those were family members. So, don't jump to conclusions about Micah yet."

"No? Demi's an eyewitness," Brady said. "That pretty damn good evidence."

"Normally, I'd agree. But not in this case."

"Then what prompts you to believe Micah's not involved?"

"I didn't say he *wasn't* involved. He might be, but I could almost guarantee he wasn't with the two men that broke into your apartment."

"Okay? How do you know that?"

"His scent wasn't there."

"Of course his scent wasn't in the apartment. He remained in the car, Forrest," Brady said. "He didn't come inside."

"That doesn't matter. Those two men came *from* his car, provided there was a car at all. Like you, Micah's an Alpha with strong pheromones. These men didn't carry his scent."

"From my perspective, that still proves nothing."

Forrest sighed. "Perhaps not. Look, I'm not trying to undermine your investigative skills, but when you allow emotions to dictate your actions, you'll be wrong every single time."

"What am I *wrong* about?"

"You're missing the greater issue at hand."

Brady turned toward Forrest and frowned. "And what's that?"

"Demi said that she called the police when those men broke into your apartment. But Cassie's the one who called you. No officers were waiting at your apartment and no one from the precinct called to let you know what had happened. Now, did they?"

"Shit," Brady said, returning his attention to the road and slowing the car. He shook his head. "You're right. If she called them, officers would've been dispatched. So someone at headquarters is involved."

"That or the mayor is. From the distance the car was parked to where Demi looked outside her door, there's no way she could possibly identify Micah. I get your anger toward Micah, but so do your other enemies. Conveniently telling you that it was Micah is a good way to throw you off the actual perpetrator's trail, and misdirects your investigation."

"That's a great evaluation," Brady said. "Forrest, what are you *not* telling me? You seem to know more information than what you're giving me. Other than the weapon on the dead councilman, do you have any true evidence of an ancient vampire?"

"Actual proof? No. A gut feeling, yes."

Brady sighed and shook his head. "Dammit. First Cassie, and now *you* with these gut feelings?"

"What do you mean?"

"You're basing the possibilities on a hunch?" Brady shook his head.

Forrest's jaw tightened. He cast an even gaze in Brady's direction. "No, it's not a hunch. Vampire Hunters are blessed with an innate sense to detect vampires but whenever we're close to encountering the ones far older than Dracula, the magnitude of the intensity is even greater. I sense the strength of an elder vampire and possibly something far worse. I get that you may not understand, but let me ask you something."

Brady shrugged. "Okay, what?"

"Was Cassie wrong about Kailey being in danger?"

The color drained from Brady's face. Regret caused him to take a deep breath. "Cassie was right. I should've listened to her. Dammit. Maybe I could've gotten to Kailey in time."

"No, Brady, don't beat yourself up over that," Forrest said. "Kailey had probably already be taken. But in the future, don't question supernatural powers you don't understand and don't be so easy to dismiss these *hunches* as you call them."

"So demons and Vampire Hunters possess a sixth sense?"

"Humans do, too. Most people never even realize it. Those who do often capitalize on it. Cassie has similar intuitions, too. All I can say at the moment is that I sense the presence of an ancient, but with its power, he or she has shielded against my ability to locate its actual whereabouts."

"I see. That makes some sense," Brady said.

"One thing I can tell you with certainty is that we need to be on guard, especially after the sun sets."

"Luckily, that's a few hours away, still."

"Mind if I ask you another question?"

Brady kept his eyes on the road and nodded. "Sure."

"How did you become a part of Micah's pack?"

"By accident, really."

Forrest chuckled. "How's that?"

"After I first realized what I was, I knew the best thing to do was to go deep into the wilderness a day before the full moon. It was the only way I could ensure I didn't kill innocent people. I drove out to some old logging roads, far from the city, but I never expected to encounter anyone. After I changed during the full moon, the cries of other wolves in the forest captured my attention. It was Micah's pack. Micah approached me face to face while the rest of the pack circled around us. Even as a wolf, I recognized Micah was the Alpha of the group, even though I didn't quite know what an Alpha was. I imagine if I'd have accepted his challenge to fight, I've have died that night."

Forrest nodded. "Probably."

"I don't mean Micah could have killed me—"

"No, the entire pack would've ripped you to shreds. Not because of his Alpha position, but because he cast a strong charisma spell over himself to hold their undying loyalty. Being an Alpha with magical power is a deadly combination."

Brady smiled. "Yeah. That's the feeling I had. Anyways, I lowered my head before him, granting him my submission. The next morning, after we returned to our human forms, he offered to let me into the pack. I accepted, mainly because I wanted to better understand what I was. He and the pack taught me a lot and helped me control my transformations. I learned I could change at will whenever I was threatened or when my anger got the best of me."

"It still surprises me that he let you in."

"Why's that?"

"He knew you were an Alpha."

"How could he have known when I didn't?" Brady asked.

"That's why he felt secure in welcoming you into the pack. Because you *didn't* know. I'm sure he was aware that eventually you'd discover it and challenge his rule, which is probably why he cast the spell over his pack, preventing all of you from turning with the full moon. Knowing Micah, he probably figured if the two of you became close friends that you'd never challenge him."

Brady grinned. "My loyalty to him as his friend did play a factor in why I waited so long to take my stand. But, by then, his spell preventing us from changing had already soured our friendship. When we weren't able to transform during the full moon, when the power of our curse is at its strongest, that further agitated me, Jacob, and the rest of the pack. A true leader wouldn't allow his pack to suffer such agonizing pain, which makes sense now, so his spell backfired."

"Yep. I'm sure he regrets it now."

"So you knew his father?"

Forrest nodded.

"What kind of man was he?"

Forrest turned to look out the window. "A great man. Jacques was the one who taught me about what I was, and he protected me as I learned."

"What happened to him?"

Forrest chuckled and lied. "It's too long ago to remember. So where are we headed anyway?"

"Nocturnal Trinity. Where else?"

"Why there?"

"Best place to get information about vampires, demons, and other preternatural beasts, isn't it?"

Forrest took a deep breath and sighed. "Also the best place for them to try to kill us, too. Not everything supernatural leads back to Nocturnal Trinity. You know that, right?"

"I think in this case, it probably does."

"Perhaps," Forrest said. "But Micah's actions have pretty much worn out your welcome and definitely *his*."

"Why? I eagerly withdrew the werewolf faction from their Order. We were never meant to be a part of them anyway. Micah's insistence was one of the stupidest things I've ever seen."

"Yep, but don't expect a royal welcoming. They like you about as much as they favor Micah or any other of the *weres*."

CHAPTER 16

Forrest rode in the passenger side of Brady's patrol car, watching the people walk, window shop, or jog along the sidewalks. Even though no vampires roamed during the day, he found that he preferred the night.

Had vampires not existed, he'd still rather spend his waking hours roaming after the sun set until the breaking of dawn. For him, the quiet softness of the early morning as the dew fell and darkness shrouded his surroundings was the best time to be awake. The silence of the night shrouded by the absence of light was his serenity. Less intrusion from the outside world troubled him, giving him more time to focus his thoughts. While most humans feared the darkness and its layered depths of night, Forrest thrived on these qualities. By all definition and his actions, he was a nyctophile.

Brady sprouted his theories aloud on Forrest's sudden deaf ears. Forrest's mind was elsewhere, probing into past memories he wished to keep buried, still looking for clues of what had come to Seattle. He didn't tell Brady he recognized the ancient being or force or entity that had arrived sometime during the past few days, because Forrest wasn't quite certain *how* to explain this sudden intrusion of something that should no longer exist, something he thought he'd destroyed nearly a century earlier.

All he could say for certain—which he hadn't and still debated on whether he should—was that the city's chance for doom was not a question of if, but when.

For some reason, Forrest's mind reflected on Flora's last moments on the earth before he plunged the stake into her cold blackened heart. Like most vampires, she had become more evil the longer she prowled the earth. During the past year, she'd spent most of her time preying upon the willing, ignorant people that spent hours lined up outside Nocturnal Trinity. But once she encountered Kailey, Flora sought to mentally torture the poor girl for reasons never explained. She could've moved her bullying tactics to her next victim the following day, like she had with all her others, but she didn't. He didn't know why Flora despised Kailey but the vampire's bitter hatred toward the girl was no secret. If he had not staked her, she'd have been the first he'd suspect in Kailey's abduction.

But Forrest witnessed Flora's last fleeting moment, eye-to-eye, when the soulless flicker of dark light in her eyes was extinguished. Her body dropped to the floor in a pile of ash, and after well over a century of slaying vampires, he understood one thing quite well: No vampire ever came back after being staked.

This made the current situation in Seattle even more bizarre. A tinge of the ancient one throbbed like a pulsing beacon, sending out its tendrils, searching and wanting, hoping, desiring to find a suitable host once again, and whenever that conduit successfully connected, an evil unlike modern civilization had ever recognized would reap and feast upon its newfound casualties.

Flora would've been the perfect host, and for that reason alone, Forrest was glad her siblings had offered her to him to slay. Her seasoned despisal for all mankind was probably what lured the ancient one to Seattle. By the time it arrived in Seattle, it might not have known that she had already met her doom, which was why he kept feeling the pulse of its reach as it sought to find her.

No doubt that some of her ashes still clung to the stake in his overcoat's inner pocket and that might explain why it kept bumping into him.

While he was thankful Flora was gone, he ached for several moments immediately after staking her. Not because he had slain a vampire, as he never regretted his duty but he did mourn for the loss of what she could've been had Lorcan not turned her centuries earlier. He had mourned Flora almost a century ago when they first met.

During his journey into the heart of the Black Forest while he was still young, Forrest had never met a woman so eloquent, so stunning, and Flora captivated him so much that several years later, he returned to find her. This was without compulsion, as he was resistant to her mind-altering embrace. No vampire could use compulsion on him or other hunters, which intrigued Flora. Perhaps, at first, she liked the thought of such a challenge.

Apparently, she was strangely drawn to him in a similar curious way. Both understood the irony of their attraction for one another. A true Vampire Hunter falling for a vampire and vice versa was not a match made in ... well, any time or place. Mortal enemies could never fully love one another. The sense of certain betrayal would always loom between them, leading each to wonder what the other's intentions was.

For approximately six weeks, he and Flora spent hours conversing. He was intrigued by her thoughts and her former ambitions before her father turned her. However, her bloodlust and ravenous appetite and thoughtless, careless slaughter of several peasants on an evening before he arrived to visit caused him to see her for the monster she truly was. She couldn't set aside her hunger, not even for him, and after he found her feeding on the last survivor of the peasant family in their own kitchen, the sight was more than Forrest could accept.

At first, she attempted to lighten the situation by inferring the peasants simply were livestock for the wealthy aristocratic vampires like her family. Such a comparison furthered the distance in Forrest's eyes and harrowed an obvious grievance in him. A look of disgust tightened his expressions, so she backtracked her statements by insisting she was merely jesting, but the damage couldn't be reversed. Forrest could never forget the carnage he'd witnessed, the fresh blood dripping from her mouth, and she was wise enough to have understood by the disappointment in his eyes. Such blood-lust was never tamed, either.

Although Flora profusely apologized and pleaded for him to forgive her, she recognized by his solemn expressions that she was his next target. Regardless of any further words, she could never convince him not to slay her because she held no remorse for her actions. He accused her of such, and though she tried to deny it, her eyes and actions betrayed her lies. A coldness reflected in Forrest's eyes that she must have recognized. She fled into the night with the swiftness of a harsh wind.

Forrest didn't pursue her. Not then. He prolonged it far longer than he should have, given her crazed hunger and total lack of empathy. When he decided to finally hunt her, she was nowhere to be found in the Black Forest.

The last place he expected to find her was in Seattle, but since she was with her five siblings, he simply couldn't have walked over to her and slain her. Her brothers and sisters were elder vampires so he'd have had difficulty slaying more than one of them at a time. Patience, in the end, paid off. She overstepped her boundaries within her own family to the degree they freely handed her over to Forrest as a peace offering.

He held no regrets in plunging the stake into her heart. A part of him wished he could've met her before her father had turned her. Of course, that would've meant she'd have passed away decades before his birth, so they'd have never met.

Forrest wondered about the unlikely truce formed between himself and the last four survivors in Flora's family. Could he allow—

"You're not listening to a damn word I'm saying," Brady said, shaking his head and laughing softly. "Are you?"

Forrest glanced at Brady. "Sorry. My mind's sorting through ... What did you say?"

"Most people view you as sullen, but that's not it at all, is it? You're a deep thinker. A brooder."

"I constantly evaluate every possibility from every angle," Forrest replied. "To live as long as I have, it pays to *brood*."

"No doubt," Brady said. "Can I ask you something?"

"Ask anything," Forrest said, "but I'm selective about giving answers."

"Are there other hunters like you in the world?"

Forrest nodded.

"Any idea how many?"

Forrest shrugged. "No. Why?"

"I'm just curious. If there are more true Vampire Hunters, why aren't more in Seattle? Seems vampires are increasing their numbers in this city. So if there are others like you, and they're not in Seattle, vampires must be a bigger problem elsewhere in the world."

"That's a fair assumption. Typically, it's rare for us to cross paths, as we are led in different directions."

"But you've met other hunters, right?"

Forrest nodded. "I had a great mentor when I first learned of my calling. At other times, hunters have hunted me."

Brady's eyes widened as he faced Forrest. "Really? Why?"

"The situation's too complicated to go into detail right now."

"I'd like to know more sometime."

"Perhaps another time, when we're not trying to find Kailey."

"Okay, sure, but that's part of the reason for why I was asking about other hunters. Do you know how to contact other hunters to help us find her and who has taken her?"

Forrest nodded and patted his side coat pocket. "Sure, I've got 'em all on speed dial. Give me a second."

"You don't have a cellphone." A second after Brady made the comment, he rolled his eyes, realizing the joke.

"Yeah, there are reasons *why* I don't. I'm not on call. I don't have a hotline number to billboard my services. Humans don't hire me. I go to where I'm needed and slay vampires. Instinct is what I follow."

"Sorry I asked."

Forrest laughed.

"If instinct brought you to Seattle, more so than Micah requesting your help, and you've not left, how many vampires have you killed since you arrived?"

Forrest sat silent for several moments. His eyes indicated he was calculating in his mind. Finally, he said, "Seventy-six."

"Seriously?"

Forrest nodded.

"I never imagined the toll would be that high, and yet, you've never mentioned this."

"The less Seattle knows of my hunts, the better my chances are for finding the vampires. But, I should add that these vampires are the neophytes. Other than Flora, I've not slain any as old as she."

"But you'd like to, wouldn't you?" Brady asked.

"I have four in mind."

"Flora's family?"

"Yeah, but my truce prevents me from my duties, for now."

Brady nodded. "You expect them to slip up?"

"If their hunger is anything like Flora's was, they're going to make some critical mistakes," Forrest replied. "It's destined to happen. And when they do, I'll be prepared. But currently, a much greater threat in Seattle must be found and destroyed first."

"And what is that?"

"That's what I've been trying to figure out."

CHAPTER 17

Kailey tugged the ropes after Raven haphazardly attempted to sever them by using the cat's jagged claws. Raven had not yet perfected the proper use of the claws, and Kailey's forearms bore the fresh bleeding scratch marks to prove Raven's insufficiency.

Kailey winced, pulling tighter, and causing the scratches to leak narrow lines of blood.

I'm sorry about the scratches, Raven projected into Kailey's mind.

"Perhaps if you *aimed* for the ropes and not my flesh?" Kailey whispered. She no longer cared if the men outside heard her talking. She'd rather take her chances fighting them once they cut the ropes to take her wherever they planned than to continue rope-burning her wrists with an inexperienced claw-happy cat.

I tried. It's not as easy as you might think. I'll gladly swap places with you.

Kailey thought about that for a moment and realized she might be acting too critical and harshly toward Raven. Becoming a cat after being human would take some considerable adjustments. "No, thanks. What's the worst I could get? Cat-scratch fever? At least the ropes seem a bit looser. They have some give."

They are frayed.

Given that her legs weren't tied, she scooted the steel framed chair until her tied hands touched the wall. She leaned slightly forward, causing the back chair legs to catch the wall. Pressing her sock-covered feet against the floor, she was able to apply more pressure against the ropes.

"Could you do me a favor while I keep trying to pry my hands free?"

The cat's rubbed Kailey's leg with the side of its head and then mewed. *Sorry. If I can, I will. What do you need?*

"See if you can pull the blindfold down from my eyes?"

Sure.

"*Without* clawing me?"

No promises, but I will be more careful.

"I appreciate it," Kailey said.

Raven leapt from the floor and landed on Kailey's lap. By instinct, the cat's claws sunk into Kailey's skin.

Kailey winced and groaned. "Dammit! I'm adding declawed to the list when I take you to the vet."

Not funny.

"It wasn't meant to be. I'm being serious."

Well, that's gratitude for you. I'm doing the best I can. Stop whining and hold still.

Raven rose on the cat's hind legs and stretched its forepaws to the blindfold, apparently more mindful of not shifting her hind feet and hoping to prevent further scratches. Using the tips of the claws, Raven snagged the cloth and tugged.

To Kailey's surprise, the blindfold wasn't secured other than a simple cross knot. Perhaps since they had ensured the rope was nearly impossible to untie, they didn't need to worry about tying the blindfold any tighter. They didn't expect her to escape. After the dark cloth fell from her face, Kailey blinked but wasn't greeted by any harsh light. The place was dim.

Raven turned and leapt to the floor.

Damn.

Kailey glanced at the floor. Raven sat on her haunches waving her left forepaw, trying to shake the blindfold loose, but her jagged claws were embedded in the cloth. Raven fought, rolled, and scampered in circles, almost fearful of the blindfold.

Kailey grinned and then giggled. The more she tried to hold the laughter inside, the wider she grinned, until she let loose and burst into laughter.

The little cat stopped moving and gave her an agitated cat stare while whipping her tail. *It's not funny.*

"You're not seeing what I am."

You know I have sharp teeth, too, right?

Kailey ignored the comment, managed to get her laughter under better control, and took several moments to study her surroundings. She seemed to be in a small office of an abandoned warehouse. Abandoned warehouses were becoming as commonplace as vampires in Seattle, so on appearance alone, she had no idea *where* they were keeping her.

A thick layer of dust covered the old desk with an obvious swath of where one of the men had rested his elbows while seated in the ratty vinyl desk chair. Unfortunately, she didn't see any sharp objects like scissors, a boxcutter, or a letter opener. Nothing that might help her get out of the rope any faster. She wanted to scream to release her built up tension but the men had been gone longer than she expected. As surely as she shouted, the two men would be inside the office and ready to torture her or worse.

Kailey looked at the door. The square wire glass window was dingy and coated with yellowish dust on the outside; not enough to completely prevent one from looking out but enough to obscure any clear view from either side, especially from a distance.

She twisted the heavy duty doorknob. It was unlocked. She twisted the locking mechanism and engaged the deadbolt and then she locked the door knob. A protective metal panel prevented one from using a credit card or another item to jimmy the lock. As long as the warehouse had been abandoned, it was far unlikely either of those men owned a key. She twisted the doorknob and it didn't budge.

"That should grant me a little more time," Kailey whispered.

Do you believe in soulmates? Raven asked.

The question caught Kailey off guard, but she didn't hesitate with an answer. "Raven, let's not get into a discussion like that, not here, not now, and well, not *ever.*"

I didn't mean it like you're thinking. Honest. It's a fair question since I had to find my soul after your succubus friend decapitated me.

"Ra-a-ven," Kailey said.

You never have lost your soul, Kailey. So treasure every moment you have it. You've no idea what it's like when it departs from your body and you lose all your compassion, the ability to love, and empathy. Once gone, immense coldness settles inside.

Kailey looked at the ragged cat with renewed sympathy. "You're right. I have no idea what that's like. That must have been horrible."

It's worse than horrible. You hate everything and loathe the living. You despise what they have and long to make them suffer worse than yourself. Why do you think Flora enjoyed playing mind games as much as she did? She thrived on hurting others the best she could, which is why she took me after Nicodemus was staked for turning me. It wasn't because she loved me or wanted to nurture me. She didn't know how to love. She knew using me was the most brutal weapon she had to destroy your mind, but I knew better.

Kailey frowned. "Knew better? Like what, exactly?"

As your roommate, I'd already seen the fighting side of you. The you that didn't take bullshit from anyone else. While you are one of the most passionate people I have had the pleasure of knowing, you also fought to survive. It was only a matter of time before Flora met her necessary fate and saw the true you.

"Raven, when you lost your soul, was every bit of your humanity gone? I mean, was there not the slightest sliver of love or compassion left at all?"

Fragments remained, I suppose. The happier times were buried deep in my thoughts or locked away in the vaults of my mind, but if ever they surfaced or you reminded me, I despised them. I shunned them. I worked harder to forget. My focus turned to causing misery because that was all I felt, all I knew.

Kailey pressed her palms together, forcing the frayed section of the rope to tear slightly. She paused, took a deep breath, and formed fists. Again, she tugged, getting a little more slack. She kept working her wrists and hands against the rope, almost like kneading dough. The stiffness of the rope lessened.

"You need to know, Raven, that I tried to get to you before Nicodemus turned you. We all did. That had been our mission, and sadly, we were too late. We failed."

I know.

"I grieved every day and was haunted each time I saw you as a vampire."

Back to my question about soulmates.

"Raven, let's not—"

I'm not nitpicking a fight over it, and I know we never were one's yin to the other's yang. I understand that fully now. I really do. I recognize what you and

Brady have is genuine; something you and I could never have achieved, and I'm good with that. I am.

"Then why even bring this up?" Kailey said, pulling fiercely at the ropes, hoping this time she succeeded in snapping them. The sooner she broke free of the ropes, the faster she could escape the warehouse and this conversation.

Because regardless of how much you oppose my love for you, it will never weaken.

"Ra-ven."

You're unbelievable at times. You know that? I have a short time to roam the earth, and I chose to find you. You. And from the looks of your current situation, you're fortunate I found you. No one else is here to help you. And I've even disregarded my need to be prim.

"You were *never* prim. You were a gothic doll."

Not the point! I'm inside a flea-ridden cat that reeks of rotten food, shit, and a host of other odors that I can't explain. I'm starving. I itch. I—

Kailey sighed. "Okay, okay! I can never put into words how much I appreciate you coming to my rescue. Thank you! But Raven, *please*, with all that's happened between us, talking about soulmates right now isn't a conversation I want. Okay? I feel horrible for all the bad things that happened to you, and talking about this now, it's preventing me from concentrating on what must be done so I can survive."

Fair enough. Okay ... what about destiny? Do you believe we're destined for what happens to us or can we change our fate?

"Raven, *please*."

Raven laughed softly. *You know what I just thought about as my ironic destiny?*

Kailey rolled her eyes. "No, but I'm sure you're going to tell me."

I'm a raven swallowed by a cat.

"Force-feeding your spirit to a cat doesn't count as being swallowed."

You have a point there.

Kailey pushed her feet against the floor and tightened her triceps, biceps, and forearms. She strained until her face was blood red and her heartbeat pounded relentlessly inside her head. She used all her remaining strength against the rope until it loosened enough for her to work her right hand free. She brought both arms around and slipped her left hand out of the rope.

Darkness swirled around her eyes. She took a couple of deep gulps of air and waited for the dizziness to pass. When the room stopped wobbling, she stared at the rope on her lap and wiggled her freed fingers.

Excited, Kailey released a slight squeal of happiness. She leaned down and reached to pet the black cat's head. The cat hissed and clawed at her. Kailey yanked her hand back quickly. "What the hell?"

It wasn't me. The cat still has reactions of its own.

"I see. Thank you, Raven, and I hope the cat understands my appreciation, too."

Some food would probably win its little heart over.

"Done," Kailey said, "as soon as we get to safety."

The office door rattled.

"Did you lock door, Serge?"

"No."

"It's locked."

"Why ya looking at me? I *didn't* lock it."

"You sure about that?"

"I swear it on both my Mama's and Papa's graves."

A car horn blared two short bursts.

"He's here early, Costel," Serge said in a harsh whisper.

"Come on. We let him in, then we break down door."

"The door is made of steel. How you break it down?"

Their footsteps thudded away from the door.

"*Shit!*" Kailey said in a harsh whisper. She moved toward the door in a crouch and rose high enough to peer through the dusty window.

The door shook again, but not because someone stood outside the door trying to get in. The larger outer warehouse door clattered and rumbled as Costel and Serge pushed it along its suspension rollers. Once the gap of the door was wide enough, a black limo with tinted windows drove inside.

Kailey's gut twisted. "Ah, hell."

What?

"It's not good. A black limo and those two men are closing the door. They'll return in a few minutes. How'd you get in here?"

From the ceiling. See the missing tiles?

Kailey looked up, nodded. Provided she could even reach the metal frame that supported the remaining ceiling tiles to heft herself up, she didn't think she could squeeze her muscled hips and thighs through the opening. But she knew without a shred of doubt she couldn't wait for them to enter the office and then try to escape. Not after the limo arrived. She didn't have any way to determine how many people might be inside.

Her instinct told her that someone bad, someone far worse than Micah, was inside the limo. And most likely, he came with an armed entourage. If she didn't escape now, she had little chance that she ever could.

CHAPTER 18

Jinn carried a small bag of garbage to the dumpster and found Jim and Terry kissing and groping one another in the alleyway behind Nocturnal Trinity. The buttons on their shirts had been ripped off and their shirts were partway rolled down their shoulders.

"Who-o-o-a. Hey!" Jinn shouted, running to them and pulling them apart. "What the hell are you two doing?"

His words went unnoticed. Their desire for one another caused them to shove Jinn aside. Jinn braced himself against the dumpster to prevent himself from falling. They didn't even know he was there.

"Ah, dammit!" Jinn shook his head. He grabbed Jim, the larger of the two busboys, looked into his eyes, and slapped Jim's face hard. "Snap out of it!"

Jim blinked and his expression was that of great confusion. Terry pushed past Jinn and grabbed Jim's hands tightly, trying to pull Jim back.

"What the hell, dude!" Jim said, thrusting his right palm against Terry's bare chest to keep him at arm's length. Terry puckered.

"Don't stop now," Terry said. "I need you."

"What the fuck?" Jim glanced helplessly toward Jinn.

Jinn spun Terry around, smacked Terry's face, and yelled, "Wake up!"

Terry shook. He looked stunned. "What's going on? Why are we in the alley?"

"Man, you looked like you were trying to kiss me," Jim said.

"Ah, hell no. You know I don't roll like that."

Jinn rolled his eyes and shook his head. He glanced at his watch. "You two have been making out for the better part of a half hour now, by my guess."

"What?" Jim said.

Jinn nodded. "Yeah, damn. I thought I'd given her a high enough dose to put her out *before* you got to her."

"What do you mean we were making out?" Terry asked, rubbing his lips and wincing.

"Look at your clothes," Jinn said. "She cast a love spell on the two of you."

Jim tried to button his shirt and realized no buttons were there. His belt was loosened and his pants were unbuttoned and unzipped. Terry noticed the same with his clothes.

Jinn laughed. "It's a good thing I showed up when I did, huh? Otherwise, I'd have gotten a view of something best not seen outside in an alley. Or anywhere, for that matter."

Jim turned and vomited beside the dumpster. Terry appeared sick, too, and his eyes revealed the wandering of his mind to try to remember the ordeal.

"Go change clothes and fix yourselves up and then get back to work," Jinn said. He sighed and fought to hold back his laughter. "I should've sent a demon to get Cassie. Damn, boys."

Before he walked inside, he leaned against the wall and laughed hysterically.

"You think this is funny?" Jim said. His hands balled into fists and he stormed across the alley toward Jinn. "I don't care if you are a demon. I'm about to put a hurting on you. This is all your fault in the first place."

Jinn's laughter stopped in an instant. He turned and his eyes glowed like orange-yellow lava. "Be warned, Jim. I don't take kindly to threats and remember that I'm a male version of what Cassie is, and either you chill your attitude in the next few seconds or I've have you two boys doing things together that you'll never mentally recover from. You'll go well past the make-out sessions and into the hard core, fellows. Unlike Cassie, I'll make you remember every single thing you do."

Although still furious, Jim took Jinn's threat to heart. He stood about ten feet away, rage burning in his eyes, but he relaxed his fists and placed his hands against the sides of his legs.

"Now, do as I told you, and the two of you get to keep your jobs. Understood?" Jinn asked, reaching for the door handle.

Terry nodded, wiping his mouth with the back of his hand.

Jim swallowed hard and acquiesced a nod.

"Be inside in fifteen minutes, or consider yourself no longer employed." Jinn entered and slammed the door shut.

Jim wiped his mouth and glared at Terry. "If you don't quit working here, I will."

"Why?" Terry asked.

"I can never look at you the same after … Knowing what happened."

Terry's brow furrowed. With genuine concern in his voice, he said, "Am I that bad a kisser?"

Jim rolled his eyes and walked away.

CHAPTER 19

*H*ours passed before Cassie finally awakened inside a dim room. She didn't immediately rise from where she lay. Through the slits of her slightly open eyes, she tried to figure out where she was after teleporting in a near unconscious state. A rose-scented candle flickered softly; the only light in the room.

Beneath her was a rough textured material that held a dusty scent mixed with the old odor of furniture and carpet that had not been vacuumed for weeks, perhaps months. The candle was the only pleasant fragrance. Other than it, the air was stale and musty.

She pushed herself into a seated position and realized she was on someone's sofa. Classical jazz music played on a radio in the next room. Under different circumstances, Cassie would've welcomed the sound. She studied her surroundings and wondered where she had teleported.

"You've awakened?" the female said in an even tone from across the room.

Cassie squinted to make out the recliner veiled in a corner of darkness. She couldn't quite make out the person's face, but she recognized the voice. "Penelope?"

"Yes." Her tone was more an apprehensive tone than that of friendliness. She seemed upset.

Cassie released a soft, barely audible sigh. She'd never been inside Penelope's residence, and she didn't even know where Penelope lived. Why she was teleported to her home remained a mystery, but at least Cassie landed in a place where she was safe.

Or was she? Fear gnawed her gut. The intrusive sensation cautioned her. Penelope was a Demon-hunter and not necessarily an ally.

After several seconds of allowing her eyes to adjust to the dim room, Cassie noticed the crossbow in Penelope's right hand. It was armed and ready to fire at the slightest press of her finger. For some reason the razored tip of the arrow was much clearer than anything else in the room.

"I appreciate that you didn't kill me," Cassie said, easing slowly back against the sofa. She was surprised to find herself still in human form, dressed like she had been when she entered Nocturnal Trinity to talk to Jinn. *The bastard.*

"The decision to allow you to live is still being contemplated," Penelope said coldly. She leveled the crossbow and aimed at Cassie's heart.

Cassie swallowed hard. Her head pounded with agonizing pain, and she was still too weak to move quickly. Teleport again? Seemed the most logic route of escape except ... she doubted she'd survive the pain since her energy was already drained. Tapping further into what little energy she retained, she'd probably rend her body in half, sending herself back to the abyss without the aid of Penelope's arrow. Unless some miracle intervened, Cassie remained at the mercy of Penelope.

"Let's not be hasty, Penelope. I've never done a thing to harm you. The fact that you haven't killed me yet is something I'm grateful for," Cassie said.

"To be frank, you're lucky I didn't. You suddenly appeared on the floor, more succubus in appearance than human, and had I been holding my crossbow or had you'd been conscious, I'd have destroyed you without question or any hesitation."

"Again—"

Penelope leaned forward, extending the crossbow. "I'm not finished speaking. If you weren't friends with Forrest, you'd already be dead. For whatever reason, he seems to trust you. His friendship with you and other demons does not sway me in the slightest. I'm a Demon-hunter. One less demon walking the earth gives me immense satisfaction. Now, tell me, why you wound up here?"

"Please understand. I'm sorry for the intrusion," Cassie said. "I teleported without any focus because if I hadn't, I'd probably be dead. Two men were trying to take me against my will. I didn't have time to focus my landing. I simply vanished from their sight, lost consciousness, and arrived here. Wherever this place is."

Penelope lowered the crossbow slightly, but kept a cautious gaze set on Cassie's heart and not her eyes. Penelope's wisdom proved she was a seasoned hunter, even after decades of imprisonment. Eyes could be deceptive, but keeping the focus on one's body movements lessened the chance of miscalculating a prey's intention to bolt by misdirection. One could manipulate an opponent by looking to the right, and then rushing to the left instead.

"This is my home. You teleported into my apartment and want me to believe this wasn't where you intended to land?"

"How could it be my intention?" Cassie asked, rubbing her temples. "I've never been here before, so I couldn't have intended to come here. I didn't know where you live. Even though I'm seated in your living room, I have no idea what your street address is."

"The one thing I've learned from demons is to believe the opposite of what they tell you," Penelope said in an even tone.

"I'm not lying to you," Cassie said. Tears crested in her eyes. "I've no reason to lie about this."

"Don't feign emotions."

"I'm not," Cassie said, pushing her anger downward, and trying not to burst into wrath at being called a liar. Such an outburst would be misconstrued as the complete opposite of what Cassie needed Penelope to believe.

Cassie forced herself to maintain a calm appearance and a gentle voice, which was nearly impossible, given the current situation. Being in such a weak condition gave Penelope the upper hand. If Cassie had full use of her strength and power, the situation would be completely different. But even then, Penelope held the power of the situation because she was the love of Forrest's life. Because of that, Cassie wouldn't kill Penelope. But she could inflict pain or mesmerize Penelope's mind long enough for Cassie to escape.

"Demons always put on a good show," Penelope said. "With lies and deception, offering gifts—"

"Look," Cassie said with a bolder voice. "I don't know what kind of demons you've killed over the years, but I assure you I'm not like they are."

"I've heard that excuse before," Penelope said in a bored tone. "It's a common phrase. All demons lie."

"As do all humans, vampires, and werebeasts," Cassie said. "You can't tell me that you've never lied. Well, you could, but then, that would be a lie, right? So don't play all smug and righteous because you're on a mission to send every demon back to the abyss. Never assume every demon is guilty of deceit or wrongdoing. Some of us never want to return to the abyss, and I happen to be one of those. So it might interest you to know that I try to help others, which is why I ended up here. At least, that's my guess anyway. I have friends, *human* friends, and my loyalty to them extends past my own self-preservation. I'd freely sacrifice myself to protect my friends. You don't believe me? How about you ask Forrest? Ask him how I aided him in finding *you*."

Penelope sat in silence for nearly a minute. One damn long minute. Cassie guessed the hunter was mulling over her words. She *hoped* she was. Since Cassie wasn't willing to alienate herself from Forrest by killing Penelope, she wagered Penelope was in the same position. If she were to kill or hurt Cassie without reason, she'd lose Forrest's trust. Forrest had experienced enough betrayal in his lifetime that he had absolutely no tolerance of it at all.

Penelope shifted uneasily and sighed. "Let's say I suspend my disbelief in your explanation. You still haven't convinced me I should trust you."

"Why not? I've not made one attempt to attack or escape."

Penelope laughed softly. "You cannot hide your exhaustion. You don't have enough strength to be the slightest challenge for me. For all I know, you're carrying on further conversation to allow yourself time to recover."

"Fine. Nothing I say convinces you of my innocence. You want to kill me? Do so, but I place one condition."

Perplexed, Penelope frowned. "What condition?"

"That you execute me in front of Forrest."

Penelope's hardened countenance softened. A moment of surprise claimed her eyes, causing Penelope to meet Cassie's eyes. Cassie's eyebrows rose and she shrugged slightly. She smiled with sudden confidence because her assumption about Penelope had been right. The hunter would alienate herself forever from Forrest if she harmed Cassie in the slightest.

Penelope brooded.

"Call Forrest," Cassie said. "I'm sick of trying to convince you that I'm on your side. Forrest knows me and my intentions. So get him here and do what you long to do. Kill me."

Penelope rested the crossbow on her lap and removed her finger from the trigger. "You really don't know how you teleported here?"

"I don't know. Honest." Cassie gave a quick rundown of the events that happened in Nocturnal Trinity and how she realized the danger she'd placed herself in by going to talk to Jinn. "So, you see, Jinn betrayed *me*. I used what little power I had left to teleport. My guess is I teleported right as I lost consciousness, so I could have ended up anywhere in the world. But I couldn't show you where this place is on a map."

"Then perhaps this arrow belongs to Jinn," Penelope said in a soft cold tone.

"No need to be hasty."

"You'd still defend him after he's betrayed you?"

"I'll put it like this. I'll never trust him again."

Penelope shook her head. "He drugged you for what reason?"

"I'm not certain."

"Then why should he not be returned to the abyss?"

"One good reason is that we don't know what kind of demon would take his place. His replacement could be far worse. Jinn's a lot of things, and he acts more for himself than others. He's an opportunist, but he's still valuable."

"In what way?"

"Information."

"Information?" Penelope's eyes narrowed.

Cassie nodded.

"Like what?"

"For starters," Cassie said, "he told me that Alec spared the four behemoths."

Penelope recoiled into her seat. Her crossbow almost slipped off her lap, but her nimble fingers wrapped around the tiller, preventing it from falling to the floor. "*What?*"

"Yes. They're still alive."

"But Alec possesses the Wrathbone dagger. Forrest gave it to him so Alec would destroy them."

Cassie whispered, "I know."

"*Bastard.*"

"That's the nickname I've given Jinn, too."

"See? I told Forrest he shouldn't have given that blade to that vampire.

Without that dagger, we're at their mercy. There's nothing we can do to destroy them." Despair rose in her voice. "*Why* did you go talk to Jinn?"

"Kailey's been taken. I hoped he might have information as to who had taken her."

"And did he?"

Cassie shook her head. Her eyes moistened. "Nothing useful."

Penelope met Cassie's eyes. "You care about her a great deal, don't you?"

"Yes," Cassie replied. "She's my best friend. I was married to her brother."

Penelope's brow furrowed. "Really?"

"Yes."

"By his freewill?"

"Of course. No bewitching. No deceit. We fell in love like ... well, like humans do," Cassie said, all choked up.

"I misjudged you," Penelope said, rising to her feet. She placed the crossbow on her chair. "My apologies."

Cassie wiped a tear from her eye. "None are needed, Penelope. Honest."

Penelope extended her hand to Cassie. Cassie accepted, and Penelope helped Cassie stand. "No quick movements and stay where I can see you. I have other weapons other than the crossbow."

"A bit jumpy still?"

"I've never extended my trust to a demon, so you'll have to forgive me if I don't immediately set my guard down."

"Gotcha. Are you going to get in touch with Forrest?" Cassie asked.

Penelope nodded. "Yes, but first, let's get you some tea and something to eat. You need to regain your strength. If we're to work together and be ... friends, I don't want you vulnerable should we encounter any of the behemoths while we search to find Kailey."

"Thank you," Cassie said.

"So tell me, what do demons like to eat?"

"Depends on the demon," Cassie said, "but I prefer most anything humans eat with the exception of pineapples on pizza. That's actually a punishment in Hell."

CHAPTER 20

*D*espite the cat's growling vehement protest when Kailey scooped it into her arms, Kailey took the cat, climbed atop the desk, and then carefully tossed the cat into the ceiling loft.

Careful!

Kailey's arms still ached from the hour of straining to free herself from the ropes. Putting the cat into the loft revealed exactly how spent her burning muscles were. After years of MMA training with an excellent trainer, she had learned how to ignore pain and mentally push herself harder to get past the aches.

Serge's and Costel's voices echoed in the outer warehouse in their native language. The trail of their voices seemed to be growing louder, which meant they returning to the office door. She didn't have much time before they discovered she'd gotten free, and certainly no time was left for the least bit of error in joining Raven above.

Positioning her feet at the proper distance on the desktop, she hoped her socks wouldn't cause her to slip when she jumped. She lowered into a squatting position with her arms stretched behind her and sprang upward, quickly reaching for the bar with her hands. If not for the desk to add to her height, she'd have never come close to reaching the metal grid bar overhead. Her fingers cleared the bar and she clung to it, gripping tighter, and pulling herself upward, in spite of her burning triceps, biceps, and her forearms.

She was almost free.

Almost. An indefinite word she hated. If one missed by *almost* an inch, it might as well be a hundred miles. A miss was a miss. Simple as that. Almost free indicated that she wasn't free yet, and if she wanted to escape, she couldn't rest until she got away from these men and the warehouse.

Kailey pulled and groaned until her navel was even with the bar, so she believed her route for escape was a great possibility, but only if she hurried.

Footsteps scuffed and echoed on the outer concrete floor.

The doorknob rattled. One of the men with a thick accent said, "She is in here, sir. But Serge locked the door."

"I did not lock it," Serge protested.

"Unlock it," a mysterious voice said.

"We no have key," Serge protested. "It was unlocked when we arrived."

"Open it!"

She gasped. The unknown male voice was haunting and sent chills down her spine.

Hurry! Raven said inside her mind.

Although Kailey was high enough to lessen the pain in her burning arms, she couldn't see a solid object to grab to help pull herself higher. The metal grid bar was already bending beneath her modest weight as it was only meant to support the light weight of rectangular ceiling tiles.

Grab the rafter beam to your right.

Her eyes adjusted to the dim lighting and she noticed the thick steel rafter Raven suggested. She reached with her right hand, grabbed it, and started to reposition her weight before the grid bar collapsed and she dropped onto the desk with a dozen or more ceiling tiles. Her eyes traced the steel beam for about eight feet before it disappeared into the darkness. She hoped she'd found a sturdy route to walk along and escape.

Something hit the door hard. Kailey figured one of the two men had tried to force the door open by shoving his full weight behind his shoulder.

"That the best you can do, Serge?"

"The door's made of steel! You try."

"See? I told you."

"You think you can do better?" Costel asked.

"No, no, no. You do it wrong. You do everything wrong."

The door thudded again.

"See?" Serge said.

"Aye, yes. See? I see you do no better."

"Like this," the third voice said.

Metal crunched. The doorknob turned without having a key and without resistance. The steel door bent near the doorknob and buckled, snapping the deadbolt. "Try it now."

The door flung open.

"She's loose, Serge!" Costel said. "Grab her! Don't let her escape!"

A hand wrapped around Kailey's left ankle like a steel vise. Panic seized her. Her breath escaped through her lips in an audible gasp that magnified into a short sudden scream. She tugged but he was too strong and was using his strength and weight to pull her downward. She kicked at his arm with her right foot, and rolled partly to her side on the rafter to give herself more leverage. The tile frame bent.

Kailey landed several hard kicks against Serge's forearm, but his grip only tightened with strength similar to that of Flora and Raven when they had grabbed her during scuffles on different occasions. Because it was daylight, he couldn't be a vampire. But *what* was he?

Kailey growled, gripping the rafter harder and kept kicking at him, missing more than actually striking.

"Don't let her get away, Serge!" Costel shouted.

"Some help then," Serge replied with a strain and a heavy hint of agitation growing in his voice.

"The both of you … get her down." The third voice came from outside the office and possibly came from the person who had been seated in the rear of the limousine. His accent was unlike any she'd heard before, even different than Flora's and her family. The man's calm voice flowed with venomous disdain and possessed an alarming authority. She imagined few people ever disobeyed his command, and if they did, they were never given a second chance to make that mistake again.

He said, "If you can't pull her down, shoot her, but don't kill her. Not yet."

Kailey glanced down to see Costel pulling a 9mm from the holster hidden beneath his leather jacket. The fluid movement of his hand informed her he was skilled using the weapon. If he aimed at her, he most likely would not miss. Still pulling and kicking, she couldn't shake Serge's hold on her ankle. Costel aimed the gun at her and closed one eye. Within seconds, she'd be shot, provided she didn't somehow escape Serge's hold.

Raven scampered across the narrow grid bar and sliced her claws deep enough into Serge's wrist to cause immediate pain. Blood seeped from the gashes, and he released Kailey's ankle. He fell backwards, apparently obstructing Costel's view, if only for a few moments, but then he stumbled into Costel.

"You idiot! Costel said.

Keeping her grip on the rafter, Kailey brought her feet upward and rolled out of their view. The gun fired and a bullet bore a hole in the ceiling tile only inches from where she lay.

Surging adrenaline pushed her to get up and move.

She moved along the tie beam in her socked feet. The metal was rough against her soles, and although she wished she was wearing shoes, she could actually balance better without them.

"Sonnabitch!" Serge said, clutching his wrist. Blood flowed through his fingers and dripped onto the floor.

"How the hell did that happen?" Costel asked.

"I'm not sure. Felt the fur of an animal."

"Rat?"

"Do rats do this?" Serge showed the deep lacerations pooling blood and then pressed it against the bottom of his shirt.

"No. Don't think so."

"Come to me," the third voice said. "Allow my touch to heal you."

"Thank you, father."

"*Father?*" Kailey whispered.

This way! Raven said, scampering past Kailey.

Raven hurried along the tie beam quicker than Kailey's feet could ever hope to move. Kailey's balance was good, but she wasn't a gymnast. Since Raven wasn't fully adjusted to walking on all fours yet, Kailey half expected her to not move so swiftly. But frightened cats were fast runners, regardless of the terrain.

Periodically, she reached a steel rafter that connected the tie beam to the roof. These offered her a solid support to grab and steady herself, but they also impeded her progress because she had to pause to step around them. A couple of times she stubbed her big toe and winced while mouthing out a string of obscenities.

Midway across the tie beam, she glanced down and noticed the catwalk.

Raven slinked against her ankle and rubbed her head against her leg.

Kailey shook her head and whispered, "How fitting."

Yep. Are you thinking what I'm thinking?

"To be honest, I don't think we have a better way to escape."

Forrest waited for Brady to show his badge to the shaken bouncer at the door. The man didn't offer any protest or use his handheld two-way radio to get permission. He caught the angered gaze in Forrest's eyes, giving Forrest a once over at his massive size, and quickly he stepped aside.

Forrest chuckled as they walked past.

Brady shook his head. "I doubt he let us in because of my badge. You could get entry anywhere, couldn't you? With that hard stare of yours, most anyone would get out of your way."

"Works well with humans, but not vampires or *weres*."

"What about demons?"

"Depends on the demon. I take it that's the direction we're headed?"

Brady nodded and they walked into the demon's trisector of the nightclub.

Forrest laughed softly. "To be honest though, I don't think I'm the reason for his fear. Something else must have happened earlier."

"And you suspect this, why?" Brady whispered.

"His wrist was bruised. I surprised he's even working the door."

Jinn carried a cardboard box of liquor bottles and set them on the bar. Seeing Forrest and Brady, Jinn's eyes revealed his sudden nervousness, but he attempted a quick rebound. He frowned and said, "Ah, now, hell no! Don't tell me that Cassie didn't give you my warning."

"Warning?" Brady asked. "What warning?"

"Ah now, don't put on that dumb cop act. I ain't buying it," Jinn said.

"Cassie was here?" Forrest asked, plopping down on a barstool across from Jinn. He placed his huge arm atop the box of bottles, gripped his massive hand over the end, and showed his teeth through an even smile.

"Yeah, about a half hour ago," Jinn said, attempting to slide the box unsuccessfully out from Forrest's arm. "Look, guys, this is harassment. I've got a job to do *before* we open."

"Harassment?" Brady asked. "We've not done or said anything that constitutes harassment. Are we making you uncomfortable?"

Forrest said, "We shouldn't be, unless you've something to hide? After all, I'm in here at least twice a week for shots. Never have you acted uncomfortable around me."

"Yeah. One of you at a time … that's one thing. I can handle that. But the two of you barging in here at the same time, *before* we're anywhere near opening? No … Unh, uh. That's a different matter altogether, especially with Brady being here."

Brady feigned having his feelings hurt. "Why's it so different with me being here?"

"Well, for one," Jinn said, pointing a stern finger at Brady, "Alec made it perfectly clear that you don't show your face inside Nocturnal Trinity unless he has need of you, unless he *specifically* calls you. And at this time of the day, I know he didn't do that."

Brady shrugged and rested his hand upon the butt of his 9mm. "So let him know I'm here. I've some questions I'd like to ask."

Jinn eyed the gun, obviously recognizing the threat.

"You know I can't do that," Jinn said, tugging at the box under Forrest's arm with both hands. He still couldn't take the box.

"Why can't you relate the message and tell him he has visitors?" Brady asked.

"Alec's unavailable until after midnight. You know that. Vampires have to sleep sometime."

"Usually during the day, huh?" Brady asked.

Forrest grinned a menacing smile. "I'd be glad to wake him."

"Don't you mean lights out?" Brady asked.

"Look," Jinn said, nervously. He whispered, "Don't even joke about that in here right now. Understand? He'd kill you in an instant if you opened his coffin."

Brady's eyebrows rose. "Hmm, and all this time I thought vampires were easier to stake during the day."

"Oh, no, you didn't mean to go there," Jinn said.

"Am I right, Forrest?"

"Usually, they are," Forrest said before he looked into Jinn's glowing eyes. "So Cassie was here?"

Jinn nodded.

Brady frowned. "If Cassie was here, I'm certain she mentioned that Kailey's missing."

"As I recall, she did mention something about that," Jinn said. He let the air grow quiet and turned his back toward Brady but kept his hands on the box.

"I'm not here to play your games," Brady said. "I want to know what you told Cassie."

Jinn froze when the slight click of Brady's gun safety was turned off.

"What do you know about her disappearance?" Brady asked in an even tone.

"Chill," Jinn said, raising his hands upward. "Like I told her, I don't know anything about it. I don't know who did it, either. But, if I hear something, I told her that I'd tell her. So please, put your gun away."

"Where's Cassie now?" Forrest asked.

"We talked and she left. That's the truth. But before she left, I told her to —" Jinn kept his voice low. "She was supposed to tell you *not* to come back. Ever."

"Really?" Forrest said. "That makes me want to sit on this barstool all the more until after midnight. Then I can sit and talk to Alec."

Jinn shook his head and tried again to pull the box free of Forrest's hold. "You really don't want to be sitting there after midnight."

"And why not?"

"Trust me."

Forrest chuckled. "I'd like to, but you seem to be keeping information from us."

Jinn glanced at Brady. "I've told you all I know. Cassie told me that Kailey's missing. Like I told her, I don't know anything about it. I swear it.

I told her I'd keep my ears open. If I heard anything, I'd call her. I'll call you."

Forrest stood, towering over Jinn from the other side of the bar. "For weeks, you and I've talked about a lot of things, Jinn. I set aside the fact you're a demon and you've tolerated me as a Vampire Hunter, and all seemed to be going well. Now, you seem to be pushing me away when I sort of thought we were becoming friends."

"Which is *why*—"

"We're going to go," Forrest said, "but if I learn that you've lied to me about anything or you've kept back valuable information, I'm coming back with Penelope. And you won't be the only demon she returns to the abyss."

Jinn didn't need Forrest to explain the threat. All Forrest needed to do was mention her name. Jinn's nervous eyes looked past Forrest toward the mirrored glass of the Demon Lounge overlooking the dance floor. He lowered his voice. "Forrest, the warning I gave Cassie to tell you … was you're not safe in Nocturnal Trinity or in Seattle."

Forrest frowned. "Meaning?"

"I don't know all the details," Jinn said. "All I know is a different sort of darkness has come to Seattle. None of us are safe, but especially *not* you."

Forrest flicked his gaze to Brady and then back to Jinn. His huge hands tightened into giant fists. "I've felt its presence. It's something dark? Like an ancient vampire?"

"I'm not certain if it's even a vampire. All I know is you're not safe, Brady's not safe, and now *I'm* not safe for telling you. Please get out and *hurry*. I don't want them seeing me talk to you."

"Are you saying that this ancient is in the nightclub?" Forrest asked.

"Did you hear those words pass through my lips?" Jinn said angrily. "No, you didn't. Now, I'm asking one more time that the two of you get the Hell out! Otherwise—"

Brady put his hand on his gun and was prepared to pull it from the holster on his belt. Since Brady had already played the threat twice, Forrest knew if Brady pulled the gun this time, he wasn't going to pretend like he was going to use it. He would probably shoot Jinn, if not kill him.

Forrest shook his head at Brady and then he leaned across the bar toward Jinn with a stare harsh enough to melt a glacier. "You know if he pulls that gun again, you'll be dying on the floor in a pool of blood. Then you can party with your friends in the abyss. You really want to play this out in such a manner?"

Jinn's eyes indicated that he didn't, but he still pointed his finger toward the exit. "Outside! Now! And to make certain you're leaving, I'm escorting you out. Now, let's get going."

Jinn leapt over the bar and landed beside Forrest.

"You sure you know what you're getting yourself into?" Forrest asked.

"I hope the two of you do," Jinn said in a near whisper. "I can't take any more of this harassment. Threatening me with a gun while you're on duty? I should call police headquarters and have them take your badge. Let's see how tough you are and what you can do outside the nightclub. I sure don't want to clean up your blood off my floors."

The bouncer opened the door, allowing Forrest and Brady to exit, but Jinn stuck close behind them.

Jinn turned to the bouncer and said, "Close the door. I'll be right back."

"You need me to get more help out here?" the bouncer asked.

"No. Now, shut the damned door!"

After the door shut, Jinn looked at Brady. The tough veneer he was using to make himself appear to be a badass crumbled immediately. His brow furrowed and his eyes filled with fear. He held out his hands and wrists. "Cuff and arrest me and take me in or take me anywhere the fuck away from this club."

Forrest looked confused, as did Brady. Forrest studied Jinn for several long seconds, wondering which personality was more genuine. A sheen of sweat cropped Jinn's brow, and for a demon to sweat was quite a feat. Something Forrest seldom witnessed. Heat couldn't do it, but fear of being sent back to the abyss certainly could.

"Just do it!" Jinn said. "Please? And hurry. I'll explain as soon as you drive me away."

Forrest sighed and winked at Brady where Jinn didn't notice. "I don't know, Jinn. You said some offensive things inside, and I'm ready to take my pound of flesh out of your hide."

"Forrest, you know I didn't mean any of that," Jinn said. "Hell, I know you know that I know I'm no match for you. I'm sorry. You gotta believe me. But, you need to know that I'm not making up the other stuff. The warning I gave Cassie to give you is on the up and up. All legit. You don't believe me? Call her and ask."

"I plan to," Brady said.

Forrest grabbed Jinn by the shoulder and turned him to face the wall. Jinn swallowed hard but offered no further words of protest. His attitude changed immediately.

"Look, now Forrest, be easy with me, a'ight? I didn't mean any of those things I said in there. If you get us out of here alive, I promise to tell you what else is going on, but believe me, you gotta get us far away from here."

"Nothing worse than a sniffling demon," Forrest said evenly. "I have to admit, though, you certainly have a good facade."

"Forrest, call me all the bad things you want, insult me until your heart's content, but let's get out of here."

"Does any of all this have to do with Kailey's sudden disappearance?" Brady asked.

"It might, but what I told you earlier is the truth. I don't know anything about her being taken or who might have done it. However, I'll do everything within my power to help you find her."

Brady took his cuffs and placed them on Jinn's hands, even though he and Forrest both knew Jinn could teleport at any second, leaving the cuffs on the ground. But, for some reason, Forrest could tell by Jinn's genuine fear that Jinn had no intention of fleeing. Something evil lurked nearby, perhaps inside the club or it was destined to arrive soon, but either way, Jinn's only safety was leaving with Forrest and Brady.

As Forrest escorted Jinn to the rear of the patrol car, he wondered *what* was coming.

CHAPTER 22

*P*artly concealed by the shadows of the lightless warehouse, Kailey realized they'd lose the safety of the poor lighting once she left her vantage point in the rafters and dropped to the catwalk. The tie beam only led to the other side of the building, and for all she knew, there might not be a ladder or another office where they could descend. And if not, few choices remained.

A twenty-five foot drop to the floor might not kill her, but she wouldn't be able to take off running. A fall like that most likely would break both her legs. By the time she discovered she had no way down and needed to head back to the center of the roof, her armed assailant could intercept her, perhaps even shoot her. As much aggravation as she had caused by her escape, Costel would probably shoot her for the fun of it.

Dropping down onto the catwalk presented another dilemma. She couldn't silence the rattling of the aluminum mesh grating when her feet struck on her landing. Plus, she'd be exposed.

Crouching down, she peered at what was below the catwalk. The warehouse was mostly empty with the huge exception of the ominous black limousine. Once she lowered herself from this position, she'd put herself into the direct view of the driver and any passengers that might not have presented themselves yet.

Kailey assumed the man who helped Serge and Costel open the office door was the man in charge, but her assumption might be incorrect. However, that person might still be hidden inside the limo.

With all the unusual, unexplainable things she'd encountered since being roommates with Raven and then moving to Seattle, she'd never imagined that after Raven's demise that Raven would find a way to move her spirit into a black cat or anything, for that matter. But due to Kailey's current situation where she'd been abducted, she felt comforted to hear Raven's voice inside her mind. Was she delusional? Had Raven really taken over a cat?

Kailey didn't want it not to be real, but a slight part of her subconscious was somewhat worried and wary that something more sinister might be at hand.

The voice patterns and the phrasing of the sentences were identical to Raven's before Raven became a vampire. Only the true Raven could possess these characteristic understandings and know the events she and Kailey had experienced as best friends and roommates. An evil spirit couldn't know all these things. It simply had to be Raven. Kailey *needed* it to be Raven.

Kailey never realized how much she missed Raven's companionship because she had been forced to hate Raven after being turned. Vampires were not even shadows of their former selves, and as Raven explained, the absence of the soul meant the capacity for compassion, love, and empathy vanished. Every vampire Kailey had encountered exemplified that to be true.

Are you going to stand there until they get close enough to nab or shoot you?

"No," Kailey whispered. "Just weighing the odds."

They don't calibrate scales of that magnitude. Jump and run. Otherwise, we don't stand a chance for survival.

Kailey reached to pick up the cat, but Raven leapt softly onto the catwalk, which was a more graceful landing than Kailey knew she'd make.

On the tie beam where she had walked from the office, shoes scuffed and a man grunted. She guessed one of the two was pulling himself up or at least, trying to. The metal frame rails seemed too flimsy to hold either man's weight, but with her recent string of bad luck, she figured the rails wouldn't collapse.

Kailey sighed. She didn't have any more time to contemplate her actions. One of them was coming for her across the beam. She jumped.

Like Kailey expected, the aluminum catwalk mesh rattled and echoed louder, even without shoes. A gun fired without hesitation but not from the rafters. Someone down below had seen her land. The bullet chinked the mesh panel less than a foot behind her.

She ran. In spite of her sore arms and her aching cold feet, she hurried along the catwalk. The mesh was rough and cut her feet. It wouldn't be a surprise to discover later that the bottoms of her feet were bleeding.

Raven scampered down the catwalk away from where the limo was parked below. Kailey hurried to catch the cat.

More bullets fired, chipping at the metal catwalk. Kailey never thought she could run so fast, and she resisted the girly scream that fought to come from her mouth. As long as her luck held out, which seemed to be lessening with each passing second, the bullets might never hit her.

Nervously, she glanced back, looked at the warehouse floor, but never slowed her pace. She counted five men firing their guns and the sixth man wore a heavy black trench coat. He wore a dress hat and dark shades and appeared a menacing height compared to those shooting at her. By his immense size, possibly taller and heavier than Forrest, she was certain he had been the one to break the locks and allowed the two men into the office, but she didn't know if someone more powerful than him remained inside the limo.

It was possible, as most leaders tended to have others do the dirty work for them.

The man on the tie beam dropped onto the catwalk with a heavier crash and rushed after her. The catwalk swayed side to side with his thundering steps.

Raven paused in stride and turned. Kailey leaned and scooped the cat into her arms, interrupting the cat's threatening hiss, and she was narrowly missed by a ricocheting bullet that hit the catwalk platform.

A barrage of bullets hailed in her direction. How the gunfire missed the man pursuing her, she didn't know. And although she'd never run so hard or fast in her life, he was erasing the distance between them with inhuman speed.

Ahead, at the end of the catwalk, was a closed door. Her only remaining hope for escape was in front of her.

"Please be unlocked. Please be unlocked," Kailey chanted inside her mind.

With the clawing cat pressed against her chest with her left hand, Kailey extended her right hand toward the doorknob. At her current running speed, turning the doorknob without slamming into the door was next to impossible. At best, if it were unlocked, she might turn it but sprain her wrist. At worst, the door would be locked, she'd slam against it, and the man would grab her. The race for freedom ended then.

"I've got her," the man chasing her said. "Hold your fire!"

Raven joined Kailey's chant. *Please be unlocked. Please be unlocked. Please be unlocked.*

Kailey's sweaty hand grabbed the doorknob. It turned! She pressed herself against the door and then yanked the door back.

"Got you!" the man huffed, grabbing her right shoulder.

Kailey turned, slightly moving with his pull instead of resisting, which lessened his grip and quickly she pivoted around with his force, striking the man's nose with her elbow. Bone cracked with a sickening series of tiny snaps.

His pain was instant. Tears welled in his bloodshot eyes. His eyes darkened, not like a wolf's but like a predatory animal. She stared only a moment, as his eyes closed due to the pain. He released her and placed his hands over his bleeding nose. Blood gushed through his fingers, and she bolted out the door before she realized what lie on the other side.

The man growled, "I'm gonna kill ya bitch!"

CHAPTER 23

The loud blustery wind whipped Kailey's hair up and around her face, suddenly chilling her. How she wished she'd worn thick pajamas with footies to bed the night before. The icy wind bit into her bare legs, taking what little warmth she had remaining.

Kailey stood on the roof, shivering. Little white clouds escaped her mouth when she said, "Where to now?"

Raven either ignored the question or the wind prevented her from hearing it.

Kailey couldn't turn back. The man inside the doorway stopped and propped against the door. He aimed his gun and was steadily preparing to fire. The only reason he was hesitant, she assumed, was because his eyes were too watery to see clearly from his broken nose.

Fur sprouted over his cheeks and his nose contorted into a slight snout. The backs of his hands were furry.

"She has nowhere to run!" the ominous voice echoed from inside the warehouse. "Don't kill her! Shoot her in the leg if you must, but don't kill her! I want her alive!"

Kailey ran. A moving target was harder to shoot. A bullet flicked off the roofing tar a little to her right. Okay, so maybe a moving target was a little bit harder to shoot, but not impossible. She cringed at how close that bullet had been. With the roar of the wind, she had not heard the gunshot, so it was possible the man was using a silencer. She had few options left, but she was not surrendering easily. Cutting slightly to the right, a sudden thought came to her mind as she ran.

Where are you going?

"I'm afraid you're not going to like this," Kailey replied.

I'm no fan of being on the roof to start with.

"Okay, then you're going to *hate* this."

With all the speed her short muscular legs could offer, Kailey sprinted midway across the roof. The cold harsh wind off Elliott Bay hammered and pressed against her, causing her to momentarily slide backwards.

She lowered her head against the wind and pushed herself to run the next thirty feet harder than she'd ever run before. Running out of roof, she didn't slow her stride.

Kailey? What are you going to do? No, you're not ... you're not going to ... JUMP!

Kailey looked into the cat's wild, frightened eyes. The sheer reflection of terror and horror wasn't all Raven's. The little cat dug its sharp claws deeper into her chest. It had been frightened enough when she rushed through the doorway onto the roof, but seeing the large expanse of the bay ahead, she feared the poor creature's little heart might explode. But should Kailey hesitate further, they were both dead. She had nothing left but to take a huge gamble and hope they survived.

The overcast grayish-black sky was angry, but the churning bay below appeared even angrier. The rabid waves frothed and lapped. Nothing about the bay looked friendly. The only invitation it offered was a cold tomb, not survival. The elements of the world seemed to be against her, wanting to erase her existence. She wanted to flip off the whole world, for all of its hardships and abuse, but she decided she'd do so when ... no, *if* they survived the fall. No need to further infuriate Mother Nature beforehand.

When Kailey's path on the rooftop ended, she jumped off the side of the building with such momentum that she almost believed she could fly. For several moments her body caught the wind and actually floated upward, carrying her further out over the bay. The swirling wind pierced her eardrums with its whistling banshee cries. The sudden pressure inside her ears diminished the outside sounds but produced a hollow ringing.

The strength of the wind weakened, allowing her to fall like dead weight from the dizzying height. She estimated that she was aloft a bit higher than a parasail chute, as she entered the deadly free fall. She adjusted her body and attempted to fall properly headfirst into a dive, but found maneuvering nearly impossible without dropping the cat.

Beneath them was the choppy waves of the bay that somewhat resembled angry hands reaching up to grab and pull her under.

Raven offered no words, but Kailey felt certain she'd heard a gasp.

The cat's claws dug deeper into Kailey's flesh as sheer terror consumed it. She wanted to tell the cat they'd be okay, that they'd survive, but even she wasn't convinced of the lie. As cold as the wind was, the water was all the more frigid. She dreaded hitting the water but knew it was inevitable. Regardless of how she tried to position herself, the impact was going to be sloppy and painful.

Ever closer to impact, Kailey took a deep breath, held it, and then she closed her eyes, preparing for the worst. She hugged the cat tightly with both arms and pivoted her body, hoping to somewhat straighten on her descent to break through the water's surface like an armless diver. The pit of her stomach tickled during the fall, reminding her of a rollercoaster on its plummet from its highest peak. Afraid to open her eyes, she braced herself, knowing the collision would come sudden. She tried to ready her mind for the pain. But no event in life could prepare anyone for what was coming.

Her stiff body slapped the cold water loud and hard with every nerve in her radiating pure agony. From a good fifty-foot drop, nothing about a bay of water was soft. It was quite the opposite. She could have collided with a concrete wall with equal pain. Being pressed between two beds of nails might have been more tolerable.

The smack jarred her. She swallowed the horrendous scream her entire body sought to release. Engulfed by the heavy water, her eyes opened. Surrounded by darkness, her body grew limp. She sank helplessly. She couldn't tell if the majority of her sudden pain had occurred due to hitting the water or because the icy water stabbed into her like thousands of little frost daggers. She expected the water to be cold, but not *this* cold. She was surprised that she didn't inhale the water from the shock of its near freezing temperature.

The water rumbled, sloshed, and echoed in her ears, distorting any sound with its odd wavy pressure. The bay seemed eager to claim a new victim, carrying her downward, and she plummeted deeper into the darkened waters.

Kailey's face burned with pain, worse than any battering she'd ever suffered in a MMA bout, and already her face was swelling. She was fortunate she had not lost consciousness. Although with the radiating pain throbbing through her entire body, death was a soothing temptation.

Because she hugged her arms across her chest, she continued downward. The shock of striking the cold water left her motionless with her mind still trying to register what was going on. Her aching, burning lungs finally alerted her to reach the surface or she'd die.

Instinctively, she kicked, fighting to slow how much farther she'd sink. The engulfing water seemed to protest her efforts until she pumped her legs vigorously, as if in a cycling spin class, which she had previously compared to Hell. After this, however, she'd never insult spin class or its instructor again.

Kailey's leg muscles burned, ached, but she kept kicking hard. Finally, she broke the barrier that prevented her from sinking deeper and her thrusting kicks pushed her upward. She thought her lungs were going to explode from the burning pain.

She kicked to rise to the top and when she broke through the water's surface, the cat was gone. She shook her head to get some of her hair out of her eyes and realized she must have released the cat to use her arms to aid her rise to the top.

Frantic, Kailey gasped for air while treading water. The choppy waves battered her back and forth, washing over her. A sense of dread and remorse filled her as she wiped strands of her hair from her face.

"Raven?" she said aloud. A wave struck her face, and a moment later, she spit out a mouthful of water. She projected, "Raven!"

No response.

Scanning the caps of the waves, she couldn't see the black cat anywhere. Sorrow filled her. She hated to know that jumping might have caused the cat's demise, and worse was the fear of not ever conversing with Raven again. She tried to recall how she was positioned when she hit the water. In her memory, she was certain she had tucked her head and tried to align her legs to break the water's surface as close to a dive as possible. Had she turned after she closed her eyes? That was possible, and if the cat shared any of the direct impact … she didn't want to think it had.

Kailey glanced toward the top of the warehouse from where she had jumped. It seemed so far away. The man stood on the edge of the roof, aimed his gun, and then he slowly lowered it. He must have possessed enough sense to realize he'd never hit her from this distance. From the distance between them, he appeared only inches tall.

She didn't understand how she'd been moved so far in the water from the docks of the warehouse where she'd jumped. Studying the side of the warehouse and the loading dock between the warehouse and the bay, the jump seemed impossible. And yet, somehow, she'd made it. The waves were brutal, bashing against her, but the current shouldn't have been strong enough to pull her out to where she was treading.

Confused, Kailey turned and attempted to swim away, despite her bruised, battered muscles. Several yards away, a dark limp figure bobbed with the waves. *Raven!*

Well ... it was the black cat. Kailey couldn't be certain about Raven until after she rescued the cat, if the cat was even alive at all.

CHAPTER 24

Cassie placed her cup into Penelope's old porcelain sink. Over time, the porcelain had accumulated so many stains, she couldn't tell what the sink's original color was. The small apartment—which couldn't have been more than a two-bedroom loft—wasn't a place Cassie could ever see herself living in, regardless of how poor the economy ever became. She was surprised the apartment met the standards to be legally rented. It seemed obvious no inspections had been performed for quite some time. Of course, it beat the streets or rat-infested basements.

The ragged wallpaper with an aged, faded flowery pattern was peeling from the walls. Some of the green-tinted floor tiles were loose while others were missing. The musty air was more unpleasant near the sink and reeked of moist garlic, onions, and other pungent odors.

"Sorry I didn't have more selections for you to choose to eat," Penelope said. Her embarrassment was genuine, but she still seemed reserved and uncomfortable talking to a demon. "I don't venture out a lot, and to be truthful, I never expected any company except for Forrest, of course."

Cassie forced a smile, wishing she had a strong alcoholic drink to wash the lingering taste from her mouth. She wouldn't have protested gargling bleach or 409. Keeping down the tidbit of what Penelope considered lunch was difficult, but at least Cassie was gaining back her strength in spite of the nauseating heartburn. Her stomach rumbled and protested with a series of nagging burps. "Sardines and … crackers. I'm afraid that's going to hold me for … quite a while. Mind if I ask you something?"

Penelope shrugged slightly. "Sure."

"Would you like for me to do some shopping for you? I don't mind getting you more food. Maybe I could bring you something new to try."

"Forrest has brought me different types of food, but I'm not too keen with most of it. It tends to be too spicy or it doesn't set well on my stomach," Penelope said.

Cassie rubbed her gassy stomach and nodded. "I understand. I imagine the food you're used to from long ago isn't the same at all."

"It isn't. We ate a lot of salted salmon during Seattle's pioneer days. Food was sometimes scarce when I traveled, so I learned to eat modestly on rations. Sometimes, we ate beef or sheep, too, but all these foods today, in such colorful wrappers and cans. It's too different. They have odd aftertastes."

Cassie smiled. "Processed food. Yep. It will take time for your tongue and digestive system to adjust."

"That's what Forrest says," she replied. "But I don't know if I *want* to adjust. The newer things can be overwhelming."

Cassie noticed Penelope's calloused hands. Dirt was under the tips of her fingernails. Some tips of her nails were chipped and jagged. Cassie reached for Penelope's hand. "May I?"

Penelope gave Cassie a shrewd, apprehensive stare.

"You can trust me," Cassie said. "I promise."

Slowly, Penelope placed her fingers atop Cassie's left hand. Cassie gently curled Penelope's fingers over the side of her index finger near her thumb, so she could better view Penelope's fingernails. With a gentle wave of Cassie's right hand, a nail file appeared.

"What are you doing?" Penelope asked with a shrewd stare. Her fingers tightened.

"See my fingernails?" Cassie said. "And how shiny and smooth they are?"

Penelope nodded.

"Yours need some work. I'm just going to help repair some of them," Cassie said. "They're a mess. Looks like you've been scrubbing floors or cutting wood."

"I did scrub the floors earlier."

"By hand?"

Penelope nodded.

Cassie pursed her lips and then she shook her head. "Times have changed, girl. The days of breaking your back to clean a floor are over. I'm definitely going to take you shopping. You can't keep destroying your fingernails like this. No need to do backbreaking work when it's not necessary."

"There's no need—"

"The less chores you bestow on yourself, the more luxury time you have to enjoy better things." Cassie gently used the nail file to smooth the rough edges of the worst fingernail Penelope had.

Penelope winced, but watched with a slight interest.

"It doesn't hurt, now does it?"

She smiled. "It feels weird. Tickles."

"I'm surprised you're not feeling a lot of pain from this nail."

"You learn to ignore pain after a while."

"You're lucky it's not infected."

Penelope studied Cassie for several moments. She gazed into Cassie's eyes a bit longer than Cassie expected her to do and then she quickly looked away.

"Is something wrong?" Cassie asked.

"Just trying to figure something out."

"Like what?"

"If this is the real you." Her fingers tightened.

Cassie eased Penelope's hand open and returned to filing. "Or course, this is the *real* me. What do you mean?"

"This isn't a guise? A mask to hide the real you. Or, you're not baiting me with kindness to coax down my guard?"

Cassie smiled. "I have no intention of ever hurting you."

"I want to believe that."

"Forrest is my friend. I never betray my friends' trust. If someone was trying to hurt you, I'd fight to defend you. I'd fight to keep you alive. Believe it or not, I'd give my life to protect you."

Penelope looked into Cassie's eyes again, somewhat bewildered.

"What?" Cassie said.

"You'd defend me, a Demon-hunter? I hunt and kill your kind."

Cassie shrugged. "Yeah, well, I'm not too fond of a lot of the demons I encounter. Most of which I wish would be returned to the abyss. I'd be happy to make a list for you sometime."

Penelope's eyes widened with surprise.

"I'm kidding … about the list, but not about how evil some demons are. Those, yes, you're doing everyone a service by getting rid of them."

"And you don't have a problem with that?"

Cassie bit her lower lip for several seconds, trying to figure out the best way to explain the situation. "No, I don't. Like Forrest, you've been chosen to perform a task to better the world. He hunts vampires and you hunt demons, so it's no wonder your two paths crossed. Call it fate or destiny, you two were meant to be together."

Penelope blushed.

"You're in love with him, aren't you?"

"Many years ago—"

"Now, your feelings for him haven't changed. It shows in your eyes."

"Perhaps, but I'm not comfortable talking about this."

"Okay, sorry. You still don't fully trust me. I get it."

Penelope shook her head. "I'm … I'm trying. I was trained to never believe a demon, as demons will say anything to convince a hunter not to kill them. We're instructed to kill them all without prejudice."

"But isn't that biased, anyway?"

Penelope frowned. Her eyes indicated her depth of thought. After a few minutes, she said, "We've never entertained the thought of any demon not being evil."

"Well, that makes it easier, doesn't it?" Cassie asked.

"In what way?"

"If every demon is automatically evil, you've no need to weigh the scales of justice that you've killed a demon that's never done any harm to anyone else. Lump them all as guilty to prevent a hunter's guilty conscience or to question one's own motive."

"You think that's what we do?" Penelope asked.

"Don't you? I mean, isn't that exactly what you described?"

After a moment, Penelope nodded. "I suppose you're right. But demons aren't humans and not given due process."

"Don't you think it's about time we are? After all, a lot of vile humans live on this earth with colder hearts and no conscience at all and they escape ever suffering penalties for their crimes. Some people are evil to the core and regardless of what religious groups would like for everyone else to believe, some of these humans weren't influenced by demons at all. They're just plain evil."

"That's a valid point," Penelope said. "But for me, after being imprisoned for over a hundred years and not witnessing the changes during that time period, I'm still having issues with adjusting. Simply talking to you, a demon, is contrary to how my mind views my duties as a Demon-hunter and how I view the world."

"I understand," Cassie said. "It takes time for one to change his or her mentality. It does, especially when mentors or organizations have influenced you to judge others in certain ways, to assume every one is identical based on appearance. It's why discrimination exists. It's why we have wars. And most wars occur due to religious reasons, when one side believes their god is greater than the other's."

"I agree. I struggled with those thoughts before I had been imprisoned, but I could never speak of those things I questioned to anyone for fear of being brought before the Council or the Church. I had no choice but to be devout in all aspects."

"So you were already mentally imprisoned. It's a bold being who rationally considers that perhaps what's being forced upon us isn't true or the appropriate cause."

Penelope nodded and peered closer at how Cassie was shaping her nails. Her intent eyes and curious smile made Cassie feel good inside. Penelope might be a ruthless Demon-hunter in the outside world, but in so many ways, she held a refined innocence like a child. Ever gaining her full trust was a milestone Cassie hoped one day to achieve.

"I happened to think of something," Cassie said.

"What's that?"

"How do you contact Forrest? He doesn't own a cellphone, and I seem to have lost mine."

"I don't have one, either," Penelope said.

Cassie sighed. "I must've lost mine when those two guys were harassing me."

Penelope bit her lower lip and blushed, slightly shaking her head.

"What is it?" Cassie asked.

Penelope pulled a cellphone from her apron pocket and handed it to Cassie.

Cassie frowned. "Where'd you find my phone?"

"It slid from your hand when you materialized on the floor."

Cassie smiled. "Great! Thanks."

"I couldn't figure out what it is or how to use it," Penelope said.

"We definitely need to modernize you."

Penelope pulled her hand back. "See? *That's* why I find it difficult to trust a demon. You're trying to seduce me with all these strange devices, mold me into something I'm not, and—"

"Whoa!" Cassie said, shaking her head. "I'm doing no such thing. If modern devices are evil, you're indicating that nothing mankind invents should ever be used at all. You really think it's a sin to incorporate the use of an invention that lessens the toils of a man or woman?"

"Change is difficult. Understanding some of these devices frightens me."

"It doesn't have to. Learning new things should be fun. But until you're more comfortable, you should take your time."

"But there are millions of things that have changed within the past century. It's like I woke up in a different world. Nothing's the way I remember it."

"Forrest will be happy to help you. As am I. Even Kailey ..." Cassie cleared her throat and fought tears. She turned the conversation for a moment. "How do your fingernails feel?"

Penelope rubbed her fingertip across the nails and marveled. She smiled. "They're smooth like soft cloth. Could you do that with the rest of them?" She extended her other hand.

Cassie winked and grinned. "Of course. So tell me, how do you contact Forrest when you need him?"

"I generally wait for him to come home."

"So he lives with you?"

She nodded. "And he checks on me twice a day."

"He doesn't stay with you at night?"

Penelope shook her head. "Most nights he hunts vampires. He seldom sleeps."

"I see."

About an hour later, Cassie had finished trimming and filing all of Penelope's nails. She painted the last of Penelope's fingernails with a glossy pink nail polish.

Penelope was intrigued. Her eyes studied each stroke of the polish brush as Cassie carefully painted. "That's an interesting color."

"There," Cassie said. "What do you think?"

Penelope marveled at her nails under the overhead lights and smiled. "I love this. Thank you."

"You have to let the polish dry, okay?"

"I owe you a favor for this," Penelope said with a broad smile.

Cassie opened her mouth to reply, but suddenly felt a harsh coldness wash over her body, chilling her. For several moments she couldn't catch her breath and struggled to move. The entire time, she pictured Kailey, and she knew Kailey was in trouble. Elliott Bay. The flash of images flooded Cassie's mind.

"We need to find Forrest or get to Elliott Bay."

"Why?"

Cassie gasped for air. "Kailey's in trouble. She's in serious trouble. If I don't find her soon, she will be dead."

CHAPTER 25

*K*ailey treaded water while holding the limp cat that Raven inhabited. The soaked cat was breathing, but still had not awakened. Raven had not spoken, either, so Kailey wondered if the cat had to be conscious for Raven to speak, or had Raven left the cat's body for good?

She held the cat close to her chest. Its shivering body was growing weaker. Even if Kailey were able to swim to shore quickly, she'd need to find a place to get warmth or they'd both succumb to hyperthermia. Chills from the water and her fading shock were slowly claiming what energy she had gained from her adrenaline surge.

The sharp wind caused the churning waves to rock her back and forth. A couple of times she attempted to float on her back to drift with the lapping water, hoping she'd be pushed to shore, but higher waves sluiced over her face, filled her nose with water, so she returned to treading. She'd swallowed enough water to sicken her stomach, and the undulating waves certainly didn't help matters.

Kailey cradled the cat in her left hand and spent a few minutes kicking and partially swimming on her right side. Her mind returned to the men at the warehouse, the man in the limo to be more precise, and she wondered who and what he was. The man who had almost captured her *wasn't* human. Some type of shapeshifter? Maybe. Or perhaps something else?

She didn't think the taller man was a vampire, as he wouldn't be out during the daylight. At least, that's what she assumed, but the limo had reflective windows and with his apparent luxury of wealth he could afford glass windows that completely blocked out UV light. And with the thick overcast sky obscuring any hope of full sunlight, her guess wasn't necessarily a good one.

Kailey was puzzled by the entire situation. Vampire or not, why did he want her? His two thugs knew where she and Brady lived, so why, if their beef was with Brady, did they find it necessary to abduct her? They could've gone after Brady at any time.

There seemed to be more than what appeared on the surface. Raven insisted she had seen Micah, but nothing indicated he was involved in this at all.

Kicking her legs vigorously to stay afloat in the battering waves was draining Kailey's strength and weakening her resolve. The cold water was sapping her body heat. She knew she had less than a half hour at best to reach the shore or she was going to surrender to the harsh weather and drown. It wasn't that she was so far from the shore as it was her finding a place to get out of the water. The piers were too high without any ladders or ropes so she needed to swim past them to reach the shore.

The docks nearest the abandoned warehouse where she had leapt from were no easier to get to, and even if she could, she was certain those men were probably scouring the docks looking for her.

"Miss!" a man said.

Kailey turned her head and looked in different directions until she saw an elderly man drifting toward her in his fiberglass fishing boat. The trolling motor couldn't be heard above the roaring wind and waves.

He eased the boat closer to her and motioned someone to kill the engine. "Looks like you could use a hand, Miss. Let's get you out of that freezing water."

Kailey looked up to see his extended hand and eagerly, she accepted. Tears flowed down her cheeks but she doubted he could even see them for all the water dripping from her hair and down her face.

At first, she didn't think he'd be able to pull her up, but he was much stronger than she expected. With one swift heft upward, he set her on the bottom of the boat. Water gushed off her and puddled around her. She shivered so hard she couldn't speak.

"Brent, get her one of those blankets under your seat. Be quick now."

"Okay, Papaw."

The chubby cheeked little boy lifted his seat and pulled a woolen blanket out and hurried to hand it to his grandfather. He patted the boy's head and then smiled at Kailey. "Name's Zeke. Here, let's wrap this around you."

"She has a cat!" Brent said with a wide grin.

"Yep. Poor thing looks like it's seen better days, too." He draped the blanket across her shoulders and then tucked it around her. "Girl, what were you thinking wearing shorts out in this weather?"

Kailey pulled her knees to her chest and adjusted the blanket to cover her legs as well. "It—it—wasn't intentional, sir."

"It's a wonder you've not already died from hyperthermia with this damned cold wind. Brent, hand me my thermos."

"Here, Papaw," Brent said, lugging it to him.

"All I got is hot black coffee, no sugar, but at least it will warm you up some on the inside," Zeke said. He poured a cup and held it to her shaking lips. "Easy, now, it's still hot. We haven't been out here too long ourselves."

Kailey gulped a mouthful of the bitter coffee, not caring if it blistered her lips or her tongue and throat. She craved heat. She slowed the next swallow after the first gulp of hot coffee burned the back of her throat and all the way down. Still, she endured the pain without complaint in favor of the warmth.

"You mind telling me what's going on?" he asked.

Kailey sipped the last of the second cup of coffee down and her voice was less shaky. "What do you mean?"

He helped her move to a dry seat near the steering wheel. He brought a second blanket and offered her a heavy coat to lay over the blankets. Her body shivered against her will, but the heavy layers helped reduce her chills. The cat shifted a bit, too.

"What do I mean?" Zeke rolled his eyes. "Young lady, do you think no one saw you jump off that warehouse over there? I'm certain I'm not the only one. Either you wanted to die or someone was chasing you. Considering that you're holding the cat and dressed like you are, I tend to believe it's the latter, especially since you didn't just plummet onto the dock. You somehow managed to reach the water. For a few moments, you appeared to sail in the air, *against* the wind, which is a phenomenal feat, especially for someone as little as you. Someone smiled in your favor. Otherwise, you'd have hit somewhere on that loading dock and be dead. Only a desperate person could make such a leap. Who's after you?"

"I—I wish I knew."

Reading the panic in her eyes, Zeke said, "Sit tight. All I'm using on this little boat right now is the trolling motor. Brent and I were going to try to catch a few fish but the wind turned out to be worse than expected. I need to switch over to my larger motor. I'll have you at the marina in a few minutes."

"Thank you."

"Don't mention it. Just glad we were in the vicinity and saw you." He reached into his back pocket and slid out his iPhone. "Hit 9-1-1 and let them know we're arriving, but if you want some free advice, I'd call a friend instead. Some of the city police … ah, nevermind, call whomever you want."

The iPhone shook in her hand. "You don't trust the police?"

Zeke chuckled. "Some I do, but others, let's just say that I worry about officers that are willing to protect vamps over the living. The trickiest part is not knowing which are sympathizers or under the control of a vampire. And there's a lot of them this day that look the other way when the vamps feed on humans."

"You know about the vampires, huh?"

Zeke grumbled without saying words, glancing at his grandson, and then he shook his head. He lowered his voice. "Yep. We know. My wife and I would move to another state to get away from the fuckers, but we can't leave our daughter and her son to fend for themselves. You know, I often wonder what's the vampire problem is going to be like when Brent's my age? You ever think of that?"

Kailey looked at Brent's chubby face as he crawled onto the seat beside his grandfather and strapped himself in, smiling the entire time. He was bundled in several heavy layers of clothes beneath his thick wind-resistant coat. His little toboggan hid his ears, but his bright blue eyes and smile warmed her heart. She smiled. "He's so cute. How old is he?"

"Almost five," Zeke said. "Look, I'm sorry for spouting off. But when you get my age and see how the world is, and then you see a young boy like my grandson, you wonder what the future holds."

"I understand. Far more than you might think."

"Please, ignore me, and call someone to meet us at the dock. And help yourself to the rest of the coffee."

"Thanks. Look, I'm sorry that you have to turn back."

"Ah, now, no apologies needed. We were headed back anyways. This weather's worse than the forecasters predicted. Can't cast a line in this. The wind's too harsh to have Brent out in it. Wife and daughter both won't let me hear the end of it, either."

Kailey smiled and dialed Brady's number and hoped he answered a number he didn't recognize for once. As the phone rang, the cat shifted under the blanket and released a soft mew. Relief washed over her that the cat was arousing, but she wondered if Raven shared the cat's body.

We survived? Raven whispered into Kailey's mind.

Kailey sighed. Fresh tears formed in her eyes.

"Barely," Kailey thought, waiting for Brady to pick up. "Whatever you do, don't look outside of this blanket until we're off the bay. I've enough claw marks and bruises. A man found us in the water and we're on his boat heading to the marina."

The cat shivered. *I'm comfortable right here, so no worries.*

The phone call went to Brady's voicemail. She declined leaving a message and dialed again. By now, she figured he probably knew she had been taken, so he might answer the unknown number on the second try. Robocallers didn't usually dial back the same number immediately, so maybe he'd get the hint that this was an emergency.

As Zeke increased the boat's speed, she pulled the blanket tightly over her head and around her face to protect herself from the harsh wind and splashing mists. She'd never been so cold in her life. The sinking feeling washed over her that even though Zeke had rescued her, she was nowhere near safe when they reached the marina. That chilled her even more.

CHAPTER 26

Cassie and Penelope descended a narrow set of rusted stairs on the outside of the three-story building. Cassie hoped they'd be able to hail a cab once they reached the street, but that was before she discovered Penelope lived in an area where most cab drivers refused to pick up or drop off patrons.

Cassie didn't blame the cab drivers, as the area held the highest crime rates in the entire city *before* the vampire population ballooned. After the vampires settled in the city's outliers, the crime rates drastically decreased, but it didn't improve a cabbie's enthusiasm for visiting the area.

Most cabbies joked that a few bucks wasn't worth risking one's neck, but the worst likelihood was in becoming one of the undead. At least ninety-eight percent of the population still had enough sense to shun the undead or feared being turned into one. But the younger generation's infatuation with Hollywood's romantic spin on the appeal of fictitious vampires had blinded them into ignoring the true nature of what being a vampire actually was. The sacrifices of what they lost were far greater than the benefits they thought they'd gain.

"I guess we're hoofing it on foot for a bit. No pun intended," Cassie said.

Penelope apparently missed the joke and gave Cassie a strange, questionable look. Penelope slung her backpack over her shoulder, which concealed her crossbow.

Cassie said, "No cabs here."

Cassie's heels clicked on the sidewalk with her long strides and for a moment, she entertained the thought of losing the shoes and turn her feet into hooves. She reconsidered since Penelope might not understand such humor and Penelope also seemed shaken weeks after her awakening while still trying to adjust to the dramatic changes of the world.

"No cabs," Cassie repeated in a near whisper, keeping her grin to a bare minimum.

Penelope hurried to keep up. "I know. That's one of the reasons I don't venture to the market for food. It's a long walk. Forrest brings provisions each evening."

Provisions? Cassie grinned. "I understand why you were low on groceries, now. And just to reinforce that I was telling you the truth earlier, this is the last place I'd ever have visualized to teleport to reach safety, and I certainly never imagined you lived here. Forrest hasn't told any of us that this is where you're living."

Penelope nodded and smiled a sheepish grin. Her voice was soft, full of innocence. When it came to fighting demons, Penelope was a different person, much bolder, and more calculated. But talking about life in general and the city, she was timid and exposed her childlike innocence, making her an easy target should some of the better masked demons discover what she truly was. Some demons had played humans so long that they often forgot they were demons.

"I want you to know you can trust me," Cassie said. But then she thought about her statement and even the most vile demon would use such a line, which was almost as bad as men's horrible, unoriginal pickup lines at bars. Cassie winced.

Penelope said, "Though it's not something I'd have thought I'd ever say to a demon, but I believe you."

"Not to sound offensive," Cassie said, immediately wishing she hadn't started with those words, which usually meant the words following the phrase would be offensive, even thought the true intent might not. "*Why* would you choose to live in this part of the city?"

She shrugged. "The price is most affordable."

"If it's about the lack of money, sweetheart, you can come live with me. I won't charge you rent. I've more than enough room. You're welcome to stay."

Penelope blushed and smiled. "While I appreciate your generosity, I must decline. I don't fear for my safety."

Cassie eyed the backpack on Penelope's shoulder and wondered how fast Penelope could pull her crossbow out and properly aim at an attacker.

"You don't? *Here*? Why not? You know that vampires have pretty much claimed this area for their own, right? That's why you don't even see a living soul out yet. Any remaining humans want to wait until the sun is fully up, just in case."

"The number of vampires have been on a steady decline. Besides, the house is safeguarded from their intrusion."

Cassie's brow rose. "Because of Forrest?"

"Yes," Penelope said.

"Ah, I see. You still don't need to live in these destitute conditions."

"I've no need for luxuries," she replied.

"This isn't about luxuries," Cassie said. "It's about the quality of life, sanitary conditions. Hon—"

"Cassie, I fear those better things you speak of would cause me to become lazy and divert my attention away from the duties I was chosen to perform."

"You realize that most demons reside in much better places than this?" Cassie asked.

"They do?"

"Damn right they do! This squabble eyesore isn't an area where a demon would consider calling home."

"Really?" Penelope looked shocked. "I've encountered and slain a few demons since we moved here. Well, *three*. Before I was imprisoned inside the magical barrier, this was the most likely place to find demons, which is why I found the few living on this street fairly quickly."

"Three?"

Penelope nodded.

"You probably got rid of the only ones staying here, then."

"You really think so?"

Cassie smiled. "In this modern age, demons lust for the better things in life. Perhaps even more than the humans do. Demons only come to the slummy rundown areas if they need to manipulate the minds of someone desperate enough to steal or murder for them. Someone who, if he or she gets caught or killed in the process of the crime, won't be missed and can't be linked to others. Gutter trash, you know? The nameless. Nowadays, it's rare a demon needs to do that because the higher class humans have less scruples than ever before. Some would do anything to get into the next higher bracket, regardless of already being wealthy."

Penelope looked confused. "Is that really the case?"

"Yes."

"The world has changed so much since I've been gone. The apocalypse can't be far away. These demons will usher the end of the world just like the prophets of old predicted."

Cassie burst into laughter.

Uneasiness settled over Penelope and her former expression of mistrust toward Cassie returned. Her voice became harsh, defensive. "Why's that so funny?"

"You really think the demons *want* this world to be destroyed? They're having too much fun. They don't want their playground demolished."

"That's the very reason it will be destroyed."

"To eliminate us?"

"Yes."

"Ah, I see, and to do that, you think the humans are going to be sacrificed along with the demons?"

"It is prophesied," Penelope replied.

"By the churches?"

Penelope nodded.

"That's your biggest flaw."

"What is? My faith?"

"No. Those who prey upon your faith and shape your beliefs for you. These churches—religions in general—are greater manipulators of humans than demons," Cassie said. "The priests, popes, and preachers have always threatened the wrath and fury of their gods as a control factor, and the leaders of these churches throughout time have far more blood on their hands than any of the demons you've ever killed. You ever think about that?"

"That's a shrewd judgment." Penelope crossed her arms and glared, but didn't slow her stride to keep up with Cassie.

Without glancing toward Penelope, Cassie said, "It's the truth. Their goal was to take over the world, still is, and for hundreds of years they slaughtered any group that refused to accept their doctrines as *divine*. That war continues even today."

Penelope put her hands over her ears and shook her head. Anger tightened her brow. "Stop with these blasphemous statements!"

"Blasphemous?" Cassie slowed her stride, falling victim to her laughter again. She leaned forward, resting her hands on her knees.

"Stop! Stop laughing!" Penelope's voice was closer to a growl. Anger spewed sudden rage in her eyes. Her countenance darkened.

Cassie refrained from further laughter, and found it difficult until she noticed how upset Penelope was. The poor girl was moments from heated tears, not of sadness, but from her festering fury and rage. Once anyone was pushed to that degree, she became unpredictable, and Cassie never intended to hurt Penelope. She certainly hadn't intended for her words to be an attack on Penelope.

Cassie reconsidered what she had said and realized what she had said had been disrespectful to Penelope's beliefs. "Look, I'm sorry. I'm not laughing at you. Truthfully. And hopefully, you're not back to viewing me as an enemy. But the sooner you realize the myths you were taught to believe more than a century ago, the better you can see the world for what it truly is."

Penelope cautiously looked toward the sky and then she scanned the tops of the buildings on both sides of the street. The dirty sidewalks were empty. The narrow side alleys where some of the homeless once built lean-tos with corrugated cardboard boxes were soulless.

Cassie sensed something seemed different. No place was ever this abandoned or silent. Not in Seattle. An ominous sensation hung over the area. Her focus on finding Kailey must have caused her not to notice or else, they had entered where its presence was the strongest.

Although uneasy, Cassie attempted to hide her sudden nervousness. She said, "I hope you realize I'm not your enemy, even though our outlooks and opinions differ."

"No, I sense you're different than other demons," Penelope said, still studying the rooftops while walking.

"Then why get so upset about what I said?" Cassie followed Penelope's searching gaze. "What are you looking for?"

"I'm afraid what you said might have caught the attention of an angel."

"An angel?" Cassie looked intently at the rooftops. Was that the presence she felt? No. Angels wouldn't be that dark.

She nodded. "Yes. I don't want you smitten for what you said."

"Have you ever seen an angel?" Cassie asked skeptically.

"Two of them."

"Really?"

"Yes, and when they appear, no demon's ever safe. Not even you."

"I don't think an angel's going to take time out of its busy schedule because I shed light on some history for you," Cassie said, even though the thought made her uneasy. "Did you see these angels recently?"

"No, it was after the Great Fire of Seattle," Penelope said. Her eyes reflected an emptiness as her mind revisited her past. "They came too late to stop the damage, but they sent dozens of demons back to the abyss and from my understanding, they aided in extinguishing the fire. That was months before I arrived. But they continued hunting and slaying the demons with an ease unlike what I had seen before. If I possessed a weapon like theirs, I could have killed hundreds more than I did."

"Wasn't the Wrathbone one of those weapons?"

Penelope shook her head. "No. It was deadly for fighting the behemoths but it's not an angel's weapon. The Wrathbone was blessed by a priest. I never had the courage to approach the angels, because they were engaged in combat with the demons. If I could go back, I'd ask for a sword like theirs, so I could help them eradicate more demons."

"Have you ever considered that their intent isn't to kill all of the demons?"

"Are you implying the angels purposely allow demons to roam the earth?"

"Don't they? If they are armed with weapons that demons hold no defense against, and all demons should be annihilated, why aren't they doing that full-time?"

"I don't know why they haven't," Penelope said. "But I witnessed their power firsthand."

"And yet, they didn't save you from being suspended in your time-resistant tomb, did they? Were you not of enough importance in the duties you performed for them to save you?"

The words cut into Penelope. Sadness came to her moistening eyes. It was apparent she had not considered the angels' failure to protect her or else, they simply allowed her fate to be sealed away. The possibility was that she might never have been released, if not for the witches', Forrest's, and even Cassie's help.

Cassie eased slowly to Penelope's side and gently placed her hand on Penelope's shoulder. She offered the Demon-hunter a smile. "Look, I didn't mean to upset you, but I've been alive and around much longer than you. For hundreds of years. Nothing hurts worse than when the real truth is brought to light. It screws with your mind and messes with your understanding. It takes time to absorb and sort through the information that's contrary to what you were taught to believe. Your mind needs time to adjust."

"I suppose." Penelope remained quiet for several moments while they walked. "Have you ever seen an angel?"

"I've seen fallen angels," Cassie replied. "And if you think a demon is ruthless, you've seen nothing that compares to the power a fallen angel possesses. Perhaps, this battle you believe about holy vs. unholy and the Light against the Dark is more of a battle between the real angels and the Fallen. The demons and humans become casualties of an eternal war."

"I've never seen a fallen angel," Penelope said.

"Trust me," Cassie said. "With your calling, you won't want to."

"I've heard of them and that the swords they carry have tarnished from their former radiance into abyssal darkness."

Cassie nodded. "Demons fear the fallen angels worse than the angels of light or hunters like yourself."

"Why?"

"The swords of the Fallen do worse than send demons to the abyss. They're completely gone into nonexistence."

"That's odd."

"What is?"

"I'd think fallen angels would protect demons, not destroy them, as they want the demons to serve them."

"I doubt a greater motivating factor exists for a demon's undying loyalty to do whatever one of the Fallen has demanded. The Fallen don't simply go around like you to hunt and destroy demons. They only use their weapons on demons that fail to carry out their demanded duties. Of course, an occasional few demons become addicted to tormenting humans and lesser demons, and that gets out of hand. Those tend to be found by the Fallen and are destroyed. My guess is that the Fallen eliminate more demons than angels."

Penelope stared at Cassie in disbelief, trying to assess all the new information.

"Come on," Cassie said. "It's too much to process for you. I think we're getting close to an area where we can find a cab."

"That's good," Penelope said. "So where I live … you don't think a lot of demons occupy that neighborhood?"

"I certainly wouldn't live there," Cassie replied with a sly grin. "Demons are master manipulators, and pass themselves off as human to hold the best jobs with the highest pay and live in condos or luxurious apartment complexes. Not in places like where you live. Your hunting ground isn't on this side of town, unless you're hunting vampires. Few demons would dare go there, and I'd say those are the ones you killed. Only demons that are hiding from the law or higher level demons or the Fallen would consider staying in this area."

Cassie stepped to a corner curb, raised her hand toward an approaching cab, and waited. Penelope stood silently beside her. When the cab slowed and stopped, Cassie opened the door and let Penelope in first. She wished they hadn't needed to walk so far to get a cab, as now she didn't know where to tell the driver to take them. She no longer felt Kailey's struggle for survival, which meant that either someone had helped Kailey or Kailey was already dead.

CHAPTER 27

*B*y the time the fishing boat drifted against the marina docks, Kailey felt somewhat warmer but longed to soak in a tub of hot water to melt away the inner icy chill that kept her involuntarily shivering from time to time. At least the boat dock was shielded from the wind by a slanted roof.

Both times she had tried to reach Brady's cell number, her call was directed to voicemail. She knew he refused to answer calls from numbers he didn't recognize but she kept hoping he made an exception.

Several of the neighboring boat owners were cleaning their boats. Zeke hitch-tied his boat to a cleat in under thirty seconds. Kailey figured he had done the maneuver so often that it was second nature and didn't require him a moment's thought.

Two older men stood on the dock wearing heavy coats, winter gloves, and worn trapper hats. Their attire made her envious, and she'd have gladly paid a thousand dollars for such a coat and hat if she was carrying the money. One of the men smoked a pipe and the other had a vapor cigarette that smelled like cinnamon. They turned slightly and greeted Zeke with broad smiles and waves.

Zeke returned their greetings before picking up Brent and setting him on the floating dock. "Tom? Darren? Could you two help me get Miss

138

Kailey up onto the dock. I don't want Brent to accidentally step off into the water while I'm getting her out."

Tom hobbled past Brent and offered his hand to Kailey while Zeke placed his hands against her back to keep her steady. The boat rocked slightly, and even though her legs ached, she was fairly certain she could get out on her own. But she was thankful for his help.

"Braving the weather?" Tom asked, gripping her hand and offering a smile. "My name's Tom."

"Good to meet you," she said with her shaky voice. "I'm Kailey."

Darren stepped beside Tom and took Kailey's other hand. "Are you nuts, Tom? They just came into the dock and looks like none too soon."

Kailey smiled at Darren. "Sorry, but I've got a cat."

"Oh, the two of you are soaked through to the bone," Darren said.

"Good heavens," Tom said, shaking his head after Kailey was huddled under the blankets on the dock. He reached for Zeke's hand. "Kailey, what were you doing swimming in this weather? And dressed like this?"

"Yeah," Darren said. "It's still a month away before the Polar Bear Club even considers it cold enough to jump into the water."

"Me and Papaw found her," Brent said with a broad smile.

Tom frowned with suspicion and glanced at Zeke. "You found her?"

Zeke nodded.

Darren slid his heavy coat off his shoulders and draped it over her shoulders.

"You didn't need to do that," she said.

"Of course I did. You'll be lucky not to catch pneumonia."

"Where'd you find her, Zeke?" Tom asked.

"Not too far north of here," Zeke said. "Come on, let's get her to my houseboat where she can warm herself, call someone to get her, and Elsa should have some clothes she can change into."

Zeke took Brent's hand in his and walked from the floating dock onto the fixed dock and turned toward the left.

Darren looked into Kailey's eyes. "How'd you manage to get into the water out there and with a cat, too?"

"I—"

Zeke said, "She fell off the tourist boat with her cat."

"And no one sounded an alarm?" Tom asked. "They usually keep better watch over their customers."

"I'm fine, now, really," Kailey said. "I'm just lucky that Zeke was nearby."

"I'm going to call that company and give them a piece of my mind," Tom said.

"It isn't their fault."

"Hell, it's someone's fault," Darren said. "You're a tourist and well, they're supposed to take better care of you than that. Where are you from anyway? Your accent certainly isn't from here. You sound like a mixture of Boston and somewhere down south."

Kailey smiled. "Good guess."

"Right this way," Zeke said, pointing to another floating dock. "Third houseboat on the right."

Kailey held Raven beneath the draped blanket and heavy coat. The bobbing of the dock caused her to wobble, but Darren stepped beside her and offered the crook of his elbow as if escorting her to the dance floor.

Not wanting to hurt his feelings, she hooked her arm with his and walked alongside him until they reached the flat deck at the rear of the houseboat.

Zeke unlocked the door and let Brent inside. Then he stepped aside for Kailey to enter. She slipped Darren's coat from her shoulders and handed it to him.

"Thank you," she said with a smile. "I greatly appreciate that. I hope it isn't too wet."

Zeke offered Tom and Darren quick handshakes, thanking them for their help.

"Gramma!" Brent shouted, running to his grandmother seated on the gray loveseat. "We found a cat *and* a girl."

His grandmother stared at Kailey with curiosity that turned into sudden horror, which slowly faded to pity. The cat's green eyes stared at everyone in the small room with intent. Its energy had returned, but it no longer fought or clawed to get away from her. It purred, but she wondered how much of its actions were its own and how much Raven controlled.

"Elsa," Zeke said, "this is Kailey."

Elsa rose from her seat and nodded. "Good to meet you. Let me get you some clothes and another blanket."

"She was in the water," Brent said. "Papaw pulled her out."

"I see," Elsa said with a gentle smile.

When Elsa returned with a change of clothes, Zeke gave a quick explanation of them seeing Kailey's leap from the top of the warehouse.

"Here," Elsa said, taking the cat and cradling it. Kailey wanted to warn her of its feral nature, but the cat never struggled as Elsa exchanged the clothes for the cat. "Go past the counter and the door to the left is the bathroom. Take a hot shower if you'd like."

"That's okay," Kailey said. "I've had enough water today."

Elsa laughed softly. "No matter. You can change in there. I have a pot of fresh chili on the stove. After you've changed, we'll sit down and eat."

"Thank you."

Zeke said, "And if that coffee didn't toast you some on the inside, her chili's hotter than the devil's furnace."

"Zeke!" Elsa said. "You want her to eat after all she's been through."

Kailey grinned and laughed. "I like spicy food, so the hotter, the better."

Kailey opened the bathroom door and gently closed the door behind her. As her body adjusted to the warmth, her bruises awakened. Her entire body ached. Her muscles throbbed and her battered face burned.

She faced the bathroom mirror and cringed. Her face was a mixtures of purple, red, and blue. It had been a miracle her neck wasn't broken when she plunged face first into the bay. She was fortunate to be alive.

After several horrifying moments of studying her face, she realized she still held Zeke's cellphone. While she appreciated their hospitality, she needed to get to Brady or at the very least, she needed to inform him of what had happened.

Kailey dialed Brady's number for the third time. If he didn't answer this time, she wasn't going to attempt another call from Zeke's phone. Three strikes, and she guessed, she was out … of luck.

"Please answer, dammit," she whispered.

CHAPTER 28

Forrest gave Brady an odd side-glance when the cellphone rang the third time. "Aren't you going to answer that?"

"I don't recognize the number," Brady replied.

"So?" Forrest said.

"You might want to answer that," Jinn said from the backseat of the patrol car. "Just in case it's Kailey. Just saying."

Brady sighed. "You're probably right."

Jinn leaned against the partition with his hands pressed against the glass, revealing he no longer wore the handcuffs.

Brady gave him a harsh glare in the mirror.

"What?" Jinn said. "You don't need to worry that I'm going to teleport. If I were going to do that, I'd *already* split *before* you cuffed me."

"That's true," Forrest said with a chuckle.

"Yeah," Brady said, "I know. But it doesn't aggravate me any less."

Brady put the phone on speaker and swiped the screen to answer the call. "Hello?"

"Brady," Kailey said.

"Where are you?" Brady asked with tears forming in his eyes. "Are you okay?"

"I escaped," she replied. Her voice choked up. "I'm at Falcons Marina."

Kailey gave the address and the number of where the houseboat was moored. Brady put the address into the GPS tracker.

"We're on our way," Brady said. He disconnected the call, pressed Cassie's number on the phone, and handed the phone to Forrest.

Forrest's brow rose.

"Give her directions," Brady said.

Forrest took the phone and shrugged.

GETTING through the city streets was quicker than Brady expected. Most of the time, when he needed to get through the congestion of the evening traffic, some smart ass always ignored his lights and siren, making it difficult to get to an accident or a crime scene in a reasonable amount of time.

Falcons Marina was about half the city away from where their apartment was. Whomever had taken her made certain a local search in the vicinity of their apartment wouldn't turn up any clues. They didn't want Brady to find her, not until they scheduled some type of meeting was Brady's guess.

As much as he wanted to pin this on Micah, Brady held enough trust in Forrest to temporarily suspend Micah as the primary suspect. Forrest was right. Brady's neighbor could not have possibly identified Micah from the front of the apartment complex to where she stated the car was parked.

If she called the police, no one from the precinct ever informed him or was waiting for his arrival. When an officer's home was invaded or a loved one was attacked, other officers possessed a solidarity need to find the perpetrators immediately. Whenever an officer was killed by a perp, the amount of anger and craving to seek immediate vengeance was unmatched. A unified desire to find and make the villain pay, sometimes physically, became the department's overall agenda. Their anger couldn't be properly measured, and even after justice was enacted, the anger might lessen, but it never completely faded away.

Overall, officers were loyal to one another as brothers and sisters in blue, through and through. When one was killed in the line of duty, all of them suffered the loss, and even consolidated for the burial service and court hearings when the perp finally stood trial. Some went so far as to sit in on parole hearings decades later to testify with reasons for why the prisoner should not be released. Good officers stood together in life and remembrance.

Under the dire circumstances, none of his fellow comrades in blue had come to Brady's aid, and he was close friends with several of the other officers, which led him to believe his neighbor never made such a call. It also made him wonder if she had been spying on his activities for some time. Had she been planted or had a vampire like Alec compelled her to feed Brady lies?

One city council member was dead and according to Forrest, the man's torture had been a slow painful way to die. Forrest hinted that some monsters fed off the agony as well as the blood.

Brady had no choice but to discount his neighbor's eyewitness testimony about Micah, for now. But Brady still believed the place where he'd find the answers to the questions gnawing his mind was in Nocturnal Trinity. With Jinn so eager to be arrested and taken away from the nightclub, Brady wasn't relying on a hunch. Something inside the club terrified Jinn, and for something to scare the shit out of a demon, it must be colossal.

Why Kailey though? What was the purpose for an unknown evil being to take her in order to get to him? That didn't make sense. Of course, as Forrest had mentioned, it weakened Brady's focus and diverted his attention in a different direction, but if they truly wanted him, this still didn't make sense.

Maybe he was taking her abduction *too* personal? Suddenly, it dawned on him that her abduction wasn't about getting him off balance. Kailey was central to their group. She was the one that he, Forrest, Cassie, and Penelope would drop everything at a moment's notice to rescue. Whatever presence Forrest sensed coming to Seattle wasn't in the city for Brady, it had arrived to eliminate all of them.

"We've got a problem," Brady said in a low whisper, glancing at Forrest. "A big problem."

CHAPTER 29

*A*fter Forrest's brief phone conversation, Cassie gave the cabbie the marina's address. She was relieved to know Kailey had escaped her captors, which explained why she no longer felt Kailey's distress. Kailey was alive, and Cassie shed tears of joy and relief. Although the news was great, Cassie needed to get to Kailey quickly before these people found her again. Cassie was certain Kailey's escape only furthered their pursuit in recapturing her. They weren't simply going to give up.

Cassie knew this wasn't over. Before a second attempt was sought, she wanted to ask Kailey pertinent questions to help identify who these people were, or *what* exactly they were. Few people were like Kailey and had friends that were demons, *weres*, a Vampire Hunter, and a Demon-hunter. Until the new enemy was revealed, Kailey would remain in the center of her hodgepodge allies, which was the safest place she could be.

"We're here," the cabbie said, looking over his shoulder at Cassie.

Cassie nodded, dug out forty bucks from her purse, and then slid the money to the cabdriver. He smiled graciously. She opened the door, exited, and then extended her hand to help Penelope out.

No sooner had Cassie closed the door, than Brady pulled his squad car into the parking spot ahead of her.

Cassie smiled when Forrest stepped to the curb and faced her. Her smile turned to immediate scorn when Forrest opened the rear door of the car and Jinn emerged.

Jinn nodded at Forrest while wiping his silk shirt with his hands. Self-absorbed, he didn't seem to notice her. Cassie bolted the distance between her and Jinn before he even had a chance to look up.

"Bastard!" Cassie shouted. His eyes met hers a second before her solid fist struck his chin. The punch echoed.

Jinn's neck twisted hard to the side and his body pivoted and swung in the same direction or his neck would've snapped. His athletic, muscular build also protected him, but she was still amazed he hadn't been knocked out cold.

An amused, entertained expression crossed Forrest's face. Her incredible strike would've flung Jinn over the front of the squad car had Forrest's massive body not been the wall that stopped him.

Forrest grinned. "You don't know *how* long I've wanted to do that."

Rattled and perplexed, Jinn wiped blood from his mouth. "Damn, girl! What the—"

Cassie reared back and slugged Jinn hard in the gut, expelling the air from the incubus' lungs. Forrest's wall-like frame didn't help Jinn this time. Jinn dropped to his hands and knees, gurgling and coughing, trying to get a word out past the sudden wheezing noise that shook inside his throat.

On his hands and knees, Jinn raised his right hand in what looked like a motion for surrender, but Cassie didn't want to interrupt his obvious pain or allow him such an opportunity to beg her to stop the punishment. With the pointed tip of her right heel, she delivered a swift kick to his stomach, and she was certain a couple of his ribs snapped. With the throbbing pain in her foot, she feared she might have broken a couple of her toes.

He arched upward with the blow and fell to his side in a fetal position, clutching his gut. Blood coated his lips and leaked from his nose. She had hurt him and he stared at her with helplessness. He was too injured to counterattack, and given his muscular tone and size, she was surprised he didn't teleport or use invisibility to escape.

Cassie prepared another kick, but Brady came around the side of the car and stepped between them, wrapping his arms around her tightly.

"Whoa, easy," Brady whispered.

Cassie pushed Brady aside. Fury blazed in her eyes. How she prevented herself from altering into her true form was anyone's guess. She kept her guard up because after the pain she had inflicted upon Jinn, he might shed his partial human appearance in an attempt to shake off his suffering. In demon form, like her, he'd be much stronger. Yet, his weakened eyes revealed his submission.

Forrest grabbed Jinn's shoulder and pulled the demon to his feet, pressing him against the side of the patrol car. Jinn could barely stand, his legs were limp, and his head lulled.

Forrest couldn't suppress his grin. "As much as I'm enjoying watching this, I need to know *why* you're trying to beat Jinn to death."

"Because the bastard drugged me!" Cassie said, tightening her fists.

"Really?" Forrest asked with genuine surprise.

Cassie nodded. Her eyes narrowed.

Forrest shrugged. "Proceed."

"No!" Brady said, raising his palm at Cassie to block her should she try to attack Jinn again.

"No?" Cassie said. "He drugged me and had two of Nocturnal Trinity's goons try to—"

"Step aside, Cassie," Penelope said, pulling her crossbow from the backpack. "He'll be no one's problem."

"Hold on!" Jinn said, barely able to stand. He leaned over, resting his hands on his knees, but if Forrest released his grip on Jinn's shoulder, the demon would collapse.

"Penelope," Forrest said, shaking his head. "No. *Not* in public."

She lowered the crossbow with disappointment and a frown of disbelief.

"Brady, this is between Jinn and myself," Cassie said. "You can't trust him."

"Did you drug her?" Brady asked Jinn.

Jinn gasped for air, nodded slightly, and then he said, "That's partially true."

"Partially?" Cassie said, taking a step toward him. "You lying asshole."

"Everyone calm down," Brady said. "The last thing we need is to make a scene. You've already caught the attention of a few people. Let's keep a low profile before this ends up on social media or in the news."

"Look," Jinn said, rising slightly. "Yes, I drugged you. But I didn't give you a strong enough dosage to render you unconscious."

"That's a lie!" Cassie said. Her teeth sharpened and her eyes burned crimson. "I barely escaped. Ask Penelope."

Brady and Forrest glanced at Penelope.

Penelope nodded. "She materialized on my floor unconscious and was half demon in appearance. She's lucky I didn't kill her."

"Cassie," Jinn said, wiping blood from his mouth with the back of his hand. "I only gave you a tiny dose of a sedative."

"Tiny?"

"Honest."

"Why?"

Jinn sighed. "Because if I hadn't, they were going to kill me and you."

"Who?" Brady asked.

"The behemoths," Jinn said.

"They're still alive?" Forrest asked.

"Yeah," Jinn replied. "That's what I was planning to tell you after we got away from the nightclub. But then Kailey called Brady so I didn't get a chance to tell you about the behemoths."

Forrest grinned and then laughed but not in a humorous way.

"What do you find funny about that?" Jinn asked.

Brady frowned. "Yeah? That's my thought, too."

Forrest said, "Alec didn't keep his end of the bargain, so now I can stake him. Hell, I can stake all four of them. The day's looking better all the time."

Jinn shook his head. "You'd have to get past the behemoths first and none of you are capable of doing that. And least of all, neither am I. Since Alec has the Wrathbone, there's little you can do to stop them. Hell, a cannonball would bounce off them."

Forrest frowned. "There are ways."

"Did you not hear me? Alec has the Wrathbone dagger?" Jinn asked.

"Which is the only weapon capable of penetrating their thick hides," Penelope said. "I told you not to give it to him."

"I know. So it's more of a challenge," Forrest said. "I've faced worse before."

"Nothing like these," Jinn said. He glanced at Cassie. "Truce?"

"Yeah, sure," Cassie said, and then she hit him in the gut again, dropping him to the pavement. "For now. Come on, let's go get Kailey."

Forrest watched Jinn spit blood on the sidewalk. Cassie strutted to the floating dock in a triumphant fashion. He was amused and looked envious of the beating she had given Jinn. He grabbed Jinn's shoulder and heaved the demon to his feet. "Come on."

"Wipe that smug-ass grin off your face, Forrest," Jinn said. "I think you're enjoying my pain too much."

"You know I am. The only thing better is if I were the one who did it."

"Really?" Jinn said. "You gotta be like that?"

"Nah, you're okay half the time," Forrest said.

"Good to know."

"Yeah, the times when we're not in the same room together."

Jinn gave Forrest an odd side-glance and then they both grinned.

CHAPTER 30

Forrest stood on the floating dock with Cassie on one side and Jinn on the other. Penelope stood directly in front of her. All of them faced the houseboat while Brady rapped gently on the door. The older gentleman opened the door and smiled.

"Ah," Zeke said. "We've been expecting you. Come on in."

Brady entered the houseboat door and Zeke's eyes widened when he saw Forrest's massive rugged physique. With friendly uncertainty, he motioned Forrest and the others to come inside.

The floating dock seemed stressed under Forrest's weight whenever he slightly moved. He imagined the boat might not balance too well if all of them tried to pack themselves inside.

"That's okay," Forrest said. "We'll stay out here."

"Are you kidding?" Jinn whispered, rubbing his jaw. "It's freezing cold."

"There's always the alternative," Forrest said. "Penelope can send you to the abyss where it's a lot hotter."

"I'm for that," Cassie said.

"No, thanks," Jinn whispered, touching the side of his face and wincing. "I'll suffer the cold. It numbs the pain."

"You sure you folks don't want to get out of the wind?" Zeke asked. "We have enough room inside."

"We'll be fine," Forrest replied. "We won't be staying long."

Zeke nodded, smiled, and went inside the houseboat, closing the door.

"Hell's not always hot," Jinn said, hugging himself against the lashing wind. His tiger's eye glow in his irises dimmed. "I should've grabbed my coat before I left the nightclub."

"Keep in mind," Cassie said. Her harsh stare showed no pity. "Things between us aren't settled. You might rethink that statement."

Forrest laughed. "And I thought a woman scorned was a terrorizing sight. Nothing compares to a succubus being scorned."

"You know it," Cassie said without the slightest tinge of a smile.

"Just so you know," Jinn said, "My boys, Jim and Terry, they ain't going to be the same after what you did to them."

Cassie tried to dismiss the comment, but her lips curled into a smile. "Is that so?"

"I had to snap them out of the lustful fog you left them in. I gotta admit that was one powerful spell you put over them. They were still going at one another about a half hour after you left."

Cassie bit her lower lip for a moment and then burst into laughter. "Serves them right."

Forrest frowned. "What exactly did you do?"

"Gave them the hots for one another," she replied.

"And they're both straight?" Forrest asked.

"They *were*. I doubt they will be now," Jinn said. "They'll be questioning their orientation for years to come. That was some shrewd thinking."

Cassie's laughter faded and her tone became frigid again. "Yeah, that was a few seconds before I teleported. Had I not been successful in either magical feat, who knows what would've happened to me?"

"Look, for what it's worth," Jinn said. "I'm truly sorry."

"You've always sought to protect yourself over any others," Cassie said.

"You know that isn't true," Jinn replied. "In fact, during our conversation earlier today, you were the one who brought it up about me helping all of you defeat Diaboch."

"He does have a point," Forrest said.

"Shut up," Cassie said in a low voice. "He works for them now."

"Is that true?" Penelope asked, turning to meet Jinn's eyes.

Jinn's eyes widened. "No, it's not. Don't be lying like that, Cassie."

"Then why else would you drug me?"

"I told you why."

"You also told me that the other behemoths tortured you," Cassie said.

"They did. They chained my wrists and ankles to a metal table and flayed large sections of my skin from my body," Jinn said. His eyes closed and he shuddered. "They mixed and poured some type of saline fluids over my wounds, causing me to writhe in pain for days while my body mended."

"They tortured you until you sided with them, didn't they?" Cassie asked.

Jinn shook his head. "No, they didn't."

"That's the only reason someone's tortured and released."

Jinn took a deep breath and then clutched his side. "If they thought they turned me, they are mistaken. Otherwise, I'd not be here with you."

"Then again," Cassie said, "that might be the *whole* reason for why you are here."

Jinn frowned. "What?"

"To find where Kailey is so you can direct them to her," she replied.

"You're being a bit *too* suspicious. You know I like her too much to do something like that. Besides, I'd not risk my life with you, Forrest, and Penelope. See where I'm standing, right? So believe me, I don't want to be near them. It's the reason I exited with Brady and Forrest in the first place. Deep down you want me guilty to justify another beatdown on me."

"Maybe so, but you've only yourself to blame since you drugged me."

Jinn nodded. "Okay, fine, I understand your logic and your distrust. I do. But you gave me one hell of a beating, too. I didn't fight back because I deserved it. But I truly was trying to protect you."

"How?"

"They wanted to take you the second you set foot inside Nocturnal Trinity but I persuaded them not to."

"By drugging her?" Forrest said. "That doesn't make any sense, even to me."

"Look, Alec sternly warned the behemoths that if they were seen by any outsiders he'd use the Wrathbone dagger to send them back to the abyss. They are truly fearful of that, and even the four of them understand that they're not fast enough to prevent Alec from using it on all of them. Hell, you know how fast an elder vampire can move."

Forrest nodded.

"So I told them that I'd help by spiking Cassie's drink and have two bouncers bring her back." Jinn straightened and groaned, putting his hands at the small of his back. "Jim and Terry aren't the brightest workers I have—"

Cassie nodded. "I can vouch for that."

Jinn grinned. "Yeah. And the amount of sedative I put into the drink was minor. I figured they'd come to get you and like you did to me, you'd beat the shit out of them. My guess is that someone tampered with the drink because you should've never gone down."

"How could they since you're the bartender?" Cassie asked.

"Before we open, I'm in and out all the time. I don't just mix drinks. I restock, take inventory, count the registers …"

"Who else works the mornings?" Forrest asked.

"Only me that early."

"So when did the behemoths discuss their plans with you?" Cassie asked.

"Yesterday afternoon."

"Then perhaps someone strengthened the dosage last night?" Forrest asked.

"Quite possibly. Damn, it'd have to have been then. There was no other opportunity."

"Who worked last night?" Cassie asked.

"Meg, but she's not like that," Jinn said.

"As I recall, she isn't too fond of Kailey," Cassie said. "And since Kailey's my closest friend, Meg probably has unspoken issues about me."

"She wouldn't do that," Jinn said.

Forrest leveled his heavy gaze at Jinn. "Can you be for certain?"

Jinn thought for a few seconds and then shrugged. "Here lately, with all that's gone down at Nocturnal Trinity, nothing seems absolute anymore."

CHAPTER 31

Kailey's eyes filled with tears when Brady stepped inside the houseboat. She ran to him and embraced him tightly. She sobbed against his chest. Her shed tears washed away her fears and the sensation of pure relief lightened the heaviness that tightened her chest.

Brady waited until she loosened her hold, and then he stepped back to look into her eyes. Instead, his attention was drawn to her battered face.

Brady placed his fingers beneath her chin and asked, "Seems like every time an issue arises, you take a beating. Who bruised your face?"

"The bay."

He looked confused.

"I jumped into the bay and landed wrong. The impact did this. The men … they never struck me."

Zeke cleared his throat. "You should have seen her jump. Never seen anything like it."

Brady glanced at Zeke. "You saw her jump?"

"Yes. If I hadn't, she'd probably have died. No other boats were adrift in that area. She leapt off an old warehouse and drifted upwards, somehow defying gravity and cleared the loading dock."

"Mew!" Raven scampered across the floor and jumped into Kailey's arms.

"Kitty!" Brent said, running after the cat.

Zeke laughed. "That cat survived the fall with Kailey."

"Really?" Brady said.

Kailey nodded.

"Yep, but I'm not so certain it'll survive Brent," Zeke said. "It seems to have taken a liking to you, though."

Kailey smiled and nodded. Raven purred.

"Perhaps you should leave it with the little boy," Brady said, reaching his hand to pet it.

"No," Elsa said. "We can't keep a cat in this boat. Not with my allergies. My eyes are already too watery and my nose is itchy."

Raven's purr turned into a violent hiss as Brady's hand neared. The cat's eyes narrowed and then it spat at him. Brady pulled back his hand.

Elsa took Brent's hand and led him to her. "And with it that unpredictable, we cannot chance it might bite or claw our grandson."

"It seems to have a split second temper," Brady said. "Perhaps we can take it to a shelter?"

"No," Kailey said. "We're not taking it to a shelter. It's hungry and needs cleaned up."

"You're not thinking about us keeping it?" Brady asked.

"For now," Kailey said. She couldn't tell Brady that Raven was inhabiting the cat, and wondered if she should ever tell him at all. But if Raven only had a couple more days to remain in the cat, after her soul left, it wouldn't matter if they took the cat to a shelter or not.

"We have too much to—" Brady glanced at Zeke and Estel and then lowered his voice. "With everything going on, we cannot carry a cat around with us."

"If you think she was running from vampires," Zeke said, "I'm pretty certain she wasn't."

Brady's eyes revealed his surprise.

"They know about vampires," Kailey said.

"Yes, we do. That's why we sold our house and bought this houseboat," Zeke said. "I've heard that vampires don't like the water or won't come onto the water or something like that."

"I don't know if that's exactly true," Brady said. "I've heard they won't cross over water, but I'm no expert. The real expert is Forrest. He's the large man outside on the dock. He could tell you."

Fear caused Zeke's voice to crack. "You mean, we sold our house for nothing? Vampires can still get to us?"

"You'd still have to invite them in," Brady replied.

Brady's right, Raven said to Kailey. *Nod your support toward Zeke.*

Kailey nodded.

Zeke rubbed his eyes in relief. "Good to know."

"Do you happen to know which warehouse you saw Kailey jump from? I need to check it out," Brady said.

"Oh," Zeke said, "I can write it down. I'm not certain the number for the warehouse, but I'm fairly certain of the dock street."

Zeke tore a small sheet of paper off a writing pad and after looking on his phone map, he scribbled down the street and handed the paper to Brady.

"Thank you for your help," Brady said. "We … We've things to attend to. Need to take Kailey to the ER to make certain she's not broken any bones or suffered any internal injuries."

Zeke smiled. "We were happy to help. Keep her safe and yourself. Please let us know when everything turns out well."

CHAPTER 32

$\mathcal{E}$ven though Irina and Nikolina could have taken the underground passageways to get to Nocturnal Trinity from Irina's estate by mid-afternoon, Irina chose to wait until closer to sunset and travel in style.

She and Nikolina sat in the back of the silver limo that displayed Nocturnal Trinity's prominent symbol on the front doors and hood. The driver entered the parking garage across the street from the nightclub. The official time for the Founders to make their appearance outside Nocturnal Trinity was a couple hours away, but Irina was in no mood to enter through the front door or tap the *fortunate* guests for the night's festivities. Instead, she wanted to access their VIP elevator inside the parking garage that they seldom used.

Irina peered through the UV-protective glass that was mirrored on the outside. Already the line of people eager with anticipation was gathering. She was in no mood to put up with the pleading desperation of these sad individuals. She wondered how humanity had waned so drastically over time. Undead creatures folks should shun and flee, they instead embraced.

The youth and most of the middle-aged people sought wealth and instant gratification, unaware oftentimes when they had achieved such. And yet, they continued their pursuits as their hunger was never quite satisfied. One could have achieved his or her first million dollars, which offered more luxuries than the commoners dreamed possible, but they weren't satisfied until they earned the *next* million and so forth and so on.

These cravings she recognized, which were far worse than any human affliction, disease, or plague mankind suffered. The longings to possess more than any other before them lessened rationalization, causing humans to cast aside the poor and weak, allowing them to live in squalor. The wealthy considered the lower class as outcasts, and not worthy to receive the slightest handout, which wasn't a new ideology to society, as parables, fables, and novels had thoroughly examined how cold the minds and hearts of the greedy were.

Irina had lived a life filled with luxuries, but had also lived almost four lifetimes' worth of days. The older she became, the more she understood that material things rusted and dimmed over time. She valued items less and less. She was unable to recall the last possession that thrilled her with excitement, and she doubted any trinket ever gifted her from this moment forward could stir immense satisfaction.

"What's troubling you, dear sister?" Nikolina asked.

The massive, muscular driver drove the limo around the sharp curves until they reached the third floor.

"I wonder why we even bother ourselves with the petty lusts of today's humans," Irina replied.

Nikolina glanced in surprise. "Whatever do you mean?"

The driver parked the car, got out, and walked to open Irina's door.

"Peasants during our youth were far more worthy of our time than these petulant leeches who hope to taste eternal death."

"Eternal death?" Nikolina placed her hand over her heart. "No wonder you live in a depressive state. You should rejoice in what we have … it's *still* life! And even the most prominent people in this world kneel before us, desiring to win our favors."

"Their sniffling groveling does not interest me. None in the least. They shall have no further favors from me, sister."

"And why not?"

"They're not worthy."

The driver opened the door, offered his hand to Irina, and she eagerly accepted.

"Thank you, Titus," Irina said.

A few moments later, Nikolina stepped out and smiled graciously. She held his hand and squeezed tightly, looking into Titus' eyes. With her other hand, she felt his thick biceps. "Thank you."

"You're quite welcome, ladies. I shall await your return."

Irina walked to the VIP elevator, inserted the key, and stepped inside as the door opened. Nikolina joined her.

"Titus has proven to be an exceptional human servant, has he not?" Nikolina asked.

Irina shrugged. "It has to be better than his former bouncer duties guarding the main door."

"He's better than Andreas," Nikolina said with a sly grin.

Irina eyed her sister shrewdly. "You're not talking about his driving duties, are you?"

Nikolina tilted her head and wailed a delightful laugh. The sound of the laughter reminded Irina of Flora, and she realized even more how much she missed their departed sister.

"Do finish your reasoning for why these wannabes visiting our club are not worthy of our eternal gift," Nikolina said. "I find it … intriguing."

"They already lack the ability to control their lusts for everything. The few we've turned are far more feral and uncontrollable than half a century ago. Raven is a prime example."

Nikolina nodded. "I agree. She was a poor choice."

"*We* didn't choose her. She's pretty much a prime example of how humans think and act during this era. Short of being staked, nothing we could've tried would've changed her nature," Irina said. "She was a lost cause *before* she was bitten by our brother."

The elevator door opened. Nikolina took a step back and flicked a nervous glance at Irina. "Wait. Why do you want to enter through the basement?"

"As I told you earlier," Irina replied. "We must see for ourselves whether or not Alec destroyed the behemoths. Either way, we'll both have the answers we desire."

"We shouldn't be here without Alec," Nikolina said.

"Do you know something you're not telling me, sister?"

Nikolina was hesitant in stepping off the elevator and reached to push the close button, but Irina grabbed her arm and pulled her out.

"Alec will be angered that we've come here without him," Nikolina said.

"And why's that?" Irina's eyes narrowed. "Since we are equal owners in

Nocturnal Trinity, no floor or room should ever be off limits to us. So tell me why we suddenly need Alec's permission?"

"It's not so much that, Irina, as it is that our snooping around shows we don't trust him."

"How is *this* snooping? Does he have something to hide?"

Nikolina's brushed her long blonde hair from her eyes. "Not that I know of."

"Then why are you so nervous and insist we get his permission? Aren't we owners of the nightclub, too? Nothing prevents us from exploring our own club. So why be nervous?"

Frustration overcame Nikolina and she sighed. "Because I've wondered the same thing about the behemoths myself."

"But you don't know?"

"No," Nikolina said. "But lately Alec's become distant, quite like you actually."

"Me?"

"Yes," Nikolina said, frowning. "For days I've tried to reach you and like he, you were not answering my calls. My suspicions got the best of me and I assumed the two of you were in cohorts toward Orsovo and I."

"Cohorts?" Irina laughed. "Never!"

Nikolina shrugged slightly and pursed her lips. "One can never know with a family like ours. Siblings have been known to ally themselves against one another."

"Nonsense, dear sister. I've not seen Alec or Orsovo, either. And you are the closest to my heart. Why think I'd turn on you? Perhaps I've been in one of my *moods*, as you insinuated earlier, but I've needed time to sort through what my future holds."

"For the longest time, I've worried about you."

Irina's brow furrowed. "And why's that?"

"You seem discontent with life, even before Flora's unfortunate demise."

"To be truthful, I'm *abhor* this life and loathe being undead."

"But why? Living generations allows us to witness progression."

Irina motioned to the narrow hallway and led the way. "I've experienced everything I've ever wanted to try multiple times. I've read books to pass the time. By books, I mean more books than what fills most city libraries. What more is there? My heart doesn't seek romance. I've tired of punishing the living and feeding off the willing and unwilling. Do you ever consider that these are reasons for why being a vampire is a curse and not a blessing? Everyone wants to live forever, but that's because it's not physically possible for a mere human. Living, after a few centuries, becomes trite."

"Dear sister, all vampires go through this phase."

"Is that so? So you've experienced this?"

"Of course. We all have," Nikolina replied. "We just don't talk about it."

"Then how do you cope without going insane?"

"Hibernation."

Irina's eyes widened. "Going underground?"

Nikolina nodded.

"None of us have done that."

"No, but we're getting nearer to the time for us to consider it, which might be the true reason Alec disbanded the factions of Nocturnal Trinity and reclaimed ownership. He's the eldest, and lately, he seems overly distracted. Instead of staking Flora, we should've sought to place her into hibernation."

"No one considered that?" Irina asked.

"It was not brought up simply because she had gone too far with her antics, possibly due to the symptoms you're experiencing," Nikolina replied. "But in her state of mind, she'd have awakened far more dangerous than she was when Forrest staked her."

"I see. Do you think Alec destroyed the behemoths then?"

"Honestly, I don't know. After he took possession of the Wrathbone dagger, only he confronted the behemoths. He never wanted the rest of us with him."

"I remember, and I thought that odd at the time, too."

"As did I."

"Then they are probably still alive, which remains a threat to our survival."

Irina walked into the dimmer passageway that reeked of stale earth and brimstone. A thin veil of smoke suspended like a winding fog above the tunnel floor.

Nikolina grabbed Irina's arm and pulled her into a corner.

"What?" Irina asked.

"Shh! We're not alone."

"Do you smell the sulfur?" Irina whispered.

"Yes. But that's not my reason for alarm. We're not alone."

"Sisters!" Alec exclaimed. "Why are you hiding in the shadows? Come, follow me. I've exciting things to share."

Irina turned quickly. Alec stood in the faint light with an odd smile. Blood dripped from his pointy fangs and a tinge of madness swirled in his eyes.

"Don't tarry," Alec said. "A party awaits. Festivities are in order."

CHAPTER 33

*L*una sat in the passenger seat of Blaze's old burgundy Monte Carlo with the window down, filing her nails with an emery board. She wore a thick leather coat with genuine silver crosses strategically sewn and superglued on her sleeves, the collar, and the vest. She wore black yoga pants that tapered into her hiking boots.

Her bobbed hair was a mixture of pink and light powderpuff blue strands. White goth foundation made her face almost glow under the faint outside security lighting that spilled inside the storage unit where Blaze kept the car parked.

Luna's lips were painted a glossy candy apple red. Heavy black eyeliner and mascara outlined her eyes.

With the car's hood raised, Blaze stood hunched over the motor, and shook his head. Usually, she loved watching him sweat over the motor while he tinkered and *played mechanic*. When it was hotter outside, he peeled off his shirt quicker. Watching the beads of sweat meander down his chest and stomach excited her. During those hot days, Luna only pretended to file her nails while her mind entertained ways of getting him to check out the back-seat with her.

It never took much for her to entice Blaze after she succumbed to her pheromones and her lustful need to be taken by him. She simply faked fretting over a lost earring and pleading for his help to find it. He never liked seeing her get dramatic, so he stopped whatever he was doing and tried to help. But he lost any shred of self-control when she leaned into the backseat wearing her leather miniskirt that left nothing to the imagination.

A smile curled on her lips, but then a swift gust of icy wind flowed through the open window. With the coming of the winter winds and freezing air off Elliott Bay, nothing about him attempting to repair the car aroused her at all. He was bundled with a sweatshirt, a thick coat, and a wool cap. And since she'd never dare sporting a miniskirt in weather below forty degrees, it was too much work and less exciting to make out on cold vinyl seats. She shivered thinking about it.

Blaze wiggled a couple of wires.

"Try it now," Blaze said.

She sighed, paused from filing her nails, and reached to turn the ignition key. Nothing.

"Dammit," he said.

She asked, "Still can't figure out why it won't start?"

"N-o-o-o."

"Might help if you were a mechanic," she said.

He looked away from the engine toward her, cocked a brow, and shook his head. His jaw tightened. She stuck out her tongue and then scrunched her nose playfully.

"I wish I could *afford* a mechanic," he replied. "You usually like coming here while I work on the car."

"That's in the summertime, Blaze," she replied, "when your name is more seasonal."

He grinned, exhaled a white cloud, and rubbed his hands together. "I see your point."

"It will be dark soon," Luna said, changing the subject. "As if it's not cold enough already. But the colder temperature isn't what we should fear."

Frustrated, Blaze slammed the car hood shut. The loud sound echoed around them. "I'm aware."

"Shh! Blaze … you should be quieter since the night is coming."

He nodded. "Sorry, but the hood doesn't latch unless I shut it hard."

"Does that really matter right now? You've never gotten it to start. It's good that Micah let you store it in his storage unit. Or the wind would cut right through you."

"Yeah, at least you have the added protection of being *inside* the car," Blaze said, resting his hands on her door.

"I'm not a mechanic, either," she said, holding up her hand, studying her fingernails. "Besides, it's taken me a couple of years to get my nails this long. I'm not chipping a nail or getting my hands greasy."

Blaze opened the door and used the handle to roll the window up. "Come on. We should get to some place safer. I'm not sure how the vampire activity is on this storage unit premises."

Luna slipped from the car and he closed the door quieter than he had the hood.

Her nervous eyes studied the outer narrow asphalt lane and then the closed unit doors on the adjacent long building. She hugged herself, in spite of the warmth of her fake rabbit-fur jacket. "It'd be freaky frightening if one of the other units was filled with vampire coffins, wouldn't it?"

Blaze took her hand and walked out of the unit. With one hand, he grabbed the handle and pulled down the rolling door. He released her hand, unhooked the open padlock from the belt loop on his ragged black jeans, and then secured the storage unit. "Why would you say something like that while we're still *here*?"

She shrugged. "I don't know. The thought occurred to me while I was sitting there. I was thinking about it, but I didn't mention it. But, it is possible."

"Yeah, but now you'll question every noise we hear while we walk to the fence gate. You always make yourself nervous before there's any reason to be."

"Yep, but it's still not dark," Luna said. "They're all fast asleep."

Blaze glanced at his watch. "Or they're awake and waiting to emerge. With the cloud cover, you might as well say it is night. They have no fear of sunlight scorching them in this weather. I heard that some vamps wear hoodies and thick garb and stalk the streets when the weather's like this. *Before* nightfall."

Luna glanced around nervously. "Really?"

"See?" he said. "You've made yourself scared."

"You're not helping the situation. You forget," she said. "I'm scared most of the time, probably because I worry about the supernatural. It's why I studied magic and became a witch, but witchcraft didn't help Eva and the other witches against the vamps. If not for you, I'd stay locked inside the magic shop day and night."

"Don't base your bravery on me." He took her hand, turned her toward him, and then embraced her tightly.

She clung to him, closed her eyes, and tried to push her inner fears away. He was right that she couldn't base her bravery on his actions and hope that he was always available. He wouldn't always be there. Though they were seldom apart, some situations might arise where they'd be separated or he needed to leave her to watch the shop while he got supplies.

Since she worked during the day, she hoped to find peaceful sleep at night, but she barely slept more than two or three hours at best each night. The lack of sleep made her more apprehensive, and she longed for sleep. But she never felt safe while asleep. Her nightmares seemed as real as her waking hours.

Luna jerked slightly during their embrace.

Blaze pulled back and stared into her eyes. "You okay?"

She forced a smile. "I'm getting by."

"Raven can't hurt you anymore," Blaze said. "You know that. You witnessed her last moments."

"I know, but Blaze, she *almost* killed me."

"Almost doesn't count."

"No, maybe not, but I cannot shake the feeling. I still feel her tightened fingers clutching me, feel the heat of her rancid breath, and the smell of death on her skin still lingers. She might be dead, but the memory of that night remains."

"I understand," he said. He gently kissed her pouty lips. "Let's get out of here."

Luna nodded and looked at the cloudy sky. No sunlight or any glimpse of the moon was visible. "You really think vamps would be out before the official sunset?"

"I don't think it's rumor for the ones venturing out on evenings like this. It probably happens, especially with the newly turned who've not learned to control their hunger. For older vamps, to challenge walking during the day has to be somewhat empowering for them. So you best hope your idea of a storage unit filled with coffins isn't true."

Luna swallowed hard. Panic brought her voice to a shallow whisper. "Let's hurry."

Blaze pulled a wooden stake from his jacket pocket.

"You think you'll need that?"

"You've gotten my apprehension up now. You realize that vamps can hear our heartbeats and smell us, right?"

Luna walked faster. "That's enough."

"Well, you're the one who brought the subject up, not me." He reached into his other jacket pocket, took out a second stake, and handed it to her. "Just in case you need this."

With nervous fingers, she took the stake and tightened her fist around it. "I want to change the subject now. Okay?"

Blaze shrugged.

"How much do you think a mechanic would charge to look at your car?"

"More than we have put aside," he replied. "Since Micah left the shop to us, business has been a rapid downward spiral. Of course, we could sell your silver crosses—"

"Don't even joke about that."

"I wasn't joking."

She glared at him. "You better be. I'd break up with you before I'd part with any of these."

"Really?"

"Yep. I never want to become a vamp. These crosses lessen my chances of being attacked. Seeing the drastic change in Raven was enough to make me more cautious. Before she turned into a vampire, she was Kailey's best friend. I wanted to be Raven's friend, too, but she despised me for no reason at all. She belittled me, mocked me, and I let her think I couldn't hear her insults. I've never mistreated anyone in my life." Tears brimmed in her eyes.

"I know, which is one of the greatest attributes you have."

"It didn't matter to her," Luna said. "She only wanted to kill me to hurt Kailey because of her jealousy."

Blaze's fingers tightened around hers. "Some people are too vain and shallow to realize the harm they cause others. You should understand that Raven was never a true friend to Kailey. The emotions she possessed while she was a human were magnified once she became a vampire, which means—"

"It means she resented me enough to kill me while being a human," Luna said. "I'm not ditsy."

"I didn't imply—"

"No, you never have, but Raven did. Others do."

"Raven's dead. Let it go," Blaze said.

"I wish I could."

A loud creaking sound of buckling metal echoed ahead of them, followed by several steady thumps in the pattern of footsteps. In the faint glow of the sodium lights, several shadowy figures moved swiftly across the rooftops of the long storage buildings to each side of the narrow asphalt lane. Their swift steps were almost silent, except for when they suddenly stopped.

Blaze and Luna stood approximately fifty feet from the chain-linked gate, which was the only way in and out of the storage unit compound without climbing over the tall fences with a half dozen strands of barbed wire at the top.

"I think you got your wish," Blaze said softly, releasing her hand.

"Vamps?" Luna whispered.

"Yep."

"It wasn't a wish. Honest. I'd never make a wish like that."

"I know," he replied. "But we cannot outrun them. Even if we were Olympic sprinters, they'll be on us in seconds. And if we could somehow manage to get back to Micah's storage unit, we'd never unlock it and get inside before they caught us. As many as there are, they'd rip the roll-down off the unit. We can only do one thing."

Luna swallowed hard. "Fight?"

Blaze nodded. "Yep. We stand our ground and fight."

"I'm not good at fighting," she said.

"When your will to live is stronger than your desire to die, you'll be surprised at how much your fighting skills tend to increase. Stay close and aim for their hearts."

"I hope you're right," Luna replied. But for some reason, she doubted his words to be true.

CHAPTER 34

*K*ailey sat in the rear of the squad car between Cassie and Penelope. Jinn sat on the other side of Penelope, as far as possible from Cassie, but after several minutes, he appeared more nervous sitting beside the Demon-hunter.

"Could you put that thing away?" Jinn asked, pointing at the crossbow.

"It's not armed," Penelope replied.

"All the same. I'm not comfortable with that out in the open," Jinn said.

Forrest was too big to sit in the backseat, so he held the shotgun position up front with Brady and besides, no one was about to challenge him to swap. "Getting a bit nervous back there, Jinn?"

"A bit," Jinn said in a near whisper. "But not nearly as bad as at the nightclub."

"The evening's young," Cassie said.

Raven sat curled on Kailey's lap, purring softly.

Kailey's eyes were closed. Her bruised face throbbed and radiated heat that seemed to increase with each passing minute. She longed for sleep, but with her adrenaline surge gone, the almost unbearable pain kept her from crossing the threshold into blissful slumber.

Cassie took Kailey's hand into hers and interlocked their fingers. Kailey didn't bother to open her eyes, but she welcomed the friendly touch. Cassie was like a sister Kailey had always wished for but never had. And even at times like this, Kailey found it difficult to accept the kind compassionate friendship this succubus held toward her. Such behavior was contrary to everything she'd ever been taught in the few churches she had attended during her youth in middle Tennessee.

What Cassie offered was a purely platonic friendship, but at times, she teased Kailey about what the two of them could share if ever Kailey expressed interest. Deep down, Kailey took the insinuation simply for what it was, playful talk, but at other times, the intent look in Cassie's eyes indicated the succubus wanted more.

But with the heartache Kailey had suffered from entering a brief flitter of a relationship with Raven, even though Kailey's instinct had warned her not to, she feared that anything beyond pure friendship with Cassie would forever end their relationship and drive a wedge between them. She didn't want to suffer the loss of another friend, and Cassie respected her wishes enough never to pursue the matter.

In many ways, their friendship mirrored the closeness of sisters that supported one another wholeheartedly.

Soft fingertips touched Kailey's face, causing her to wince.

"Sorry," Cassie whispered, sliding back her hand.

Kailey opened her eyes and turned her head slightly to face Cassie. Cassie smiled.

"I can heal you," Cassie said.

Kailey attempted to smile but the pain prevented it.

"Yeah," Jinn said, "but you have to drink her blood and give her some of yours in return."

"Is that true?" Kailey asked.

Cassie sighed. "Unfortunately, yes."

Kailey tried to hide her gag reflex but failed. The idea of drinking blood, anyone's blood, sickened her. "I'm sorry, but I can't. I—I just can't."

"It's not the same as a vampire. You won't become marked by me," Cassie replied.

"Sorry, no. Please don't be offended."

"I'm not. I understand," Cassie said but her voice echoed her disappointment.

Jinn laughed.

Cassie shot a hateful glare at him, rendering him immediately silent.

"I just don't like to see you suffer pain," Cassie said. "Well, not *that* kind of pain."

Raven flexed her forepaws, exposing her jagged little claws. *Is she the reason you turned me down?*

"No," Kailey replied.

Can't say that I'd blame you. If I had my human body back for a day, I'd love a go with her.

Cassie stared at the cat and then to Kailey. "Was that your cat?"

Kailey's battered swollen face prevented her from any clear expression of shock. "What do you mean?"

"Did that cat speak to you?" Cassie said.

"This cat spoke?" Kailey asked. Her eyes opened wider and she hoped she could successfully feign surprise. "Look, I'm the one with the head trauma, remember?"

"I sensed a foreign entity relaying a message or trying to pass energy to you," Cassie said.

"As did I," Jinn said, turning slightly in his seat to examine the cat.

"Guys, don't play games with me," Kailey said. She nervously scratched behind the cat's ears. "My head's spinning and I need some ibuprofen."

"We're not playing," Cassie said. "At least, *I'm* not, but if Jinn sensed it, too ..."

"I swear. No lie," Jinn said. "That's not a normal cat."

"If you were a witch, Kailey," Cassie said, "I'd dismiss it as a familiar or a cat possessed by an imp. However, that's not the case. An imp, Jinn or I, could identify."

With little emotion and no interest in the cat at all, Penelope said, "It's not an imp."

"You're all serious?" Kailey said, showing slight uneasiness. Her uneasiness wasn't a complete fabrication, however, as she did fear Cassie and Jinn might discover the cat was housing Raven's soul. With Raven's last moments of brutality as a vampire, she didn't think anyone inside the patrol car was in a complete forgiving state of mind, just yet. Kailey had been sorting through the whole ludicrous idea of Raven talking to her via feline and she wanted to categorize the interactions as stress-related mental derangement. But if two demons sensed the cat's dialogue, Kailey's mind might still favor the sane side of the maniacal scales.

And from what Forrest had told her about Penelope's hatred of demons, if the cat was possessed by an imp or some other type of demon, her reaction would have been similar to Jinn's and Cassie's. Kailey marveled that Penelope was seated between two demons in the backseat of a car. She supposed almost anyone could change, but Penelope might simply be waiting for either demon to give her a reason to slay them. The young lady kept her emotions in check and appeared reserved because of her innocence.

"Kailey, I'm quite serious about this," Cassie said. "You know I wouldn't make up a story, especially after what you've suffered through today."

"Do you know what the cat said?" Kailey asked.

"No. I have no defined understanding of its words," Cassie replied. "I didn't interpret the words. Jinn?"

Jinn shook his head. "No idea."

"Then how do you know it spoke?"

"You ever hear mumbling voices coming from another room?" Cassie asked. "Like when someone is speaking to you, but not loud enough for you to understand what they've said?"

Kailey offered a slight nod.

"That's the case with the cat. I could hear what I know to be words but at a different octave or in a language unfamiliar to me. I doubt that makes sense."

"It sort of does," Kailey replied.

Whew! Cat's not out of the bag yet!

Kailey frowned at Raven, *"Behave, Raven, please."*

Really? You're going to tell *a cat what to do?*

"No," Kailey thrusted her thoughts hard toward Raven, making her head hurt worse. "I'm asking you not to act out. We have enough distractions without you deliberately trying to gain the curiosity of Jinn and Cassie."

And if I don't?

"We're dropping you at the nearest shelter."

The cat's mouth opened with a quick gasping sound.

Cassie and Jinn exchanged glances and then they focused on the cat again.

You wouldn't.

"Try me," Kailey replied. "If you were and are truly my friend, prove it to me now by being more a cat than a smart ass."

Fair enough.

Forrest cleared his throat. "Kailey, what can you tell us about the people who took you? Anything that can help me … us … better identify them?"

Silence hung in the car for several long moments.

Kailey's head ached. Digging through her foggy memories only added to her fatigue. Whatever they used to sedate her caused her mind to swim. But they needed information. If she wanted to prevent the chance of being taken again, she needed the information. Her brow furrowed and her eyes watered.

Brady glanced into the rearview mirror, making eye contact with her. "My neighbor swears that Micah was at your apartment. Neither Forrest nor myself detected the slightest hint of his scent. Was Micah there? Did he have anything to do with your abduction?"

Tell him! Raven said.

Even though the words weren't aloud, Kailey's ears rang from the harshness of Raven's tone. Kailey jerked slightly.

Cassie rubbed the back of Kailey's hand. "Try to remember, honey."

"I never saw him or heard his voice," Kailey said.

I know it was him, Raven pleaded.

Kailey pushed her thoughts at Raven. "You might have seen Micah at the warehouse, but I did not. I never saw him after I awakened."

You don't believe me? Raven asked.

"It's not a matter of my believing you—"

Cassie frowned at the cat, glanced to see Jinn was doing the same, and then both demons turned their attention toward Kailey.

"What's going on?" Cassie asked.

"What do you mean?"

"With the damn cat," she replied. "You can't tell me you don't sense it because whatever it's doing is focused on you, and not on anyone else in the car."

Cassie reached toward the cat, and Raven hissed and bowed her back.

Watch it, bitch!

Cassie snatched back her hand but her eyes flickered with fierce heated anger. "A lot of vicious energy is radiating off this animal."

"I agree," Jinn said.

Kailey wanted to tell Cassie about Raven, but now wasn't the appropriate time.

"So Micah wasn't there?" Brady asked.

"I barely remember what happened when the intruders burst through our apartment door," Kailey replied. "I was fighting and trying to escape."

"Did you ever see their faces?"

Kailey nodded, looking into the mirror to meet his gaze. "When I was escaping, I saw their faces. I have a general idea of what they look like, but could I identify them again if I saw them? That's doubtful. Most of my memories from the warehouse are a blur, as I was more focused on getting away from them."

"I understand," Brady said. "Okay, so focus on what you can remember. Other things might come to you later. For now, concentrate on the more vivid memories."

"Both of the men who tied me up. Well, I assume they were the ones that did," she said. "Their accents are foreign and thick."

"What kind of accents?" Forrest asked, glancing over his shoulder.

"Not quite Russian or German," Kailey said, her mind trying to recall their word patterns. "Broken English, so I'm guessing English isn't their first language. I really don't know."

Forrest glanced at Brady. "Probably from the old country."

"Yours?" Brady asked.

Forrest shrugged. "Quite possibly, or from an old Germanic region, which reinforces what I've assumed for several days now."

Brady looked into the mirror at Kailey again. "What more?"

"Whoever sent these men after me has a lot of money," Kailey said. "Or at least he wants everyone to believe he has."

"In what way?"

"A limo arrived at the warehouse," she replied. "And the one being escorted had armed men, possibly security or bodyguards, but he expressly ordered that I not be killed. He didn't care if his men shot me, so long as I wasn't killed."

Brady shook his head in anger and then looked at Forrest. "Does that make any sense to you? Why do they want her? Their reasoning can't be to pull me into a fight. They took her from our apartment, but they waited until *after* I left for work. If I was their target, they'd have not waited for me to leave. Don't you believe there's something more for why they want her?"

Forrest nodded. "It would seem that way, since the man gave the order not to kill her but didn't mind if she was injured in their pursuit to get her back. They want her alive, but I don't think they intended for you or us to ever find her."

Cassie smiled and squeezed Kailey's hand. "They don't realize she's surrounded by good friends that aren't human."

Kailey's stomach tightened. She felt sick. "But why do they want me?"

"There's only one way to know for certain," Forrest said.

"And what's that?" Brady asked.

"We find them and make them talk," he replied.

Cassie grinned. "Sounds like a good way for me to beat out some of my aggression."

Jinn rubbed his jaw and looked out the side window. "At least it won't be me this time."

Brady said, "Kailey, is there anything else you remember that might aid us in finding their whereabouts?"

"One of the two men guarding me was disgusted that I had been with a werewolf," Kailey said. "He said that he could smell Brady on me."

"Ooooh," Cassie squealed, squeezing Kailey's hand before winking at her.

Kailey frowned at the succubus and whispered, "Stop."

Yes, please. Raven emitted a low growl. *Before I hurl a juicy hairball on your lap.*

Kailey's stomach turned. "For that reason alone, he wanted to kill me."

Forrest shook his head and groaned with discomfort.

"What is it?" Brady asked.

Forrest faced him. "Nothing hates werewolves more than vampires."

"I don't think he's a vampire," Kailey said.

"No, *he's* probably not, but that doesn't mean he's not a servant for one," Forrest said. "Someone's put a lot of time and effort into capturing Kailey. The limo didn't belong to Nocturnal Trinity, did it?"

Kailey closed her eyes and thought. "No, I don't think so. The limos the nightclub uses are silver. This one was black, trimmed with gold, but also a vintage model."

"That's good information, actually," Forrest said.

"Why?" Brady asked.

"The presence that has come to Seattle is ancient," Forrest replied. "An older car indicates the owner isn't materialistic like those in Flora's family or the younger generation. His power is what he flaunts. Nothing more.

Wealth has no appeal, and he certainly doesn't need it to gain attention. He asserts his dominance by the overwhelming power of his aura."

"I want to check out that warehouse where they took Kailey," Brady said, "but we need to get her to a safe place where they won't easily find her."

"Shouldn't you take her to a hospital?" Cassie asked.

"We need to," Brady replied. "Just know it's the first place they're going to look."

"Jinn and I will stay with her and keep her safe," Cassie said.

Jinn nodded. "Be happy to."

Kailey shook her head. "No. I'll be fine. No hospital."

Brady looked over his shoulder at her. "You sure?"

Kailey stared at him in disbelief. "You remember what happened the last time you took me to one? No, I'll be fine with Cassie and Jinn. I trust them."

Brady turned and watched the road. "Then we need a safe place to hide you. It can't be any of the department's safe-houses since we can't trust that all of the officers are not somehow tied to the corruption of the vampires. Some might be under compulsion."

"Penelope's house would be a good place," Cassie said. "No one would look in that neighborhood for her."

Penelope's brow rose, she leaned a bit forward, and gave Cassie a questionable stare. Cassie shrugged and grinned.

"That's probably the best place for Kailey to hide," Forrest said.

"I don't like the idea of hiding," Kailey said softly.

"Can you think of a better alternative?" Brady asked.

Kailey chewed on her lower lip for a moment and then she shook her head.

Forrest typed the address into the squad car's GPS. He turned and smiled at Kailey. "Then that's where you'll stay."

CHAPTER 35

"Wake me when we get there," Kailey said. "I'm tired."

Cassie nodded. "Sure."

Before Kailey closed her eyes, the cat stared up at her with its green eyes.

You're taking a nap? Now?

Kailey closed her eyes and pushed her thoughts to Raven. "No. I said that so Cassie and Jinn quit asking me about you."

You need to tell them about Micah.

"I can't," Kailey replied. "I didn't see or hear him. And if I bring it up now after denying it, they'll question why. Now's not the time to reveal that you've decided to occupy a black cat. Other than myself, no one else will share the happiness of knowing you're not completely gone yet. Cassie might harm the cat, hoping to somehow destroy you. She takes the violent battering you inflicted on me quite personal. It's doubtful I could talk her out of whatever she'd do."

Fine. Do you really mean that? That you're happy I'm not gone?

"I did, but you're still trying to bully me, even though you're inside a cat. I'm reconsidering my feelings and—"

Sorry.

"It's just part of who you are, Raven. Nothing will change it. Ever. Regardless of what form you take, you're always going to try to manipulate and bully me. How much longer before your spirit departs this world?"

You want me gone?

"That's not what I said. I wondered how much longer, in case you suddenly stop talking. When I grabbed the cat from the water and you didn't speak for quite some time, I feared the crash into the bay had somehow exorcised you from its body."

The cat almost drown. But the fear it suffered during the fall, I'm surprised its little heart didn't explode. When it lost consciousness, I did, too. I thought my final time had come. I'm afraid that if the cat's spirit leaves its body, I'm not able to keep it alive. Of course, I have no way of knowing that. No one does, I suppose, as I've never read of this in any spell book. And you know how witches love their familiars. If a spell existed that enabled their pets to live prolonged years, any witch would cast it immediately.

"I suppose so."

I also feared not talking to you again as well.

Those were the last words she heard before she fell asleep. Completely drained from the surge of adrenaline and fighting to stay alive, her mind lofted on the soft pillow of slumber. Perhaps there, unexpectedly, she'd remember more about her abductors.

CHAPTER 36

$\mathcal{I}$rina stared in disbelief at Alec. Although she didn't startle easily, his sudden appearance caught her off guard. She hoped her face remained void of expression, but since she feared wrinkling her skin, she had—over decades of practice—perfected her ability to *not* show any emotion. With the ability to age for centuries, she didn't want to *look* her actual age—ever.

Nikolina was not any less surprised, and because of Nikolina's nervous eyes, Irina believed her sister held no previous knowledge of Alec's activities in Nocturnal Trinity's underground tunnels.

"Festivities?" Irina finally asked, breaking the abnormally long silence. "Have you lost your manners completely, or do you wish to boast to everyone that you've fed recently? That's untidy, even for you."

Alec grinned, nodded, and then taking a silk napkin from his vest pocket, he wiped the fresh blood from his lips and teeth. Drops of crimson mottled his otherwise white ruffled shirt and his black tie. "Beg your pardon. Sometimes feeding gets the best of me. But yes, dear sisters, tis a time for celebration."

Nikolina laughed nervously, tilting her head back slightly. Her wavy long red hair flowed down her back.

"And what, pray tell, are we celebrating?" Irina asked. "Seems you were content in us *not* knowing about the gathering."

Alec extended his palm to her. She graciously accepted with a pleasant smile. "Oh, come sisters, let's not spoil the surprise."

Irina felt her stomach flutter from sudden nervous energy. The moment was eerily similar to when they entrapped Flora. Nikolina took Irina's free hand into hers and then squeezed hard enough to cause Irina to look at Nikolina.

Nikolina's brow rose, and her eyes resembled a frightened animal caught inside a snare. *Was she experiencing the same trepidation?*

Best proceed with caution, Irina thought.

For either of them to flee their brother wrought severe consequences. Nikolina lips trembled, and Irina understood that her sister couldn't whisper her fear because Alec was close and would hear her.

"What frightens you, Nikki?" Alec asked with absolute concern. "You seem a bit apprehension, which is never how you react around me. What troubles you?"

"I did not know you'd returned," Nikolina said softly with a slight shrug.

"I've never left Nocturnal Trinity," Alec said with a broad smile. "I've been here the entire time."

"In the basement?" Irina asked.

Alec nodded.

Nikolina frowned. "I thought you had gone on business, out of town?"

"Whoever told you that? Certainly not me," he replied. He motioned with a nod toward the darker stretch of the passageway. "Come."

"Dear brother," Irina said, tightening her grip on his hand. "You're dressed as if attending a funeral."

"A funeral?" Alec gave a hearty laugh. "Dear, no! This is cause for cele-bration. No one dresses to the nines for a funeral."

"No one dressed to the nines tends to eat sloppily, either," Irina said coldly with a shrewd stare at the blood droplets on his shirt.

"Touché," Alec said, glancing at the bloodstains. He grinned. His voice sounded giddy, as if inebriated on a drug. His piercing dark eyes stabbed into hers. He had fed far more than usual and was evolving into a frenzied state of mind. "At times, we lose full control when we celebrate. Don't you agree? But what kind of host would I be if I didn't partake with our guests? Come, see for yourselves. We've delayed long enough."

Guests? Unannounced guests. Private festivities?

The smell of brimstone grew stronger. Moans and groans of immense pleasure echoed further down the passageway. The way Alec tugged her hand displayed his eagerness for returning to the pleasures inside the room, and his fervor undulated severe trepidation in her.

She glanced once more at Nikolina who remained frightened. Clearly, she had no idea what was taking place in the room down the hallway, either. Her reaction made it obvious that Nikolina didn't know Alec was still inside Nocturnal Trinity during the time she believed him gone. Neither she or Nikolina wanted to follow Alec, but in his current frame of mind, an outright denial to follow could seal their fates like Flora's. They could not flee. They had no other choice except to follow.

If what was going on in that room was nothing more than fun and games, Alec was aching to return. But should something more sinister be taking place, Alec was under the influence of his bloodlust and unable to remain rational. And should Irina and Nikolina decide to run, a chase was something that would simply heightened his euphoria.

With great reluctance, she decided not to run, which might have been her worst, most recent mistake.

CHAPTER 37

$\mathcal{L}$una pressed her back against Blaze's. She held the stake so tightly her knuckles ached. The number of vampires increased minute by minute on the rooftops of the storage buildings. If not for the sodium security lights, the vampires would not be visible. At least two dozen vampires were watching them, and Luna had never tasted the sour bitterness of fear on her tongue before.

She hunched over and vomited.

Several vampires laughed and a couple of female vampires squealed with delight.

"Keep your focus," Blaze whispered. "Fear's an aphrodisiac for them."

Luna wiped her mouth with the back of her shaky hand. Even if she were a professional at staking vampires, she couldn't picture a way that she and Blaze could survive the coming onslaught. They were far outnumbered.

Two vampires stepped from the edge of the roof and landed on the ground with the light grace of a feather, unshaken by the fall, and their eager eyes indicated their evident hunger. The male vampire wore black jeans, a gray T-shirt, and a leather jacket. The female, despite the cold, wore a short vinyl skirt, a short black halter top with her midriff exposed, and black fuzzy boots. Luna was somewhat envious of her attire.

Luna gasped, realizing she had seen these two individuals before they were turned into vampires. Almost nightly, only a few months prior, these two stood in line with the other hopefuls to be chosen outside Nocturnal Trinity when she and Blaze had worked undercover for Micah. She imagined the others on the rooftops were former vamp wannabes, too, who had gotten their ill-gotten wishes and perhaps were pissed to learn their new reality.

Buyer's remorse, as it were.

"I don't recall ordering out," the male vampire said. His fangs protruded in an instant. "It's nice when your food delivers itself to you."

The female vampire laughed softly. Her maddened, intent eyes studied Luna with delight, and she licked her lips. A second later, the tips of her fangs appeared more evident and strangely, longer.

Luna realized the female's gaze was directed solely at her neck, and in a way, Luna was thankful. Direct eye contact could have been far more dangerous if the vampire sought to use mind control. Perhaps hunger and the sudden increase in Luna's heartbeat aroused the newly turned vampire, making her forget her power to pull a person into a deep trancelike state of mind. From what Micah had told them, young vampires had a harder time of using compulsion. It sometimes took years for them to master the hypnotic art.

The edges of Luna's vision darkened and a wave of dizziness passed over her. Her heart thudded harder and inner fear beckoned her to lose consciousness. She averted her gaze, making certain she didn't make direct eye contact, as she was already vulnerable to the terror seizing her. Yet, she wondered how she was supposed to defend herself when she was limited in watching the vampire.

Eyes could be deceitful, though, so Luna kept her gaze on the vampire's pale chest, trying to picture where the heart was. She wished she'd paid more attention in anatomy courses now.

Was the heart more to the right or the left?

In a heartbeat, the female stood an inch from Luna. By instinct, Luna plunged the stake into the vampire. The female shrieked and shoved Luna hard.

Luna stumbled back two steps and collided against Blaze who prevented her fall. Luna stared at the dripping blood on the sharp tip of the stake and then turned her attention to the vampire with a large hole near the center of her chest. Her undead enemy stared at the gaping hole and watched with curiosity as blood leaked from the wound.

"Sorry," Luna said with an embarrassed smile and a slight shrug. "I missed. I can't believe that I missed. I'm kinda new at this."

The vampire seethed. Never had Luna seen such rage in another being, not even in Raven. The vampire's eyes turned completely black, veins swelled across her forehead, and her fangs protruded to incredibly long, sharp points.

"I guess we're both new to this," the vampire replied. "But this time, I won't be as careless."

Before the vampire rushed at Luna for a second attack, two male vampires stepped off the storage unit roof and stood behind her.

"If she misses," one of the two said, "rest assured that we won't."

The angered female glanced back at them. "Have some faith in me, okay?"

The hole in her chest mended remarkably fast. Her soulless eyes shimmered like wet obsidian. She licked her lips. "Let's try this again."

Luna swallowed hard and took a deep breath. She slid her right foot back slightly to brace herself. Blaze apparently was sparring with the male vampire. She couldn't be certain, but she wasn't about to take her attention off the female attacker to check his progress.

As much as Luna tried not to look into the vampire's eyes, their strange appearance made it nearly impossible to look away. The mesmerizing black pools, though frightening, held an alluring quality, manifesting her hypnotic power to make what should be terrifying into something more pleasant and strangely seductive.

Luna focused on the vampire's chest, but like before, the vampire rushed her in lightning speed and grabbed Luna's shoulders and pulled Luna toward her. Luna's attacker released her in an instant, howling in pain while staring in horror at her smoldering hands. Burnt outlines of the crosses melted the skin of both palms. With the distraction, Luna took the time and opportunity to drive the stake through the vampire's heart with better accuracy.

As her enemy dissolved to a pile of smoky ash, Luna wanted to smile but noticed the other two vampires taking slow steps toward her. For some reason, her index finger throbbed with vicious pain, which drew her attention. She looked and discovered her fingernail had not only been chipped, but was torn near the base of the cuticle. The sharp pain felt like a needle had been driven under her fingernail.

"Dammit!" Luna said, cringing.

"What?" Blaze asked, panting. "Are you okay?"

"The damned bitch ripped my fingernail nearly off!"

One vampire facing her stared in disbelief. "That's all you're worried about? Your fingernail?" He turned with a laugh at his comrade.

The lunacy of her statement didn't even register with her. Getting bitten or her neck snapped by the vampire would have been far more severe, but all she could think about at that moment was how many years she nurtured her nails in order to get them to the length and shape they were.

Luna growled and ran at the closest vampire, catching him off guard. Fueled by anger, she drove the stake into the vampire's heart. The one standing nearby dove at her with his arms outstretched, hoping to wrap his arms around her, she guessed, but she fell forward hitting the asphalt, causing him to lunge over her. She rolled with the stake in her hand, sat up, and pushed herself to her feet.

Even as quickly as she had been in her actions, her speed was no match for the half dozen vampires that formed a semi-circle in front of her. They moved incredibly quick and a moment before, they had not been there. Six against one were impossible odds unless she possessed Forrest's slaying skills but she was nowhere near his caliber. She only lasted this long simply because she and Blaze spent an hour a day sparring and practicing due to Micah's persistence, long before Micah had chosen to disappear.

A vampire behind her screamed, and Luna paused long enough to see it drop to fiery dust after Blaze staked it.

How many had he killed during her distraction? She hoped far more than she. They each held a stake while pressing their backs against one another. Usually, feeling the warmth and closeness of Blaze's touch calmed Luna, but not tonight. She feared this was the last time they'd be together. On the other side of Blaze stood eight more vampires slowly pressing their way closer and tightening the circle around them.

"Since you've taken several of our coven," one scarred vampire said, "we won't kill you. You'll both become like us. We need to increase our numbers."

Luna and Blaze exchanged worried glances.

"Not if we have anything to say about it," a deep voice said from the shadows.

The vampires turned and peered into the shadowed recesses between two buildings. Their curiosity seemed greater than Luna's. Raspy breathing echoed whispers in the shadows, making Luna fear what was about to emerge.

CHAPTER 38

*L*una held her breath, not sure what had spoken or when it might reveal itself. The good thing was that the vampires' interests in her and Blaze lessened. Blaze pulled Luna closer, holding her hand.

From the shadows came furry creatures running on all fours. Werewolves. At least a dozen. Their claws scratched the asphalt, creaking a cacophony that sent chills down Luna's back. The vampires retreated slightly, leaving a narrow break in their formed circle, which was enough for her and Blaze to run through and possibly escape, but neither of them could move. Her feet seemed frozen to the pavement, but Blaze studied the approaching werewolves. He was mesmerized by their presence. She figured he was hoping to identify one of them as Micah or maybe figure out if he knew any of them.

One of the sprinting werewolves growled, fiercely glanced at Blaze, and said, "Get the hell out of here, now!"

She almost didn't move. One of the werewolves looked familiar to her, but after careful consideration, she realized it wasn't who she had thought. Blaze's grip tightened around Luna's fingers and without further hesitation, he pulled her with him as he tore into a jog.

Growls and screams filled the night air behind her. Her heart thundered inside her chest, and she kept her eyes on where Blaze was pulling her, even though her curiosity begged her to look back. But then bloodcurdling shrieks pierced the air and disturbed her, making her want to get far away because she didn't want to view the carnage.

Blaze reached the gate, slid a card through the security reader, and the lock on the gate clicked. He pushed the door outward, waited for her, and then slammed it closed. Not that it mattered since the vampires were capable of leaping over the fence. But for some reason, she felt better seeing the gate closed than left open.

Everything blurred around her: the shrubs, the parked cars, the wind-blown debris swirling on the ground. She didn't slow her pace until they reached a street with better lighting. She panted, never letting loose of Blaze's hand, holding onto him like she might a ring buoy in treacherous ocean waters. Her side ached, her throat burned, and inhaling gulps of the cold air, she thought her lungs might explode at any moment.

Blaze's footsteps staggered but he kept moving forward. She wondered if he hurt as much as she. Probably. Neither of them did much active exercise, certainly not jogging or sprinting or stamina training of any sort.

"*That needs to change,*" she thought.

"You saw him, didn't you?" Blaze said. He released her hand and his clumsy jog slowed to a lazy walk.

"Who?" she asked, stopping to gulp in air.

"Micah." Blaze leaned over with his hands pressed against his knees, trying to catch his breath.

Shaking her head, she said, "No, I didn't see Micah."

"You sure? I swear it was him."

Luna nodded. "At first glance, I thought it was him, too. But right before we took to running, I realized it wasn't."

"He was the spitting image of Micah," Blaze said.

"Maybe an older relative?" Luna asked, looking at her torn fingernail and wincing. "The man back there had scars, deep wrinkles, and grayer hair. Unlike Micah, that werewolf has been in a lot of fights. Micah always sought peace over battles."

"You're right." Blaze sighed. "Damn."

"What?"

Blaze stood and shrugged. "Just hopeful is all."

"I know. I miss Micah, too."

Blaze shook his head. "I never expected this sort of behavior from him though."

"What do you mean?"

"I realize he's one to seek peace above hostility or a battle, but he radically changed after Flora and Raven were destroyed."

"He was uninvited to Nocturnal Trinity's inner circle by Flora's remaining brothers and sisters. Brady okayed the werewolves' departure."

Blaze sighed and offered his hand to Luna. She smiled and interlocked her fingers with his, heading on down the sidewalk.

"I know," Blaze replied. "But I questioned Micah's motive when he insisted the werewolves be added to the Council of Nocturnal Trinity in the first place."

"You never mentioned that."

"No. What's the point? My opinion won't sway Micah or Brady. Now those two are enemies of one another."

Luna frowned. "You really think they are?"

"Whatever loyalty they held for one another died the night Raven and Flora were turned to ash," Blaze said.

"Neither spoke to the other," Luna said. "So how do you know?"

"Their behavior toward one another. The thick silence that hung between them that night. When Alec told Micah to clear his office, Micah left that task to Brady and Forrest. No one has seen Micah since. You'd think the aftermath would have drawn the pack closer together. Instead, lines were drawn, as I imagined they should've been earlier on. Demons and vampires are not allies to werewolves."

"Not all demons are enemies," Luna said.

"Cassie is a rare exception," Blaze said. "But you saw the monstrous demon in the basement of Nocturnal Trinity, right?"

"The behemoth?"

Blaze nodded.

"Yes. How could I miss it?"

"I never knew anything like that walked the earth."

"Me, either."

"So you see my point?"

"Which point?"

Blaze sighed. "With demons as powerful as that, the last thing the pack needed was for Micah and Brady to go their separate ways. The pack needs unity now more than ever."

"Then let's get in touch with Brady and—"

"No," Blaze said. "Not until we hear from Micah first."

"Why? We might never see Micah again. And if Micah left the city for good, you and I are defenseless."

"We've got to learn to defend ourselves sometime," Blaze replied. "We've got to become adults."

Luna stopped walking, yanked her hand free from his, and glared into his eyes for several moments. Then she rested one hand on her hip and pointed in the direction they had come from. "You realize had those werewolves not come to our defense, we'd both be dead, right?"

"Yes, I'm—"

"How many vampires did you kill while I was fighting for my life?" she asked.

Blaze looked down, embarrassed. "Just the one."

Luna's mouth gaped.

"I know," he said, shaking his head. "I should've been able to kill it and help you."

"Don't you have holy water in your pockets? Silver crosses? All you used was your stake?"

"To be honest, my mind blanked." He shook his head. "All I could think about was not getting his long fangs into my neck. I wish I had remembered the holy water. That could've given us a better advantage."

"I'm calling Brady or Kailey when we get back to the shop," Luna said.

Blaze sighed. "Have some patience. Micah's bound to show up sometime."

"Blaze, we're not cut out for this shit. We're fortunate they didn't turn us into one of them. You can fend for yourself if you want, but I can't do this."

"You've got me," Blaze said, hurrying to catch up with her.

"That doesn't give me a lot of assurance right now. And don't *ever* tease about selling my silver crosses again. Without these, I'd be undead."

"Fine. Look, I wish you could have more faith in me."

"I've little faith left in anything or anyone these days. While you forgot to use holy water, I didn't even think to cast a protective spell around us. See? That's why we need to be in a bigger group. You froze up and so did I. Now, let's get back to the shop so I'll feel a bit safer. We're too exposed on the street. The vampires are getting much braver and growing in number."

CHAPTER 39

andlelight brightened the edge of the narrow corridor in the
basement of Nocturnal Trinity. The intense pleasurable moans
lowered into a brief moment of faint whispers, followed by an eerie silence.
A familiar power undulated from inside the doorway, slithering its unseen
chill-bump inducing tendrils up the walls and across the floor like twisted
strands of ivy. Irina sensed a trap and wasn't quite certain whether she
should expect anything less from Alec.

In her present frame of mind, she held high suspicions about everything
and everyone.

Irina exchanged glances with Alec. His smug look didn't lessen, nor did
it call into question what was going on in that room. He knew what was
transpiring and he flaunted that he held knowledge for things she had yet to
unearth. He capitalized on her ignorance, as he and the others had during
her youth in the Black Forest castle.

Seeing his expression in the dim lighting of the corridor made her
question why Alec had ever allowed them to hand Flora over to Forrest to
begin with. Their traits and personalities seemed more alike than
Nicodemus and Flora, now that he had ascended into Nicodemus' leadership position. Was she and Nikolina the next to suffer such fates? After
Flora died, neither Irina or Nikolina took her place in leadership for the
female vampires. They shared their place without either making a claim

for Flora's responsibilities and deeds. She figured Nikolina didn't want the role. Irina didn't want it for herself, either. She loved her privacy far more than recognition.

"Is that the room you wish to show us? The old storage room?" Irina asked, watching the ominous door.

"Through the lit doorway, sister," Alec said. He released their hands and swept to the edge of the doorway in a blurred instant. He waved his hand for them to cross the threshold. "After you, dear sisters."

Vampires never rushed into a room without a cautious examination of what was inside first. Such was an unwritten and unspoken rule. The philosophy should be common sense to anyone, whether vampire, were-wolf, or demon.

Irina peered into the room with Nikolina pressed against her back. Nikolina seemed almost fearful of leaving any distance between them but Irina feared Alec might shove them into the room with the behemoths. After sweeping her gaze across the room, she determined the behemoths were being held elsewhere. They weren't inside the room.

Nearly a dozen well-dressed men stood in small circles talking and oblivious to Nikolina and Irina's arrival. No other women were inside. Well, none that were still alive. She quickly discerned these men to be vampires. Elder vampires. She wondered why they were at Nocturnal Trinity.

Warmth cascaded and spilled through the doorway. Wood crackled and burned from inside a hearth. If the fireplace had been in this section of the nightclub since it was founded, she never recalled seeing it. Of course, since the room was one of their supply storage rooms, boxes and crates might have blocked her view of the fireplace.

A long antique banquet table with claw feet stretched down the center of the room with eight matching chairs on each side. At each end of the table were larger wooden chairs with arm rests. The detail of the hand-carved furniture sent a chill through her. The furniture was familiar. The set was identical to theirs in their castle when they were children. She doubted the design could be matched by any modern woodworker anywhere in America, as the woodcarver for this set was a peasant from their village centuries earlier. For this to have survived ...

Three nude females lay deathly still in fetal positions along the tabletop. Without closer examination, she knew they were dead and quite possibly the ones that had made been making the euphoric sounds of pleasure during the last moments of their lives. Most likely, these women had been intoxicated through compulsion of their feeders.

The women's flesh was tinting paler under the glowing candle chandeliers. Without stepping into the room, she detected the absence of their heartbeats. None offered the slightest breath. The flesh of their necks were chewed into pale ribbons. Two men dressed in vintage suits and top hats lingered over one cooling body. Dark blood coated their chins and most of their cheeks. They smiled contently. Apparently, their bloodlust had become beyond control during their feedings.

Irina didn't recognize either man, but she did sense the overwhelming power of their age. She understood that offending them was not in her best interest, but their reasons for being unannounced guests disturbed her. Why had Alec secretly invited them to Nocturnal Trinity without alerting his sisters?

With some difficulty, Irina pretended to ignore them and downplayed their importance, which was nothing less than how they acknowledged her sudden entrance into the room.

Three other men, also in stylish vintage clothing, stood at the fireplace conversing. The one in the center wore a cape and she stood at his back. Studying the room, the clothing, and the atmosphere, she seemed to think she had stepped backward through time. A part of her longed for the simpler things in life before the innovation of technology had disfigured social interactions, connecting the most vile of human interactions that once were seldom encountered.

Classical music played softly, and she half expected to see a small string quartet playing to further set the mood. Instead, they settled on listening to the streaming music of someone's smartphone.

Alec watched her facial expressions with curiosity. His excited grin didn't waver. He eagerly awaited her opinions.

Irina marveled, lost in the elements, and realizing her mind was absorbed by the room, she turned to face Alec. "Since when did we add a banquet hall?"

"Ah, do you like it?" Alec said.

Her gaze returned to the decor. She pursed her lips but didn't reply.

"When did you do this?" Nikolina asked with a hint of anger in her voice. "Why weren't *we* informed?"

"I suppose the room could use a female's touch in design, but with limited time for our guests' arrival, we had to make due," Alec said. "Don't be angry, dear Nikolina."

"I'm more angry you didn't invite us to these … festivities," she replied.

Irina couldn't care any less for not being invited to decorate. She didn't want her time wasted by designing a room she probably wouldn't spend any time loitering in. It was horrible enough to dredge up memories she tried to keep buried.

"You don't recognize it?" Irina said to Nikolina.

"Recognize what?" Nikolina asked.

"The table. It's identical to the one in our castle in the Black Forest."

Nikolina turned her gaze toward the table. After a few moments, she nodded. "It does look identical."

Alec grinned. "It *is* the old table."

"How's that possible?" Nikolina asked.

"I won't bore you with the details," Alec said with a smug smile.

"Who are our guests?" Irina asked.

"You don't recognize any of them?" Alec asked, somewhat shocked in his tone and his inquisitive stare.

"Should I?" Irina studied their faces once again, but still saw no one she remembered. Of course, most of the banquets at their castle she'd missed because she'd been locked away in her room. To Alec and perhaps Nikolina, these were frequent guests at the castle they might well remember. She didn't.

"Look closer. These are guests from the old country," Alec said. "I know it's been centuries, but surely you should have some recollection of their faces, at least."

Fury creased her brow. She almost tore into a loud tirade, reminding Alec of her mental torture, but now wasn't the time. *Remain cordial*, she reminded herself. She tightened her lips and restrained her heated urge to lash at him, which was easy. She took a deep breath and feigned a broad smile.

Playfully, Irina reached out and placed her hand on his forearm. Then she hooked her arm in with his. "No, dear brother, I'm afraid the past escapes me for the moment. But please, introduce me?"

"Quite certainly."

CHAPTER 40

$\mathcal{A}$fter Alec introduced her to the two men at the dining table, Irina was none the wiser to the others inside the room. No names or faces stirred remembrance. Yet, they boasted in their German accents of Alec's success and his eye for detail and nonchalantly cast aside any notion to divulge information about her. They passed her over, as her father had done all her early life, which was suitably fine by her. She never liked the haughty natured aristocrats her father nestled his affairs with anyway.

What are you up to, brother? she thought without looking at him. It seemed odd that after more than a century Alec suddenly seemed interested in reviving old ties with their father's former advisors. *Is this why you dissolved our Council with the demons and witches?*

When Alec led her to the three men standing near the fireplace, she still was at a loss. She recognized neither man, regardless of their status in old Germany. They held less importance to her than she did to them. She was tired of wasting time with high status vampires she didn't know, and Alec had yet to explain his reasons for inviting them. It was highly unlikely they had stumbled on the knowledge of Nocturnal Trinity. Although she offered polite smiles and curtsies as Alec introduced her, she sighed on the inside. None of these people meant anything to her, but then the third man who stood with his back to her turned around.

Her mind screamed in horror but outwardly, she remained steadfast and stoic in appearance with a remarkably frigid stare, absent any blink or the slightest flinch of widening from terror. Her feigned smile weakened. She paled a shade lighter than her vampiric alabaster skin already displayed. Cold fear stabbed through her but none of her reflexes revealed it. Her thoughts struggled on whether to flee, attack, or shriek. Somehow, she chose to do none of those. Instead, she offered her nervous hand and presented herself with a slight curtsy and humble bow.

Irina swallowed hard and her voice almost refused to be make a sound. Clearing her throat, she finally gasped the question, "Father?"

"Irina!" Lorcan said with a huge smile and a hearty laugh. He took her hand into his and kissed the back of it. Despite his well-trimmed beard, his dimples were evident. His eyes bore like hot steel, with a ring of fiery red pinpointed at the center of his pupils. He was the monster she remembered, the man she had loathed most of her years in the castle after he had turned her, and much to her displeasure, he hadn't suffered his demise. His skin was near rosy, which meant he had fed well recently, but apparently not in the presence of the other guests. His mouth, teeth, and beard were not stained with blood. "It has been ages!"

When Alec had led them down the corridor, her thoughts were that she'd learn what she had suspected: The behemoths were still alive. She held no doubts. She never anticipated such a shocking revelation. She never expected to see her father, and she wondered why Alec had not killed the behemoths, which led her to question whether all of this was nothing more than an illusion. A sick, maddening nightmare that had somehow twisted itself into her reality.

She stared into her father's eyes without flinching, a feat she never imagined possible. She was almost mesmerized by the overwhelming power flowing from him. Yet, she silently asked, *Why are you here?*

"Indeed it has," Irina finally found the courage to say. "I feared you'd met your demise since none of us have heard anything from you in, like you said, *ages.*"

Though she said the word, *feared,* she actually meant *hoped.* Because now that he was alive, old hidden fears clawed their way from the dark cellar of her memories.

Lorcan released her hand, took a slight step back, and then looked her over. With a reluctant tone, he said, "My, you're far more lovely than I remember."

"Father!" Nikolina said, interrupting his gaze and rushing in front of Irina to fiercely embrace their father. The action was genuine with fondness and happiness. Neither emotion Irina could portray without making her nauseated stomach turn even more.

"Nikki," Lorcan said softly, running his hand through her silky red hair. He pulled free of her tight embrace and placed his fingers beneath her chin, looking at her with immense pride. "Ever as fiery as I recall. Dear heart, it does me good to see you after all these years."

Irina slipped away from them and edged near Alec who stood with a content smile.

"Dear sister," Alec said. "You look like you've seen a ghost. Are you not happy at our … little family reunion?"

"I'm surprised to learn that he's still alive," Irina whispered.

"As was I," Alec said softly.

"You almost seem disappointed, Irina, to discover I never met my demise," Lorcan said.

"No, father. Not in the least," Irina replied, realizing a whisper in the presence of an ancient vampire might as well have been shouted through a megaphone. "I am surprised, as I said. For anyone to be silent for so long … generally, it doesn't bode well. I, like the rest of us, had hoped you'd have emerged long ago. After a century of your absence, how else should your own children view the quieted circumstances?"

"Yes, father," Nikolina said. "Where have you been? After we gathered together, we'd given up on ever learning your fate, so we moved to America."

"My intention was to find you before the twentieth century began, but my servants feared for my safety and kept me in hibernation," Lorcan replied. "By sheer accident, one of my human servants happened upon Alec in Vancouver and told him about my long undisturbed sleep. After long discussions, Alec requested my servant send word to awaken me."

"How fortunate for us," Irina said, forcing a bright smile. She glanced at Alec. "And where is our brother, Orvoso? Has he learned of the good news?"

Alec grinned. "Yes, he's bringing another guest and should arrive shortly."

"So kind of you, Alec, for *not* sending an invitation to us," Irina said in a harsh tone.

Lorcan frowned. "Did you not have word of tonight's feast?"

"No," Irina said. "I did not."

"Nor did I," Nikolina said.

"And what is the meaning of that?" Lorcan asked, approaching Alec. "They're of no less importance than you. After all, family's family, and the blood of my blood should always be bound together. In the future, do not make such errors in important matters."

"Mere oversight, father," Alec said. He snapped his fingers to get the attention of the servants standing at the far corners of the room and motioned them to clear the table of the nude corpses. They nodded and hurried to obey his directives. "I barely had received word of your arrival to Seattle. Had it not been for your servants' delivery of your furniture ahead of time, we would not have had such an elegant dining experience."

"I commend you on your choices for the lovely blood centerpieces," Lorcan said. "They served their purposes quite well."

The other four men raised their goblets of blood toward Alec.

Alec nodded and smiled.

"And who is the guest Orvoso is bringing?" Lorcan asked. "Seems his arrival is a bit … late."

"Seattle's mayor," Alec replied.

Irina and Nikolina exchanged curious stares.

"Mayor? What's the purpose for his delay?" Lorcan asked.

"Seattle's a busy city," Alec said. "Perhaps, he's been detained due to his duties or waited until the sun completely set."

"Waiting for the sun to set?" Lorcan's slight frown surrendered to a short rumble of raspy laughter, unlike the laugh she remembered from long ago, making Irina wonder how long her father had been awake. "Is he a babe in training?"

Alec nodded. "He's only been a vampire for a few months."

"His skin and resolve should toughen over time," Lorcan said. "However, mayor or not, he needs to understand that he shall never expect *us* to wait for *him*."

"He's aware," Alec said.

Lorcan studied Alec for a moment. "Is he your spawn or Orsovo's?"

"Orsovo's," Alec replied.

"He willingly sought to become one of us?"

Alec nodded. "Oh, he begged and pleaded, because he knows we've allowed few into our circle. We're selective in our choices. Perhaps a bit *too* selective."

"The less attention you bring to yourselves, the better," Lorcan said. "I learned the hard way, and it's a wonder all of you hadn't been staked or beheaded before I went into hibernation. Initiating large numbers of prose- lytes at once is foolish. They're too ravenous in their hunger and cannot control the rage that burns within. Trying to do so becomes distracting and makes one vulnerable. A large coven of vampires must be built over a lengthy period of time."

Irina pursed her lips, almost hesitant in speaking, but finally she asked, "And where is your coven?"

Lorcan's eyes narrowed at her question. Anger flickered within his glowing irises. Regardless if he ever tried or not, her father could never quash his disapproval of her. She never understood why he disfavored her in comparison to her brothers and sisters. She was his least favorite and for some reason, he seemed to resent her. His feelings were never subtle.

"You and your siblings are part of my brood," he replied in a gravelly low voice. "My inner coven."

"Surely, there are more than us," Irina said. "A coven is never so slight in number, especially when you've been absent for so long."

"There are a few others," Lorcan said. "In the old country. But none related to you."

Irina pondered the statement, fearful that she might be reading too much into it, but did he have children from another marriage that were later turned into vampires as well? Additional ones he considered to be a part of his coven could be those he had chosen and turned and not be related through genetics.

She held her father's gaze without looking away and discovered a lot about herself had changed after more than a century. She was bolder. She'd no longer be browbeat and intimidated by anyone, not even her father, which seemed to anger him even more.

The veins in his forehead and neck swelled. The others in the room stood and watched in silence, and Irina realized her attitude was an embar- rassing insult to his prominence. Most in the room probably considered her actions as that of a spiteful brat, but they didn't understand the agony her father had put her through as a child. The longer she stared, the more she challenged him, but for a reason she couldn't understand, she wasn't about to back down.

Nikolina causally stepped forward and purposely lost her footing, stumbling into Irina hard, and causing Irina to break her staring contest. Irina's jaw tightened and her piercing eyes filled with fury as she grabbed Nikolina and steadied her.

"What are you doing?" Irina asked.

Nikolina grabbed Irina's elbow, held tightly, and turned away, leading Irina away with her. "What are *you* doing, besides embarrassing yourself?"

"I did nothing wrong," Irina said.

"Irina ..." Nikolina's disappointed tone was like she was an adult speaking to a child.

Conflicted, Irina said, "What did I do?"

"You looked like you wanted to go to war against him," Nikolina said softly.

"I asked him some simple questions. Nothing more. I wasn't accusatory with my words or my tone. I didn't ask anything that should've offended or angered him toward me. *He* became hostile, not me."

"But you refused to be submissive—"

"Submissive?" Irina's eyes darkened. Her fangs showed. The thoughts of her unknown punishment and being locked away for years by her father wrought her inner rage. She fought to suppress her anger and not allow it to show, which proved most difficult. "We've not seen him in over a century. We didn't know he was even alive. And besides that, I'm an adult. He's a stranger to us. You expect me to be submissive?"

"He's our father," Nikolina said.

"Yes, and until several minutes ago, as far as any of us knew, he was dead."

"That's beside the point."

"Sorry, we're late," Orsovo said.

Lorcan's angered glare ceased in an instant. He turned and smiled. He motioned everyone to the table. "Finally, let us be seated."

CHAPTER 41

*I*rina almost stormed out of the banquet hall, rather than stay in the room where she felt unappreciated and unwanted. She retraced her words with her father, and nothing she said should have angered him to the degree it had. Unless, he was trying to hide something.

Or was it because she had not fawned over him the moment she was introduced to him like Nikolina had? But why should she? She didn't possess any pleasant memories concerning him. All he ever bestowed to her was heartache and sheer misery; and of course, the curse of being undead, which was a different type of misery altogether. Her dismal undeath might not have affected her like it did, had her earlier years pressed under his mental torment not been so cruel.

Lorcan sat at the head of the table with Nikolina hurrying to claim the chair immediately to his right. She swept with her gown flowing and plopped into the chair, quickly smoothing the ruffled silk around her legs. Alec grinned at her and took the chair directly to their father's left. Orsovo sat beside Alec, in hierarchical order.

One of her father's guests gestured with his hand, offering Irina the chair next to Nikolina. Irina declined by shaking her head. Instead, she chose to wait until everyone else took a chair before she sat the farthest from her father, which placed her directly across from Seattle's mayor and close to the exit.

Before seating herself, she still contemplated departing the meeting, but doing so would surely bring her father's swift wrath and possibly that of his servants and vampire associates. She wasn't a fool. The men in the room weren't the only ones that had accompanied Lorcan. Most likely, the others were enjoying various entertainments upstairs, either at the bars or lounging in the VIP room, or seducing willing, eager wannabes mingling near the dance floors.

Their distance from her father's presence at the banquet table was of little importance or concern for Lorcan. Depending on their association with her father, he could summon them in an instant to carry out whatever punishments toward her or other disruptive guests he found necessary. Not that Irina worried about any severe repercussions, as she was not subservient to him. But rather than invite unneeded hostilities—figuring her father's stay in Seattle was short-lived because his long extended absence indicated he favored living independent of his children—she'd attempt to play the *good little girl*. That thought alone repulsed her. She didn't want her father to believe she longed for him to extend his stay because she was content with his absence and had mentally buried him long ago.

The mayor's expressions were similar to an eager child awaiting a birthday party. His bewildered eyes studied each person seated at the table, and he was overly eager to nod or smile in a friendly manner. Nothing less than what any politician might do when meeting new potential donors or hoping to gain supporters.

His silvery-gray hair was mottled with splotches of black and complemented his artificially tanned face. Hardly a sign of crow's feet tugged at the edges of his dark brown eyes. Certainly the mayor had persuaded Orsovo to turn him at the most opportune time before his body aged further. To most women and men in Seattle, the mayor's handsome face and toned body made him attractive without the power of compulsion to persuade favors from his benefactors. Combine his allure with matured compulsion and he became a dangerous person.

The mayor kept adjusting his tie and didn't seem able to fully settle himself in the seat. Finally, his attention turned to Lorcan at the head of the table, their eyes met, and a calmness overtook the mayor.

Lorcan bridged his long slender fingers and rested them on the table.

Slowly, his eyes studied each face in the room, but he averted even the slightest glance at Irina, further agitating her. He smiled.

"First, let me thank Alec and Orsovo for gathering everyone together at such short notice," Lorcan said. He glanced at the mayor. "Forgive me, but we've yet been introduced."

Orsovo stood and placed a gentle hand on the mayor's shoulder. "My apologies, father. This is Mayor Thomas Scottridge. Mayor, our father, Lorcan von Hirshmacht."

The mayor rose with a hearty, gracious smile and extended his hand toward Lorcan. Lorcan gave a dismissive glance at the mayor's hand and instead of shaking it, Lorcan presented his curled hand, exposing the prominent silver signet ring with its ruby-eyed wolf gleaming in the light. When the mayor met Lorcan's intent, almost glowing eyes, the mayor lowered his gaze and submissively kissed the ring.

Irina slightly shook her head in disbelief. Her stomach felt sick. Uneasiness washed over her and tightened her chest. Her siblings, however, watched with broad delightful smiles. The sensation of being the outcast of the family choked her longing to return to the strengthened bond she had learned to love with her siblings' Unity in Nocturnal Trinity. Lorcan didn't belong here and somehow he was wedging his place into theirs, and in the process, Irina was being squeezed out again.

A sly grin spread across Lorcan's face. "Please, be seated, Thomas."

Orsovo and Thomas sat promptly.

"My reunion with my family has not come without immense heartache," Lorcan said. "In fact, upon my arrival, I was saddened at the loss of my eldest son and daughter. Alec aptly informed me of their demise, and like the trustworthy son he's always been, he apprised me of what transpired. I want to find the one responsible for ultimately causing their deaths. I will not be satisfied until my vengeance is quenched."

Irina crossed her arms. *I suppose Alec didn't clue you in on those details, just like he and Orsovo didn't inform Nikolina and I of your arrival or this meeting?*

Thomas smiled. "My office is at your disposal."

Lorcan turned and leveled a glare at the mayor that made Alec and Orsovo visibly shudder. "You don't understand your place. Did Orsovo not inform you?"

"Of what?" Mayor Thomas asked. His brow furrowed in confusion. He shook his head and nervously offered a weak, polite smile.

"The office you hold *is* my office. You're simply the figurehead. Nothing more. Whatever I need done in this city shall be done without question. Orsovo may have been kind enough to bestow upon you our gift, but that gift came with a hefty price."

"Price? No, he never mentioned anything of the sort," Thomas looked at Orsovo. Orsovo smiled mischievously.

"If you wish to keep the office," Lorcan said, "you must agree to these terms."

Thomas straightened his tie and swallowed hard. He glanced at Orsovo with a look of slight betrayal, but the smugness on her brother's face didn't lessen. "I see."

Lorcan nodded. "Should you ever waver from what you're told, the gift you were given shall be taken away."

"That's possible?"

Irina rolled her eyes. *Can you not detect such a threat?*

Lorcan sighed. "Yes. It means you'll be staked and exist no more. If you become useless to me, you cease to be."

Thomas considered the option with nervous eyes and slowly nodded. His eyes indicated his confusion had fled and he snapped to full understanding. "My office will do everything you request."

"That's better," Lorcan said. "As soon as a couple of the state senators join us, the less we rely on you. You might well play an important part in attracting them to our cause. But, until then, I've need of your services to help us find the culprit responsible for Flora and Nicodemus' deaths."

Culprit? Irina frowned. "Father?"

Lorcan turned his gaze to her, as did Nikolina and Alec. Her brothers' eyes darkened. All three seemed to fear what she was about to say.

"Yes, my dear?" Lorcan said.

"Has Alec not informed you of his role in Flora's death?" Irina asked.

Alec's eyes narrowed into a death stare directed at her.

Nikolina gasped and shot a look of agitated desperation at her sister. She appeared shocked that Irina had presented the question.

"His role?" Lorcan asked, a bit rattled by the news.

Irina nodded. "Yes. It was Alec who suggested we offer Flora to Forrest."

Lorcan turned to Alec and his voice growled like a fierce beast. "Is this true?"

Alec's face became void of all expression. No words came from his mouth. He lowered his head and nodded.

"You told me that a young woman named Kailey was responsible." He faced Irina again. "And did you mention the name, Forrest?"

Irina nodded, but like Alec, she was unable to offer words.

"Forrest Wollinsky?"

Softly, Irina said, "Yes."

CHAPTER 42

For the better part of five minutes, Irina sat in silence, as did the others seated at the table. Lorcan fumed. His face contorted, destroying the attractive, almost seductive visage he presented to society and his true monstrous appearance was enough to make demons tremble.

While Irina loathed her father and lacked any compassion for him, she found herself wondering why she had so easily betrayed her brother by announcing his role in Flora's death. Her jealousy toward Flora while her sister blazed because Flora always seemed to be the center of everyone's attention, regardless of where she was. Her illumination was a lighthouse beacon while Irina always pictured her own light to be nothing more than the dim flickering flame of a candle. But with Flora's light extinguished, Irina ached at the increased darkness surrounding her.

Perhaps Irina told her father in the hope that she might receive greater attention or at the very least, she'd get partial affection from the man who acted as though he hated her existence. Offering her eternal undeath had not been his gift as it was considered for the rest of her family. It was meant as a curse and a lasting punishment.

Irina despised that the rest of her siblings found favoritism while he constantly refused to acknowledge her presence except to castigate or belittle her in front of them. With the news of Alec's role in Flora's death, she discovered a bit of satisfaction watching her father's wrath and disappointment turning to someone else for a change.

With lightning speed, Lorcan grabbed Alec's tie and pulled his son partway over the table and flipped him onto his back without rising from his chair. In a flash, Lorcan pressed a weapon to her brother's throat. In horror, she recognized it to be the Wrathbone.

Why did you give father that weapon? Irina took a sharp breath. *You fool!*

Stunned, Irina didn't know what to do or say. She never intended to turn her father's wrath against Alec. She certainly didn't seek Alec's death.

Nikolina placed her hands on her cheeks and gasped. "Father, no."

Orsovo rose but didn't fully stand. For him to stand completely upright would be viewed as a direct challenge. Something Lorcan *never* tolerated from anyone, especially not from his children. "Father—"

Lorcan ignored them. Blackness filled his eyes. His fangs glistened in the light. Never had her father appeared so hideous before her. With his evident rage, he probably never heard Nikolina or Orsovo pleading for Alec's life.

Lorcan pressed the dagger against Alec's neck, indenting his alabaster skin. Alec's eyes widened for a moment and then tightened shut as if in a plea for mercy while offering his complete submission. The slightest resistance or attempt to escape their father's hold would result in Alec's immediate death.

Alec or any vampire didn't have to be staked to be killed. No vampire ever recovered from decapitation. With the razored edge of the blade and the incredible strength of her father, Alec ceased to exist should her father combine the two elements in one swift slash. A narrow line of blood seeped from the slight groove formed beneath the blade. Despite his anger, her father somehow managed his restraint. But she doubted the outcome would be the same if she were the one beneath the blade.

"Why did you betray Flora and me?" Lorcan asked. His mouth widened and his fangs appeared even larger. Madness stirred in his eyes. Now, she held no doubt Flora had always been his favorite.

Lorcan seethed. "Your own flesh and blood? You offered Flora to my worst enemy? For what? Why?"

Alec opened his eyes and raised his hands in surrender, careful not to forced himself against the gleaming blade. "Let me rise so I may explain."

Lorcan remained still, not moving, as if frozen in place.

Irina looked across the table at Mayor Thomas. Terror petrified the mayor who occasionally eyed the doorway that exited into the dark corridor. She wondered if he was calculating his odds of reaching the corridor before her father ripped his head from his shoulders.

The mayor seemingly realized that the *gift* he had begged and bargained Orsovo for was not as promising and beautiful as he might have imagined. After all, if Lorcan was ready to cut off his own son's head for family offenses, a newly turned vampire stood far less a chance of pleading his case to be spared for the slightest transgressions. His hands trembled.

Irina realized the slight smirk on her face and quickly became solemn. She imagined her father would get anything he wanted without question or objection from the mayor.

Everyone's attention turned to the head of the table where her father still had not moved. As intense as his glare was, Irina was surprised her father hadn't bore a hole through Alec's forehead. Rigid and frozen, neither looked away from one another.

After several long, silent moments, Lorcan eased the blade from Alec's neck. Alec took a deep breath and by instinct, his hand went to his throat, but other than that, he dared not move.

Alec's eyes showed an uncertainty she'd never witnessed in him before. For as long as she remembered, he always beamed confidence and carried himself proudly without fear. The way he looked at their father indicated that his invitation for Lorcan to come to Seattle had been an unfortunate mistake, and like Mayor Thomas, Alec's liaison offered to Lorcan wasn't filled with the promises of prosperity he had hoped. The festivities—the term Alec had proudly boasted—were at an end and a coup d'etat for Nocturnal Trinity was inevitable. By giving the Wrathbone dagger to their father, Alec had granted Lorcan supreme power. Essentially, he had gifted their nightclub they had worked so hard to make successful to their father.

Lorcan licked the blood from the edge of the Wrathbone. Still hideous in appearance, he flicked his gaze at Alec. "Explain your reasoning. You have five minutes."

CHAPTER 43

*I*rina adjusted slightly in her chair, careful not to draw any unnecessary attention to herself and fearful their father might yet decapitate Alec at the slightest distraction.

Alec pushed himself upright in a cautious, slow manner. The slight fear in her brother's eyes indicated his uncertainty in what their father might do.

Bent over Alec like a hungry predator ready to pounce, Lorcan never took his eyes off his son.

Alec slid into his chair, straightened the wrinkles on his dress shirt, and then he adjusted his tie, attempting to regain his composure.

Lorcan never blinked. The heat of his intense anger never lessened, either.

Trying to regain his composure, Alec motioned to the armed chair. "Father, please, be seated, so I can explain."

"Explain? Was Nicodemus' death at your hands as well?"

"No," Alec replied without hesitation. "He died long before Flora."

"Why?" Lorcan slid into his chair and placed his arms on the rests, reminding Irina of her youth when she still held some respect for her father *before* he turned her. He was no longer that man, and she was no longer a frightened child. And now, after more than a century, he was acting like he presided over them.

Alec sighed. "Over the past few years, Nicodemus and Flora have played games with some of our chosen patrons."

Lorcan bridged his fingers and rested his chin atop them. "What sort of games?"

"Mind games usually. For the years we've owned the nightclub, over time, we learned to discern those who were skeptical and more curious about what goes on inside the club rather than having genuine interest in becoming one of us. So Nicodemus and Flora scanned those eager for the club to open and picked a vulnerable wannabe from the waiting line, invite him or her inside, and for a few hours, they terrorized their victim by chasing them through the darker areas of the nightclub," Alec said. "Making the person believe they were about to be ripped apart and eaten. All in good fun."

A slight grin spread on Lorcan's face. Irina read the thrill of pursuing a victim he was apparently entertaining in his mind, but she understood that the ending in his game would be to drain the quarry until the last drop of blood was taken.

Lorcan laughed softly. "Those two were always jokesters. Had they not already been royalty, they'd have found success in entertaining other kings and queens."

"No argument from me," Alec said with a dour expression. "But like I mentioned, the games usually only lasted a few hours and when their pursuit ended, Flora revealed that the victim was part of an elaborate prank. Afterwards, the shaken guest was given a consolation prize and a permanent membership card to return any time he or she wanted. Few ever came back."

"You're out of time," Lorcan said, rising slowly. "And yet, you've given me little information."

Alec's brow leveled. "I'm getting to that. That *game*, as they called it, was what got both of them killed."

Lorcan straightened in his chair. "It did? How?"

"Kailey Yates."

"Yes, she's the young lady you informed me about. She won't be a problem much longer. I sent my servants to capture her."

Alec looked surprised.

Irina stiffened, and somehow prevented a gasp from escaping her mouth. Nikolina gave a nervous side-glance to Irina.

"You've already sent servants to get her?" Alec asked.

Lorcan nodded. "They lost her near the bay earlier today, but since night has fallen, they'll not make the same mistake twice. So tell me how she caused my eldest son and daughter to be killed."

"Flora had chosen Kailey because she was timid. The last place the girl needed to be was inside Nocturnal Trinity. She didn't even believe in vampires or demons when she was brought inside. Flora savored playing the game with Kailey, nearly scaring her to death, but then we learned that Kailey's brother was the man we'd murdered. She came seeking revenge, and while it should never have happened, she succeeded."

"She killed them?" Lorcan asked.

"Not directly," Alec said. "All would've been fine except that Flora refused to let it pass that Kailey had actually gotten the better of her in the mind games. Instead of Kailey's fear increasing, Kailey found the courage to stand her ground. So regardless of Flora's attempts to shatter Kailey's resolve, Kailey persevered and grew stronger, despite the odds. Strangely, she gained powerful allies."

"That's true," Nikolina said.

Lorcan broke his gaze from Alec and turned toward her. "How so?"

"We pleaded with Flora to let it go and pick another guest to play her games with, but Flora refused," Nikolina said. "She didn't like being outdone or outsmarted."

"This still doesn't explain why you handed her over to Forrest," Lorcan said, turning his attention back to Alec.

"Because," Alec said, "she was drawing too much attention to us. After Forrest arrived, other shifter hunters came to Seattle to kill as many vampires as possible. Had we not met a truce with Forrest by offering Flora as a sacrifice, he'd have slain us all."

Lorcan's upper lip snarled. "And did Forrest accept this offering and agree not to slay any more of you?"

Alec nodded. "He did."

"You realize how much it pained Forrest to stake Flora, don't you?" Irina said. "She and Forrest had been—"

"Yes, I know." Spittle of disgust flew from Lorcan's lips. "I know all about Forrest. He's been a thorn within a festering sore for far too long for our entire family. He's part of the reason we fled our castle. If he's met a truce with the rest of you, that makes him vulnerable. He will not break his word.

A true Vampire Hunter never does. Invite him to Nocturnal Trinity where we can corner him and this … Kailey. Then we torture and slaughter them slowly."

When Brady parked his squad car outside the rundown three-story building where Penelope and Forrest resided, Kailey leaned up and tried to widen her eyes for a better view. In the glow of the streetlights, she couldn't have seen much more if her face wasn't swollen. Although she was sore, she wasn't in as much pain as when Raven had nearly beat her to death in the fighting ring months earlier.

Her face was bruised because she had hit the water at a bad angle and since she hadn't broken her neck or back, she considered that somewhat of a miracle.

I see why … mmm … cats loved to be … ahh … ooh … petted so much. Yeah, right … there.

Kailey blushed and took her hand off the cat, not even realizing she had been stroking its fur.

Oh, don't be a tease! Pet me some more. Please! You've no idea how good that feels to a cat.

"Raven!" Kailey said aloud in a soft, scolding tone.

Cassie turned and frowned at Kailey. "Excuse me?"

Kailey sighed and shook her head. "Sorry. Bad memories."

Bad, huh?

Kailey closed her eyes and projected her thoughts. "Raven, the last few weeks of your life … well, your time after you became a vampire … were actual hell on earth for me. You did worse to my face than this. You almost killed me."

I know. I'm sorry. For like, the millionth time.

Brady opened the rear door of the squad car and let everyone climb out. He took Kailey's hand and helped her to her feet. The cat hissed and slashed at the back of his hand, narrowly missing.

Brady shook his head. "I think your cat hates me."

Your boyfriend is sharper than Sherlock, hon. Don't let him get away.

Kailey forced a weak smile, partially feeling guilty for not revealing to Brady that Raven's spirit was inside the cat. "Yeah, when I take her to the vet for a flea dip, I'm going to see about getting it declawed."

You wouldn't dare!

"I warned you before and besides, I owe you one," Kailey thought to Raven.

Yes. You do. Without these claws, you'd never have gotten out of those restraints. You know that's true.

"Maybe so, but you're not making this easy for me."

What do you mean by that?"

"You're distracting me, and everyone here thinks I injured myself worse than I have. I know you said that Micah was there, so don't remain angry because I didn't tell them. There's the slight possibility you're mistaken, too."

The cat re-ow-ed in agitation. *Fine. Fair enough. I'm sorry for clawing at Brady. I promise I'll behave myself around him from now on.*

"Thank you, Raven."

Brady hooked his arm around Kailey's and led her toward the rusted stairs at the side of the building. He glanced at Forrest. "You're staying in *this* part of the city?"

Forrest shrugged. "I don't see any problem with it. I've lived in far worse over the years."

"I hope you got a good deal on the rent," Brady said.

Forrest grinned. "Let's just say that the owner and I reached an understanding."

"Meaning?" Brady asked.

"He's no longer in charge of the grounds. He's a part of it."

"A vampire?"

"Was."

. . .

Cassie was the last to reach the stairs behind Jinn and Penelope. Penelope followed behind Jinn a few paces with her finger resting against the trigger of the crossbow as she walked ahead of Cassie. Cassie wondered how their arrival looked for others in the area if they saw the patrol car and were watching them ascend the stairs.

Jinn glanced warily over his shoulder with apparent concern. "Please point that thing elsewhere, okay? If I were going to try to attack you or flee, I'd have done so inside the car where you didn't have adequate room to use that damn bow, if that were my intentions. Ask Cassie."

Cassie laughed from behind Penelope. "You expect me to vouch for you?"

Jinn shook his head. "Now's not the time to tease, Cassie, not when she's got that bolt pointed at me, all right? Besides, you know it's true. I'm safer with all of you than I am on my own or if I go back to Nocturnal Trinity. Shit, if I go back to the nightclub, I'm good as dead. I guess that wouldn't break Penelope's heart any. Ain't that right, sweetheart?"

Penelope didn't reply. Her harsh stare made him recoil slightly.

"Anyhow," Jinn said. "By now, I'm certain the behemoths are aware of me getting the word out that Alec didn't slay them. So, either way, I'm safer with the lot of you. The behemoths will kill me the instant they locate me."

"The behemoths can't leave Nocturnal Trinity," Cassie said. "The witches' runes prevent them from leaving the premises."

"Well, that may be true, but I'm not about to take my chances. You understand? I completely understand they've marked me for death. I've no qualms about dying from those I expect to kill me, but for this little sweet Demon-hunter with the itchy trigger finger? Uh-uh. You realize how embarrassing it'd be to get accidentally killed by her slipping or something? Can't explain that to the other demons in the abyss. 'So, Jinn, how'd you get sent back here?' 'Oh, this fine looking Demon-hunter sneezed and unintentionally pulled the trigger on her crossbow. Next thing I know, I'm down here.' Mm-hmm. No, that won't be good at all."

Cassie wailed with laughter.

"Yeah, I see *you* think it's funny," Jinn said. "For me, it's not a laughing matter."

A grin spread on Penelope's face.

"Oh, now, it's contagious!" Jinn said. "Ah, come on, make a truce with me or something. Just please aim that arrow elsewhere."

"Penny," Cassie said. "You can trust him, for now, at least."

Penelope looked over her shoulder with a questionable stare. She tried to return to her normal serious look but she still seemed humored by Jinn's antics. Like Jinn or hate him, his charisma could lower someone's guard or charm the pants off almost anyone. It was part of his demon charm. One that he capitalized on to remedy most any situation, dangerous or otherwise, but in this case, Cassie believed him.

Seeing the brief smile on Penelope's face was new for Cassie. All she'd ever seen was Penelope's hardened scowl, which hid the glowing beauty Penelope actually possessed.

"You're sure he won't welch?"

"I'm fairly certain," Cassie replied.

"So you trust him?"

"Hell, no. He and I still have some issues to settle. Once all of this is over, provided the behemoths don't rob me of the opportunity, I'm going to finish my beatdown on him."

Jinn sighed and shook his head. "Look, let's just call it even. You got some hard licks in on me, but not the kind of licks I'd *prefer* you—"

"Hey!" Cassie frowned.

"Easy, now," Jinn said. "No need to get all bent out of shape. It was an innocent joke."

"Nothing about you is innocent. On second thought, Penelope," Cassie said. "Shoot him."

Penelope looked confused but turned with the crossbow and leveled it at Jinn.

Realizing that Penelope was going to do it, Cassie quickly placed a gentle hand on Penelope's shoulder. "I'm only kidding."

"No!" Jinn said, flinging his hands up to cover his face while trying to shield his chest with his arms. He peeked through his fingers to see Penelope lower the bow. "Don't ever say something like that. Not to *this* Demonhunter. She doesn't know when you're joking. Sheesh! She was going to shoot me. You saw that, didn't you?"

Penelope lowered the bow. "He's right, Cassie. I was a second from pulling the trigger."

Cassie waved her hands and nodded. "You're both right. I'm sorry. I won't ever make that joke again."

Jinn took a gulp of air and placed his hands on his temples. "Whew!"

Penelope placed the safety on, disengaging the crossbow.

"So the next time I say that," Cassie said, "you can know I mean it without any question or hesitation. Okay?"

Jinn frowned. "Wait a minute ... *what?*"

"Just clarifying," Cassie said. "I won't ever say it as a joke. If I ever say it again, I mean it."

"You're carrying this grudge much harsher than I expected," Jinn said.

"Think about what you did, Jinn. Really think about it. You drugged me and allowed me to venture out of the nightclub where any perv could have found me unconscious." She walked past Penelope and tapped her index finger against Jinn's forehead. "When that registers inside your tiny selfish brain, maybe you'll understand my unrelenting resentment."

Cassie brushed past Jinn striking her shoulder against hers, knocking him slightly back. Near the top of the stairs, she waited for Forrest to open the door. After Forrest unlocked and opened it, he let Brady and Kailey enter first. Still fuming, Cassie stepped inside.

A part of her knew she should attempt to make peace with Jinn to strengthen their team while they searched for the people who had abducted Kailey, but his gratuitous actions were unforgivable. She didn't believe she could ever dismiss what he had done.

CHAPTER 45

Not much more was said at the banquet table, but Irina was thankful her proximity to Alec was at a good distance. His radiating anger sent harsh waves at her, washing over her. She held little doubt of the scolding he and her other siblings were ready to thrash on her, but she didn't care.

It had not been her idea to cater to their father's demands. Even had she known Lorcan was alive, she never would've sought him out. At least not on friendly terms. She'd have done everything possible to avoid ever crossing his path. She wouldn't have extended an invitation for him and given their nightclub to him. Perhaps that was Alec's reason for the secrecy of the festivities.

Alec and Nikolina acted like Irina had betrayed them. She hadn't. In actuality, it was the complete opposite. Didn't Nikolina realize that Alec and Orsovo had betrayed all of them? Not only had Alec given Lorcan the Wrathbone dagger, Orsovo had delivered the mayor of Seattle to Lorcan as well, which was a greater gift than receiving the honorary key of the city. Seattle was now under their father's control. Mayor Thomas' every action was at Lorcan's discretion or command. In her view, her brothers had betrayed them all.

Essentially, she and her siblings had lost their rights to Nocturnal Trinity. They might as well have signed the deed over to Lorcan. Even though she exposed what had happened to Flora—their father's *beloved*, precious daughter—to Lorcan, she didn't expect her father to wrap her inside his good graces, not that he possessed any. He would never embrace her with fatherly compassion. He probably wouldn't protect or shield her from Alec's wrath, either. She never expected he would. She didn't mention Forrest to unleash her father's wrath on Alec. She couldn't stand the thought of losing another brother, further weakening their strength in Unity. However, the mantle of that unity had further cracked after Lorcan's arrival, and it was only a matter of time before it completely shattered.

"Tell me, Alec," Lorcan said. "Was there no other way to preserve your lives without sacrificing Flora?"

"I could see no other way," Alec replied, meeting their father's gaze. "She was beyond control. No amount of pleading on our part convinced her to settle down. The decision came with a heavy heart then and the burden of her loss weighs heavily on me ... well, *all* of us ... now. We thought after Nicodemus' death that she'd cease her obsessive behavior toward Kailey. But she only got worse. She had darkened beyond all control."

Lorcan took a goblet of blood from a tray that a server offered. He shook his head. "I see. Her need for vengeance is similar to mine."

None equals yours, Irina thought. *Is that why you came, father? To settle old scores?*

Irina wasn't aware if her father knew about Forrest's arrival to Seattle but due to conversations she had with Flora long ago, she knew Lorcan despised Forrest. Lorcan's goal was to see the young Vampire Hunter dead.

In exchange for Forrest sparing Lorcan's life, Lorcan gave Forrest information on where an even more powerful vampire resided. He had done so in order for Forrest to meet his demise. He never surmised Forrest to successfully slay a master vampire since he was an unseasoned hunter. However, Lorcan knew if Forrest succeeded, Forrest would return to slay her father.

Later, after learning of Forrest's survival and his brief emotional romance with Flora, her father attempted to slay Forrest. Lorcan failed. Afterwards, her father fled from the Black Forest entirely. While the irony of a Vampire Hunter and a vampire finding extreme attraction for one another was somewhat humorous, the entire ordeal angered Lorcan.

Was this the opportunity Lorcan had finally been hoping for? Lorcan was much older and more powerful than he'd been when he first met

Forrest. But, so was Forrest. Forrest was only a child when he encountered her family in the Black Forest. Most assumed Forrest's judgment and fighting abilities lacked the seasoned experience the older Vampire Hunters possessed, but such was not the case. Forrest was blessed by higher powers or held a supernatural insight other hunters did not.

Lorcan sipped from his goblet and set it on the table.

Alec sighed. "I'm sorry, father. I realize the importance of her loss to you."

"No, you don't," Lorcan said in an even tone. "Had you placed her into hibernation, she'd have settled down. You do realize that, don't you?"

"Hibernation?" Alec sighed and slowly shook his head. "To be honest, hibernation never occurred to us."

That's true, Irina agreed.

"It's something each of you need to consider," Lorcan said. "The long sleep clears your mind, allows you to mend. When you emerge, you're incredibly stronger than you were beforehand. After you've fed, that is. Now that I'm here, the four of you can hibernate for a decade. My servants will protect you. I'll tend to the affairs of Nocturnal Trinity while you're all asleep."

Irina noticed Alec's obvious flinch, which was the same as Nikolina's and Orsovo's. The information revealed Lorcan's true motive. He wanted to set up a new throne to reside over their foundation and use it for his empire in Seattle. Unlike her and her siblings, Lorcan was ruthless and lusted for political power. If left alone while they hibernated, he'd turn Seattle into a city of darkness where vampires ruled the night. Any remaining wandering humans would serve as food.

Unlike their father, they were selective in turning humans into progeny. Their subtle approach was necessary. Overexpansion too quickly would draw the attention of Vampire Hunters from around the world, bringing a war Nicodemus and Flora had even warned about before they were slain. All six of them realized that if they wished to live a luxurious lifestyle, they needed to blend in with humans and hide in plain sight.

Nocturnal Trinity's reputation was taken by most as a place where fan fiction came to life and where those intrigued by the thought of becoming vampires was more fantasy than reality. The predominant reason for not going public about the owners being real vampires was a misdirection to thwart possible invasions from Vampire Hunters or hunter wannabes.

Each of the siblings had turned vampires and nurtured them to remain faithful. Even Irina had a half dozen progeny that traveled from the old country with her. But like Nikolina and her brothers, their broods lived in the outskirts of Vancouver where they could hunt more efficiently and oversee their other nightclub: The Dusty Casket.

This nightclub didn't prominently display its association with vampires. It didn't need to. Since Vancouver received tourists from around the world, their broods were dined on visitors without drawing attention to themselves. If they accidentally drained a foreigner and disposed of the body, the authorities had a difficult time tracing the victim's last steps. In cases where their victims didn't die from enthusiastic feeding, the vampires erased the blood-bags' memories, further keeping the vampires and the nightclub unnoticeable.

Irina wondered how many of her father's other coven were in Seattle with him. Her memories of his egotistical attitude were no different than how he flaunted his power while seated at the head of the table.

Silence hung over the room. Her stunned siblings were probably still trying to absorb their father's suggestion of hibernation. That their father made such a request should inform what his true intent was. He wanted to regain his power and rule over them. She, for one, refused to allow it. Nocturnal Trinity was theirs. After decades of hard work making the establishment an attraction for Seattle's own, she wasn't handing it to him. Not without an intense battle.

Lorcan laughed.

Alec, Orsovo, and Nikolina stared at him with slight confusion.

"Why are you speechless?" Lorcan asked. "There was a time when all of you placed your trust in me. In a vampire's mind, that's not a long time ago. I offer you rest so your bodies and minds can recuperate, giving you vigor and lessening the pull from the edge of madness that wishes to possess you as you age."

Alec flicked his gaze to Nikolina and then to Orsovo. Perhaps his distaste and slight anger toward Irina prevented him from looking for her reaction. After several seconds, Alec said, "That's an immense proposition. One that requires us to discuss and debate amongst ourselves."

Lorcan's eyes narrowed. His jaw tightened and his lips parted slightly, revealing the tips of his fangs. "Debate? Are you indicating that I don't have your best interests at heart?"

Irina sat at the edge of her chair, desperate to hear Alec's reply.

Uneasiness widened Alec's eyes beneath his furrowed brow. He had already been a second from being turned into ash by their father. It went without saying that none of them could trust their father, especially not Alec. And now Lorcan wanted them to hibernate so *he* could attend to their affairs?

Alec cleared his throat. "That's not the implication at all, father. But Nocturnal Trinity is a business, *our* business, that needs our touch and for at least one of us to remain awake and on the premises at all times. We've worked too hard to establish this nightclub and keep its ... semi-untarnished reputation. We cannot simply hand it off to someone else. Not even you."

His statement was partially true but also a challenge. Often, they were all away from the nightclub at the same time, but he was correct that the nightclub operations wasn't a matter her father could oversee. She released a slight sigh, easing back into her chair, hoping their father bought his words.

Lorcan kept a hardened glare on Alec for the better part of a minute before acquiescing a nod and waving his hand slightly in the air. "Ah, perhaps you're right. I'm *not* a businessman. Those affairs bore me. And it's not right for me to barge into your establishment making harsh changes. We've been separated too long, and we should spend time reacquainting ourselves before such an endeavor occurs."

Lorcan stood. Two of his human servants rushed to each side of him. Their intent gazes studied Irina and her siblings. While they were not as powerful as Lorcan's children, Irina sensed their ability to block oncoming attacks should any of them decide to rush their father. The other elder vampires rose from their seats as well.

Alec took a cautious rise and Orsovo was quick to edge to their brother's side. For Irina, it was difficult to discern the scene, as it remained obvious an unspoken, unseen line had been drawn between the generations, and with the sharp glare Alec sent her direction, she found herself on the outside of them all.

She didn't see Alec as an ally for the moment, and she wondered if Nikolina's earlier cordial attitude would fade, too. Another fear nudged her conscious and that was in wondering if Nikolina's visit had been more to detect where Irina stood after Flora's sacrifice. Unfortunately, Irina had revealed all of her cards. She held nothing secret, which might have been her worst mistake.

With Nocturnal Trinity's Unity down to four siblings, she didn't believe Alec would contrive to have her staked. They might insist she be placed into hibernation, but not before their situation with Lorcan was resolved. The current circumstances indicated their father's intentions weren't to play nice or to come for a hearty family reunion. Was that what Alec had foolishly expected?

Lorcan wanted to return to his status of power and authority like he once held. He savored and thrilled maintaining his despotism from more than a century earlier. Hibernation had not lessened his thirst for blood or his want to reign over the *lesser* humans.

"Father," Alec said. "We've prepared a place for you to stay."

We? Irina frowned.

Alec smiled. "Do you wish to see the nightclub in all its splendor? The evening crowd's coming in. Perhaps you'd like to see those eager to be *chosen* for the night? I'd be happy to escort you."

Lorcan cocked a brow and promptly responded with a dismissive shake of his head. "No. I've other places to see. I've made previous arrangements of where to stay during the day."

"Where?" Orsovo asked with a curious frown.

Lorcan sighed while one servant adjusted Lorcan's long cape. "Trivia matter, son. Until we're more comfortable with one another, it's best that I reside at a location unknown to all of you."

Irina smirked and didn't attempt to hide it. *So you do fear us?*

"For this evening," Lorcan said, "I wish to spend it with Mayor Thomas and see the city. This will give me time to inform him of my proposals."

Thomas stiffened in his chair at the suggestion and was unable to hide his fear.

Lorcan smiled at the mayor. "It's clear, at least, to the mayor, as to whom is in charge."

CHAPTER 46

*K*ailey held Raven and crossed the threshold into Forrest and Penelope's apartment.

Well, this is the perfect place for a cat. No need for a litter box, either. Smells like they already have one. I'm guessing a meth house smells better.

"*Neither of us would know that, so behave,*" Kailey said to Raven.

You smell that funky smell, too, right?

"Of course I do, but unlike *you*, I'm too polite to mention it."

Brady eased beside Kailey. "Everything okay? How are you feeling?"

Kailey forced a weak smile. "I'm fine. Honest. Go do whatever it is you and Forrest need to do."

Kailey lowered Raven gently on the floor.

What the hell, Kailey? Get me off this grimy floor. There might be mice or rats.

"Earn your keep, then," Kailey said with a sly grin.

That's not funny.

Kailey walked over and looked into a small mirror on the wall. Seeing her reflection, she grimaced and shook her head. She touched her swollen cheek and winced. "Damn. It's always my face that takes the pounding."

Brady slipped up behind her, rested his head on her shoulder, and looked into the mirror to catch her gaze. He squeezed her hips and pulled her tight against himself. "It's not *always* your face that takes a—"

Kailey's mouth gaped. She frowned and placed a finger to her lips. "Shh!"

Ewww! I need cotton for my ears and a place to vomit.

Brady kissed her cheek. "Forrest and I need to check out the warehouse where they kept you. I'll call you once we get there."

Kailey gasped.

"What?" Brady asked.

She patted her rear pocket and then realized she wasn't dressed in the clothes from earlier. "Shit! I don't have my cellphone."

"You probably lost it in the bay," Brady said.

Kailey shook her head. "No. I'm pretty sure I didn't have it on me after I untied myself. It might still be in the apartment."

"The only cellphone in our apartment was smashed on the floor, but it wasn't yours. I placed it into a bag for evidence."

Kailey looked worried. "Then they must have taken mine if you didn't see it."

"If they took it, that's actually a good thing."

"Why?"

"We can trace it," Brady said. He hugged her tightly. "Stay with Cassie and Penelope. They'll keep you safe."

"What about Jinn?" she asked.

Brady sighed. "Under the circumstances, he's probably safer if he rides with us."

Kailey grinned and nodded. "You're probably right."

"Jinn!" Brady said. He motioned toward the door. "You're going with me and Forrest."

A look of relief and appreciation replaced the heaviness of his worry. "The first good news of the day. It's not any other day that I'd actually look forward to riding in the back of a squad car, but given my current company, I'm the happiest demon in Seattle."

Brady grinned. "Don't get too cheerful. The warehouse might have more danger than here."

"You keep that attitude," Jinn said. "I'm inclined to worry about that later. I'd rather have your weapons and Forrest protecting me than a crossbow, trigger-happy Demon-hunter eyeing me down."

"If you're thinking of us as bodyguards," Forrest said, "you're only fooling yourself."

"Now, wait," Jinn said. He pointed at Brady. "It's his duty, as a sworn officer, to protect us from danger. After all, I'm a bartender, not a fighter. I'm certainly not an investigator and I've never fired a gun."

Brady shook his head. "Then it might be best that you stay out of sight, don't you think?"

"You got that straight."

"Come on," Brady said, opening the door. "Let's go."

CHAPTER 47

The black limo pulled into the alleyway and stopped behind Nocturnal Trinity. Serge and Costel sat stiff on the leather seat with their backs straight while facing Dr. Litman.

Serge's wide nose was broken. Dried blood stained his upper lip and the side of his head. Costel held a blood-soaked handkerchief to his right temple. Neither offered a word but both stared at the doctor, trying to analyze what the aged millionaire was thinking.

Dressed in an elegant suit with the jacket unbuttoned and opened to reveal the 9mm holstered at his side, Dr. Litman wore sunglasses that further heightened his intimidating features. He sat holding his cane upright with both hands. His silence was his most frightening attribute because no one knew what actions he might take. He chewed the nub of a cigar.

Someone that ranted all the time often made their intentions known and held few secrets. A man that sat in silence was difficult to read, unpredictable, and often quite dangerous. Unable to see his eyes through the dark lenses was even more menacing.

After Serge and Costel searched the docks at the marina for over an hour and still had not found Kailey, they were ordered at gunpoint into the rear of the limo by Dr. Litman's three armed bodyguards. A few times when Serge and Costel attempted to explain their mistakes and shortcomings and their inherit fear of water, Dr. Litman's bodyguards pistol-whipped them for refusing to jump off the warehouse roof into the bay when Kailey was still in sight.

On land, Serge and Costel moved with stealth-like precision and defined the perfect example of what a cat burglar was, even in human form. But water might as well have been hydrochloric acid because of their innate fear of it.

In pain and partial worry that the limo ride would be his last, Serge reached and rubbed the back of his neck. His fingertips touched the steel collar that encircled his neck. Locked by the magic of an Eastern European witch, Serge was unable to loosen the links to free himself. Not even with his Amur-*were* strength could he or Costel break their collars, allowing them to turn into their werecat or rare Pallas forms. Costel was imprisoned in the same manner. The collars prevented them from transforming.

Regardless of what they wanted to do while they wore the collars, they were enslaved to Dr. Litman to perform whatever duties he required of them. Although stronger than mere men in their human form, they possessed only a slight fraction of the strength their *were*-forms held. Otherwise, they could've taken down Dr. Litman and his tyrant bodyguards, guns or not.

"You had one duty to fulfill," Dr. Litman said. "And yet, you failed to achieve that."

"You hired us to kidnap Kailey," Serge said. "We *did* that."

"Yes. You were also required to *keep* her until we arrived," Litman replied. "But, she escaped by the time I got here. And when she fled, you did little to apprehend her. You disobeyed direct orders to get her after she got onto the roof."

Costel stiffened in his seat with a sickened expression on his face. "But … she jumped into bay. We … we cannot swim."

With one swift motion, the back of Litman's hand struck Costel cheek with enough force to break teeth. Costel winced and placed his hand to his face. Blood coated his lower lip.

"Have you ever tried to swim?" Litman asked through tight lips.

"You know what we are," Serge said. "It is impossible. You expected us to dive into the bay? No. We'd rather die than jump into *shallow* water."

Dr. Litman smiled. "That *is* an alternative."

"Look, sir. We did what you asked," Costel said, rubbing his jaw. "We found and captured her."

"You failed miserably at that, too. Part of the job was for you *not* to make a scene. Now, police are combing the streets near the apartment, looking for clues, looking for you," Litman said.

"Not our fault, sir," Serge said. "We entered through upper floor window, quietly and without being seen by anyone."

Litman's face tightened. "Reports indicate the front door was splintered and broken down."

Horror filled Costel's eyes. "Yes, that's true. But not by us."

Litman's jaw flexed. "Then by whom?"

Serge shook his head. "We do not know. The intrusion caused us to take girl out de upper window, which was never our intention. We planned to leave through the front or back door on lower level."

"Did you see the intruder?" Litman asked.

"No," Costel replied. "But his scent was … it was … I don't know how to explain it."

"Werewolf?"

"No. Not a werewolf," Serge said, nodding. "Not sure what it was."

A cellphone rang, causing Serge and Costel to jerk and flinch. No one else in the rear of the limo moved.

After the third ring, Dr. Litman leaned forward toward Serge. His voice was harsh, strained, and low. Yet, even with his thick accent, he was perfectly understood. "Perhaps, you should answer that."

Serge's eyes widened. Due to his fear of Dr. Litman, he failed to feel the phone's vibrations. He patted his back pocket and brought the phone out. "The phone is not mine, sir. It belonged to the girl."

An intrigued smile crept across the old man's face. "Let it go to voicemail. Playback message should they leave one. I'm guessing whoever it is, will. Perhaps you two aren't so useless after all."

Serge nodded and the phone shook in his nervous hand. After less than a minute, the message symbol lit up, displaying a message in the box. Serge touched the message icon and the number necessary for the playback.

"Uh, Kailey, this is Luna. We … we need your help. We've kinda gotten ourselves into … a situation. We need a place to go. A safe place."

Litman smiled and nodded. He lowered the mirror glass partition behind Serge and Costel. "Driver, take us to Nocturnal Trinity now."

CHAPTER 48

Forrest followed Brady and Jinn down the rusted stairs. The staircase creaked and rocked under Forrest's heavy footsteps. Jinn glanced over his shoulder several times with nervous eyes staring at Forrest's huge boots.

"Take it easy," Jinn said. "I don't want to fall and have you crumple me on these stairs. You'd crush me to death."

Forrest grinned.

Jinn shook his head. "I'm not kidding."

Midway down the stairs, Brady stopped.

"What's wrong?" Forrest asked.

"That Jeep parked across the street," Brady said. "Have you seen it before? Does it belong to one of your neighbors?"

The midnight blue Jeep's tinted windows prevented them from seeing if anyone was sitting in the vehicle. It was a newer model, too.

Forrest eyed the Jeep and shook his head. "No, I've not seen it before. It's too new for anyone in this area to afford. Why?"

Brady eased his hand to his 9mm and unlatched the strap. "It followed us for several blocks while we were on our way here. At first, I thought they were tailing us but they turned right a few streets back."

"Maybe they suspected you had noticed them," Forrest said.

"Could be and they circled back." Brady placed his hand on the butt of the gun.

"Ah, shit," Jinn said, crouching down slightly, trying to make himself look smaller.

"Hide behind me," Forrest said. "I never thought I'd see a demon tremble as badly as you do."

Jinn squeezed around Forrest. "I'm a lover, not a fighter."

"Both seem questionable to me," Forrest replied.

Brady pulled his 9mm and hurried down the last few steps to the sidewalk. The Jeep's headlights came on and the driver sped away.

"Come on," Brady said, holstering his gun and running to the squad car. "Let's catch them."

CHAPTER 49

Irina wanted to whisk herself from the banquet table and sprint into the night, to get as far from her family as possible. But she knew Alec would stop her before she got outside the nightclub. It wasn't that he was necessarily faster, but her evening attire and shoes weren't favorable for running.

Although her father expressed his need to leave for the evening, a half hour of being interrupted by other vampires in the room slowed his departure. His gracious smile and handshakes seemed genuine on the surface, but Irina knew him. When he set his mind for leaving an event, he loathed others that slow his retreat. Yet, he kept his faux mannerisms alive because he needed to maintain an attractive image due to his recent arrival. Not only did he want his diplomatic ties with those from the old country to remain favorably fused, he desperately needed those in Seattle to desire his presence. Without their lustful needs for him, his idea for a new rule stagnated. The Trojan Horse approach was something a lot of the elder vampires used before launching their autocracy.

Once their father achieved his new pinnacle, he'd squeeze her and her siblings completely out of the picture. She saw his ruse for what it was. Why couldn't Alec and Orsovo?

After Lorcan made his proposal known to her family and their guests, he couldn't maintain an immediate reign over thousands of new vampires without the aid of other ancients to control the vile nature of the feral, younger ones. But knowing her father, he'd not trust her or her brothers and sister to lend their help during his coming to power. Such was too risky, as even Alec and Orsovo would refuse to sit idly by, watching their father taint and rule over the city and the prosperous nightclub all six of them had established.

Jilted family members were the worst enemies anyone could ever have. Their secretive plots to get satisfactory revenge ensued without question, often without the slightest outside hint of their intent. While scheming, the scorned continued their warm smiles and cordial attitudes, but all the while their inner thoughts calculated the best ways to carry out their goal of toppling the person they despised the most. Irina knew this to be true because the memories of her youth when she had attempted to eradicate Lorcan's terror once and for all still lingered fresh in her mind. With his unexpected arrival shockingly jolting her emotions, new ideas to fulfill seeing his demise beckoned her immediate attention. Plots she must exact by herself because she no longer fit or seemed welcome inside their Circle of Unity.

Lorcan and the mayor were almost to the door when one of the night-club bodyguards stepped into the room and said, "At Lorcan's request, I introduce to all of you: Dr. Litman, Serge, and Costel."

The three entered the room. Lorcan approached Litman with arms raised and placed his hands on Litman's shoulders, giving a hearty squeeze and a broad triumphant smile. "What a joyous occasion! You bring good news?"

Alec's eyes studied them with curiosity and then he flicked his gaze to Orvoso and then Nikolina and Irina. None of them recognized these three men, either.

Lorcan lowered his hands from Litman's shoulders, and Lorcan stared past him. His smile faded and disappointment crossed his brow. "Where's Kailey? You did bring her?"

Even in the dim lighting of the room, Litman wore his shades, which Irina thought odd. He removed his fresh cigar from his mouth, lowered his head slightly, and said, "They let her get away."

Lorcan's eyes darkened and his voice deepened. He turned toward the two men. "Is that true?"

Serge and Costel looked at one another with wide eyes and vehemently shook their heads.

Serge explained the events that had occurred and how Kailey escaped.

With a smile stretched on Lorcan's face, he backhanded Serge before anyone saw his hand move. The impact of the strike lifted Serge off the floor and spun him over backwards. Serge landed on the floor facedown with blood leaking from the sides of his mouth.

For several moments, Irina worried that his strike had killed the man. After a moment, Serge coughed and sputtered, slowly pushing himself partway up.

Lorcan pointed his finger at one of his guards. "Restrain both of them. Make certain they're unable to get free. I'll deal with them later."

Alec whispered to one of the nightclub's wait staff and motioned toward the dark corridor. Irina assumed Alec was telling her where the two men should be held for the night. What some folks with weaker constitutions called torture chambers, others laughingly called pleasure chambers. It simply depended on one's preferences.

Litman puffed his cigar. "What are your plans for them, Lorcan?"

"Lately, we seem to be lacking entertainment, doctor, that today's generation has never seen and wouldn't understand," Lorcan said. "What they consider entertainment lacks imagination and initiative."

"Entertainment?" Alec asked with a furrowed brow. "What does that have to do with these two men's failure to capture Kailey?"

Lorcan's dark eyes bore into Alec's. His voice held a serpent-hiss quality when he spoke. "I don't condone failure. I favor enacting some punishments in ways where I savor immense joy from watching the chastisement unfold."

"What type of punishment?" Litman asked.

Lorcan glared at Serge and Costel. "Slow death."

"Please," Serge begged, pressing his hand together in a prayerful manner. "Give us another chance to correct our failure."

A smile curled Lorcan's narrow lips.

"Death?" Litman said, chewing his cigar. "That's harsh even for you. The worst I recall you inflicting was the Cat-o'-nine-tail."

"Oh!" Lorcan's eyes grew wide in excitement. Saliva formed at the edges of his mouth as he savored the past and inhaled deeply. "Those were glorious days, were they not? To relive them …. But no, I've something much bloodier in mind."

The elder vampires came closer, piqued by sudden interest and arousal.

Serge and Costel paled.

Litman frowned. "Will they survive?"

A hearty deep laugh rolled from Lorcan. "If they survive the punishment, they're pardoned from their death sentences."

"What do you have in mind?" Litman asked.

"A brutal challenge. A battle for survival. How well do you think the two of them would fair being pitted against a behemoth?"

Litman seemed to be staring at Serge, but wearing the sunglasses, it was impossible to know. He chuckled under his breath, and then walked toward Lorcan. "The two of them against one behemoth?"

"Does it matter?" Lorcan asked.

"For betting odds, yes. It makes all the difference in the world. But for them to actually stand a chance to fight longer than a minute, you'd best place both in the match against one behemoth. Otherwise, you'll find few who'll bother betting the odds."

"Doctor," Lorcan said. "I've matters to attend with the good mayor here. Do you mind accompanying us and later, we can further discuss the details?"

Litman smiled. "Not at all."

Lorcan nodded and looked at Alec. "I'll leave you to take care of your nightclub business and rejoin you later."

CHAPTER 50

"If this is supposed to be a chase," Forrest said, "perhaps the person driving the Jeep should make it more challenging, don't you think?"

Brady grinned. "It's almost as though the person wants to get caught."

The driver kept slowing to a near stop and then gunned the engine whenever Brady came within a few feet of the rear bumper.

"Either that," Jinn said, "or he's trying to set you up."

Brady glanced into the rearview mirror. The headlights of three motorcycles turned onto the street and sped toward the squad car. "Yep. We've got company."

Forrest crouched in the seat so he could look into the sideview mirror.

Brady tossed his cellphone to Forrest.

"What the hell's this for?"

"Call Kailey."

"Why?"

"This distraction might only be to give someone else time to take Kailey," Brady replied. "Since the Jeep was waiting on the curb when we left the apartment, they know where Kailey is."

Forrest picked up the phone and studied it as the foreign object it was. His brow furrowed with confusion.

"Here," Jinn said. "I'll call her."

Forrest handed him the phone and nodded. "Thanks."

"You need to catch up with the times," Jinn said.

Brady nodded. "That's what I've been telling him."

Forrest laughed. "It'll never happen. I enjoy my privacy. Not to mention how dangerous it would be to forget to silence a phone and it ring just a second before I was going to stake a vampire."

The Jeep sped away, causing Brady to increase his speed.

Two of the motorcycles sped along side the patrol car. The Jeep took a right at the intersection and the bikers made certain Brady followed.

The narrow alley dead ended. Brady parked behind the Jeep and the three bikers parked around the car.

Jinn nervously whispered into the phone, informing Kailey to remain alert. Afterwards, he disconnected the call and slid the phone over the seat to Brady. "If the two of you don't mind, I'll keep my ass in the car. Okay?"

Brady and Forrest ignored him and opened their doors at the same time. Before they were able to stand and exit, the bikers blocked them. Wearing helmets, Forrest figured, to hide their identities.

Brady pulled his 9mm and aimed at the man closest to him. "This can go one of two ways."

"No need for violence," a voice from near the Jeep said.

Forrest's eyebrows rose from his recognition of the man's voice; a voice he treasured from his youth.

"We didn't lead you here to attack you," the man said. "I need to talk to Forrest."

"Jacques?" Forrest asked, standing and shoving the biker out of his way.

The man grinned.

Brady frowned at Forrest. "You know him?"

Forrest nodded. "He's my cousin and Micah's father."

Brady said, "I see the resemblance."

Forrest took long strides toward Jacques. They embraced.

Jacques stared up at Forrest. "Damn, you never stopped growing. You've turned out to be a bear of a man."

Forrest grinned. "You don't know the half of it. To be honest, I didn't know if you were still alive after all these years. From my understanding, werewolves aren't immortal."

"I've aged, albeit a bit slower than most werewolves."

"How? Might I ask?" Forrest said.

"As with most everything in life, there are loopholes," Jacques said with a grin. "That's a discussion for another day. Buy me a fifth sometime and I'll tell you."

"Fair enough," Forrest said. "What brings you to Seattle?"

"I'm trying to find Micah," Jacques replied.

Brady holstered his gun, closed the car door, and joined Forrest.

CHAPTER 51

When Lorcan left the banquet room and ascended the spiral rock stairs that led up to the nightclub's dance halls and bars, Irina waited with Alec, Orsovo, and Nikolina until the elder vampires had gone to the upper floor.

Irina mentally braced herself. She read the harsh temper flaring in Alec's eyes. Orsovo's weren't much different. She expected to be berated, to say the least, but never had she witnessed fiery hatred coming at her from all of them at the same time.

"You—" Alec said, pointing a stern finger.

Irina placed a finger to her lips and then touched her ear. "Now's *not* the time. Father's hearing is far better than ours."

Her siblings flinched and their eyes widened for the briefest moment.

Irina smiled and whispered, "Now, before you lay the blame, it's best we see what the wolf you brought into our fold desires. He never shares his spoils. If ever he gives anything, what he requires in return is far more costly."

Alec's jaw tightened. He turned on his heels and proceeded up the spiral stairs with Orsovo close behind. Nikolina paused only long enough to look into Irina's eyes. Her sister's eyes moistened with tears. She appeared torn, unable to decide which side of the newly drawn line she wished to stand.

Irina predicted Nikolina would eventually side with their brothers, rather than oppose Alec's stance.

Before Nicodemus and Flora had been staked, none of Irina's siblings ever placed much confidence in what her views were. Her opinion was always the last to be asked, which further kept her alienated as she'd been in her early years as a vampire. She existed only as a last resort within the family but never felt like she properly fit. At least with the decision to invite their father with open arms, the blame could not befall her, a fact she couldn't wait to point out.

At the top of the stairwell, Alec, Orsovo, and Nikolina slipped to the side of the room near the wall. The blinding flashes of laser lights and the pulsing, electro tech music mesmerized the bouncing, dancing wall of people in their late teens and early twenties. Nothing outside of the nightclub mattered to this mob. They had no worries about their day jobs, the economy, world matters, or mortality. The vibrations prompted them to dance, to laugh, and their urges to fulfill their sexual lusts. From overhead vents, mists of overpowering pheromones sprayed periodically, further enticing the desires of the young males and females to tempt them to dance closer and closer.

With all the normal amenities to increase the hunger of the the rave party, tonight everything was about to change, but not for the better.

Lorcan smiled broadly, parting the crowd with his arms outstretched. He spoke in a tone that drew the reception of the young men and women. Slowly, their dancing stopped. They stared in awe at him, pressing toward him with almost empty but pleading eyes. The DJ stopped the music.

Lorcan turned to the mayor, leaned to the side of his ear, and whispered something. The nervousness on the mayor's face faded. He grinned and licked his lips. He took the hand of a young fit woman dressed in a skintight, black leather bodysuit, and she didn't resist. With eagerness, she came to him and pressed herself against the mayor's side. She kissed his neck, his cheek, and then she pushed her lips against his with a deep kiss. While kissing, she slid the mayor's hand to her buttocks. He cupped her ass with a tight squeeze. She pressed against his crotch.

The young man that had been standing beside her, apparently not captured by Lorcan's compulsion, grabbed her hand and tried to pull her back. She yanked her hand free and swatted him away, eagerly kissing the mayor.

"That's my wife!" the man shouted. His face reddened from his heated anger.

"Not for tonight," Lorcan said. "Tonight, she belongs to the mayor."

The man rushed at the mayor, but Lorcan caught him by the throat and lifted him off the floor. Lorcan grinned, shaking his head. With a swift twist, he snapped the man's neck and dropped his dead body to the floor. No one in the crowd noticed; not even to the man's wife, who kissed the mayor deeper.

Lorcan turned to the mayor. "My mistake. She's yours for as long as you desire."

Another young woman rushed to the mayor's side. He pulled free of the widow's kiss, gasping for breath, and smiled. He wrapped an arm around each woman and headed toward the exit with Lorcan at his side.

Fury tightened Irina's brow and her narrowed eyes focused on Alec. Taken back, Alec caught her gaze and turned, heading back down the stairs. Before Orsovo or Nikolina could follow behind him, Irina broke in between them, hurrying down the stairs behind Alec.

CHAPTER 52

*I*rina followed Alec downstairs to the banquet room. Never had she felt the heat of anger. She had experienced angered and wrathful stares, stern enough to make her flinch, but never actual heatwaves radiating through the air, directed at her.

Alec stopped at the head of the table. He turned and faced her.

"What have you done?" Irina said. "*Why* would you even consider bringing our father to Seattle?"

"I may not have thought this through," Alec said softly.

"You think?" Irina said. She frowned and shook her head. "Of course you *didn't*. You've always based your decisions upon *impulse*."

Orsovo rushed to Alec's side as Irina pointed a stern finger at Alec.

"You handed *everything* we worked so hard to make a success and now, he's ruined it," Irina said.

Alec shook his head. "No, I did not."

"No?" Irina said. "You gave him the Wrathbone dagger, which gives him control and power over the behemoths, or did that not cross your mind? Without that dagger, we cannot kill the behemoths, as you promised Forrest you'd do. The behemoths might wager with father to have him spare their lives. In return, they could offer to kill us if our father demands it."

"Father would never—"

"No? You've not spoken to him in nearly a century. You've no idea what he's capable of. None of us do."

"He's been in hibernation," Orsovo said.

"So he *says*. But none of us know whether or not what he said is true."

"You think he'd lie to us?" Alec asked.

"To gain power, he's capable of doing anything," Irina said, "or have you forgotten the peasants he slaughtered during their revolt? He killed women and children and babies until the men in the villages finally surrendered and obeyed."

Alec broke their gaze and stared at the floor with regret.

"Don't tell me you were a part of that?" Irina said.

"At the time, I believed the cause was justified," Alec said.

Irina's eyes widened. Her stomach twisted. "Justified? That clarifies why you didn't have any qualms about sacrificing Flora to Forrest to save your own life."

"That's not true."

"Isn't it? You're no different than our father, which appalls me."

Alec lifted his head and stared at her in anger.

"What did he promise you in exchange for the dagger?" she asked.

"You're out of line," Nikolina said.

Irina hurled a flaring look of anger at her sister. "*I'm* out of line? Earlier this evening, you expressed your regret over siding with Alec in Flora's death. And now you're siding with him again?" She pointed at the stairwell and glared at Alec. "We've got a mess to fix upstairs now, since father killed that man in front of everyone."

"I'll take care of it," Alec said.

"How? Compel them all?"

Alec shrugged. "We've done similar before."

"We've never killed anyone on the dance floor. In the VIP rooms, humans have died from time to time, but usually it occurred with one of the wannabe guests. That's easier to fix, by simply turning the person. That cannot be done with this man.

"Father allowed the mayor to pull the man's wife away, seemingly *against* the husband's wishes but not of her own since she was under father's compulsion. If you somehow find a way to turn him, he's not going to forget watching his wife kissing and hugging the mayor. Turn him and you'll have to kill his undead body. You don't quieten that kind of rage."

"I said that I'd take care of it," Alec said, placing his hands on his hips.

"And with today's technology," Irina said. "Someone probably recorded it on a smartphone. The incident might already be viral on social media."

Alec shook his head. "Phones are required to be left at the door."

"Yes. That's our rule, but with some of these people's cellphone addictions, it's far more likely that several people got into Nocturnal Trinity with a cellphone still on his or her person. It wouldn't be the first time someone left a dummy phone with the greeter."

Alec sighed. "Orsovo, get to the front door and make certain every person is checked before leaving the club for an extra phone on his or her person. Take any phone someone snuck in and destroy it. Have the man's body moved to our VIP room until we can figure out a solution."

Orsovo nodded and headed toward the stairs.

"Satisfied, Sis?" Alec asked her.

"Not in the least. You've placed us all in immense danger."

"Irina, you're overreacting."

"No, brother, I'm not," she replied. "Did you not hear his implications? He wants all four of us to enter hibernation."

"That's not going to happen," Alec said.

"Maybe not, but it reveals his intent. He wants us gone so he can be free to take over. He looks at the opportunity to seize our groundwork from us so he's in charge. And what knowledge did you have that he was trying to capture Kailey?"

"None."

"Don't lie," Kailey said. "You're in this deeper than you wish us to know. How much did you know? What are you *not* telling us?"

"I told father that Flora was dead because of Kailey, and that's not a lie."

"It's not the complete truth, nor is Flora's death Kailey's fault."

Alec leveled an intent stare at her. Like Nikolina had tried to read her thoughts, Alec was attempting to do the same. She shielded her mind.

Alec's upper lip curled in a snarl. "Siding with the human, are you?"

"No," Irina said. "I'd give the remainder of my undead years to have Flora back in our Circle of Unity instead of me. But as you told father, and this is true, Flora overstepped her boundaries. She had gone to a very dark place, even for a vampire. Even if she had succeeded in killing Kailey, it's doubtful her fall into darkness would've lessened."

"I know," Alec said. "Which is why I made the decision to sacrifice her to Forrest. I actually regret that now, too."

"But you failed to address that to father."

"I was in the process of figuring out the best way to tell him without losing my life in the process," Alec said. His eyes grew dark. "As you saw, the way *you* divulged the information to father almost ended my existence. Or is that what you were hoping for, dear sister?"

"Not at all," Irina said truthfully. "I harbor no ill-will toward you. I do hold regrets. Perhaps hibernation would've helped Flora, if we kept her in that state until Kailey's natural life ended."

"Perhaps," Alec said, reflecting on her words and slowly nodding.

"Now Kailey's in a worse situation. Father won't stop pursuing her until she's dead. Surely, even you've not forgotten his bloody vengeance."

Alec straightened his tie and his eyes went distant. "I locked those memories away, best I could. The hands of my youth were covered with the blood of the innocents. Peasants, mostly. I did things I hoped never to recall."

Irina swallowed hard, wondering if their father had sent Alec to kill the man she'd hoped to marry.

Alec gave her a regretful smile. His voice reflected his regret as well. "Those horrifying memories are returning, now that you've reminded me. Had I remembered father's true nature, I'd have kept Kailey secret. Honestly, I didn't think he'd send people to abduct her. But had they succeeded in killing her, that wouldn't have necessarily been a bad thing."

Irina cocked a brow. "Oh? Why not?"

"We could've tied up loose ends."

"You reneged on our promise by keeping the behemoths alive, and you wish to fault Forrest for the agreement? Rather than take the dagger back from father and kill the behemoths, you think you can kill Forrest instead?"

"Do you think any of us can take the dagger back from father?"

"You should never have given it to him in the first place."

Alec nodded. Worry tugged at the sides of his eyes. "Yes, I see that now."

"And don't forget that Cassie's one of Kailey's closest friends. You harm or kill Kailey and she'll make you wish for Hell."

"Anything else, dear sister?" Alec asked.

Fury darkened Irina's eyes. Her voice grew cold. "Tell me why you gave him the Wrathbone."

"To be honest, I'm not certain."

"There has to be a reason," Irina said.

Alec sighed. He rubbed his chin, his eyes deep in thought. Finally, he met her gaze. In earnest, he said, "Because he's our father."

"You owe him no allegiance after more than a century of not knowing if he was even alive," Irina said. "It's no wonder Flora took Nicodemus' place after his death, because you've not half the spine of either of them."

Alec's jaw tightened.

"Is that—" Irina's eyes widened. She gasped. "*That's* why you wanted Flora dead! You knew you'd never have power over us until she was gone."

Nikolina's gaze darkened as she turned toward Alec.

Alec shook his head. "That's not true."

"You're spineless and pathetic," Irina said. "But knowing you're not capable of residing in power over the rest of us, you handed our father everything."

"Irina, I regret our decision about Flora. I do. I never thought about hibernation. And I suppose, since I'm being confronted for my actions, I gave father the Wrathbone because I harbor guilt over Flora's death. I'm truly sorry."

Irina cocked her head as she evaluated his body language and the tone of his voice. His last three words weren't something she'd have ever heard from their father, or Flora, for that matter.

"I'll figure out some way to get back the Wrathbone."

"You realize father sent the men to capture her, *not* kill her, which means you should fear what happens once he finds her."

"Why?"

"He wants answers first. Although she doesn't know much more than Flora's intent and whatever Brady has told her, should father compel her for answers, she might give him even more reasons to kill you."

Involuntarily, Alec's hand went to his throat. Hardly an etched line remained where the dagger had parted the skin. Soon it would fade but the memory of the ordeal would last for years. "I feared he was going to earlier."

"As did I," Irina said. "I wanted to rush to aid you, but even I'm not *that* fast."

Alec sighed. "It's good you didn't try. The slightest provocation would've been my death, Irina."

"That's why I didn't move. The longer you allow father to roam Seattle, the weaker we become," Irina said. "Right now, he's still building his strength. With what he did upstairs to control the dancers, it's obvious that he's almost returned to the height of his power."

Nikolina took a goblet of blood from the table, turned, and sat against the edge of the table, delicately balancing the glass stem between her fingers. "I agree with Irina."

Irina placed a hand over her chest and faked a gasp with widened eyes. "Finally, she speaks, and actually tosses some support *in* my direction."

Nikolina sipped the blood, licked her lips, and then pursed them. "All of us have the power to control a crowd of one hundred people."

"Yet, father didn't compel all of them," Irina said.

"That could've been intentional, though, rather than weakness or a mistake," Nikolina said.

Alec flicked his gaze at her. "What makes you say that?"

"Maybe he wanted to prove a point of his power by allowing the husband to remain uncontrolled?" Nikolina replied. "And killed him to show the elder vampires his ruthlessness without hesitation? No vampire has ever attained a throne by showing pity or mercy."

Alec nodded.

"That makes sense," Irina said. "Who were the elder vampires?"

Alec frowned. "You don't remember them?"

Irina shook her head. "Should I?"

"They frequented our castle in Germany," Alec replied. "Quite often, as I recall."

"No, I don't remember them." She explained to Alec about how their father had locked her in her chambers for years.

Alec rubbed his chin. "I'm sorry, sister, I—I never knew."

"Nor had I until this afternoon," Nikolina said.

"Father's always despised me," Irina said. "Even tonight he made it evident that he does not and never has favored me. Regardless of what transpired, I was always the scapegoat and I paid a heavy toll for everything. I tried for years to be a dutiful daughter, seeking to find favor in his eyes. That is, until he made me a prisoner inside our own castle. But he's never given a reason for my mistreatment or why he despises me so."

"It's because you have a different father than the rest of us," Alec said.

Irina took a step back in horror and gasped. "What?"

"Alec!" Nikolina said with a harsh glare. "How dare you!"

Irina's stomach knotted and ached as though someone had kicked her. She glanced at Nikolina and then to Alec. Both refused to meet her shocked, curious gaze. "Is this true?"

The silence built around them. The room seemed to spin so Irina walked to the table and sat to keep her weakened knees from buckling. "Nikki, is this true?"

Nikki set the goblet of blood on the table and placed a consoling hand on Irina's shoulder. "Yes. Sadly, yes, it's true."

Irina's face whitened.

CHAPTER 53

"Why didn't any of you ever tell me?" Irina asked, fanning her face with a vintage silk fan.

"We never thought it necessary," Alec replied.

"Not necessary?"

"No, of course not," Alec said. "We've never viewed you as anything less than our sister, even though our fathers are different. It's never mattered in the past and it certainly doesn't matter now. You're our sister. You're one of us."

Irina closed her eyes, took a deep breath, and then slowly sighed. "This explains so much though. All the reasons for why father has never held any affection for me and never will. Now I better understand why he treated me like he did before we were forced to flee the Black Forest. But that means mother—"

Alec nodded. "Yes. She was unfaithful."

"Then who is my father?"

"Hans Bauer. He was a peasant that worked in the stables and took care of the horses," Alec said. "Father was often away on diplomatic errands and came home to find them together."

"So my father wasn't a vampire?"

Alec shook his head. "No."

Irina bit her lower lip, imagining her father's reaction when he discovered her real father in bed with her mother. Irina had seen Lorcan quite angry during her youth, as though he detested her existence, which apparently, he did. But she couldn't imagine the rage that consumed him for such betrayal.

"What happened after father found them?" she asked, even though she wasn't certain she truly wanted the details. "Did he kill my father?"

Alec's cheeks puffed with air before he sighed. "Eventually."

Nikolina shook her head. "Are you sure you want to know?"

"I need to know. I must know," Irina said in a whisper. Her eyes were contrary to her words. She then flicked a near accusatory gaze at her sister. "You know what happened, even though you're several years younger than me?"

"I don't know the full details like Alec does," Nikolina replied. "But I expect the details are gruesome."

"I still don't understand why you couldn't have told me the truth much earlier than tonight," Irina said.

"Like you," Alec said, "I believed father had met his fate long ago. I never expected to see him again. Given that, why should I add to the peril of your past? If he were dead, how does *not* knowing hurt you?"

Compassion burned in Alec's eyes. The softness of his words actually comforted her. For the briefest of moments she entertained the idea that he held her best interests at heart, that he genuinely cared. Yet, she resisted the urge to be persuaded by his words. After all, he had not informed her and Nikolina of their father's arrival or the fact that Lorcan was still alive.

Alec's projection of concern for her might be authentic, but she wasn't foolish enough to disregard other motives he might hold secret. The best factor in his favor was how close he had come to being killed by Lorcan. His near decapitation wasn't staged. The jovialities seconds prior to her blunt revelation of how Flora's death had actually played out couldn't have been predicted. Their father's heated rage occurred in the spur of the moment. In an instant, Lorcan had been ready to kill his eldest living son and heir. While Alec's flair to suppress his emotions was greater than most, no one could dispute the obvious fear in his eyes when Lorcan pressed the Wrathbone dagger to Alec's throat.

Regardless of his current intent, Irina quietly chose to keep her façade to place her trust in him until she held no question of Alec's ulterior motives, should he have other hidden secrets.

Irina smiled. "I understand that you didn't wish to add more weight to my heavy burdens that continue to weigh upon me. I appreciate that, brother. But still, now that he's returned, I need to know what transpired long ago after Lorcan discovered our mother's affair."

"I expected no less a response from you," Alec said with a broad smile. "But understand the details might haunt you."

"I'd be haunted more by the burning questions concerning the incident, if I don't learn the truth."

"So be it," Alec said. "According to mother, when father walked in on them, father clutched Hans by the throat and flung him across the room. Hans hit the plaster wall with such impact that he crashed through to the other side and hit the banister of the stairwell. By all means, he should've died instantly, but being a stablehand and a farmer, his muscular stature prevented him from sustaining worse injuries.

"Hans was alive, but physically he wasn't any threat to father even before his injuries. Mother said that Hans attempted to stand but father stood over him in a split second. Father again took Hans by the throat and lifted him off the floor. Father held him over the edge of the banister and was ready to release him and him drop three floors to the marble tile below. Mother screamed.

"Her scream ushered Nicodemus and I from our rooms to find father holding the naked man over the rail, preparing to let him go. When father saw us, he somehow restrained his urge to drop Hans. Instead, he dragged Hans down the stairs and decided to make a public example out of him to the peasants in the surrounding village." Alec paused for several moments. "Sister, are you sure you wish to know more?"

Irina nodded, even though she was apprehensive to learn the truth. She realized that she couldn't hate Lorcan any less than she already did. However, she understood her hatred toward him might magnify with greater significance.

"I must know," she said.

Alec studied her eyes intently. He seemed hesitant in discussing the matter further. But after she refused to look away, he acquiesced. "Father forced Hans to sit and be restrained to a spiked iron chair where he suffered for hours before finally bleeding to death."

Irina closed her eyes and winced. "And what punishment did our mother endure?"

"She was forced to watch Hans' torture until he died."

"That's all?" Irina asked, opening her eyes to meet his again.

Alec shrugged. "Isn't that enough?"

"Well, yes, of course. That'd be torture enough for anyone to suffer," Irina said. "But with father's nature ... I expected some type of physical abuse on her, too."

"She bore you," Alec said. "But after you were born, he never allowed her to see or hold you. She never knew your touch, nor you, hers."

Irina's eyes widened. "The woman who nursed and raised me wasn't my mother?"

"No. She was a replacement, a wet nurse, and she loved you as though you were her own."

Irina nodded. "Yes. I remember her vividly, until my sixth birthday and then she went away. Then I came to live in the castle."

"She left at the same time our mother gave birth to Nikki," Alec said.

Irina glanced at Nikolina and said, "I remember mother died after bearing you."

Nikki nodded.

"That's what we were told," Alec said. "But that might not how she met her fate."

"You think that father killed her?" Irina asked.

"I believe so."

Tears heated the edges of Irina's eyes. For the first time in decades, she wept.

"I'm sorry," Alec said. His eyes revealed his sympathy.

"As am I," Nikolina said.

"No," Irina said, fanning her face with her hand. "I needed to know. Thank you for telling me. Now, if you'll excuse me, I need some time to myself."

CHAPTER 54

Forrest towered over Brady and Jacques. Both men could hide behind Forrest and not be seen. He was an imposing figure, even to those he valued as family and friends.

Forrest was at a loss for words as he stared into his uncle's eyes. The wrinkles on Jacques' face had grown deeper over the years. His eyes were tired from the strain on his soul. Forrest remembered some Jacques' faint facial scars. Other scars must have occurred after Jacques and his wife departed London and traveled to Canada. Werewolves weren't known for peaceful lives.

"I've not heard anything from Micah in weeks," Forrest said.

"Nor have I," Brady said.

Jacques leaned against the Jeep, crossed his arms, and sighed. "That concerns me."

"Why?" Forrest asked.

Jacques' eyes narrowed with the fierceness of a wolf as his gaze pierced into Forrest's. "I've had a lot of bloody nightmares lately."

"About Micah?" Forrest asked, tilting back his hat and scratching his forehead.

Jacques nodded. "Yes. Dark, dreams of despair. Monsters and such. I fear something bad's happened to him."

The armed entourage with Jacques paced the alleyway. None bothered to remove their biking helmets, but several times they looked up to scan the rooftops.

Jacques glanced at Brady. "You're the one who took over the pack?"

Brady winced. "I wouldn't say that I *took* it from Micah. His leadership … Let's just say, he made others leave due to his bad decisions."

"What kind of decisions?"

Brady explained the factions of Nocturnal Trinity and how Micah forced the Unity to accept the werewolves into it. He briefly detailed Micah's magical, forceful hold over his pack's shifting abilities, including Brady's, and how it had created a partial revolt.

Jacques rolled his eyes and shook his head. "He should stick to shamanism. That's his true calling. He's an Alpha, but some people aren't cut out for leadership."

Forrest chuckled. "That's true."

Jacques smiled. "Brady, how did he react when you separated the pack from Nocturnal Trinity's Unity?"

"He was pissed. I truly expected he'd seek revenge for what happened."

"Most weres would," Jacques said, "but not Micah. He's a firm believer in not harming others, unless forced to do so. I imagine after he cooled down, he realized your actions were rational and in the pack's best interest. Perhaps he's licking his mental ego wounds? But, it's imperative that we find him."

"Why?" Forrest asked.

"Before I answer that," Jacques said, "answer a question for me, Forrest."

"Sure, if I can."

"Have you had any nightmares recently? As long as you've lived and survived as a Vampire Hunter, I'm guessing your insight to detect danger has sharpened. Any premonitions? Anything supernatural that's stirred uneasiness inside you?"

Forrest ran a hand through his beard and looked away. He nodded. "I've sensed an ancient presence combing Seattle during the past few weeks. And this morning, it was stronger than ever."

"Ancient? Like what?"

Brady stared at Forrest with sudden curiosity.

Forrest crossed his arms. "I'm not certain. Whatever it is, I've encountered it before. Long ago."

"And you don't remember what it is?" Brady asked.

"No. I'm not sure. I've the sensation that I've fought it before. I thought I had killed it."

"But you don't remember?" Jacques asked.

"No."

Brady frowned. "How could you not?"

Forrest shrugged. "I've killed a lot of supernatural creatures during the past century."

"Is it a vampire or demon?" Jacques asked.

"It might be either. I'm almost convinced it's something worse. The dark evil enveloped around it are far more powerful than a demon or an elder vampire."

Jacques bit his lower lip and shook his head slightly. "My nightmares suggest a dark being that's stronger than any demon or vampire I've encountered. Your assumption that it might be a different creature is a good one, but it's not a good thing if that's true."

"I know." Forrest sighed.

Jacques glanced into the rear of the patrol car and then gave a shrewd stare at Brady. "Why do you have a demon in the back of your car?"

"Occupational hazard nowadays," Brady said with a grin.

Forrest chuckled. "I almost forgot about him."

Brady took a sharp breath. "Forrest, could this ancient be one of the behemoths?"

Jacques' brow rose. "Behemoths?"

"Four of them live in Nocturnal Trinity," Forrest said.

"Four? Damn."

Forrest nodded. "Yes, but they're not what I'm sensing."

"So whatever this is," Brady said, "you're implying it's *worse* than those demons?"

"It's definitely worse," Forrest said. He looked at Jacques. "When's the last time you talked to Micah?"

"I don't know when you disbanded the werewolves from Nocturnal Trinity, but I'd say that I last spoke to Micah *before* that occurred. He'd have made mention of that."

"But he hasn't afterwards?" Brady asked. "Do you think he's in trouble?"

"I'm more worried about his welfare after talking with you two than I was before," Jacques replied. "You've no idea where he might be?"

Brady shook his head. "No more than you."

Forrest said, "While it's unlikely, Micah might have returned to his magic shop. It wouldn't hurt to check."

Jacques nodded. "We tend to stay close to the familiar things. If I didn't fear Micah was in danger, I'd have never come. As a precaution, most of my pack traveled to Seattle with me. They're scattered around the city, keeping watch. There are far more vampires in Seattle than you might know about, Forrest."

"I'm aware," Forrest said softly.

"Phil," Jacques said. "Frank. Come here."

Two of the motorcyclists walked to Jacques.

"Give them the address of the shop so they can use GPS to get there before we do," Jacques said.

Forrest gave Jacques a questionable stare. "You're into all that technology?"

Jacques smiled and patted Forrest's arm firmly. "Of course, Forrest. You've got to keep up with the times."

Brady laughed. "I keep telling him that."

CHAPTER 55

*L*una and Blaze sat on the curb outside the magic shop. She stared at her broken fingernail with sadness in her eyes. The painful tear near the quick of the nail throbbed. She shook her head, knowing she'd lose the nail. She'd fret over the loss later, but for now, her busied thoughts were more concerned with survival.

After seeing the vampires, she no longer felt safe. For some reason, she had kept the fantasy that the vampires lived in Nocturnal Trinity. To see so many on the streets like a gang frightened her.

No matter how much Blaze insisted he'd fight to protect her, the confrontation with the young vampire coven proved he didn't possess the ability to do so. He'd frozen during battle and so had she. Neither of them had the fighting experience to remain collectively calm and use their available weapons and skills without hesitation. The harshest reality was without the werewolf pack's intervention, she and Blaze would be dead.

Luna stared at the cracked asphalt without blinking or glancing up. Her focus reflected on how she and Blaze had been surrounded in the storage unit yard. She wondered about the werewolf pack that had rescued them. None of the werewolves she recognized, except that one held an uncanny resemblance to Micah. Where had this pack come from? Did their battle against the vampires cost them casualties? Did Brady know about them?

More than ever before, she wished Micah was here so she could consult his advice and seek his magical protection. She was more comfortable talking to him than Brady, and that was only because she'd spent more time with Micah. She trusted Brady since he was a cop and Kailey was in love with him. Kailey possessed sound judgment. But since Kailey and Brady's relationship was still young, Luna didn't want to bother them.

Luna checked the time on the phone. "It's been quite a while since I left the message for Kailey, which is unusual. She normally calls me back within a short amount of time."

"We should probably go inside. I've a feeling that tonight's not a good night to be outside," Blaze said.

Luna studied the narrow alleyway. A cold wind brushed the loose dirt and debris along the asphalt, causing a nerve-tingling scraping sound. She shuddered and hugged herself. For a moment, she thought she'd seen an elongated shadow disappear into the darkness.

Although she loved living in the spare room at the back of Micah's magic shop, she hated its location, especially after dark. Twice, she'd called the city, trying to get them to install sodium safety lights along the alley, but each time, they denied her request, which seemed odd. The city grew darker week after week. She noticed that more and more alley lights had been busted, most likely by vampires, allowing the predators of darkness safe stalking paths to capture those foolish enough to enter after sunset.

The intense darkness frightened her, and the possibilities of what was hidden in the darkness, watching them, unnerved her even more.

Blaze's suggestion to go inside wasn't a bad idea. His voice didn't tremble with fear, but she shook inside.

"Are you coming?" he asked, rising to his feet.

Luna wanted to follow him, but something scraped the rooftop farther down the alley close to where the shadow had vanished. "Did you hear that?"

Blaze shook his head. "No. What?"

Her eyes widened, and although she wanted to bolt to the magic shop door and rush inside, her intuition warned her that they'd never make it.

"Shh!" she said, placing her finger to her lips. "We're being watched."

"Did you see something?" he whispered.

Her eyes met his. With a slight shaking of her head, she said, "No. But I heard it."

"From where?"

Luna nodded to indicate the direction.

Blaze studied the alley.

"It's on the roof," she said.

"The wind's strong this evening, Luna."

"I know," she replied. "I think it traveled past with the breeze about a minute ago. It used the wind to mask its presence."

Blaze reached for her hand. "Look, you're probably still shaken over the vampires at the storage facility. I know I am. So every noise you hear probably sounds suspicious."

"No," Luna whispered. "It's not that."

"Are you sure? I mean, you made yourself nervous *before* the vampires appeared."

Headlights appeared at the far end of the alley. She stood. "Maybe that's Kailey."

"I don't think so," Blaze said. "Come on. Let's get inside the shop."

"How can you tell if it's her or not from this distance?"

Blaze grabbed her hand. "Kailey would've returned your call by now to find out what's wrong. Not once has she ever arrived unannounced."

"Few people drive down this alley after dark."

"All the more reason to be skeptical," Blaze said.

Blaze pulled her away from the asphalt and waited until the vehicle came into sight. It was a dark limo. "See? Not her. Let's go."

The limo swerved and parked at the side of the magic shop. The passenger window lowered and the overhead light revealed the driver's face. He was probably in his mid-fifties with a pleasant face. He asked, "Are you Luna?"

Luna swallowed hard and nodded. "Yes?"

"Kailey said that you called. I was sent to pick you up." The man's voice glossed with a smooth, rich and charming tone.

"Run!" Blaze said in a stern whisper.

Blaze tugged her hand but she stood still. The driver's voice lured her. She wanted to flee with Blaze and her spirit scolded her, screeching inside her head that she needed to get away, but her feet refused to budge.

The man's eyes beckoned. His devilish smile was tempting, reassuring. She hated that her fear of this man equaled her desire to seek his embrace; not in a romantic way, but as a daughter felt the safety inside her father's hug. This alarmed her. Was he compelling or bewitching her?

"Why run?" she replied. "Let's—"

"Surely you don't believe him. Do you? Think about it. Kailey wouldn't send a limo to pick you up!"

The man stepped out from the driver's side and opened the rear limo door, ushering her toward the door with a sweep of his hand. He wore an expensive suit and cap. In spite of his smile, his dark eyes indicated his sinister intent, but she failed to see the danger. She felt the warmth of his charm and longed to hear the honey-richness of his voice. "Please, Kailey awaits."

"She's in the limo?" Luna asked.

"See for yourself."

"It's a trap," Blaze said. He tugged her hand effortlessly.

Luna bit her lower lip. Deep inside, she knew she should run, but she needed to know for certain that Kailey wasn't in the limo.

Blaze wrapped his arms around her, picked her up, and turned to run. "Kailey's not in the limousine, Luna. Snap out of his mental embrace."

"Let her go," the driver said in a soothing tone. "She's coming with me."

"Luna, fight his mind control."

Luna didn't respond. Her eyes longing gazed at the driver. Even though Blaze held her feet off the ground and was carrying her toward the magic shop, she didn't feel or sense him anymore. Instead, for a bizarre few moments, she felt like she was flying.

Blaze cradled Luna in his arms. His coaxing words fell on her deaf ears. She was spellbound by this limo driver and he couldn't understand why.

Blaze had encountered a few dozen vampires since the time he began working for Micah and studying the strange disappearances that were occurring inside the Nocturnal Trinity nightclub. He recognized when a victim was under compulsion. He'd seen it enough to know Luna's wasn't compelled. But somehow, she was under this man's seductive charm, which wasn't magical in origin, either.

Had this man merely compelled Luna, Blaze didn't doubt that he'd have been compelled as well. That lessened the chance of Blaze interfering with the man luring Luna to the limo. Blaze didn't need to look inside to know Kailey wasn't there. The man's actions and words betrayed him; at least to Blaze.

"Put her down," the man said, rushing at Blaze.

Motorcycle engines revved down the dark alleyway, fast approaching the shop. Blaze shook his head. "What now?"

The sound of the engines partly surprised the driver and he gaged his interest on the two bright headlights brightening the alleyway and coming in their direction. The man didn't seem to recognize the riders and appeared agitated that he would need to deal with additional distractions.

"Shit," Blaze whispered. While he might escape one individual, he doubted he'd successfully get inside the shop before the driver or one of the cyclists blocked his path. He didn't know anyone that was a motorcyclist, so as far as he was concerned, the riders weren't necessarily coming to aid him.

The driver cast a nervous look at the slowing motorcycles and frowned at Blaze. "Put her down, now! I don't want to kill you, but—"

Blaze adjusted Luna's weight in his thin muscled arms and sprinted. While he ran toward the magic shop door, he realized that with Luna in his arms, he couldn't possibly get the door key from his pocket to unlock the door. The man advanced in almost a blur. Blaze turned and glanced around to see where else he could run. Before he could make a decision, a solid punch to the jaw dropped Blaze.

He landed on his back with Luna landing atop him. His breath was painfully thrust from his lungs and the back of his head smacked the ground. His sight dimmed and set everything around him into a dizzying spin. Nearing unconsciousness, he watched the man pull Luna to her feet and wrap his left arm around her, persuading her hypnotized mind to return to the limo with him.

As much as Blaze wanted to protest, he was still gasping for breath. His head throbbed. He rolled helplessly to his side, trying to push himself partway up. He hoped to get to his feet before the man tucked Luna into the rear of the limo. Even if Blaze stood, he doubted he could run steady enough or fast enough to prevent the man from driving away.

Blaze growled and fought his pain. He forced enough air to shout, "Fight him, Luna! I love you!"

His last three words jolted her from her near trancelike state. Instead of allowing the stranger to calmly lead her to the limo, she stopped walking and turned toward Blaze. Angered, the man gripped her arm and pulled.

Luna resisted and tugged herself from the man's grip, freeing herself. Her pleading eyes were on Blaze. He figured she wanted his help but also seemed to realize he was injured.

Before she took another step, the man wrapped his arms around her waist and tried to pick her up. Luna screamed and fought. She flung around with her elbow and struck his face. He cried out in pain. Blood trickled from his nose and mouth. As he staggered backwards, she backhanded him. The loud slap left an immediate imprint on his cheek. One of her jagged rings ripped through his skin. He growled and he lunged at her, reaching to grab her throat. She bit his hand.

In agony, the driver yelled, yanking his hand back and rubbing it. His pain turned to heated anger. His reddened, bleeding face contorted slightly. "You sorry little bitch."

Blaze rolled onto his stomach and tried to push himself up, but collapsed due to the severe pain pounding the base of his skull. Swimming darkness clouded his vision and fought to consume him. In the fleeting moments of his consciousness, he witnessed a creature that could only have been a waking nightmare.

The driver and Luna looked to the sky with horror widening their eyes. Large black feathery wings, spanning at least ten feet across from the tip of one wing to the tip of the other, were attached to the shoulder blades of what looked like a man. As much as he wished this creature to be an angel sent to rescue them, he knew this wasn't an angel. Not a demon, either. Perhaps it was something in-between?

Whatever it was, it glided downward.

Luna and the man screamed. The two motorcycles screeched to a stop, burning trails of rubber on the alleyway.

Blaze lost consciousness.

CHAPTER 57

$\mathcal{L}$una trembled, unaware that she was screaming, unaware anything else in the world existed. Mesmerized, she was too transfixed on this winged creature's red eyes to realize the two motorcyclists had skidded to a stop and swung off their bikes.

The men pulled off their helmets and tossed them aside. Perplexed, they exchanged confused glances as they turned into werewolves. Another rider slowed and stopped behind them.

Luna's scream faded into a hoarse cry. The creature's red eyes shrank. The horrifying appearance it held changed. In disbelief, she frowned. Micah? Fear chilled her. Shaking her head, she stopped screaming and dropped to her knees, covering her face with her hands. Peeking through her fingers, she recognized Micah's facial features, but this wasn't Micah.

It hissed. A forked tongue slithered out between rows of jagged teeth. Evil loomed in its gaze. It studied her for a moment and then turned a hungered stare at the limo driver.

FORREST HAD FELT an ancient's presence for several weeks. He was reluctant to hunt for the being, because he knew it was a waste of time. When the creature wished to be found, it would appear. But Forest understood the creature might never appear and return to wherever it had come from.

Brady drove through the narrow alley at a dangerous speed. The taillights of the motorcycles brightened, so Brady eased off the gas and applied the brakes. In the wash of combined headlights, a huge winged creature glided and landed on the pavement.

Brady blared the patrol car's horn, slowed to a stop, and shone his spotlight on the winged creature. By instinct he flung open the door, pulled his gun, and aimed. He stepped around the door and his finger tightened on the trigger.

Jacques parked his Jeep behind the patrol car.

"Brady, no!" Forrest said. "Luna's too close. You might shoot her."

Brady noticed Luna and lowered the gun slightly.

"What the fuck is that thing?" Jinn asked, slumping in the rear seat.

"An enemy far worse than me," Forrest said, glancing over his shoulder. He opened his door and grinned. "Stay down. Unless you want it to kill you. If it strikes you with its weapon, you won't see the abyss. You'll cease to exist."

Jinn's eyes widened. He gasped. "It's one of the Fallen?"

Forrest nodded. "Yep. Stay hidden, Jinn. I want to be able to hate on you when this is over. Never say I wouldn't miss your company."

"Yeah, funny, Forrest. But don't worry, I'm one with the patrol car."

Forrest slammed the car door and laughed.

Luna fell to her side. The creature glanced at the bright headlights and the fierce spotlight from the patrol car. It shrieked like a predatory bird before it struck its prey.

"What the hell is it?" Brady asked, stepping to the side of Forrest.

"Something I thought I killed long ago," Forrest said in an even whisper.

Brady frowned.

Jacques stepped to the other side of Forrest and forced a smile. "You actually fought one of the Fallen?"

Forrest nodded. His eyes narrowed. "Yep."

Jacques shook his head. "And lived to tell about it. I knew when you were a boy that you were going to be an exceptional Hunter."

"Fallen?" Brady said. "Like a fallen angel?"

"That's what most folks call them," Jacques said. "But they're really from a different dimension. An ancient society some believe once lived on this planet."

Brady gave an incredulous stare. "Am I going have to search your car for marijuana or peyote?"

Jacques grinned. "Before you became a werewolf, did you think such creatures like us existed?"

Brady shook his head. "No."

"Be prepared to learn many more mysteries during your lifetime, provided we survive this."

"I get other paranormal creatures might exist, but the *different* *dimensions*? I've a hard time accepting that."

"Do you believe in a Heaven and a Hell?" Jacques asked.

"I've heard of them," Brady said, smiling. "Hard to believe either exists unless you actually see them. I've no plans for an early reservation for either."

"All right. Let's say you did believe in them. Wouldn't you consider those places to be in dimensions of their own? It's not like you can physically walk into Heaven, right? If one could, everyone would rush through the gates."

Brady nodded. "I see your point."

Two of the werewolves approached the winged beast with caution.

"Stay outside its reach," Forrest told them. "It has a nasty bite and a nastier sting."

"What?" Brady asked.

Forrest stepped forward. "Gadif! Remember me? I see your wings healed back nicely."

"Forrest," Jacques whispered, grabbing Forrest's arm. "You've no weapon capable of fighting it."

The Fallen creature straightened at the sound of Forrest's voice. It recognized him. Its human face contorted, becoming more birdlike with eyes blacker than a raven. It growled and shrieked an earsplitting, piercing cry.

"He's still fond of you," Brady said.

From the car, Jinn shouted, "Forrest has a memorable personalty, ya know? That's why everyone's *always* eager to see him again."

Forrest took another step toward Gadif. The winged creature clutched the limo driver by the throat and took to flight, disappearing into the dark cloudy sky.

"Dammit," Forrest whispered.

"We need to be better prepared to fight it," Jacques said.

"How can you kill it?" Brady asked.

Forrest watched the night sky. "The best way is to use its own weapon on it. But *taking* its weapon is easier said than done. I speak from my personal experience."

Brady's cellphone rang.

"Yeah?" Brady said. "We're at Micah's magic shop. Why?"

Forrest turned to listen.

"How far out are you?" Brady asked. He was silent for a moment. "Ah, that's fifteen minutes away. Sure, we'll wait for you."

"Who was that?" Forrest asked.

"Jacob. Remember the three witches that were once part of Nocturnal Trinity?"

Forrest nodded.

"Jacob's bringing them here. They've some important information to discuss."

"About what?" Forrest asked.

Brady shrugged. "I guess we're about to find out."

CHAPTER 58

Forrest squatted beside Blaze. Blaze opened his eyes. "You okay?"
Blaze nodded slightly, but his eyes remained disoriented.

Forrest helped Blaze to his feet and handed Brady the key to the front door of the magic shop. Luna clung to Blaze, supporting him like a human crutch. She wept uncontrollably and her eyes stared straight ahead in shock. Although he was in severe pain, he did his best to console her.

"Come on, you two," Forrest said. "We'll get you inside, make some tea, and get you warmer."

Jacques held open the door and let everyone enter ahead of him. Forrest offered a grim smile in passing. Were it not for the Fallen creature and figuring out who was behind Kailey's abduction, he'd love to sit and catch up with his uncle Jacques. He imagined the two of them could talk for several days and still not tire of listening to and telling stories.

But Jacques wasn't here for reminiscing. His concern was to find Micah. His worry tightened the wrinkles around his eyes. Whenever Forrest made eye contact with Jacques, Jacques turned away. His pain was too heavy. Forrest simply hoped when all this was over that he and Jacques could spend time together talking over a few drinks.

Without Jacques' advice and help when Forrest was a child, Forrest wouldn't be alive. Jacques was the one who had told Forrest about his calling of being a Vampire Hunter on the day a vampire had viciously attacked and nearly killed Forrest's father. Jacques' arrival on that day couldn't have been timed better. The revelation opened Forrest's eyes to the supernatural world surrounding him.

Jacques traveled with Forrest and his father for over a year before Jacques decided to sail to North America. With Forrest's father being a hopeless drunk, Jacques' absence weighed upon Forrest. He needed and wanted Jacques to continue traveling with them for moral support and as a mentor, even though Jacques was not a Vampire Hunter.

Not long after Jacques' departure with his new wife, Forrest lost his father and nearly lost his own life, but fate wasn't finished with Forrest or perhaps the deities simply wanted to punish and torment Forrest even more by keeping him alive.

Forrest thought about Micah and Micah's path of peace as a shaman. An odd choice for a werewolf to make, Forrest thought, but maybe Micah hoped to make and maintain his inner beast docile. But his path was far different than Jacques', as Jacques had been Catholic *before* becoming a werewolf.

Forrest understood grief. He had watched his father nearly die at the hands of a Baron vampire that had also killed Forrest's mother, only to later actually witness his father's death by another vampire. Forrest's grief, however, was short lived, and was quickly replaced by an insatiable need to seek vengeance. It hardened Forrest, encasing his heart within a massive shield of detachment. Love and emotions tended to distract from his goal to slay vampires and distractions made a Hunter vulnerable.

Jacques never asked about Forrest's father, probably because his father would have already died of natural causes nearly a century earlier, since he was a mere mortal. Forrest planned to eventually tell the tale of his father's demise to Jacques after they found Micah. Forrest had dealt with the loss, so he didn't need to mention it.

The others in the shop remained solemn. Jacques stood in a corner with several members of his pack. Blaze and Luna sat on the floor holding one another. Brady must have had Jinn come inside the shop rather than stay in the patrol car. Brady seemed unable to wipe the bewildered look off his face.

Forrest thought about the Fallen creature and the battle between them nearly a hundred years earlier during the first World War, somewhere in Austria.

Based on the Fallen's massive towering size, Forrest would've thought it invincible, until he actually fought the creature. To a normal human, perhaps it was indestructible. During their fight, after Forrest had broken its wings and legs, he flung its corpse off the side of a building and watched a war tank drive over it, crushing its body and leaving its remains in building rubble.

Even now, Forrest was certain it had been dead before it ever hit the street. Seeing it alive confused him. Was it immortal after all?

What bothered Forrest more was that it wasn't the ancient presence he sensed in Seattle. As disturbing as it was to see the Fallen beast, the supernatural power Forrest felt wasn't coming from it. He'd have recognized it as the source since they had been standing in such close proximity outside the magic shop. He didn't have any idea how or why this creature was alive and had arrived in Seattle, of all places. All Forrest knew was that he needed to find and destroy it. If it happened to kill demons and vampires before he did, all the better. Most likely, though, its pursuit was indiscriminate.

CHAPTER 59

*I*rina walked through the dark narrow corridor that led to the elevator where she and Nikolina had entered Nocturnal Trinity. Her mind was numbed by her shock and she felt hollow inside, knowing that Lorcan had killed her real father long ago. And her mother's affair and pregnancy were why Lorcan had killed her mother, too.

Irina had hated Lorcan before, but she loathed him far worse than ever.

Her footsteps were almost silent. The corridor was deceptively silent as well, and when she extended her finger to press the elevator button, Alec swept around in front of her.

"Where are you going, dear sister?" he asked. His intent sinister eyes searched hers.

"Outside."

"Why?"

She reached past him, pushed the button, and then she took a step back, waiting for the doors to open. "Father's gone."

"So?" Alec asked, shrugging. "Seems that's a better time for you to be here."

Irina shook her head. "The worst time, actually."

"Oh? Why's that?"

"He has the Wrathbone and the behemoths are still alive and well. I imagine their anger toward us, particularly *you*, is high enough they'd like to see us all dead should they escape."

Alec smirked. "Escape? It's not possible."

The elevator doors opened. She stepped inside and Alec slipped into the elevator with her without a second's hesitation.

"Dear brother, did it ever occur to you that father might have already freed them? Thus, seeing to it that we all meet our demise this evening while he seeks entertainment elsewhere with the Wrathbone safely in his possession."

Alec's brow furrowed. He swallowed hard. "Why would he do that?"

"It might be better to consider why he *wouldn't*."

"I'm sorry father mistreated you for all those years," Alec said, "and had the rest of us known, we'd have done what we could to free you. He punished you out of spite for mother's affair. It clearly was wrong and nothing justifies such cruelty. But he's not such a monster that he'd kill all of us."

"Those who lust for absolute power have no need for love, compassion, or mercy." Her gaze burned into his. "Bet you wish you'd kept your oath to Forrest now? I also imagine you probably wish you'd kept closer ties with the werewolves."

Alec forced a smile. "I'm trying to see the humor in your fictitious premonition about the behemoths being loose. You *want* to see me uneasy. Perhaps you want me to show signs of fear, but I've no reason to fear the behemoths."

"You've more reason than the rest of us do," she replied.

"Why's that?"

"You were the one who chained them to hold them against their wills. Remember? You took the Wrathbone from Forrest but you refused to let us approach the behemoths with you. The only way you could have gotten those behemoths to surrender themselves to be bound was by threatening to use the weapon on them. So yes, brother, if they're free, they're coming to find you first. Myself, I need to find Forrest and let him know our father is in Seattle."

"Do you plan to tell him about the behemoths?" Alec asked.

"He probably already knows."

"If you tell Forrest about father, Forrest will attempt to kill him."

Irina smiled. "Yes, I know. For the first time in my life, I've this bubbly feeling inside; something I've only heard about and recognized in pitiful humans. I find it most enjoyable. So, I've no qualms telling Forrest about father. Forrest has an old score to settle, and for how father treated me for decades, I hope Forrest is the victor."

Alec stared at her in disbelief. "Really? You hope that?"

"Of course. Don't you?"

"I'm ... torn. You realize that makes you almost as vile as he."

"No, it makes me better."

"How?"

Irina smiled. "How else can we get the Wrathbone back?"

Mayor Scottridge's entire body stiffened. He pressed his back against the leather seat of his Cadillac limo sedan and tilted his head upward, gasping in ecstasy. Sex before his turning had never heightened with such ravenous pleasure. He grabbed handfuls of the widow's hair as she knelt between his knees. Never had the heat of a woman's lips and mouth aroused him with intense vigor. He ached and feared he'd explode. Strange groans escaped his lips mixed with partial agony and immense gratification as she released his held back anguished satisfaction. He shuddered and his body relaxed.

After a heavy sigh, he opened his eyes to see Lorcan and Dr. Litman seated on the opposite seat watching. He flinched, seeing them there. Caught in his pleasurable rapture, he'd forgotten they were in the limo. The widow wiped her mouth and curled on the seat beside Scottridge, nuzzling her face against his chest. Her hands clung to him with unsatisfied longing and need.

"Looks like you picked a good one," Lorcan said. His eyes were blackened and the sharp tips of his fangs prominent, apparently reveling in his own arousal. "Quite … uh, skilled."

Dr. Litman took a handkerchief and wiped beaded sweat from his brow and then his upper lip. Litman wore shades, hiding his eyes. He turned to

Lorcan. "This younger generation holds far more experience than women in your past."

"Then I've awakened at a most opportunistic time," Lorcan said, grinning.

Scottridge panted, licked his lips, and attempted to straighten the widow's tousled hair with his fingers. "Oh, I never dreamed ... anything like this could be so damn good. I'm afraid if I were still human, I'd have had a heart attack just now."

Lorcan smiled. "Stick with me, mayor. It only gets better from here. Money, fame, any woman, or *man*, that you want. Pleasures galore, my new friend. Together, we're going to build a greater Seattle than the world ever imagined."

Scottridge rubbed the widow's cheek and smiled down at her. "I look forward to it."

The limo braked hard, causing the mayor and the widow to be hurled forward. They crashed into Litman and Lorcan. Then the car sped forward, sending all four of them into the floor between the seats.

Angered, Lorcan rose and pressed the intercom. "What the hell are you doing?"

"Sorry, sir, but something odd landed on the road ahead of us. I had to swerve to miss it."

"*What* landed on the road?"

"I—I don't rightly know. It was massive and ... it has huge wings."

Lorcan reseated himself and brushed his suit jacket with his hand, as did Litman. Scottridge was perplexed. He hardly understood the radical changes he had undergone in becoming a vampire. He was aware of demons, werewolves, and other vampires, but that was the limits of his awareness of the supernatural world he'd allowed himself to take new citizenship in.

His fangs involuntarily appeared and his eyes narrowed with a raging resolve to fight whatever was outside his limo that posed a sudden threat. For whatever reason, fear didn't overshadow him, even though he'd been a timid person before Orsovo turned him. The only real fear he suffered since he'd become a vampire was the clear threat Lorcan had given when he told Scottridge that he was only the mayor in appearance, but the office and acts passed were solely Lorcan's.

Yet, Scottridge sensed a darkness from outside the vehicle, much different than what Lorcan and his children were, and Scottridge understood that whatever it was, was pursuing them.

The roof of the limo buckled beneath a heavy thud. The widow cowered and screamed, still laying in the floor. The driver swerved the car side-to-side, apparently trying to unbalance whatever was buckling the roof. The driver hit the brakes again. The tires squealed and the car struck the side of a building, coming to a dead stop. The horn blared.

Scottridge pictured the driver dead and slumped against the steering wheel, but he didn't know if that was the case since the dark partition was still up.

Footsteps moved across the car's roof. Metal crunched and the horn ceased. The following moments of silence hovered in what seemed to be hours. The mayor exchanged glances with Lorcan and Litman.

Lorcan didn't seem fearful, but he was cautious. Without any of them speaking, each watched the roof as though wondering the same thing. Had the creature left?

The roof crumbled and thudded with the limo shaking slightly. The footsteps stopped directly over them. Again, silence that made even the undead's skin crawl. Lorcan's fangs appeared like sharpened picks. An echoing hiss eased from his throat and slithered out his mouth. Perspiration beaded Litman's brow.

The silence fled in an instant to the screeching of bent, torn metal. The roof peeled back, revealing the giant horrifying winged creature staring down at them. Its strange red birdlike eyes studied each of them.

Lorcan flashed his fangs and growled. His face contorted into the most unhuman form. Litman pulled the hidden short sword from his walking cane. Scottridge wanted to ask what this thing was, but words failed to become audible.

Scottridge snarled, fear and rage rose inside him, but he kept his eyes locked with the creature's. Such a beast, he never thought existed. Although the mayor was a neophyte vampire, he felt the vigor of greater strength than he'd had while merely a human. Since Lorcan was an elder vampire, as Orsovo described before introducing them to one another, Scottridge expected Lorcan's strength to be even greater. He wondered how Lorcan fared in a fight with this winged beast.

By all accounts, Scottridge expected that the three of them could fight this hellish foul creature and survive by at least injuring it enough to make it flee or they might be fortunate enough to kill it.

Litman stood and rammed his sword through its thigh, igniting its rage. The tip of the blade emerged and blood leaked from around the wound. Litman tugged the blade but wasn't able to yank it free. The Fallen creature reached down, grabbed Litman by the throat and hurled the heavy man somewhere down the street.

Scottridge glanced to Lorcan, hoping for some advice on how the two of them should attack. Lorcan's brow furrowed and in the blink of an eye, he was gone, leaving Scottridge and the widow in the car.

Stunned, the mayor searched the car, baffled that an elder vampire with such immense strength would flee and abandon him.

Scottridge was still learning what he was capable of as a vampire. Since no manual existed, he had hoped Orsovo and Lorcan would aid him in the necessary knowledge. Instead, he was left to fend for himself against a being that possibly lacked any vulnerability.

The Fallen shrieked in triumph, reached down and wrapped its massive right claws around the mayor's throat, and ripped Scottridge's head from his shoulders. Only a moment of pain registered with the mayor as intense heat blazed through his undead body.

No time to gasp a protest. Mayor Scottridge ceased to exist.

CHAPTER 61

$\mathcal{D}$r. Litman hit the ground about forty yards from the limo and rolled a half dozen times. He was surprised to be conscious after all the violent bouncing his obese body suffered.

Although his mind was alert, his body wasn't responding to his internal panicked desire to push himself to his feet and run. As bad as his left leg and right arm ached, he suspected both were broken, so he wasn't going to escape by running from the Fallen creature should it approach.

Rolling to his side, Litman discovered his vision was blurred. He patted his face and realized his glasses had fallen off when he struck the ground. Squinting, he noticed an obscure object a few feet away, which were probably his sunglasses. Without the sunglasses, even the most subtle flashes of light caused severe pain. His eyes could never adjust without the protective lenses to shield them. Despite his pain, he struggled to pull himself across the asphalt by crawling with only his left arm.

Panting, he took the glasses and put them on. The Fallen creature stood on the floorboard of the limo. The short narrow-bladed sword he had thrust into its leg didn't seem to affect it at all.

Litman caught a blur of movement as Lorcan escaped from the limo. Lorcan didn't pause to search for Litman, nor did he even look back for Scottridge. He fled, shooting through the shadows without a thought of helping the mayor or Litman.

"Bastard," Litman whispered. "I should've staked you while I had the chance."

Anger stirred inside Litman, but in his physical condition, he was helpless to pursue Lorcan. He couldn't even get to the limo in time to save Scottridge if he wanted; not that the mayor held any vital importance to Litman.

Still partially lying on his side, he watched in horror as the Fallen beast ripped Scottridge's head from his body. The head and body disintegrated into fiery ash.

Litman rolled over onto his back and groaned. He tasted blood as it seeped from his broken nose and trickled down his throat. Pain pulsed through his body. A moment later, the Fallen stood over him.

"Where's Kailey?" it asked in an odd voice. A human face materialized over its former birdlike one, almost like a mirage but Litman knew the reflection was real.

The question puzzled Litman, as Litman had been pursuing Kailey as well, at Lorcan's direct request. Had Lorcan summoned this Fallen creature to kill the mayor and Litman? Was that why Lorcan fled instead of fighting?

"Bastard," Litman whispered.

"Where's Kailey?" it repeated.

Litman shook his head. Pain radiated down his neck and into his spine. "I don't know. I've been looking for her. Did Lorcan summon you?"

The human face frowned. "Who is Lorcan?"

Litman gasped. "Never mind. Spare me, and I'll help you hunt for her."

"I've no need of you," it replied, placing a clawed foot to each side of Litman's head.

"In that case." Litman stretched, ignoring the burning pain in doing so, and he gripped the hilt of the short sword protruding through its leg and twisted.

The Fallen creature shrieked and howled in agony.

Knowing the blade held no chance of killing the monster, Litman placed more pressure anyway.

The winged beast flapped its wings. The muscles in its arms, chest, and back swelled in response to its rage. It lifted its uninjured leg and brought up its foot. With a swift stomp, it crushed Litman's head.

CHAPTER 62

Cassie stared out the window of Penelope's apartment. Kailey sat on the old cushioned chair, and slumped forward with her head resting in her hands. The black cat was curled on the arm of the chair.

Little had been said after Brady and the others left. An ominous feeling washed over Cassie. Like she had sensed Kailey was in trouble earlier in the day, that uneasiness seized her again, even though Kailey was within sight.

No one walked the streets, but she didn't expect to see any humans foolish enough to venture this area of the city after sunset anyway. Only demons and other paranormal creatures roamed. However, not seeing them didn't mean they weren't lurking outside. She couldn't shake the dark presence she'd perceived from earlier in the day when she and Penelope went to get a cab.

While Cassie held the curtain to the side of the window, Penelope slipped up beside her.

"You sense it, too. Don't you?" Penelope said softly, apparently not wanting to alarm Kailey.

Cassie let the curtain fall and cover the window. She nodded. "Do you think it was watching us earlier today?"

Penelope nodded. "I do. Was it one of the Fallen?"

Cassie shrugged and pursed her lips. "I cannot say for certain, but that's the sensation I recognized. How's Kailey doing?"

"She's still suffering a lot of pain."

Cassie bit her lower lip and pulled back the curtain again. "I'd like to say that she's safe here, but I don't think she is. None of us are."

"What should we do?"

Cassie sighed. "We wait. What else can we do? Maybe Brady and Forrest will return soon. Until then, we keep check on things outside."

Penelope glanced at Kailey for a moment and then she whispered, "I'm uneasy about that cat Kailey found."

"I am too," Cassie replied.

"Are you certain it's not a demon?"

"It's almost impossible for even the best shapeshifting demon to fool another demon."

"But it can happen?"

"Yes. Sadly, from time to time they go unnoticed by their peers. I still don't think the cat is or has a demon. It doesn't seem to want to cause her harm. It's a little protective of her, too. Like I said before, if Kailey was a witch, the cat responds to her like a familiar would, and that would be normal. The closest Kailey's been to a witch was ..." Cassie turned her head and her eyes narrowed while she studied the cat.

"What's wrong?"

"*Raven*," Cassie whispered. She released the curtain and walked toward the chair where Kailey sat. Cassie stopped and shook her head. "No, it's impossible."

"What?" Penelope said.

"The cat smacks of Raven's magic and aura, but it's not possible since I cut off Raven's head and she became smoldering ash. No remnants of Raven remained. No vampire ever returns after being decapitated. It can't happen."

The cat eyed Cassie. When their eyes met, the cat's eyes widened with alarm. The cat rose, bowed its back and stretched, and then climbed on Kailey's lap.

Cassie came closer. Her heels clicked on the floor. "Kailey, you mind if I ask you something?"

Kailey lifted her head, winced, and slowly pressed her back against the chair. "Sure."

The cat looked up at Kailey for a moment. Kailey shook her head slightly, and then the cat's eyes narrowed at Cassie.

"Where'd you find the cat?"

"In the warehouse. I grabbed it when the men started shooting at me. Why?"

"You risked your own life for a stray cat?" Cassie's eyes narrowed.

"Yes. Why?"

"You sure there's not more to the story?"

Kailey rubbed her eyes. "Like what?"

"Did it belong to Raven?"

Kailey jerked with shock and then frowned. "No. What ever made you think that?"

"Because I sense part of her is either infused with the cat or Raven cast a spell on it before she was slain."

Kailey adjusted in the chair and winced. "Cassie, I like that you worry over me sometimes—"

"A *lot* of times," Cassie said.

"And I appreciate that. But my head hurts so badly. The last thing I need is something else to trouble myself over. I'm not sure why you'd think that about the cat, but—"

"I'm sorry, Kailey," Cassie said. "You need to get some rest."

CHAPTER 63

Forrest stood with his back leaned against the inside wall of the magic shop. He faced the door. Jacques stood beside Forrest and drank hot tea. Neither spoke, allowing their thoughts to dictate their time. Both had developed patience for brooding and evaluating situations and circumstances.

After Jacques finished the tea, he set the cup and saucer on a table beside the loveseat where Blaze and Luna sat. She pressed the side of her face against Blaze and sobbed.

Jacques leaned toward them and smiled. "Do you two remember me?"

Forrest walked closer, wondering where they might have seen Jacques before.

Luna wiped away tears and glanced at him. She nodded. "Were you at the rental units when the vampires attacked us?"

"I was," Jacques replied with a broad smile.

"Thanks." Blaze weakly offered his hand to Jacques. While Jacques shook it, Blaze said, "You saved our lives. How many vampires did you slay?"

"Sixteen. The others fled. Next time, don't stay out past sundown. You took out a few, but you'd never have survived against the whole lot."

Brady eased the front door of the magic shop open, allowing Jaclyn, Raine, and Gillian to walk inside. Jacob came inside afterwards. Brady shook Jacob's hand and the two gave a quick brotherly embrace.

Jacques smiled at Luna. "You two can't seem to avoid the beasts, can you? First, vampires attacked you, and then the Fallen beast."

Luna became quiet. Her sobbing suddenly silenced. Her haunted eyes stared blankly.

Jacques flicked his gaze to Blaze. "What's wrong with her?"

Blaze cleared his throat. "That winged creature scared Luna far worse than all the vampires did."

"Why?" Forrest asked, stepping closer. "Tell us, Luna. You're safe with us."

Luna shook her head as though being aroused from deep sleep. She dried her eyes and nuzzled her head against Blaze's shoulder. With a sob-filled voice, she said, "That monster's face was Micah's."

Jacques' attention snapped to her. "Wait. What do you mean its face was Micah's?"

Luna turned slightly. Her red puffy eyes leaked tears. "It had Micah's face."

"That's impossible."

"I'm afraid it's not," Jaclyn said. She introduced herself and Gillian and Raine. "Did you know Micah?"

Jacques' eyes narrowed, darkened, like a wolf's.

Forrest detected by the tone of her voice and since she'd asked the question in past tense, most likely it meant Micah was dead. He placed a gentle hand on Jacques' shoulder.

"Micah's my son," Jacques replied. "What happened?"

She motioned to a round table with four wooden chairs. "Perhaps we should sit down for this."

"Recently, I've had nightmares with that Fallen creature in some of them. At least, I assume that's what the monster was. I never quite made the connection, until earlier. Micah's dead, isn't he?" Jacques said, looking into her eyes. "How did he die?"

Jaclyn's eyes moistened. She placed her hand atop his after he seated himself. "The creature killed him."

The floorboards creaked under Forrest's weight as he walked to the table. His facial features were grief stricken. "How?"

Jacques kept his eyes locked on Jaclyn. "Where did he encounter this creature?"

Jaclyn, Gillian, and Raine became uneasy, shrinking back together, fearful to reply. Finally, Jaclyn straightened and said, "We summoned it."

With indignation, Forrest and Jacques said, "What?"

CHAPTER 64

Forrest formed massive fists and leveled a glare of pure spite at the trio of witches. He fully understood why Gadif was back, but it wasn't the Gadif Forrest had killed. Jaclyn was a necromancer.

Fuming, spittle flew from Forrest's lips. "I fought that beast years ago. I killed it. It was *dead*. You didn't summon a Fallen being. You resurrected an undead version of it. How could you be so foolish?"

Jaclyn lowered her eyes. "In our defense, Forrest, Micah tricked us."

"*What?*" Jacques said.

"How?" Forrest asked.

Gillian nodded, folding her long delicate fingers in a prayerful manner. "It's true. He requested our help to summon an old vampire slayer to help him destroy the last four founding vampires of Nocturnal Trinity. We believed him."

"And you three offered to help?" Forrest asked.

"If you could rid Seattle of Flora's siblings, wouldn't you?" Jaclyn asked.

Forrest nodded. "Of course, but it's best to weigh the price beforehand. *Not* afterwards."

"Again, he tricked us."

"What was his deceit?" Jacques asked. The creases around his eyes deepened. Unlike Micah was known to have been, Jacques did not possess a peaceful, pleasant tone.

Raine leaned forward on the table, somewhat nervous. In a meek voice, she said, "When we arrived to help with the incantation, he'd already drawn the large circle with symbols and runes. He insisted he'd done so to save us time, but he had actually hidden another written spell beneath the first protective circle. His work was meticulous. It must have taken him half a day or more to draw it. His artful hands created such a spectacular pattern that we didn't notice the hidden spell."

"We trusted him," Jaclyn said, "so we didn't further inspect his work, which now we understand to be a costly mistake."

Jacques sighed. "If he wrote the spell, why did the Fallen creature kill *him?*"

"Since it's a necromancer's spell, a blood sacrifice is required. When the Fallen creature appeared in the center of the circle, Micah freely offered himself without a moment of hesitation," Gillian said. "By this time, we couldn't do anything to stop his actions. The beast pulled Micah into it. That's why Luna saw his visage. Micah's inside it."

Forrest and Jacques exchanged concerned glances.

Jaclyn wiped tears from her eyes. "I'm sorry. I truly am. We had no fore-knowledge."

"What was Micah's true purpose for summoning this beast and not a Vampire Hunter like he said he would?" Forrest asked.

Raine lowered her gaze. "He wanted it to kill Kailey."

"What?" Brady said. He walked to the edge of the table and glared at Jaclyn, but she refused to meet his gaze. "Why would Micah want to kill Kailey?"

"Revenge," Jaclyn whispered.

"Revenge?" Forrest said, confused.

Jacques shook his head. "No. That's completely contrary to Micah's nature."

"It's the truth," Gillian said.

"I cannot accept that," Jacques said. His jaw tightened.

"I understand," Raine said. "We thought the same, too, which is why we didn't mind aiding him with the summoning to bring forth an old Vampire Hunter. Micah had always fought for peace and issued love to others. But, he wasn't the same after we joined our magic for the incantation. He was darker. He wanted revenge. He wanted Kailey dead."

"Dead? But why? Revenge for what?" Brady asked.

"He said that she was the reason for the total disruption of everything we held dear and sacred in Seattle. Her arrival to Seattle was the beginning of the evil chain reaction that disrupted our lives."

"That's nonsense," Brady said.

"Normally, I'd agree," Jaclyn said. "But he traced it all back to when she arrived in Seattle to find out who had killed her brother. Kailey came for vengeance and everything else tumbled afterwards like a long winding line of falling dominoes. Had she never arrived, life as we knew it would've never altered to the degree it has."

Raine nodded. "Because of her, Micah had to release the pack from his spell that imprisoned their wolves."

"Which he should've done to start with," Brady said with anger rising in his voice.

"Because of that," Raine continued, "Eva died and Raven was turned into a vampire. Forrest ended Nicodemus' reign over Nocturnal Trinity, but that only led to more problems with Flora and Raven. Then problems arose with the behemoths. He insists that one issue led to another. Nothing was resolved. It simply got worse. He blames Kailey, and as much as I hate to agree, he's right that these problems started from the day she arrived. I don't agree that she should be killed. And although situations have grown worse, they're ultimately getting better."

"Why didn't you stop him after the Fallen arrived?" Forrest asked.

A grim expression tightened Jaclyn's face. "We could do nothing. The Fallen creature absorbed Micah, but because the creature had yet fully materialized, it moved like a ghostly figure without physical qualities. It passed through the wall with Micah. I'm guessing it has taken a physical form by now?"

Jacques sighed. "Unfortunately, yes."

"Then he's searching for Kailey."

Brady crossed his arms, fighting his internal beast's urge to turn. "And killing her does what exactly? It's not like he can change everything back."

"Actually, he can," Gillian said.

In unison, Brady and Jacques asked, "How?"

"Through a dimensional portal—" Jaclyn said.

"Bullshit!" Brady said.

"His grimoire indicates it's possible," Gillian said. "It dropped from his robe after he sacrificed himself."

Jaclyn sighed. "He spent an extensive amount of time with the research. But a lot of his information came from demons."

Forrest nodded. "Micah's right. Some of these dimensional creatures can alter time."

"Seriously?" Brady asked.

"Ever hear of Deja vu?" Forrest said.

Brady turned and scanned the room. "Jinn!"

Jinn came from the side room and crossed his arms.

"Have you heard what all's been said?" Brady asked.

"Even the best demon cannot block out all of your yammering?"

"I need a favor," Brady said.

"Ah, I see, now the incubus is *needed*? I have to agree with the consensus that Kailey set the world on its ear by coming to Seattle and sticking her nose where it doesn't—"

Forrest formed fists and stepped toward Jinn.

Jinn's eyes widened. "Of course, *my* opinion doesn't matter. I'm at your service. What do you need?"

"Teleport to Forrest and Penelope's apartment. With Cassie's help, the two of you teleport back with Kailey and Penelope," Brady said.

"That's a big order to fill."

"I realize that."

"I don't think that you do," Jinn said. "Teleportation is quite draining via one's self. Teleporting to a place and then back again with another person? Hell, man, that's a heavy energy drain. Not to mention that Cassie's already done this twice in less than a day—"

"Death's a heavier drain," Forrest said. "Either you help us or we'll let you sort out your differences with the behemoths."

"No, no. I'm not saying I *won't* do it. I'm saying that I might *not* be able to do it."

Forrest frowned.

"But, with my good nature and all, I'm willing to give it a go."

Jinn closed his eyes and flexed. His carved tattoos glowed like molten lava. A second later, he was gone.

A worried expression furrowed Brady's brow. "You think he went to do that or did he flee?"

Forrest sighed. "We can hope that he's on our side and did as you asked. For now, all we can do is wait."

CHAPTER 65

Kailey shrieked and Cassie's eyes widened when Jinn materialized in the center of the room. Penelope grabbed her crossbow off the table and spun toward Jinn.

"It's me!" Jinn said, staggering slightly. "Brady sent me! Don't shoot!"

Kailey said, "Why'd Brady send you here?"

"Your life is in danger," Jinn said.

"Tell us something we *don't* know," Cassie said, resting her hand on her hip.

"No, I mean right at this moment. Like, right now." Jinn looked at the door.

"What do you mean?" Kailey asked.

"That Fallen creature was summoned by Micah with the help of the three witches. Somehow, Micah's inside it. He summoned it so he could kill Kailey."

Cassie's jaw tightened and her eyes blazed red. "What?"

Jinn nodded. "It's here to kill Kailey."

That bastard! Raven said.

"Why me?" Kailey looked confused. "Micah has no reason to kill me."

"We don't have time to discuss it. But, it's true, girl. Seriously, it's true. Brady sent me to teleport you back and he wants Cassie to bring Penelope." Jinn shot a quick glance at Cassie.

Cassie shook her head. "More than anything, I'd like to help, but because of your damned drugging me incident, I teleported twice within hours. I don't have the physical energy to do it again. I could die."

"We're all going to die if we stay here," Jinn said.

Cassie sighed. "Jinn, take Kailey back. I'll stay here with Penelope and we'll fend off the Fallen creature."

"Look, Cassie, I'm not allowing you to stay behind," Jinn said.

"So you *want* me to die?"

"No."

The outside metal stairs creaked and groaned.

"Shit!" Jinn said. "That's the Fallen beast, isn't it?"

"It's not Avon," Cassie said.

Raven laughed. *I'm beginning to like her.*

"Okay, there might still be a way I can lessen the mental and physical strain on you," Jinn said.

Kailey stood, cradling the cat in her arms, and winced.

"How's that?" Cassie asked.

"We form a circle," Jinn said. "A tight circle. I pool some of your magical energy into mine, and the vast strain falls on me. But, you must promise me something in return."

Cassie cocked a brow and pursed her lips. "Oh? And what's that?"

"No future beatdown over what happened earlier." Jinn offered a hopeful smile. "We call it even?"

Cassie stared at him with scorn.

The metal stairs groaned and bent. A loud crash echoed outside the upper apartment door, which meant the stairs had collapsed.

Jinn nervously looked at the door and then flicked his questioning stare at Cassie.

Cassie shook her head. "Okay, fine!"

"Everyone join hands," Jinn said, waving everyone closer. He looked at Kailey. "You're seriously going to take the cat?"

Hell, yes! Raven said.

Kailey offered a slight nod, afraid to further her splitting headache.

Cassie sighed. "Kailey, you and I need to talk about that cat."

Aww, Raven said. *Don't blow it. I was just getting to like you.*

"The stairs might've collapsed," Jinn said, "but that doesn't mean we've a lot of time."

Kailey stood between Cassie and Penelope and held hands with them. Jinn stood directly across from her.

Cassie said, "Where are we teleporting to?"

"Micah's magic shop," Jinn whispered. "Everyone's been there, right?"

Kailey and Cassie nodded.

"What about you, Penelope?" Jinn asked.

"Once."

"Okay, good. Everyone close your eyes and focus on the shop. Inside is preferable. Visualize it. Think of nothing else," Jinn said softly. "Keep picturing and keep a firm hold on one another's hands."

A coldness washed over Kailey and what seemed to be a circling wind spun around her. The floor beneath her disappeared. She flexed her right foot and nothing but air was under her. She gasped. The pit of her stomach tickled, but like striking her funny bone against something, she found no humor in it.

Wind howled around her. She wanted to open her eyes, but fought the urge, uncertain if some type of debris might cut her eyes.

The wind ceased suddenly. Her feet plopped on the floor, jarring her slightly. The cat leapt from her arms. She opened her eyes. They were inside the magic shop. Cassie lay sprawled on the floor, unconscious. Blood leaked from her nose and mouth.

Horror seized Kailey. She rushed to Cassie and knelt beside her.

"Please be okay," Kailey whispered.

Although weak and profusely sweating from exhausting his strength, Jinn knelt beside Cassie, too.

"Here," Gillian said. "Move aside. After Jinn informed us of the dangers with teleportation, we mixed up a healing potion."

Kailey backed away, allowing Gillian to use a dropper to feed the liquid into Cassie's open mouth.

CHAPTER 66

Irina walked through Nocturnal Trinity and stopped at the bar in the Demon sector. Maggie wiped the bar with a towel and stopped when she noticed Irina's approach.

Irina's graceful steps appeared as though she glided on air. Ignoring the seated guests at the bar, she directed her attention at Maggie. "Where's Jinn? I need to speak to him."

Maggie grinned, showing her pointy yellow teeth. "Haven't seen him this evening. He left with Brady and Forrest this morning."

Irina frowned. "Jinn left with them? Voluntarily?"

Maggie shrugged. "I wasn't here. I was told their conversation became confrontational and that Jinn challenged them to meet him outside. Jinn never returned."

Thinking aloud, Irina said, "Did they take him into custody?"

"Wasn't here. Don't know," Maggie said in a deeper, agitated tone.

"Thanks," Irina said. In the blink of an eye, she was gone.

Irina entered the vampire VIP room silently. Her thoughts were on why Jinn had left the nightclub with Brady and Forrest, more out of curiosity than concern. But if he were still with Forrest, the advantages were in Irina's favor. She wanted to talk to Forrest so she could inform Forrest about Lorcan's arrival. She only wished to talk to Jinn to ask where she might find Forrest.

After the death of the behemoth, and Jinn's betrayal—at least in Alec's eyes—Jinn suffered horrendous torture from the remaining behemoths while her two brothers watched. She imagined Orsovo and Alec held no pity for Jinn. Nikolina never said whether she'd accompanied their brothers or not. However, Irina conveniently made herself unavailable.

Alec and Orsovo kept portions of Jinn's skin and had them tanned. She knew her brothers' dark streaks were like their father's, but lately she discovered that their evil continued to magnify more and more the longer they lived.

Overall, Irina liked Jinn. For a demon, she favored conversations with him over the majority of the visiting mature vampires. He was witty but blunt, and he never hesitated to help her when she asked, but that was before her brothers allowed his torture. After he healed, he never fully viewed Irina without skepticism and suspicion. She didn't blame him.

Irina detested how Alec and Orsovo treated Jinn after he banished Diaboch to the abyss. She wouldn't have objected if he'd sent all of the behemoths to the abyss. They made her uneasy and she always believed they were scheming to teeter the balance of Nocturnal Trinity in their favor before Alec dissolved the Circle of Unity.

She eased the VIP door closed. To her relief, no vampires or desperate wannabes were seated in the lounge and for that, she was thankful. The evening was still early, but she expected within the next hour or so that the lounge would be packed. For a vampire, time was limitless; but being in the lounge to get what she needed without being noticed, she didn't have much time at all.

Irina glanced at the lounge door and craned her neck slightly, listening for any sounds outside the door. Content that no one was at the door, she pressed her palm against a small panel near the darkest corner of the room. It clicked, moving inward. A narrow panel slid into the wall, barely giving her slender body enough room to squeeze through.

Once she moved past, the panel sealed shut again. She stood inside their hidden office. She hurried to the polished desk.

"Where is it?" she whispered, searching through the desk drawers. She shook her head. "It has to be here somewhere."

After looking through the last desk drawer, she turned to the filing cabinet. The third drawer down, she flipped over a flat manila file and found a rectangular silver device that was similar to a cellphone but larger. She picked it up and sat in the plush desk chair. She pressed a button and waited for the screen to load.

Not only had Alec and Orsovo allowed the behemoths to peel large portions of Jinn's skin from his arms and legs, they inserted a GPS tracker into each of his upper thighs after Jinn lost consciousness. If Jinn went rogue again, they wanted to make certain they knew his whereabouts at all times. The one thing her brothers hadn't counted on was Irina's eavesdropping and her learning about their shady scheme and the tracking device.

A red dot blinked on the screen. With her index finger and thumb, she zoomed in to see the location on Seattle's city map. Then, to her surprise, the dot vanished. After zooming out, she found that the dot had moved halfway across the city in the blink of an eye. Surely, it was a glitch.

"Odd," Irina whispered.

The battery light indicated the tracking device needed charged, so she plugged it into the adaptor beside the desk. She figured the sudden movement was perhaps nothing more than an anomaly due to the low battery.

While giving the charger time, she looked at the split computer screen that showed live footage from twelve different cameras at various vantage points inside and outside of Nocturnal Trinity. None of the cameras showed the room where the behemoths were being kept. She half expected the reason was so she and Nikolina never discovered them still alive. She wished she could view the room without physically entering it, which she would never do alone for fear of being overpowered by the behemoths. Since Lorcan possessed the Wrathbone, she could fight the behemoths for days and never harm one of them.

Irina watched each camera for several seconds in order of its box on the screen. When she got to the twelfth, she noticed a small arrow pointing downward. She touched the arrow on the screen. The screen with the twelve different cameras flipped upward and six more camera angles filled the next split screen. Her mouth fell open.

The behemoths were somehow caged inside glowing silvery-barred cages. They weren't dead, but they weren't able to get past the enchanted bars. Any time their hands touched a bar, the behemoth yanked back its hand and roared. She wondered who had placed such a powerful spell on the cages since the witches were no longer a part of the Circle of Unity.

Irina glanced to the next camera screen. Serge's and Costel's wrists were locked inside cuffs held by chains above their heads. The chains were only long enough to allow the tips of their toes to touch the floor.

Her father wanted to pit these two shifters against one behemoth, which sounded almost like a fair fight. Seeing how they were being held captive, compared to the behemoths, these two didn't have a chance to survive. Even if they weren't hanging and shackled, one behemoth could rip them apart in less than a few minutes.

Lorcan didn't intend for them to survive. The blood and gore of the match would cause all the visiting elders to praise the host of these festivities. Even though Alec had done the majority of setting it up, the glory would befall Lorcan, and she despised him even more for taking the spotlight.

The tracking device beeped. Jinn's dot returned to its original place on the map, but this time she didn't believe it was a glitch.

Zooming in, Irina retrieved the address.

"Micah's Magic Shop?"

It made sense somehow. Her intuition told her that she'd find Forrest there. On the computer screen, she brought down the screen of the original twelve camera angles. She took a moment to find the live footage of the hidden camera in the vampire lounge. To her relief, no one had entered yet. She rose from the desk chair and slipped to the narrow panel. Now, if only she could get out of Nocturnal Trinity without any of her siblings noticing.

CHAPTER 67

"Will Cassie be okay?" Kailey asked, frantically meeting Jaclyn's gaze.

Jinn's brow furrowed with concern. Kneeling beside Cassie, Jinn placed his hand to her forehead. "Come on, girl. Pull yourself out of this. You're a lot tougher than this."

Jaclyn placed a hand on his shoulder. "Give the potion time."

"We might not have that kind of time," Forrest said.

Jinn stood. "Forrest's right. We don't."

Forrest grinned. "Good to see you're coming around to my kind of thinking."

Jinn ignored the jab. "Tell 'em, Kailey. That Fallen creature was already outside Penelope's apartment door."

Kailey nodded.

"You saw it?" Forrest asked.

"No," Jinn said, "but the rusted stairs broke away from the side of the building and crashed. I figure it *has* to outweigh you, Forrest. Don't take that as a compliment, by the way."

Forrest said, "Then it won't be long before it comes back here."

"Damn," Brady said.

Jinn swallowed hard. "How would it know to return here?"

"Two demons suddenly leaving the same apartment?" Forrest shrugged.

"Being what it is, I've no doubt it can follow your path like a hound tracks a rabbit's scent."

Jacques scratched his bearded chin. "We cannot keep running away from it. We must stand against it and fight."

Forrest nodded. "I agree."

"Is there a way to destroy it?" Jacques asked.

"When I killed it before," Forrest said. "It wasn't undead, so my method won't work a second time."

"How *did* you kill it?" Brady asked.

"I crushed it to death." He looked at Jaclyn. "The blame for this creature being alive again is on you, regardless of your ignorance to what you thought Micah's plans were."

Jaclyn sighed and closed her eyes, remaining silent.

"Look," Brady said, "we don't have time for trial and error. It's probably flying to our location now. How do we destroy it?"

Jaclyn looked at Gillian. "There's really only one way."

"How?" Jacques asked.

"We reverse the incantation," Jaclyn replied. "The only problem is that we'd need another powerful witch."

"Why?" Kailey asked.

"Four of us summoned it here. We need four to banish and send it back from where it came."

Me. Pick me! Me! Raven said.

Kailey ignored Raven. "What about Luna?"

That peabrain?

Kailey frowned at the cat.

Jaclyn shook her head. "No, while she could handle lesser spells, she's not mastered magic to what's required for her to participate. Besides, look at her. She's suffered too much trauma to be effective with any task."

Kailey glanced at Luna and saw the shattered expression on the young lady's face. Blaze kept one arm around her and his cheek pressed against her forehead. Luna was in no shape for minor magic.

Pick me, Raven. Please?

The cat mewed continuously.

Cassie opened her eyes, shook her head, and stared at the cat. She scooted away from it. "What's wrong with your damn cat, Kailey? Can't you quieten it down?"

Tell them, Raven said. *I'll help any way possible.*

"Is that even possible?" Kailey asked, staring at the cat.

"Is what possible?" Brady said.

Yes! Raven purred and paced back and forth with odd little cat cries.

"I think your cat has worms," Cassie said, trying to get up.

Hey! Raven hissed and spat at the succubus.

Kailey scooped Raven up. "We have the fourth witch right here."

"You know you're holding a cat, right?" Jinn said, cocking a brow. "Did the teleport swirl your brain, too?"

"It sounds crazy," Kailey said, "but Raven possessed the cat after her vampire form was slain."

"*What?*" Brady and Cassie said together.

Forrest frowned. "That's impossible."

Kailey explained what had happened and how Raven had helped save Kailey from Serge and Costel at the warehouse.

Brady placed a hand to her cheek and stared into her eyes. "Are you … okay?"

"I'm fine. My aches have subsided."

Jinn said, "So, you're saying Raven's in the cat and I'm guessing that she's able to speak to you even though she's a … cat."

"Yes. Telepathically. Believe me, when she first spoke to me, I thought I'd gone crazy."

"Girl, I've not quite given up on that theory," Jinn said.

Cassie frowned at the cat. "I knew there was something odd about that feline. Even if what you say is true … After all you've gone through, Kailey, how could you possibly trust her?"

"Look, all of this I'll discuss later," Kailey said. "But time's not on our side. Jaclyn, Raven believes that she can still aid in the incantation as a cat. Is that true?"

Bewildered, Jaclyn offered a shrug and an uneasy smile. "I don't know. I've never heard of what she's done as having happened before. She found her soul after losing it when she turned into a vampire. I don't know if she can or not. All we can do is try."

"Where did you do the incantation?" Kailey asked. "Don't you need to use the circle of protection Micah had used?"

"We can't," Jaclyn said.

"Why not?"

"The rain has probably washed it away by now," Jaclyn replied.

Kailey's heart sank. "You said that it probably took Micah *hours* to draw the circle with the hidden spell. We don't have that kind of time, and if rain washed it away, there's nothing we can do."

"The rain might've washed it away," Gillian said, "but each of us took pictures of it with our phones."

"What good does that do?" Kailey said. "It would still need to be drawn."

Jaclyn smiled and stood. "What we need is a solid summoning circle to superimpose the image onto and we can perform the ritual."

"And where are you going to find one of those?" Brady asked.

"We all know where one is, but getting access is greater problem," Gillian said.

"Where?" Kailey asked.

Jaclyn grinned. "In the basement of Nocturnal Trinity. Where else?"

CHAPTER 68

"*N*octurnal Trinity?" Kailey said. "It'd be a cold day in Hell—pardon the expression Cassie and Jinn—before they'd let all of us inside."

Forrest cracked his knuckles. "We take the underground tunnel we used the first time we attacked the vampires and demons. That's the closest route to that stone circle, provided it's been repaired."

Jinn said, "It was repaired."

"You know this for certain?" Jaclyn asked.

Jinn nodded. "Yes. They used parts of my flesh in the sacrifice to fix it."

"Ugh," Cassie said with a slight shiver. "Sorry, Jinn."

Blaze timidly walked to the table. "Forrest, there's someone at the door. I figure you should be the one to decide whether or not to let her in."

Forrest frowned. "Who is it?"

"Irina. She pleaded for me to invite her in. She says that it's urgent. But since you're the Vampire Hunter, I'm leaving that decision to you."

"Thanks," Forrest said. He pulled a stake from his coat pocket before looking at the others. "I'll be right back."

At the door, Forrest greeted Irina with a stern frown. She glanced at the stake in his huge hand but didn't flinch, nor did she flee. He rather admired her boldness since she knew who he was. With his peripheral vision, he looked for movement in case she had not come alone. His insight detected no other vampires lying in wait.

"Forrest, I've only come out of urgency, as an ally and not an enemy, contrary as that sounds," Irina said. "I'm prepared to offer the rest of my undead days to you should you choose to stake me. I won't fight or resist, but please, hear me out first."

Of all Flora's siblings, Irina was the one he knew the least about, which meant he'd still keep a close eye on her movements. Yet, he discerned no malice in her words and a sincerity few vampires kept after becoming one of the undead.

Forrest half shrugged. "I'm listening."

"Yes." Irina nodded, offering a meek smile that made her pale skin and brilliant eyes even more pleasant. "A great evil has arrived in Seattle, as I'm sure you're aware."

Forrest nodded. "I've felt it for a couple of weeks. We're preparing to kill it."

"It?" she asked with a confused frown. "To what are you referring?"

"The Fallen beast."

"Ah, I see." Her expression didn't change. She remained confused.

"Is that not why you've come?"

Irina shook her head. "No. I was speaking of ... father."

"Lorcan?" Forrest's voice deepened and his jaw tightened. Rage set in his eyes. "He's in Seattle?"

Irina nodded and smiled, almost gleeful in seeing Forrest's heated anger.

"*Why* is he here?" Forrest asked.

"Alec invited him."

"So you've known that he was still alive?"

She shook her head. "No. We all thought him dead. Alec only found out recently. I only found out hours ago, and by accident I should add. Honest."

Forrest studied her eyes, trying to read them. Nothing about her tone or gaze indicated she had come to deceive him. He wondered if her slight happiness surfaced because she'd gotten a rise out of him by mentioning her father's name. "So what is it that you want?"

"Slay Lorcan, Forrest, and do us all a favor."

Forrest's brow rose. He didn't expect such a request and he couldn't hide his surprise. "You want me to slay your father?"

Irina released a short hysterical burst of laughter mixed with a mournful tone. A delirious moment one often suffered after tragic news, right before a heavy downpour of tears gushed out. Her eyes shimmered like rare jewels. "You see, Lorcan killed my *real* father a couple hundred years ago. Lorcan raised me to believe he was my father, but I learned the truth today. Not to say that I've not wished death on him ages ago. I plotted to kill him often because of his constant brutal treatment on me. I despise him above any other."

"And what of your brothers and sister? How does this bode with them? I've already slain Nicodemus and all of you offered Flora to me. How would they view me after I've slain Lorcan?"

"Father ... *Lorcan* almost cut Alec's head off earlier today. He wants to put the four of us into hibernation."

Forrest frowned. "Hibernation?"

"Yes. For *our* benefit, he said. But I detect he's lying. He wishes to rule Seattle and then the state. I won't stand for it. I can't allow it. Alec fears him greater than ever before. He won't stand against father—he *lacks* the backbone—but he won't shed a tear if you or someone else slays Lorcan."

"I see. And where is Lorcan now?"

Irina sighed and straightened the front of her dress with her hands. "He left Nocturnal Trinity with the mayor to discuss plans and get a tour of the city. Orsovo turned the mayor, more as a ploy to run the politics and control the city. Lorcan has eagerly capitalized on subduing the mayor as his own pawn."

Forrest's jaw tightened. Lorcan's hope to control the city possibly explained why one of the city council members was dead. He probably objected to the new decisions that the undead mayor was suggesting. The weapon could only have belonged to Lorcan, so Forrest could claim that puzzle solved. Lorcan had probably stashed all his medieval weapons and traps ages ago. Torture, to him, was all pleasurable games. He'd never trash such devices.

Irina seemed uncomfortable with Forrest's silence. She straightened slightly. "Will you do your duty as a Vampire Hunter and slay Lorcan? I know you've probably longed to drive a stake through his heart for betraying you nearly a century ago. I'm ... I'm sorry for the loss of your father. I'm also sorry for rambling so, as this is off the subject, but you and I have that loss in common. Fueled together, we can rid the world of him."

Forrest stepped outside the magic shop and pulled the door shut. Despite her being so much shorter and dainty in appearance, Forrest didn't question how deadly she could be in one unguarded split second. He read in her mannerism of the aching heartache she'd endured under Lorcan's control and he held no doubt she sought revenge on an equal level as he did. Perhaps more. She and Forrest shared an identical goal. Both would be thrilled at Lorcan's demise.

Irina nervously unfolded her hands at her waist. She closed her eyes and calmly pressed her hands against her legs, giving him an unblocked angle to stake her. "Please? Give an answer before shoving that stake through my heart. Surely, you can offer such a courtesy."

Forrest cleared his throat and loosened the hold on the stake. "I give you my oath as a Vampire Hunter this evening. I'll slay your father, but I'll not slay you tonight, Irina. I will, however, ask a favor in return."

Her eyes opened in surprise and her brow furrowed. Her reply came as a hushed whisper. "Anything."

"To kill this Fallen undead beast, we need access to your summoning stone beneath Nocturnal Trinity. Jinn informed us that the stone had been repaired."

She nodded. "It has."

"To get there, we need a distraction."

Irina smiled and offered a curtsy. "I'm honored to assist you."

CHAPTER 69

Forrest stood outside the magic shop with Irina. He almost expected her to sprint into the night, but she lingered. He wondered if she were waiting for his invitation into the magic shop or if she had more she needed to say.

"There's something else, isn't there?" Forrest asked.

Irina met his gaze and nodded. "Father has an entourage of elder vampires from the Black Forest."

"How many?"

"A half dozen."

Forrest crossed his huge muscled arms and frowned. "So we should expect a battle?"

Irina pursed her lips. "The elders came at Alec's invitation, to his *festivities,* as he termed it. After Lorcan almost cut off Alec's head, my brother is no longer pleased that he hosted the event at Nocturnal Trinity, nor does he look forward to being in Lorcan's presence again. The elders arrived, I'm guessing, to pay their respects to Lorcan's long absence. Whether they'd risk their lives to protect him, I cannot say. They seemed indifferent at the chaos that occurred over dinner and kept their thoughts to themselves."

"Chaos?"

Irina explained Lorcan's bitter heated reaction to Alec handing Flora over to Forrest. "Flora was father's favorite."

"I know," Forrest replied. His eyes softened. "I remember."

"Their goals and attitudes were also identical. With the news, that's why Lorcan came close to decapitating Alec. After he refrained, he set his new ambition on hunting and killing you. But, he also sent others to take Kailey."

The news was somewhat expected but jarring as well. This meant, both Lorcan and Micah held near identical missions and they weren't even allies. Each blamed Kailey, as though she were the stern hand of Fate that destroyed unfinished, impossible plans. Forrest knew Micah and Lorcan would never work in direct cahoots, but their ideology was the same.

"Two of the men that had taken Kailey are still alive, but they're being held prisoner in the basement of Nocturnal Trinity." She pointed at the limo parked near the shop. "I believe that limo belongs to the man hired to take Kailey."

"I'm not sure who the driver was, but the Fallen creature carried him off into the night. I'm fairly certain the man's dead."

"If it's Litman's limo, *he* left with the mayor and Lorcan."

Forrest shrugged. "Jinn told us that Alec never sent the behemoths back to the abyss. Is that true?"

Irina nodded. "Yes. Those two men are being restrained to be thrown into a pit with one of the behemoths later. I suppose fat—Lorcan wants to prove his ruthfulness to the vampire elders."

"Would Alec return the Wrathbone to me, so I can do what he promised he'd do?"

Irina bit her lower lip. "Alec gave it to Lorcan."

"What?" Rage exploded inside Forrest. He fought not to yield to his grizzly beast that was suddenly clawing its way to the surface.

For the first time since Forrest stepped outside to speak to Irina, her eyes filled with fear and she took a few steps back.

"Why did he do such a foolish thing?" Forrest asked.

Irina shrugged. "Duty? Obligation? Fear? He regrets the decision, especially after Lorcan placed the dagger to Alec's throat."

"That's a bit late for regret."

"I agree. Although Alec assumed Nicodemus' position after you slayed him, he's not good at making leadership decisions."

"Then why didn't you challenge him?"

"I didn't know he was giving it—"

"No, why didn't you challenge him for rank? Why allow Alec to reside over Nocturnal Trinity?"

Irina sighed. "I held no interest in assuming it, nor did Nikolina. Orsovo … He's not much better in his decisions either. My thinking is that Alec wanted to appease Lorcan, hoping to strengthen our inner circle in Nocturnal Trinity."

"You realize that will never occur, right?" Forrest took a deep breath to further calm himself. "After your trinity shattered, you have little hope of ever mending it. Too much mistrust is what crushed your Circle of Unity in the first place. Now, none of you could set aside your skepticism toward others to rebuild what was lost. You'll hold suspicions at all times."

"I was willing to suspend my mistrust by placing my trust in you," Irina said. "And that's far more than I'd do for any of my half siblings."

"Only because we share a common goal."

"No," Irina said. "Not *only*. Lives were lost under my father's reign. Those who were most precious to us. I've held in my regret for so long, but more so for the things I never followed through with."

"Like what, exactly?"

"I was being honest in my admission of plotting to kill Lorcan."

"What stopped you?"

"I wasn't callous enough?" she shrugged. "Truth be told, had I known Lorcan had killed my real father and that he was a fiendish imposter in my life, I'd have been better calculated. I've have destroyed him without hesitation or question. Because I didn't, we both lost."

Forrest studied the sparkle in her eyes and smiled. "Is it a bad thing that you aren't calloused and cold like Flora and Nicodemus?"

Irina laughed softly. "For a vampire? Those aren't qualities one lacks."

"Maybe not. So back to my favor. Can you help us get to the summoning stone?"

"Yes. I think I know a way."

"One more question," Forrest said.

Irina nodded. "Okay?"

"Do you think you can get your siblings to side with us in the slaying of your father and the other elders?"

"It's possible since none of us wants Nocturnal Trinity to be taken over by other vampires, demons, or witches."

Forrest extended his hand to her. She reached for it without hesitation.

But Forrest wasn't offering to shake her hand. Instead, he took her icy cold hand into his and walked to the door.

"I invite you inside," Forrest said. "We've much to discuss but little time to act. The Fallen creature also wants Kailey dead. It's already been at the shop, so I've a feeling that it's already on its way back. Since it's also undead, killing it might be impossible."

CHAPTER 70

Forrest opened the door and allowed Irina to enter the shop first. All eyes flicked to her but everyone remained silent. Some stared at Irina with skepticism. Others seemed suspicious of her intent.

Although weak, Cassie stood and stepped in front of Kailey.

Forrest stepped forward and said, "Irina has come to ally herself with us."

"For what reason?" Brady asked with his arms crossed. "According to Jinn, Alec never kept his word, so why should we believe she will."

"Because she's given me vital information that also concerns Kailey's well-being. Not only does Micah hope to kill her, but a near ancient vampire does as well."

"Who?" Kailey asked, peering around Cassie.

"My father," Irina said.

Before a barrage of questions ensued, Forrest said, "I've dealt with her father, Lorcan, nearly a century ago. He's part of the reason for my father's death."

"And my real father's death," Irina said.

Everyone held their silence but their facial expressions expressed pity.

"You have my word that I will do everything possible to help slay Lorcan. Not only did he kill my real father, he later killed my mother for her unfaithfulness."

Jinn cleared his throat. "Of all the remaining founders of Nocturnal Trinity, I'd vouch for Irina over all the others. She's never betrayed her word to me."

"Thank you, Jinn," Irina said.

"Look," Forrest said. "We'd best leave this shop. Gadif's already been here. He most likely is tracing Jinn's teleport passage and could arrive at any time. We have another obstacle."

Brady frowned. "What?"

"Lorcan has the Wrathbone."

Penelope growled.

"And at least six elder vampires are inside Nocturnal Trinity," Forrest said. "Since Lorcan has the Wrathbone, he can use threats to get the four behemoths to do whatever he demands. Jaclyn, get any supplies you might need and let's load up in the vehicles outside. If the keys are in the limo, we'll use it, too."

Jacob smiled. "If the keys aren't inside the limo, I can hotwire it."

Brady shook his head and grinned. "Jacob, call any available pack members and have them meet us at Nocturnal Trinity."

"Not at the front entrance," Forrest said. "We must enter through the underground tunnels."

"No," Irina said, "I've a way to get inside faster. Tell them to meet at the third floor of the parking garage across the street."

Forrest motioned toward the door. "Let's load up and finish this."

CHAPTER 71

Kailey sat in the rear of the limo with Raven curled on her lap. Cassie was seated beside Kailey. Jaclyn, Raine, and Gillian sat across from them. Irina rode in the passenger seat with Jinn driving.

Kailey projected her thoughts to Raven. "Are you certain you can help with this summoning incantation?"

You think I'd lie about that?

"No. Not intentionally. I'm just wondering since you've never done it before, how you know that you can?"

Kailey, I studied magic most of my life. I've studied things I never disclosed to you. Black magic, gray magic, white magic ... the vein of magic doesn't matter. I've studied each extensively. Being near Salem made that easy. I visited elder witches that allowed me to read tomes older than the country we live in. Some allowed me to practice with them. With your life in danger, believe me, I wouldn't volunteer to help them if I didn't know how, because the consequence could be your death. You know I'd never risk chancing that.

"Okay," Kailey thought. "I trust you."

Cassie gave Kailey a side-glance. "The cat's talking to you?"

It's Raven! The cat narrowed its eyes.

Kailey smiled. "Yes."

Jaclyn adjusted herself in her seat. "I know you're not a witch, Kailey, but we will need you to stand in with Raven at the summoning stone since you're the only one that she speaks to."

"Okay? What do you need me to do?"

"Nothing major. Just hold her and repeat the chant with her."

Kailey nodded. "Sure. But how are we going to get the Fallen creature to us?"

"We're going to summon it."

Cassie's eyes widened. "What?"

Jaclyn smiled. "Yes. We summon it to the circle and then after it appears, we will begin the chant to banish it from this Earth forever."

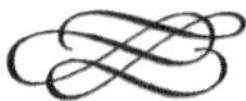

CHAPTER 72

After twenty minutes of riding in the rear of the limo, Kailey grew apprehensive as Nocturnal Trinity came into view. Dozens of people lined the street and sidewalks, ever hopeful that they'd get an invitation to enter.

Just like old times, eh? Raven asked. *People* dying *to get inside.*

Kailey didn't reply. She swallowed hard against the sudden burning tears welling in her eyes. She took a deep breath and fought those tears. The memories of the first day Kailey stood in that line haunted her. And the reason for why Micah wanted to kill her by summoning the Fallen beast made sense.

She marveled at how she'd never noticed it before or why she'd never made the connection. She hated to admit it even now, but Micah was right.

The unraveling of the nightclub, Micah's pack, and the death of the eldest vampire founder, Nicodemus, all occurred because she had stood in that line. Had she not allowed her investigative reporter's quest for knowledge overtake her, a lot of people and supernatural creatures would still be alive or undead, whichever the case might be.

And that was only the first wave she'd been involved in. The next was with Flora and Raven. Despite Raven's warnings not to go or to stay in Seattle, Kailey needed to know why her brother had died. The real reason. *Not* speculation. Determined to find the truth had cost the lives of innocent people. Some bystanders. Her former best friend. But even that didn't deter her media nosiness to pry and poke at situations most would never disturb.

Would she have fared better if she'd simply attended her brother's funeral and returned to Boston without discovering the truth? Perhaps. Could she have mentally coped with her loss? Never. Her need to know would've gnawed and eaten at her mind until she couldn't logically reason and cope with life.

"My fault," she whispered to herself. "All of this is my fault."

What's your fault? Raven asked.

Kailey straightened and gently placed her hand on the cat's neck. "What happened to you, the nightclub, the vampires, the werewolf pack dividing."

Nonsense.

"But it is true. None of these things would've occurred had I not started it all by standing in that line and Flora picking me."

If not you, something else would've happened to set it into action. Think about it. It was destined to happen without you ever coming here. The divisions in their so-called unity had already cracked. They weren't on a solid foundation anymore.

"Maybe."

No maybes about it. Don't allow *Micah* to make you wallow in self-pity. You'd not have Brady or Cassie, right?

"True. But you'd still be a living breathing witch in the sexy bod."

Look, I'm on your side, so don't try to make me agree with Micah. Do I have regrets? Sure. But Kailey, each decision I made. Hell, each decision we all made came from ourselves. No one forced us. Don't you see?

Kailey sighed. She loved Raven for being supportive and setting aside rightful grievances. "I'm sorry, Raven, for things falling apart. Thank you for coming back to rescue me."

The limo stopped on the third floor of the parking garage. Jacques parked his Jeep beside the limo and Brady parked his squad car.

Irina got out and hurried to the rear of the limo and opened the door. The others exited their vehicles and gathered near the limo.

Irina said, "I think we might all fit in the elevator, but once it opens on the basement floor, I can't promise we won't run into the elder vampires that came to pay tribute to Lorcan."

Forrest grinned and handed Brady, Jacob, and Blaze wooden stakes. "I'll exit first, just in case."

CHAPTER 73

When the elevator opened at the basement of Nocturnal Trinity, the shadowed corridor was empty. Forrest stepped across the threshold and Brady placed a hand on the door to prevent it from shutting.

Forrest stood still and listened. Overhead, the ceiling rattled from the pounding rave music and heavy dancing footsteps, creating a pulsating vibration that moved down the walls. The sensations made it difficult to detect any soft approaching footsteps down the corridor, but his insight didn't alert him to any vampires being nearby.

The smell of death lingered, however, which indicated vampires had gone through this passageway recently. Most likely the elder vampires Irina had warned him about. The coppery odor of blood tainted the air, too. Dead bodies were in the vicinity.

The harsh scent of brimstone permeated the tunnel. He sensed the presence of the behemoths. They weren't too far away, but the best he could tell was they weren't roaming freely, either. Of course, Penelope would inform them if they were. He wasn't certain how he'd destroy the demons since Lorcan had the Wrathbone, so the best solution was for all of them to avoid the behemoths. Depending on where they were being kept, it might be easier said than done.

The familiarity of Nocturnal Trinity's underbelly hadn't changed much.

The dismal atmosphere Forrest recognized. Although Alec had verbally forbade Forrest from entering the lower levels of the nightclub again, Forrest knew he'd eventually return. He couldn't help but grin.

Forrest glanced back at Irina. "I think we're good."

Irina stepped from the elevator and stared down the dark corridor. She pointed. "The summoning stone is down that hallway. Be aware that one opening to the left is where Alec held Lorcan's party. I don't hear any sounds coming from that room, but others could enter the room from the inside stairs that lead to the dance hall above."

Brady said, "Our pack members are on their way."

"Have them come in through the old passageway," Irina said. She looked at Jinn and handed him a set of keys. "You know where that door is. Go unlock it and then meet us at the summoning stone. We'll need some help guarding the stone once the incantation begins."

Jinn stared at the keys in his hand and nodded.

Irina looked at Forrest and then the gathered group behind him. "I'll be right back."

In a flash, she zipped down the darkened corridor. Forrest was about to worry that she'd betrayed them, but a few seconds later, she stood in front of him again. "No one's in the banquet room. The doors to the other rooms in between it and the summoning room are now closed. Before I closed them, I checked to see if anyone was inside. The behemoths are caged, so they shouldn't interfere. Since Lorcan has the Wrathbone, it's highly unlikely Alec will free them. Jinn, why are you still standing here?"

"All right, I'm leaving," Jinn said.

"I'm going with you," Cassie said.

"Whoa, ya don't trust me?"

"Not particularly," she said, tightening her grip on a wooden stake. "But that's not my reason. Too many hindrances could occur between here and the doorway. It's best we go together."

Jinn frowned.

"She's right," Forrest said.

Jinn grunted. "All right. Come on."

Jinn and Cassie hurried down the corridor.

"Any idea where Alec is?" Forrest asked.

Irina shrugged. "I'm not sure. With the music pounding, he's probably with Orsovo and Nikolina. They're probably mingling with the crowds or in the VIP lounge. Lorcan left the nightclub a couple of hours ago. He never disclosed whether he was coming back before sunrise or not. He indicated he had made arrangements elsewhere. That doesn't mean he won't return."

Forrest's eyes narrowed. "Let's hope he returns after the Fallen creature is banished."

Forrest knew the moment after he released the words that the things people hope for the most, seldom occur.

Kailey held Raven at Raven's request. For her new temporary life as a cat, she didn't want to get her paws dirty? Kailey had almost rolled her eyes at the remark, but she knew Raven would call her on it, so she refrained.

For all her life, Kailey had tried to treat everyone with kindness, holding onto the myth of 'reaping what one sowed', only to find that two powerful supernatural individuals were plotting to kill her. Hardly the appropriate reward for good mannerisms. Her life seemed nothing more than a physical contradiction.

She'd have never suspected Micah wanted to kill her. He'd offered his pack's aid to rescue her. He never showed malice except after Brady made the decision to separate the werewolves from Nocturnal Trinity's Circle of Unity. She reasoned that Micah's anger should've been directed at Brady, not her. But that wasn't what she wished to happen. Then again, it was probably as she had thought earlier. Harming her made Brady more vulnerable.

Kailey stroked the cat's neck, more to calm herself than to appease Raven. She projected her thoughts. "Raven, do you still think you saw Micah when I was tied up at the warehouse?"

I do.

"But that's impossible since we know the Fallen beast consumed him."

Yeah, kinda weighs against my argument, doesn't it? What I might have witnessed was his in-between transformation from the ethereal plane to the physical. I swear Micah noticed me for a moment, but I don't think he recognized me. I was sorta adjusting to my new form as well.

"Possibly," Kailey thought. "If he was in his physical form, there was nothing to prevent him from killing me while I was tied up."

I agree.

Jaclyn stopped outside the open door of the room with the summoning stone. "Everyone inside. Forrest, if you and Brady would stand guard at the door that would be appreciated. I'll assign positions around the circle in a few minutes."

He and Brady nodded.

Jacob looked at Brady. "I'll go find Jinn and Cassie. When the others arrive, I'll lead them here."

"I appreciate it," Brady said, clasping Jacob's shoulder.

Blaze helped Luna through the doorway and they walked to the far corner and sat down. Even though they held wooden stakes, neither looked prepared to fight a crippled ant.

Jacques stepped into the room with the witches. "How long before you're prepared?"

Raine smiled, taking her cellphone from her robe pocket. "Once we've transcribed the protective circle and Micah's hidden spell atop the summoning stone, we'll take our places and begin the incantation."

Gillian began smudging the room. Jaclyn took blessed white chalk from her pocket to outline the new circle around the summoning stone.

Jacques frowned. "That's going to take too long."

"Not as long as you'd think," Raine said.

"How's that?"

"All three of us will project the image atop the carved summoning circle from our cellphones and use a spell to imprint a glowing image of Brady's old circle and spell."

"You can do that?" Forrest asked, looking through the door.

Jaclyn smiled. "Yes. The app was designed by a High Priestess so witches could send protective and summoning circles to other covens. It won't take long to get the imprint, but we still don't know if it will work. I've never had the assistance of a cat possessed by a former human witch."

CHAPTER 75

J inn and Cassie passed the room where the behemoths were caged. Jinn was thankful the door was closed. His nervousness showed in his eyes. Cassie placed her hand on his forearm. He wished he could say that it eased his nerves, but even though the behemoths weren't able to physically assault him, it didn't prevent them from taunting him.

"Jinn, free us or we'll do worse to you than before."

"Ignore them," Cassie said.

The scars on Jinn's arms and legs where they had peeled away his skin burned and throbbed with pain.

"We should have killed you," another behemoth said.

The four behemoths laughed.

"I would've killed you, Jinn, had Alec not forbade me."

Cassie cast a glance at his troubled eyes. "Ignore them. You're safe now."

A deep chuckled rumbled. "He's never safe for as long as we reside inside Nocturnal Trinity. He's our puppet. We're his master."

"Don't listen to them," Cassie said. She grabbed his hand and pulled, trying to speed his pace.

Fear seized him. His mind took him back to the memories of them using long razored blades to filet long strips of skin … He shook his head.

Tears heated his eyes. He pressed with his mind to block their words and laughs. His feet moved faster. The farther from the behemoths' prison cells they moved, the less their voices could be heard.

"I'm sorry, Jinn," Cassie whispered. "I never knew."

"Don't worry over it." He pointed. "There's the door."

ALEC SAT in the vampire VIP lounge with his feet propped on the back of another chair. A young wannabe vixen rubbed his shoulders and kissed his neck, whispering her pleas.

Another young lady brought him a warm goblet of fresh blood. As she handed it to him, she pulled her hair from her neck and exposed her neck. "If you'd enjoy feeding on me instead?"

The question hung on the air but he remained stoic as though she'd said nothing.

Nikolina sat half curled in a plush sofa chair.

Alec figured she was thinking about their father, too. He started to ask her feelings about the events that had occurred in the banquet room when the VIP door flung open, striking the wall with full force.

Lorcan glared at Alec. "Did you send it after me?"

Alec lowered his feet from the chair and sat upright. "Send what?"

"The Fallen beast."

Alec's brow furrowed. "I don't know what beast you're speaking of."

Lorcan stood over Alec with the Wrathbone dagger drawn.

"Father!" Nikolina said, rising to her feet. "Neither of us know what you're talking about."

Perplexed, Lorcan studied Alec's eyes and then shot a glare at her. Slowly, he lowered the dagger. "The mayor's dead and so is Dr. Litman."

Alec stood. "What? How?"

"This Fallen creature. One of the ancients attacked the mayor's limo." Lorcan paused and ran a hand through his frazzled black hair. He didn't show fear, but he was obviously confused. "It ripped Scottridge's head from his shoulders with less effort than it would have required me to do."

Alec's phone buzzed inside his pocket. He took it out and read the screen. "Nikki, we have a breach in the basement."

She frowned. "What?"

"An intrusion."

Lorcan's eyes narrowed. "You mean this nightclub is being invaded?"

Alec nodded. "Yes. Now, if you'll excuse us."

"Excuse you?" Lorcas smiled, licked his lips, and showed his fangs. Excitement gleamed in his dark eyes. "Looks like the festivities have just started."

CHAPTER 76

*J*inn inserted the key to unlock the passage door. A small blinding light blinked and a sharp chirping sound squealed.

"When did they install a security alarm?" Cassie asked.

"Beats the hell out of me," Jinn said.

She clasped her hand around his. "We'll have to run back to the others. This alarm means Jaclyn and the other witches are going to need a lot more protection than what we originally thought."

"Shit," Jinn said. "You think Irina set us all up?"

"I want to say no, but it's still too early to tell."

"Have you recuperated enough to run?"

Cassie grinned. "Whatever potion they gave me has restored my energy. You think you can outrun a succubus, Jinn?"

"Of course. But the real question is whether I'd *want* to outrun you."

Her brow furrowed.

"I rather like watching the view from behind."

She gave a shrewd stare and pointed her finger at him. "Now, Jinn—"

In a flash, he left her behind.

"Crude, Jinn! You *needed* the head start!"

ALEC HURRIED down the stairs with Nikolina and Lorcan following him.

Orsovo remained in the hidden office where the security camera screen was. Their brother would join them soon after he wiped the VIP visitors' minds of him emerging through the hidden panel.

"Invigorating," Lorcan said with a slight grin. "Does this happen often?"

"No," Alec said, slowing his pace after leaving the stairs. He didn't want to alarm the guests by seeming in a hurry, but since Orsovo had given him the names of the intruders, he expected they'd not to be in a great hurry to leave the nightclub. They were here for a reason, and he wondered why they had forced their way inside.

"That's a pity," Lorcan said. His voice was haughty and rather snobbish. "It's been ages since I've enjoyed the thrill of the hunt. Both of you and your siblings have lost the knack for such sport. It's withered away. Of course, why bother, right? Your prey, if you could justify calling them that, offers themselves to you. There's no hunt. It's quite lazy actually, this modern generation."

"Times have changed, father. Laws forbid it."

"Indeed. But that presents an interesting factor, doesn't it?"

"Meaning?"

"It's no secret this nightclub has vampires. Who'd be so foolish as to invade your establishment?" Lorcan asked.

"Those you've wanted to find."

Nikolina gave a nervous glance at Alec.

"Whom exactly?" Lorcan asked.

"Kailey and Forrest Wollinsky," Alec said.

Lorcan laughed. "Surely you jest, son."

"Not at all. Orsovo's the one who has a visual on them as we speak."

Lorcan rubbed his hands together vigorously. "Tonight I shall do what I should've done a century ago. Have you ever drank the blood of a Vampire Hunter?"

Alec and Nikolina both shook their heads.

"It's invigorating. You'll find nothing else more satisfying."

They approached the walls that resembled dancing waves of people. The guests were lost in their own trances. The rhythm of the music swayed some, but others were captivated by the spritzed pheromone cocktail floating within the billowing machine fog.

The crowd rocked back and forth in an undulating series of waves, making it difficult to cut through.

"Can we move along any faster?" Lorcan asked.

"It'll only take a few more minutes."

"I could make it faster," Lorcan mused.

"No, father," Alec said. "We mustn't make another scene. We already cleaned up your earlier mess and wiped the memories of those here. It's too risky to attempt it again."

Lorcan placed his chin on Alec's shoulder as they walked and whispered, "How I wish I'd arrived when Nicodemus and Flora were still alive. I dare say they held more fortitude than the rest of you combined."

"Other than Flora's obsession to torment Kailey, both kept themselves quite reserved in their pursuits."

Lorcan hissed and slipped in stride beside Alec. "Carry on then, son. Introduce this Kailey to me. I want to look into her eyes as I rip out her throat."

CHAPTER 77

Forrest turned toward Irina when the loud chirping alarm shrieked down the tunnel. He pulled a wooden stake from his pocket. "You betrayed us?"

Irina shook her head. Her eyes widened as she glanced over her shoulder in response to the alarm. Her expression indicated the sound was unexpected to her, too. "No, I swear I didn't. We've never had any alarm like that. It must be new."

Forrest's jaw tightened. He glanced at the summoning circle and then to Jaclyn. "How soon?"

"We're ready to begin once everyone's in place." Jaclyn pointed. "Kailey, stand on the west of the circle and hold Raven. Gillian, stand to the north. Raine, to my right at the south. Now, for the rest of you, keep guard and remain silent. Forrest?"

He turned to meet her gaze. "Yes?"

"You must watch the door, but remember, we're summoning the Fallen beast *into* the center of this circle. After he materializes, we'll begin the banishing spell. He will fight to break free of the binding spell. No one should underestimate that. The spell might be effective for only a short amount of time. If our circle gets broken … he will attack all of us. Be ready to fight him."

Forrest nodded and adjusted his feet so he could watch the door and the witch's summoning circle with his peripheral vision. Penelope stepped near the circle and placed a sharpened wooden bolt into her crossbow. With her accuracy, she could stake a vampire in an instant.

"If I may ask," Jacques said, "what happens to Micah after all this occurs? Is there no way to free him from the Fallen beast before you banish it?"

Jaclyn shook her head. "No. Micah's already dead. What you see of him is his apparition. He gave the ultimate sacrifice in order to have his wishes granted. Magic comes at a price. Sorcery ... it comes at a greater price."

KAILEY SWALLOWED HARD AND THOUGHT, "SHIT."

What's wrong? Raven asked.

Kailey projected her thoughts. "I just thought about something."

What?

"When that creature emerges, he's going to be only feet away. He's going to kill me."

He will be bound to the circle.

"And if he isn't?"

I've read the inscriptions. They've ensured its hold. That is, unless the circle gets broken.

"I'm telling you that it's going to come right at me to kill me."

Not if I can help it.

"What about Micah?"

What do you mean?

"Will the inscription prevent him from attacking me?"

Yes, it should.

"Should?" Kailey bit her lower lip. "For a spell to work properly, doesn't the spell need to be specific? Did they account for Micah or could he be ... I don't know a better way to put it ... Could he be a loophole and bypass the binding?"

Kailey, you've always worried too much—

"And you've never worried enough."

Look, the Fallen beast is far more powerful than Micah. The beast consumed him, so it controls him.

"And you possessed a cat, but *you* control *it*—"

You're overthinking this.

"I don't think I am."

Focus on the center with us while we work the spell. Alert us if anything happens, okay? Let us witches do our witchy business.

"Fine. I hope you're right. If you're wrong, it's been nice talking to you again."

FORREST SENSED several undead in the corridor. Most likely, vampires.

"Forrest," Irina said.

"What?" he asked in a stern, almost unforgiving tone.

"They're coming. My brothers, Nikolina, and most likely Lorcan, but I'm not sure. They're getting closer."

Forrest detected more than just her family, but he said nothing. He held a stake in each hand and whispered, "I know. I'm aware of their arrival, too. I shall take it that they've sided with your father?"

"That remains to be seen," Irina said.

Forrest shrugged with an indifferent look in his eyes. "Perhaps. But should any of your siblings come to attack me, your family will become smaller."

Irina looked into his eyes and then she smiled. "I'm fine with that."

Eerily, he held no doubt that she was.

CASSIE AND JINN stood outside the doorway. The witches chanted. Cassie used her shadowed form to blend into the wall unnoticed by the human eye and was invisible to most vampires. She tapped Jinn's arm hard.

Jinn visibly jumped. His nervous eyes focused and took on his shadowed form. She wondered if his fretting was due to being so close to where the behemoths were. Their stench of brimstone permeated the corridor.

She had no idea what potion Jaclyn had fed her while she was incapacitated, but whatever it was, it was like magnified demonized steroids. She'd never felt more alert. Her muscles were pumped. Adrenaline ran through her at an invigorating height.

Cassie was uncertain how Jinn might react once the incantation began and the Fallen beast entered the summoning circle. Their best hope was to remain invisible. Should the beast break free, its duty and first priority would be to kill them since they were demons.

Jinn had always been the macho bartender with the sarcastic jabs.

Human females swooned over him, which only increased his ego and his confidence. She'd never known him to be fearful, except to the behemoths and rightly so. Any lesser demon could never hold its own against them. She was troubled though. Jinn's demeanor had been partially broken due to the cruel torture he'd endured. She almost felt bad for her earlier beatdown on him. Almost. He should've never drugged her, even if he had been pressured by the behemoths. She'd managed to escape, so with everything else Jinn had suffered, she figured she might bury her remaining animosity and let it slide.

He'd indicated his dosage wasn't potent, and someone else must've tampered with the drink. Only one individual despised her enough to be so underhanded. Maggie.

Cassie never understood Maggie's disdain and jealousy, except that Cassie was a seductive succubus and Maggie was not. It was rare for her to entice a human to her bed. Most men could never get past her frightening jagged demon teeth and that was something Maggie couldn't change.

Whenever Cassie worked the bar, she always got higher tips, more flirty men and women, and people simply requested Cassie to make their drinks. So jealousy might well be the factor.

Footsteps echoed down the corridor. Cassie slipped through the door and stood behind Kailey. A rising wind blew dust away from the summoning stone. Cassie kept her eyes focused on the center of the circle. She doubted she could defeat a Fallen creature—Gadif, Forrest had called it —but she'd do whatever was necessary to protect Kailey. The most important thing was for Cassie to prevent the Fallen creature from drawing its weapon. Should the blade strike her or Jinn, neither existed anymore.

Irina's fangs lengthened and she hissed when Alec, Orsovo, and Nikolina stepped from the shadows. She stood between the doorway and her siblings.

"Well, well, well," Lorcan said, easing around Alec. While she assumed her father might have been with her siblings, she wasn't certain he'd returned to Nocturnal Trinity. She wondered why he'd returned so soon, and how he could mask his presence from her. Lorcan's dark eyes pierced into hers. "Alec, we seem to have a traitor in our midst."

Alec tilted his head to the side and stared into Irina's eyes. His lips were an even smile, his gaze deceptive, but she was wary to where her brother's loyalties lie. The six vampire elders stood behind her siblings, and being as she didn't know them, she automatically viewed them as enemies. Anyone who favored her father could never be her true ally.

Anger rose inside of Irina. She spat at Lorcan's feet.

"Know your place," Lorcan hissed. "Treacherous attitudes are not tolerated *in my house.*"

The emphasis on those words set a raging fire inside her. "You're the traitor, Lorcan. You're a murderous tyrant. It's time for your existence on this world to come to an end."

Lorcan glanced over his shoulder to her siblings and to the vampire council elders. "See how this defiant one greets her father after all these years?"

"You're *not* my father," Irina said.

Lorcan jerked and faced her with darkened eyes. Fury tightened his thin face. He looked ready to rip her apart but for some reason, he held back. Perhaps doing so ruined his performance for the vampire council behind him. His jaw grew firm and he spoke through tight lips. "Feisty. I like that."

"Irina," Nikolina said, "what's the meaning of your betrayal? Why have you sided with Forrest?"

Alec placed his hand on Nikolina's and shook his head.

"Forrest's only here for Lorcan," Irina said. "He offers a truce to us in exchange for father."

"A truce, children, did you hear that? A truce offered to vampires *from* a Vampire Hunter? Do you not detect the irony?" Lorcan's smile broadened. His eyes gleamed. "Surely, that's not worth the paper it's written on or the breath required to speak the words. Even you're not so stupid to believe such a tale? I'm up for settling old scores, Forrest. But first, I must admonish a rebellious child."

"I'm *not* your daughter. Alec revealed the truth to me."

Lorcan's eyes darkened like black obsidian. His fangs grew and he revealed the ancient hideous monster worming its way to the surface. "I should've drained your blood long ago, you bastard child. Alec has learned his place, as you can see. So shall you."

Irina hissed and lunged at Lorcan. He grabbed her by the throat and flung her down the corridor without any effort. She shrieked and disappeared into the dark silent corridor. He turned immediately to face Forrest.

. . .

FORREST STEPPED INTO THE DOORWAY. With his immense size, there was no getting inside the summoning room without moving him and moving him was nearly impossible for any faction. He hoped Lorcan at least tried.

"It's been a long time, Vampire Hunter," Lorcan said. "You've been full of surprises, even when you were a young boy. You should have died on the same day as when your father perished."

Forrest's eyes narrowed. "You're right about one thing."

"What's that?"

"Your mistake was not fighting me when I was younger and less skilled. You might've had an advantage back then. I must've set fear into you after slaying the other master vampire, eh? I mean, if you weren't strong enough to slay him and I was? That must've been a trifle embarrassing, don't you think? Why else would you hide yourself into hibernation for so many years?"

Lorcan's hideous face tightened. His black eyes turned red. "Meet your rightful fate this night."

"I have every intention to accept my fate. However, my fate is seeing you become a pile of ash. But know this, you're going to suffer some incredible pain first in honor and memory of my father. Every bone of yours I snap, he'll rejoice at your pain. You're going to beg me to stake you and put you out of your misery."

"Beg?" Lorcan hissed. Madness swirled in his eyes. "Come at me, Vampire Hunter. We'll see who'll beg for mercy."

CHAPTER 78

Forrest had learned over his century of slaying vampires to never strike at an elder vampire first. Make the vampire attack. Patience usually paid off.

Although Lorcan was wary of the two stakes in Forrest's hands, his inner rage seemed to have convinced the vampire he was invincible and he'd be the victor. He came at Forrest in a flash, but foolishly didn't realize that despite Forrest's massive size, Forrest was agile and incredibly fast. All Vampire Hunters were.

Before Lorcan could reach Forrest, the Vampire Hunter's massive fist crushed Lorcan's nose and sent him spiraling across the hall and against the wall. The solid slam stiffened the vampire's body for a moment. Forrest could've easily staked him, but he wouldn't have any pleasure with that. He had meant what he said. He planned to inflict as much pain as possible before finally slaying Lorcan.

Forrest grinned and shook his head. "For an ancient vampire, you're pathetically slow. Maybe it wasn't a good thing to take such a long nap? You're sluggish."

Lorcan wailed in pain and anger, pressing his back against the wall, and holding his nose. Blood leaked from his twisted nose. If not for the wall to brace him, Lorcan would've dropped to the floor.

Although vampires could live forever and suffer extensive physical damage without dying, they weren't completely immune from pain. Unlike humans that backed away from a fight after their pain became too great to continue, vampires fed on the pain. Forrest expected Lorcan's rage to increase at any given moment. But rage didn't aid a vampire's fighting abilities, especially against a seasoned Vampire Hunter.

Forrest glanced at Alec. A half grin spread on Alec's astonished face. Since Alec had extended the invitation to Lorcan to come to Nocturnal Trinity, Forrest was rather surprised not to receive a glare from Alec. But then again, as Irina had told Forrest, Lorcan had almost cut Alec's head off, revealing Lorcan's true nature. That threat better explained Alec's inaction.

Lorcan noticed his son's smile and bloody spittle flew from Lorcan's mouth. "You'll not defend your own father?"

"Is that what you want?" Alec asked. "Your son to fight your battles? This fight is yours, father. It's what you wanted. It's what you requested. You want to take over our nightclub? To make this *your* home? First, you must lead by example."

Alec crossed his arms and stepped back. Nikolina gave Alec a confused stare. Orsovo showed no emotion, but he didn't look like he'd intervene, either. The six vampire council elders eased closer with eagerness in their eyes.

One of the vampire elders looked at Lorcan and said, "Carry on, Lorcan. If you wish for us to give our support to your new resurrected reign, you must prove your strength and your worthiness. Nearly a century has passed since we last witnessed any of your power. Yet, our power and rank in society has grown exceedingly well without you. We host respectable banks and businesses around the world. Your long absence indicates weakness, making me question if your *hibernation* stemmed nothing more than as an excuse to not face Forrest Wollinsky. Prove you're worthy to still preside over us."

Perplexed, Lorcan wiped blood onto his ruffled shirt. "If you've come to witness bloodshed, Hans, you shall see it!"

The vampire elder seemed unimpressed by Lorcan's haughty statement.

Lorcan darted toward Forrest with such swiftness, only a whirl of dust rising from the floor could be seen. In spite of his speed, he was unable to reach Forrest. Instead, Forrest rammed the two wooden stakes into Lorcan's gut, intentionally too far from the heart to slay him, but deep enough to cause Lorcan injuries and sufficient pain. Lorcan gasped. His eyes widened.

"Hibernation has made you weak," Forrest said. "Or is it because you fear me?"

Inside the summoning room, the witches' chants grew louder.

Forrest held the ends of the wooden stakes and grinned as Lorcan looked up into his eyes. Forrest yanked the stakes free, dropped them on the floor, and gripped a fierce massive hand around the elder vampire's throat. He clutched tightly, lifting Lorcan off the floor.

Lorcan grabbed Forrest's wrist with both hands and fought unsuccessfully to lessen the hold. Blood saturated the vampire's shirt and soaked into his slacks. Veins swelled on the vampire's face and across his forehead. Lorcan sputtered unable to talk.

From his peripheral vision, Forrest noticed none of the elder vampires or Irina's siblings had budged. They simply looked on with interest, but for some reason, Forrest seemed to believe they wanted Lorcan slain.

Perhaps Lorcan had played dead for too long, and since all the vampires had adjusted without needing him, it suited them better if Lorcan had never awakened. None seemed willing to cede their rightfully earned power and properties to the rebirth of a long believed-to-be-dead legendary vampire.

From Forrest's other side, shadows approached at a fast pace. As they came into view, Forrest recognized Jacob and the six werewolf pack members behind him.

A gurgling sound rattled in Lorcan's throat. Blood dripped from his mouth. Despite his injuries, the vampire still tried to pry Forrest's grip from his neck.

Forrest glanced at Brady. In a low deep voice, he said, "No one intervene. Lorcan's mine. Should any of these elder vampires or Lorcan's children try to stop me, execute them."

Brady and Jacob nodded.

Hans sighed and then spoke in a dignified, stately tone. "No need for idle threats, Forrest, as we're not interested in participating in your scuffle. You may proceed with our blessings."

Lorcan stared at Hans with pure hatred and perhaps would've spieled vile threats if he could voice the words.

"Good to know," Forrest said. He grinned at Lorcan and shrugged. "I guess it's just you and I."

Forrest flung Lorcan partway down the hall, but not as far as Lorcan had thrown Irina. He wanted to keep the vampire in sight. Lorcan landed on his back and rolled to his side. He clutched his abdomen and pulled back blood-drenched hands. He sat up and glared at Forrest, moving to balance himself on his hands and knees.

"Lorcan!" a harsh, deep voice bellowed. "Free us and we'll fight for your cause."

Lorcan knelt and rubbed his throat. He forced a smile and darted toward the voice.

"He's going to free the behemoths," Alec said.

Forrest took a deep breath and held it. The odds were fixing to change, and most likely for the worst.

CHAPTER 79

Kailey held the cat while the witches chanted. She felt like she was inside a vacuum, a void of some sort, and her skin pimpled with sudden chills as the circling air around her grew colder.

Magical power rose around her, forming a thin shimmering wall that wasn't fully visible. She doubted she could've seen the wall had she not been invited to be part of the circle. Raven chanted with the three witches and apparently, she'd been right. Even while residing inside the cat, she could aid them with the incantation.

After several minutes, Raven's spirit left the cat. Standing directly in front of Kailey was Raven's transparent apparition of how she had looked when she was alive. She looked like a hologram.

Kailey's heart ached. She didn't know how or why Raven's spirit stepped outside of the cat, but it proved to Kailey that she hadn't been teetering on the edge of insanity. She had been conversing with Raven. Raven really had possessed the cat and come to rescue Kailey.

The center of the summoning circle turned crimson, slowly widening. Heat rose from this point and she swore flickering flames licked their way through the opening. A giant birdlike head pushed up through the fiery hole. The opening widened. The Fallen beast's shoulders emerged. The towering creature was rising through the hole.

Fear gripped Kailey, but the witches continued chanting with their eyes closed. She wanted to scream but feared doing so might break the binding spell, and the creature would kill them all for trying to capture and banish it.

How could she warn them? Did they even know its body had risen inside the circle? It was far larger than she'd ever imagined.

Suddenly, the ground shook. Kailey sensed the floor's rocking was due to forces *outside* the protective circle. She glanced away from the rising beast and saw shadowed forms of Cassie and Jinn running to the far wall where Luna and Blaze sat huddled and holding one another.

Bricks and blocks broke away from the wall with a thunderous crash. Chunks of brick and mortar blasted across the room. The floor shook and renewed terror seized Kailey.

Three behemoths ripped through the wall and stood at the edge of the summoning stone. The Fallen creature appeared in its fleshly form. Its massive wings unfolded and spread outward like what most viewed an angel to bear. The bird face faded. Micah's face appeared in its stead. He smiled a most unfriendly smile. Evil possessed his features. His hateful gaze pleaded for bloodshed. *Hers.*

Forrest entered the room and headed toward a crazed vampire with its fangs projected.

One of the behemoths struck the magical circle and reached for Jaclyn. The shimmering magic veil shattered and melted away, showering down like iridescent dew droplets.

"Run!" Kailey yelled.

Her scream alarmed the witches, snapping them from their chanting trance. Already, the Fallen beast stepped away from its summoned portal. The behemoth shoved Jaclyn aside. She turned and flung her hands upward. For a moment, while still atop the summoning stone, Kailey watched a blue arc of light form a curved magical barrier around Jaclyn. Gillian and Raine lent their magical aid to help shield her. The behemoth struck at the bluish dome, but was unable to penetrate her shield.

Kailey turned to run, but the Fallen creature gripped her wrist and pulled her to it. Micah's face held a eerie smile as he looked down at her.

Every emotion ran through Kailey, as she knew she was moments from death. Her will to fight drained and a frigid wave encapsulated her.

The gentleness of Micah's eyes she had remembered months ago was no longer present. Only one question pounded inside her mind and finally she had the boldness to say it. "Why?"

Micah replied, "They've already told you my reasons for wanting you dead. Your time has come."

CHAPTER 80

When Lorcan disappeared into the shadows of the corridor, Forrest didn't bother pursuing. He didn't need to get cornered in the room with the four behemoths and Lorcan. Holding his ground outside the corridor held a greater advantage. He preferred to let the battle come to him.

With the witches' chant echoing its rhythmic chorus and a fiery hole opening in the center of the circle, Forrest expected Gadif to materialize soon. Watching from the doorway didn't benefit the witches should Gadif emerge and somehow break free of the binding spell.

Forrest advanced into the summoning room and waited. He needed to be closer to defend the witches because no Fallen beast would simply stand idle and allow itself to be banished.

At almost the exact moment the Fallen creature fully emerged, the behemoths crashed through the wall and separated, Lorcan walked through the piles of busted bricks and stone with bold determination set in his eyes. The four behemoths made him braver.

Although Forrest wanted to laugh, he realized Lorcan actually held the advantage now.

Cassie grabbed Luna and vanished while Jinn disappeared with Blaze.

Forrest met Lorcan's gaze and shook his head.

Lorcan grinned. His pointed fangs lengthened. He had healed somewhat, but still he wasn't at his full strength. "You never expected a vampire to fight fair, did you?"

"To be honest, I hoped you wouldn't," Forrest replied. "You never did before. Why should I expect that you would now? You seem the type to allow your entourage to fight your battles for you."

"Still troubled over the loss of your father? How long did that plague you?" Lorcan took a few cautious steps closer. "You realize a child never becomes an adult until after the parents have perished, right?"

Forrest's eyes narrowed. The taunting didn't bother him. He expected nothing less. A vampire lacked true emotions, so they enjoyed using their prey's emotions against them in a way to weaken them. But Forrest had long accepted the loss of his father, so he didn't understand why Lorcan was hoping to jab at a painful wound.

Forrest smiled. "Then tonight your remaining children enter adulthood."

Lorcan laughed. "We shall see."

"Remember when I told you that I was going to make you suffer horrific pain before I staked you?"

"Yes." Lorcan hissed.

"I must confess something," Forrest said.

"What's that?"

"I never intended to fight fairly tonight, either."

"Oh?" Lorcan's brow theatrically rose, just like the feigning of his voice's tone. "So what surprises do you have in store for me? Coming out of hibernation is like a birthday for a vampire."

Forrest dropped the two wooden stakes into his coat pockets. He turned his neck to one side, causing it to pop loudly. He rolled his shoulders.

When he made eye contact with Lorcan, the vampire produced an amused smile, eagerly awaiting but foolishly not expecting whatever Forrest held in store.

The heavy overcoat Forrest wore prevented others from seeing the thick grizzled fur forming on his arms, legs, chest, and back. Lorcan's confusion increased when Forrest's slight sideburns suddenly spread and covered his face.

"Did your children not tell you of the were-grizzly that lives inside me?"

The blank expression that covered Lorcan's face indicated they never had.

Forrest roared, revealing large teeth. His face lost all human resemblance and he stood in his monstrous grizzly form.

He batted Lorcan with a huge paw. The impact slung Lorcan into the air and across the room. Before the vampire hit the ground, Forrest followed and smacked him again.

The vampire spiraled and crashed atop a large rock from the crumbled wall. He tried to move away while Forrest bounded on all fours and landed atop him.

Forrest pressed his thick sharp claws beneath his weight into the two gaping stake wounds of Lorcan's gut. In confused disbelief, Lorcan stared into Forrest's dark bear eyes.

"How?" the vampire whispered.

Still human enough to speak, Forrest said, "On the day I killed your nemesis vampire as you requested I lost my father. I lost him, but I gained what I long considered a curse. Except tonight, it isn't a curse."

Forrest shoved his thick claws deeper. Lorcan howled in pain and gnashed his teeth.

Forrest curled his paw into a fist. His claws ripped and sliced through the vampire's entrails. His grizzly form backed away, pulling a long section of Lorcan's guts out onto the floor. Forrest opened his huge mouth, roared again, and then he bit deep into Lorcan's left quadriceps, striking bone.

Lorcan reared back his head in sheer agony. His fangs lengthened. In response to the pain, Lorcan flung himself upward and forward, possibly hoping to bite Forrest, but the bear shook the vampire's thin body vigorously as if it were nothing more than a straw-stuffed scarecrow.

A metal object jostled free from the vampire's inner vest pocket and slid across the stone floor, but Forrest didn't stop violently shaking Lorcan until the vampire's femur snapped loudly. Then Forrest released his leg and roared in triumph.

Lorcan gasped and winced in agony. He coughed and sputtered and whimpered.

Vampires healed fast, but with the severity of Lorcan's injuries, he'd need a feast of blood to overcome and mend his torn broken body. Forrest knew he couldn't escape.

He relaxed and focused, shunning his grizzly beast to go dormant. Forrest pushed himself to his feet and stood over Lorcan. He met the vampire's gaze and pulled a wooden stake from his coat pocket.

"For decades," Forrest said, "I've longed to cross paths with you. I wanted you to suffer for what you've done, for the suffering you've caused, not just to me, but to your family and all the peasants in the villages surrounding your castle. I could batter you for hours more but I'd have no more pleasurable satisfaction than what I've already experienced."

Forrest dropped to one knee and raised the stake overhead. He locked eyes with Lorcan. The greatest pleasure would be in seeing the last moment of the vampire's undeath extinguished.

"Forrest, no!"

He turned to see Irina limping through the door toward him. The scratches and scuffs on her arms were healing. Her right foot was twisted slightly inward. During her landing, her leg had been severely broken.

Forrest lowered the stake. She stared at Lorcan with tears cresting in her eyes. They spilled as narrow meandering streaks of blood down her cheeks.

If Lorcan might've taken the moment as one of his rescue, that thought fleeted from his gaze when he realized Irina stood over him. Her tears came from intense anger, a fury too extreme to hold inside.

Irina glared at him. The look was enough. She needed no words. Kneeling on the other side of the man who'd killed her real father, she reached for the stake. Forrest offered it to her. She shook her head. With Forrest's huge hand gripping the stake, she cupped hers around his hand and lead his hand over Lorcan's heart. She lowered the tip of the stake, pressing it where the heart was, and then she nodded at Forrest.

Forrest lifted the stake up while she held his hands. Together, they drove the stake through Lorcan's heart.

After the body withered into a pile of smoldering ash, Forrest became aware of the ensuing battle around him. He rose and helped Irina stand. As he turned, two behemoths struck him with their shoulders and carried him toward the broken wall. He struggled to fight them off but his feet didn't reach the floor. Few creatures he'd encountered matched the strength of these oversized demons. Irina dropped to the floor and dug through her father's ash.

"Where's the dagger?" she gasped, desperately digging and patted through the ash. "It's got to be here."

Alec sprinted and grabbed one behemoth's massive arm and fought to pull it off of Forrest. Brady and Jacob rushed to help.

Forrest managed to free one arm, but the other behemoth struck him with enough force that it drove him down onto the floor. Its heavy weight pressed against his chest. The heat of its brimstone breath washed over Forrest's face. Flames flickered inside its nostrils and its eyes. It was almost like opening the door to an incinerator.

Brady and Jacob pulled at the behemoth but were flung away with a swift backhand. When they struck the ground, both growled. The snapping of bones and sinews indicated they were turning. But even in their *were* forms, Forrest viewed their help as useless.

Two arrows struck the behemoth's throat. The tips caught in between its scales but didn't pierce through its skin. The behemoth laughed and knocked them away. Forrest took a wooden stake and even though he knew the effort was useless, he rammed it against the demon's gut.

"That tickles Vampire Hunter," it said. "Now, you die."

CHAPTER 81

Kailey would've pleaded for her life if she'd have thought it would've made a difference. Reading Micah's intent, she knew words were useless. Pleas would only entice his desire for revenge.

"You're the reason for all this chaos," Micah said. "Look around. Carnage has bloodied Seattle because of *you*. The longer you stay, the more you've unbalanced life in this city."

Kailey tried to pull her arm free, but it yanked her closer and placed a hand around her body. She tried to squirm but the tight fingers constricted her attempt and hampered her breathing.

The witches returned to their chanting but outside of the summoning stone. Kailey figured they were casting protection spells on Kailey, but she didn't think their magic was going to help.

She wanted to protest Micah's poor evaluation about how she'd made the situation in Nocturnal Trinity worse, but she'd only be lying. She knew he was right. Things were thrown off course because of her coming to the nightclub. So, she couldn't argue that point. Even he'd perceive the lie. What she could argue, provided she could speak, was that killing her didn't change the situation. It didn't reverse it. And if it were possible, that somehow through the dimensional portal that he could turn back time, he'd probably offset everything else but not for good.

Events in life had courses to follow and crossroads presented decisions

344

everyone had to make. Simply because one person made a decision or chose a particular direction didn't necessarily mean that they'd done it for selfish or evil purposes. Each decision was part of a greater chain reaction. A misstep altered the future, but who's to say what difference the future would've been by taking the alternate route?

Hindsight was what most people looked back on with regret. Retracing the steps to find where the mistakes occurred for why the current problem existed was fine, if those steps were one's own. The nerve of him to try to discern and dictate where *her* steps needed to be undone so that *his* future was better. It was utter foolishness and outright selfishness. She chose her path to obtain justice for her brother's death. It had nothing to do with Micah or his failed leadership of his own pack.

And had Flora's unfounded obsession to torture Kailey ended sooner, none of this would've occurred, either. Why didn't Micah cast the rightful blame on Flora? Flora ended up paying the ultimate price. She was destroyed due to her own actions.

Kailey bared her teeth and tried to pry free of his grip. Oh, the vitriol she wished to spew if only she could spout the words.

The Fallen creature stiffened suddenly. Its free hand reached over its back to draw its sheathed weapon. The strange blade gleamed an icy blue flame with black smoke-like waves rising from it. Micah's face suddenly retreated and Gadif lowered her to the floor. It turned and left her.

CHAPTER 82

Forrest found breathing nearly impossible beneath the heavy weight of the behemoth. Alec and Orsovo exerted their strength in an attempt to knock the demon off the Vampire Hunter. Forrest appreciated their effort but even the strength of two elder vampires couldn't budge the behemoth.

The demon wrapped both hands around Forrest's throat and squeezed.

Its fiery eyes flickered. "Flora was our friend, our overseer. You slayed her and demanded that Alec return us to the Abyss."

Forrest tried to laugh but the demon's grip was too tight. He remembered Flora's early obsessions with summoning demons, so it didn't surprise him if she'd developed some type of friendship with the behemoths when the Circle of Unity was at its strongest. Now that the Circle's strength had weakened, the behemoths viewed their existence as threatened, and rightly so.

His face heated and he imagined his skin was a ripe plum purple. He didn't think this would be the way he'd meet his demise. And yet, here he was about to be crushed to death by a behemoth. He figured there were worse ways to go.

He patted the floor and touched the large chunks of jagged stone that had fallen from the broken wall. The stones would be no more useful than the wooden stake he'd tried to ram into its gut. Then his fingers touched cold metal that was tucked against one busted block and his mind retraced his fight with Lorcan while Forrest was in his grizzly form.

A metal object had fallen from Lorcan's jacket pocket and slid across the floor. During the bear's rage, Forrest had almost missed the sound.

The demon roared and in response, the grizzly inside Forrest struggled to emerge. His grizzly wanted to fight to save Forrest, but Forrest knew even the bear couldn't kill the demon. Besides, his massive bear paws prevented him from grasping the dagger.

Forrest's fingers felt the blade and slid it under his hand. Then he found the hilt and wrapped his fingers around it. Fighting his dizziness, he used his fleeting strength and plunged the dagger into the behemoth's gut. Its eyes widened with surprise and Forrest grinned.

The demon released Forrest and tried to stand. Alec and Orsovo grabbed Forrest under his arms and slid him away from the demon before it burst into flames and chunks of its fiery body dropped to the floor. Forrest gulped huge intakes of air and coughed.

Another demon roared in pain, capturing Forrest's attention. Alec and Orsovo helped Forrest to his feet and balanced him upright between them.

Forrest held the Wrathbone dagger but realized he didn't need it. Gadif was executing the other behemoths.

After Gadif pierced through one behemoth's tough skin, he turned and slashed through the third one, which left one remaining behemoth.

The last one backed away from the Fallen beast. Still taking deep breaths and exhaling hard, Forrest handed the Wrathbone to Alec. Alec took the dagger and looked into Forrest's eyes. Alec acquiesced a meek nod and stepped forward, plunging the dagger into the behemoth's back.

Gadif turned his attention to Forrest. Forrest was still struggling to regain his breath and his strength. The two stared at one another for a few moments as if measuring each other up. He half expected another battle against the Fallen. Drained, he didn't think he could defend himself against Gadif, let alone set an attack.

Finally, Forrest took a deep breath and a step forward. He readied himself to turn into his grizzly form. "Are we good, Gadif? Or—"

Gadif's strange undead eyes studied Forrest for a moment and then the Fallen one turned away. The large pole of his weapon dragged on the stone floor. Forrest wasn't certain if Gadif remembered their previous battle since it had returned as one of the undead. Perhaps its kind didn't hold grudges?

Gadif's birdlike appearance faded and Micah's face returned. He headed to the summoning circle. Brady rushed toward the Fallen creature.

"No!" Jacques said. "He'll kill you."

"I'm not going to let him kill Kailey."

"Stand back," Jacques said. "Let me handle this."

Brady was hesitant. Kailey sat where she'd stood in the circle and rubbed her throat.

"Are you sure?" Forrest asked.

Jacques responded with a nod.

CHAPTER 83

Kailey pushed herself to her feet before Gadif reached the edge of the summoning circle. After it killed the behemoths with its weapon, she'd dropped to the floor in relief. The Fallen creature had regained its control over Micah, and she figured she was safe. But once more Gadif surrendered itself to Micah.

"Run, Kailey," Jaclyn said. "Over here!"

"To us," Gillian said, waving her to the witch trio.

Kailey ran. When she reached them, they huddled around her.

Kailey said, "It took over Micah and killed the behemoths. Why would he place Micah back in charge now?"

"A deal's a deal," Jaclyn said.

Kailey frowned.

"Micah offered himself to the Fallen creature in return for letting him kill you. That's the only reason Gadif has gone dormant," Jaclyn said.

Cassie and Jinn sat in an unoccupied booth near the demon bar with Blaze and Luna.

Jinn was weak and shaken from teleporting again, but Cassie didn't suffer the lag as she had earlier in the day. She attributed it to the potion Jaclyn had fed her. However, something strange had also occurred. Although her physical body had come to the demon sector with Jinn, Blaze, and Luna, her shadowed form remained in the summoning room. She watched helplessly as Micah grabbed Kailey and drew the weapon. Cassie reached for Kailey but she couldn't touch Kailey.

Cassie tried to scream but no sound came. It was an odd sensation to be in two places at once. Well, divided into two places at once. Then, with nothing to explain her rejoining her body in the booth, she found herself whole again.

Behind the bar stood Maggie with her back to their booth. She'd never noticed their appearance.

Jinn placed his elbows on the table and rested his head in his hands. He groaned.

"Jinn, stay with Luna and Blaze," Cassie whispered.

"Where are you going?" Jinn asked without glancing up.

"Got some business to take care of."

JACQUES HURRIED and stepped in front of the beast. Micah's fierce gaze caught his father's and then softened.

"Micah," Jacques said. "You don't need to do this."

"Yes, father, I do."

"A true shaman would not act in this manner. A shaman wouldn't shed the blood of an innocent person."

"She's not innocent. She's the spark that ignited the blazing fire."

"That's not true, and you know it," Jacques said.

"Move, father, or you'll leave me no choice but to kill you."

"Listen to yourself, Micah. We've always been close. Never would you have made such a threat. You've allowed evil to replace peace."

"Move," Micah said.

"You're going to have to kill me if you plan to murder her in cold blood." Fur covered Jacques arms and face. His jaw and nose contorted. "But you won't kill me so easily."

"We shall see," Micah said.

FORREST STEPPED AWAY from Orsovo's assistance and he thanked both brothers. Penelope sifted through the behemoths' ashes, looking for rare gems. She apparently realized her bolts would do no harm to the Fallen.

Frustrated, Alec said, "How will we get him to enter the stone circle in order to banish him?"

Forrest shook his head. "Are you kidding? It's not going to cooperate. But I've an idea."

"What?" Alec asked.

"Help Jacques distract Gadif or Micah or whatever it has become. Keep its focus on you," Forrest said. "Whatever you do, don't get cut by the blade. It's more effective than a stake. One cut and well, you get the idea."

Alec and Orsovo nodded.

CASSIE WALKED behind the bar and leaned against the countertop. Maggie turned and her eyes widened. She took a sharp breath.

Cassie's eyes narrowed. "You seem a bit surprised to see me."

Maggie swallowed hard and cleared her throat. She attempted to regain her hardened exposure but her hands shook. She took a rag to wipe the bar and refused to make eye contact. "Well, yeah, when you slink up on someone like a cat, what do you expect?"

Cassie gloated. "I think it's more than that."

"What'cha mean?" Maggie asked.

"Don't be coy."

Maggie gave a questionable stare. "About what?"

Cassie shook her head. "You really aren't good at faking human emotion facial expressions, are you?"

Maggie shrugged.

"Let me spell it out for you, then, you demon strumpet," Cassie said, stepping toe to toe with her. "You didn't expect to see me because you figured the behemoths had taken me to torture. You were the one who placed the extra sedative in my drink. What deal did you make with the behemoths in exchange for handing me over to them like you did Jinn?"

Maggie's jaw dropped.

Cassie didn't need to guess further. Maggie would've become defensive if Cassie's accusation was false.

Maggie tried to step back but Cassie grabbed the collar of Maggie's leather jacket and held fast.

"I'll let you in on another little secret, sweetie," Cassie said. "All of the behemoths are dead, forever."

Tears darkened Maggie's eyes. "Dead? No, you mean they've been sent to the abyss."

Cassie grinned. "Do I?"

"Yes, you can't *kill* them."

"Wanna bet? Or better yet, how about I show you?" Cassie wrapped her arms around Maggie and vanished.

CHAPTER 84

orrest eased as quietly as a man of his immense size could, making his way behind Gadif without being seen. With Micah temporarily controlling the Fallen beast, Forrest hoped he might steal its weapon. Micah haplessly carried it, perhaps not understanding the power it possessed, or that the weapon could destroy any of the Fallen.

Alec and Orsovo had joined Jacques to intercede and protect Kailey as best they could.

With the circle having been broken, Forrest couldn't see any way for the witches to regroup and reset the protective circle. Gadif certainly wasn't going to stand inside the circle and allow it. Micah would kill them for attempting the incantation because he'd view their actions as a threat.

The only way to destroy the Fallen beast now was to kill it with its own weapon. While it sounded easy enough, few had ever been successful, at least that's the tales he'd heard. The Fallen were rare to encounter and usually only appeared during or after a major catastrophe. However, to his knowledge no Fallen beast had ever allowed a *were* creature to enter and share its power, either. With Micah trying to reach Kailey, this might be the only opportunity Forrest had to steal the weapon.

Forrest crept up behind Gadif and leaned forward to grab the pole-arm and yank it from the Fallen's grasp. He was less than two meters from the shaft.

Cassie suddenly appeared in front of Gadif with Maggie clutched in her arms. Cassie pointed to where Penelope sat on her knees searching for gems in the remnants of the behemoths' stone corpses. "Look! All those charred rocks are what's left of the behemoths and—"

Cassie looked up, terrified. The Fallen beast towered over her and Maggie. "What the—?"

The demons materializing at the feet of the Fallen must've caused Micah's form to recede. The Fallen's birdlike head reemerged. Cassie ran, leaving Maggie in its path. Before Maggie could decide what to do, Gadif raised the pointed blade of the pole-arm and slashed the demon in half.

Gadif turned to find Cassie and Forrest lunged, grabbing onto the pole-arm and wrapping his arms around it. His unexpected weight against the wooden shaft of the weapon knocked it from Gadif's hand.

Forrest held fast to the shaft, rolled, and slowly rose, stumbling to regain his footing. He was still slightly dizzy from his near choke-out match with the behemoth.

Alec charged Gadif and wrapped his arms around one of the Fallen's wings. Gadif shrieked with the piercing cry of a diving hawk. The sound echoed off the ceiling and walls, causing almost everyone to cover their ears.

Forrest winced and fought the pain, not dropping the weapon shaft. He feared if he dropped it, he'd never be able to lift it off the floor.

Orsovo gripped the lower edge of Gadif's other wing and yanked hard on the black feathers. Gadif tried to flap his massive wings to shake off the two vampires. While its attention focused on the vampires, Forrest balanced the heavy weapon and staggered toward the Fallen beast. Forrest needed more speed, as it was too awkward and long for him to run with it.

Irina stepped beside him and lifted the weapon, lessening the weight and strain on Forrest's muscles. Brady hurried and did the same. It looked as though they were carrying a battering ram to bash through a sealed gate.

Jacques ran past Gadif while the two vampires struggled to twist and hold its wings, enraging it.

Jacques exchanged glances with Brady. Forrest read the hurt in Jacques' eyes.

Forrest whispered, "You don't have to join us in doing this."

Jacques heaved the pole-arm upward. "I'm afraid I must. I tried to reason with him, Forrest. I tried. He's beyond rationality. What he's become is no longer my son."

"I know," Forrest replied. He whispered. "At the count of three, we charge and aim for the gut. One ... Two ... Three."

Gadif howled as the sharp glowing blade sliced and plunged through his abdomen and protruded out through his back. His wings stretched and arced, sending Alec and Orsovo reeling. The Fallen gripped the shaft in both hands, trying to pull it out.

Forrest dropped to the floor.

A howling breeze whirled. Gadif seemed to fold into himself, growing smaller and smaller as a dark portal opened. When the wind ceased, Gadif was gone and so was the portal. The weapon was no longer there, either.

Exhausted, Forrest lie on his stomach and looked around the room. Too tired to rise, he simply closed his eyes and drifted to sleep. He didn't question his safety or that the battle was completely over, but it didn't matter. Even a Vampire Hunter reached extreme levels of exhaustion that he could no longer fight sleep.

CHAPTER 85

After Gadif disappeared, Kailey left the witch trio and hurried to the circle where the little black cat sat.

Kailey reached for the cat. It hissed and clawed at her hand before scampering out of the room. "Raven?"

The cat fled and never hesitated to look back before disappearing.

Sadness caused Kailey to ache inside. She felt like her insides were being ripped to shreds. She stepped on the spot where she'd seen Raven's spirit exit the cat. She felt no warmth. Just cold emptiness and the departing of a friend.

Kailey projected her voice. "Raven? Are you still here? Please, don't leave me."

Nothing but silence returned.

Kailey closed her eyes, fighting the burning tears. Brady slipped up from behind and wrapped his arms around her. She stiffened for a moment, until she realized it was him. She leaned back against him and sobbed. He kissed her tear-stained cheek.

"Are you okay?" Brady asked.

Her eyelids tightened and hot tears streamed down her cheeks. She shook her head.

"What's wrong?"

"Raven's gone," she said with a quivering voice.

Cassie stepped in front of Kailey and placed a hand on Kailey's shoulder. "I'm so sorry, hon."

Kailey sobbed and her body shook. Cassie leaned in, kissed her cheek, and hugged her close.

Cassie's sweet scented pheromones alleviated some of Kailey's stress and soothed her into an almost dreamlike state where she seemed to drift over a field of exotic flowers. Kailey pressed against Cassie and dug her nails into Cassie's blouse. Before she succumb to the full power of the perfume, Kailey jerked back and pushed away from the succubus. Even though nothing was seductive in the calming effect, Kailey needed to keep her senses. She needed to feel the pain of loss so she could grieve.

Jaclyn, Gillian, and Raine approached.

Kailey looked at Jaclyn. "Where'd Raven go?"

"She's not with us?" Jaclyn asked.

Kailey wiped her eyes. "I saw her spirit leave the cat during the incantation. That was only moments before the behemoth broke the circle. When I tried to pick up the cat, it ran away. She's not inside it anymore. She's not replied to my thoughts, either. She's ... gone."

Jaclyn placed her hands on Kailey's cheeks. "Perhaps her time on Mother Earth was over?"

"I suppose, but we never said our goodbyes."

"You remember that she tried to kill you, right?" Cassie said. "She did mean horrible things to you, Brady, Luna—"

Kailey nodded. "She apologized for all the bad things she did to us. She was genuinely sorry or else, she'd not have helped us. Without her help, you'd have never found me. I had hoped to have more time to talk to her."

Still holding Kailey's cheeks, Jaclyn kissed Kailey's forehead. "Without her help, we'd have never summoned the Fallen beast here. I sensed her power. So she was here. Had she not been regretful for her actions, you're right; she wouldn't have aided us. The battle might have lasted far longer and it's quite possible that a lot of people would've been killed."

"I know," Kailey said, nodding. "Is there any way you three could somehow check to see if she's still in the nightclub?"

Jaclyn folded her hands at her waist. "No more than you can. We never knew she was with you until you informed us."

"I knew something was wacky about that cat," Cassie said, wiping a tear from her eye. "At least she made peace with you."

"But we all benefited from one thing," Jaclyn said with a smile.

"What's that?" Kailey asked.

"You were blessed by the touch of a familiar."

CHAPTER 86

The following night Forrest sat at the banquet table in Nocturnal Trinity. Jinn and Cassie sat to each side of him. Irina, Nikolina, Alec, and Orsovo were seated on the other side of the table.

Forrest sat directly across the table from Alec. "Do you now understand why you should've used the Wrathbone on those behemoths?"

"Yes. My apologies. No grudges, please. The Wrathbone is yours to keep, too." Alec held no smugness in his voice or facial expressions. He seemed more dignified and wiser. Perhaps Lorcan had been correct about children maturing after the parents passed on.

"I appreciate it. I hope you've no plans to invite more behemoths to join what's left of your Circle, which seems to keep getting smaller," Forrest said.

"The only two demons we'll trust with such inclusion are the two seated at the table tonight," Alec said. "I gave an invitation to Brady and Jacob. My olive branch to the werewolves."

Forrest shook his head. "They politely declined. Brady remains adamant about not being a part of Nocturnal Trinity, at least not until he finds out who on the police force is a mole."

Alec nodded. "Please inform Brady the invitation's open should he change his mind at any time."

"I will."

"I invited the witches and they declined as well."

"Witches have tended to be the first to die in this nightclub whenever an attack has occurred or have you forgotten?" Forrest said.

"No, I've not. And what about you, Forrest?" Alec asked. "Will you become a part of—" Alec burst into laughter. "I'm sorry. It so contradicts what each of us are."

Forrest laughed deeply. "Yes, it does. For the betterment of your establishment, it's not in your best interests or mine that such a union occurs. At least not openly."

"I agree," Alec said. "We both have reputations that must be maintained. Neither side would argue that, now would we?"

"No. And understand something else," Forrest said, peering directly into Alec's eyes. Since Forrest resisted vampire compulsion, Alec was slightly nervous holding their gaze.

"What's that?" Alec asked.

"By all accounts, I should not enter into any truce with you since you failed to destroy the behemoths."

"Yes, I understand that."

"However, I believe you've realized the error of your decisions after Lorcan set you straight."

"Indeed," Alec replied.

"But, this is the point I'm making. One more major misstep in judgment that places any of my friends or myself into harm's way, and the truce I've extended ceases to exist. Is that clear?"

Alec nodded.

"While it is something no other Vampire Hunter has done—aligning with vampires—I believe we can coexist in Seattle. Now, what about the two shifters Dr. Litman traveled with?"

"We released Serge and Costel under guard and sent them to Romania where they came from," Alec said.

"Do you think that wise?" Forrest asked. "After all, they were the ones who abducted Kailey. Did you run this by Brady?"

"No. Neither seemed a threat, other than being forced to carry out orders from Dr. Litman. Since Litman's no longer alive, it's doubtful they're on the prowl. Besides, both are a large cat shifter but the collars they were forced to wear prevented their transformation. We've no idea where the key is for the collars, so they're stuck with them."

"I suppose that's a good thing," Forrest said. "And what of the elder vampire council?"

Alec shrugged. "Sometime during all the chaos, they fled. They've not made contact and I doubt they will."

"They didn't seem to favor your father's reappearance."

"No, they didn't," Alec said.

"Understand something else, though," Forrest said. "None of those elders are included in this truce. Should any of them return to Seattle, I'll know and I'll find them. You know what happens to them then."

Alec nodded. "Suitably fine."

"I wish to thank you," Irina said. "For helping us slay father."

"Yes," Alec said. "He's always been ruthless, cold, and unforgiving. I must say I never anticipated his desire to kill us, his own children."

"That's what mongrels do. They kill and eat their own."

"I also appreciate that you didn't seek to slay us after slaying our father," Alec said. "Especially since I didn't uphold our former truce. You could've killed us but you chose not to."

"Likewise. After Gadif vanished, I fell into a deep sleep. You had every opportunity to end my life if you had chosen."

Irina smiled. Her eyes sparkled. "To the contrary, we helped the were-wolves get you to a limo and driven home."

Jinn folded his hands atop the table. "Are we supposed to get used to this charming flowery display between forces that should be mortal enemies?"

Alec's eyes narrowed. "Do you have a problem with it?"

"Oh, hell no," Jinn said. "It's not what I expected, is all."

Forrest shrugged. "As you have seen, I'm a man of my word. Even after you failed to keep your word, Alec, I didn't pursue you."

"I know. Thank you."

"I can't go as far as saying we're all close friends," Forrest said, "as it contradicts everything I was taught. From this day forward, I offer you this. I won't consider you my sworn enemies provided you don't murder humans or force feed off of unwilling guests. There's never a shortage of those overly eager youthful fools begging to become your food. I suppose that breaks no laws."

Nikolina grinned. "In return, Forrest, we'll make it a point to inform you and Brady should any of the younger vampires go rogue. We'll also give you whatever information about them you need."

Forrest nodded. "Then, we consider this our new truce?"

Irina smiled. "Indeed."

TWO DAYS LATER.

Kailey sat with Cassie inside a corner coffee shop at a booth near the window. Brady was on duty.

Kailey stared at the cold cloudy sky. A mix of sleet and rain sluiced against the window, matching the tears staining her soul.

"Aren't you going to drink your coffee?" Cassie asked.

Kailey glumly shook her head and mumbled, "It's gotten cold."

Cassie grinned and stuck her finger tip into the coffee. Seconds later, steam rose off the coffee's surface. "Voilá! Problem solved."

Kailey waved her finger in the air. "Whoopee."

Cassie placed her elbow on the table and propped her chin on her palm. "You still hung up on Raven?"

"Confused is all."

"Why?"

Kailey shrugged. "I miss talking to her."

"You have me, right here," Cassie said, waving. "In the flesh, too. Nothing like a wavering ghost or a filthy cat."

"I know you're here. It's just … Raven made my life miserably interesting at times."

"And you miss *that*? Hey, I can make you miserable if you want." Cassie scrunched her nose. "Or, if you prefer, I could rise the heights of your pleasure to the point you forget all the pain and loss."

"Thanks, but … no. That's not what I meant about misery. For a few years Raven and I were close friends, then she was jealous and bitter, which grew into her trying to kill me—"

Cassie gave her a shrewd stare. "You realize your argument is getting weaker by the second."

Kailey laughed and snorted.

"See? That's more like it."

Kailey sipped her coffee. "Hmm. Better. I just wonder *where* exactly she went. She said that while she was a vampire, she was still a witch, but she wanted to be staked because she hated how empty she felt inside and how she had treated us as a vampire. She placed a spell so that when she died, her residual spirit could search for her soul."

Cassie's eyes beamed. "Really? She said that?"

Kailey nodded.

"Wow."

"But where did she go to find it?" Kailey asked.

"She never told you?"

Kailey shook her head. "We never had ample time for her to tell me. Have you ever heard of such a thing?"

"No. And I wouldn't know where to even start looking."

"I hope she's gone on to a better place or plane or dimension, but I still miss her."

"It's natural to mourn for those who've died."

"I know," Kailey said, "but I'd already done that twice. Once when she became a vampire and again, after you ... well, you know."

Cassie reached across the table and patted Kailey's hand. "Look at it from a more positive view. She found her soul and was able to make amends. Isn't that better than her being slain as a vampire without any hope of eternity?"

"What's eternity? Does it really exist?"

"Depends upon your exit," Cassie said. "Those four behemoths no longer exist on *any* plane. Vampires suffer a similar fate since they have no soul."

Kailey nodded. "Yes, and that's my point in a roundabout way. If Raven could find her soul, what's to prevent vampires from doing the same?"

Cassie sat back against the seat. "O-o-o, now *that* could be a huge problem. For now, though, why not set those thoughts aside and let's go see a movie or do something. No need grieving over Raven a third time, not since she redeemed herself."

Kailey sighed.

"Come on," Cassie said, standing and reaching for Kailey's hand.

Kailey took Cassie's hand and then scooted from the booth. After paying for the coffee, she and Cassie went outside and opened their umbrellas.

Cassie was right. Kailey had grieved more than her fair share for Raven over the past year in different ways. Raven was gone, and Kailey was certain that she was gone for good. Raven still didn't respond to Kailey's projected thought, and it was time to dismiss the notion that Raven would. She didn't sense any familiarity of Raven at all.

Kailey hoped that wherever Raven went that she could finally rest in peace.

THE END

ACKNOWLEDGMENTS

A special thank you to KC Riley-Gyer for the extra set of eyes to catch my mistakes, which is her superhero ability. Typos and wrong word choices whisper her name.

ABOUT THE AUTHOR

Leonard D. Hilley II grew up a quiet, shy kid with an inquisitive mind. Learning to read at an early age, he fell in love with books. He read every book he could get his hands on and stacks of dark comics about ghosts, monsters, and creepy things that stalk the night.

Like a lot of boys, he caught beetles, wooly bears, butterflies, and had an ant farm. When he was ten, his interests in science increased even more after seeing a professor's insect collection. Soon he set out on his quest to build his own collection. He also learned to rear butterflies and moths to obtain perfect specimens. He learned botany, gardening, and set his goal to become an entomologist.

At eleven, he saw Star Wars. His imagination soared. Soon after, he discovered Roger Zelazny's Chronicles of Amber. Six months later, he had written the first draft of a novel. A novel he later discarded, but the characters stuck with him. Years later, these characters came to life in Shawndirea, which Hilley intended to be a novella for Devils Den. The characters, however, refused to be ignored and took the opportunity to unveil Aetheaon in their first epic fantasy. Lady Squire: Dawn's Ascension was quick to follow.

Shawndirea was Hilley's farewell to butterfly collecting, and those who have read the novel understand why. He has taken Ray Bradbury's advice to heart: "Follow the characters." He does. He follows, listens, and take notes—often never knowing where they're going to take him, but he's never been disappointed in the results.

Hilley earned a B.S. in Biology and an MFA in Creative Writing to combine his love of science and writing.

Sci-fi Titles: Predators of Darkness: Aftermath, Beyond the Darkness, The Game of Pawns, Death's Valley, The Deimos Virus.

Epic Fantasy: Shawndirea (Aetheaon Chronicles: Book One), Lady Squire (Aetheaon Chronicles: Book Two), Frosthammer (Aetheaon Chronicles: Book Three), Shadowfae (Aetheaon Chronicles: Book Four), and Devils Den.

UF/PR: Succubus: Shadows of the Beast (Nocturnal Trinity Series: Book One), Raven (Nocturnal Trinity Series: Book Two)

YA UF/Paranormal: Forrest Wollinsky Vampire Hunter; Forrest Wollinsky: Blood Mists of London; Forrest Wollinsky: Predestined Crossroads.